D0442941

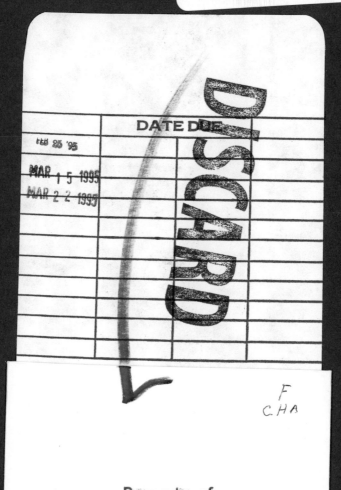

# THE
# SNARES
# OF DEATH

*Also by Kate Charles*

A Drink of Deadly Wine

# KATE CHARLES

# THE SNARES OF DEATH

**THE MYSTERIOUS PRESS**

Published by Warner Books

A Time Warner Company

*for*
*Michael*

First published in Great Britain in 1992 by Headline Book Publishing PLC.

Mysterious Press books are published by Warner Books, Inc., 1271 Avenue of the Americas, New York, NY 10020.

A Time Warner Company

The Mysterious Press name and logo are registered trademarks of Warner Books, Inc.

Printed in the United States of America
First U.S. printing: December 1993

10 9 8 7 6 5 4 3 2 1

Library of Congress Cataloging-in-Publication Data

Charles, Kate.
    The snares of death / Kate Charles.
      p.    cm.
    ISBN 0-89296-498-7
    I. Title.
    PS3553.H3228S65   1993
    813'.54—dc20                  92-50899
                                     CIP

*Author's Note:* As in *A Drink of Deadly Wine*, certain ecclesiastical liberties have been taken. St. Mary the Virgin, South Barsham, is a product of my imagination (as is the village itself). Wymondham Abbey, though, and the town of Wymondham, are quite real. And improbable as it may seem, Walsingham and its Shrine do exist, and largely as I have depicted them. I do hope, though, that the Guardians of the Shrine of Our Lady of Walsingham will forgive me a bit of artistic license, particularly in the descriptions of the College.

The Psalms at the beginning of each chapter are taken from *The Book of Common Prayer.*

# PART ONE

# Chapter 1

*Lift up your heads, O ye gates, and be ye lift up, ye everlasting
doors: and the King of glory shall come in.*

*Psalm 24:7*

On a chill February morning, less than three months before he
was to die, the Reverend Robert Dexter packed his suitcase for
a weekend trip. "Elayne!" he shouted. "Where are my clean
shirts?"

There was no reply. "Elayne!" he repeated, his voice rising
in irritation.

After a moment a young woman came to his bedroom door.
"I don't think she's here, Daddy."

Dexter's face softened but his voice retained its annoyed
edge. "Where is she, for heaven's sake? Doesn't your mother
realize that we're leaving in a few minutes? And she promised
me that those shirts would be ironed . . ."

Rebecca Dexter smiled at her father. "I've ironed them for
you, Daddy. Shall I bring them up?"

Returning her smile, Dexter shrugged off his residual anger.
"Thank you, Princess. Have you packed?"

"Yes, I'm ready to go. And I've been through your morning
post—there's nothing that won't keep until Monday."

The front door closed quietly, but Bob Dexter heard the click of the latch and followed his daughter onto the landing. "Elayne! Is that you?" he demanded, his frown returning.

The face that Elayne Dexter raised was startled. "Oh, Bob!"

"Where have you been?" he scowled furiously. "Don't you realize that it's time to leave? The London traffic . . ."

"I'm sorry, Bob." Her voice was conciliatory but she was unable to meet his eyes.

"Where have you been?" Dexter repeated.

"I . . ." Elayne hesitated fractionally, then went on. "I popped down to the news agent. To cancel the papers for the weekend." She held her breath: would he believe her?

Losing interest, he turned away. "Oh, very well. But you should have done it yesterday. There really is no time to waste today." He paused at the bedroom door to add, deliberately, "At least Becca has ironed my shirts for me."

Elayne flushed. "Yes."

"Come on, then. I hope you've packed. When Bob Dexter says he'll be somewhere at three o'clock . . ."

"Yes, Bob." And Elayne hurried upstairs to change her shoes. There could be trouble if Bob were to notice her wet feet; the pavement between the vicarage and the news agent's was perfectly dry.

Several hours later, his wife and daughter settled into their hotel, the Reverend Robert Dexter pulled into the car park of the Gates of Heaven Printing Company. He glanced at the clock on the dashboard and nodded in satisfaction: three o'clock. Just on time. He left his overcoat in the car, for although it was very cold, the walk from the car park to the building's entrance was a short one. The building was quite new, and purpose-built; the glass doors, etched with full-sized representations of the Pearly Gates, slid apart quietly at his approach.

The receptionist just inside the door recognized him, as well she should. Noah Gates, of course, employed only born-again Christians at Gates of Heaven. "Good afternoon, Reverend Dexter," she said with an admiring smile. He recognized her admiration and was glad he'd left his overcoat behind. Without it, he knew that he cut a very impressive figure in his charcoal-grey suit and pale blue clerical shirt with the wide expanse of dog collar. "They're in the boardroom—I believe you know the way." Bob Dexter returned her smile with a confirming nod and pressed the button to call the lift. The boardroom was on the top floor, a glassed-in box in a position to command the best views of Fakenham and the surrounding Norfolk countryside. As Bob Dexter entered the room he was conscious of the atmosphere of anticipation; it was as though they had been waiting for him, and he felt it was right that it should be so.

Noah Gates, naturally, was seated at the head of the oval table. He didn't rise, but gestured toward the empty seat at his left hand. "Hello, Bob. I believe that you know everyone here." Bob Dexter looked around the table at the faces and nodded. "And you remember my son Toby."

"Yes, of course. How are you, Toby?" He reached across the table and gripped the hand of the young man sitting opposite, on his father's right. The young man's handshake was a bit weak, Dexter thought, but from what he knew of him he was a good lad.

"Very well, thank you, Reverend Dexter. And you?"

"Just fine. Just fine." He shifted his attention around the table, acknowledging the greetings of the half-dozen or so men who were gathered there. They all looked very much alike, clean-cut and well-scrubbed and wholesome, with an air of having bathed in Harpic, and he was hard put to remember all of their names.

The preliminaries out of the way, Bob Dexter took his seat and looked at the man at the head of the table. Gates sat silently for a moment, fixing the men one after another with his stare, his eyes like small flinty black pebbles in an impassive face. The man's appearance was as uncompromising as his manner; short and compact in stature, he had dark hair untouched by gray, made even darker by the hair oil with which it was slicked straight back from his forehead. His color was high and choleric, and the small pursed mouth was set above a pugnacious jaw. Noah Gates was clearly a man who meant business, all the time and in every way.

Several years ago Herbert N. Gates had been just a successful Norfolk businessman, founder of the Gates Printing Company of Fakenham. But at his sudden and enthusiastic conversion to Christianity, both he and his company had been re-christened: he became Noah Gates, and his company Gates of Heaven. And the focus of the company had changed. Most of his money had been made from printing salacious magazines—not actually pornographic, he was quick to explain, though the distinction was not always immediately evident, especially to those untutored in such things. Now, however, Gates of Heaven was dedicated to the furtherance of the Word of God, and though its profits were not so great as they had been, Noah Gates counted himself a happy man, and a blessed one.

Gates cleared his throat. "There will be plenty of time for chitchat later over coffee," he began. "But now that we're all here, we'd better make a start." He picked up a pencil, brand-new and sharpened to a precise point, and drew a circle on the pad of paper in front of him. "This is a cancer," he announced. "Here, on our very doorstep. I don't need to tell any of you gentlemen what this cancer is, or what its source is." He looked around again, then back at the paper; with a sudden movement he stabbed the pencil into the middle of the circle. "WALSINGHAM!" he thundered. "The Whore of Babylon!"

Toby Gates jumped slightly; Bob Dexter glanced across the table at him almost pityingly.

"We all agree, gentlemen, that this cancer must be stopped. We've all worked together on this in the past, the last few years at their National Pilgrimage." His voice was calmer now.

"But now is the time for a really concerted effort. We must mobilize our forces. We must concentrate, this year, on wiping out this abomination once and for all!"

He stared at them challengingly but no one spoke. "You might ask how this can be accomplished. It may seem a difficult task, even an impossible one. Idolatry has survived—has flourished—in that detestable place for hundreds of years. But I believe—" he paused impressively. "I believe that we are instruments of God's will in this matter, and I have asked Him for guidance." Again he paused. "God has spoken to me. Through the Holy Spirit, and through His Holy Word, He has spoken." Noah Gates closed his eyes and quoted, softly at first but swelling to a climax and then finishing on a whisper, " 'Their idols are silver and gold: even the work of men's hands.

" 'They have mouths, and speak not: eyes have they, and see not.

" 'They have ears, and hear not; feet have they, and walk not: neither speak they through their throat.

" 'They that make them are like unto them: and so are all such as put their trust in them.

" 'But thou, house of Israel, trust thou in the Lord: he is their succor and defense.

" 'Ye house of Aaron, put your trust in the Lord: he is their helper and defender.

" 'Ye that fear the Lord, put your trust in the Lord: he is their helper and defender.

" 'The Lord hath been mindful of us, and he shall bless us: even he shall bless the house of Israel, he shall bless the house of Aaron.

" 'He shall bless them that fear the Lord: both small and great.'

"God will be with us," he finished. "We cannot fail."

At last someone spoke; it was one of the men at the far end of the table. "But how, Noah? What can we do differently?

We've tried for years—we've tried talking to them, we've tried reason, we've shown them the Holy Scriptures, but they've hardened their hearts."

Another added, "It's true, Noah. They don't listen. Last year at the National Pilgrimage I spoke to so many of them. They wouldn't even take our tracts! They just shook their rosaries in our faces!"

"O ye of little faith!" Gates said, sorrowfully. "I tell you, God will be with us." He stood, turned dramatically and unfurled a banner on the wall behind him. In letters several feet high on a background of fluorescent orange it proclaimed MISSION: WALSINGHAM. Pointing to the letters one by one, he intoned, "Mary, Idols, Saints: Stamp It Out Now! This is our new battle cry!"

Toby looked down at the table, saying nothing. When his father had outlined his plan to him several days ago, he had protested, "But it's ungrammatical! Surely it should be stamp *them* out now?" His father's scorn had been withering: "Who cares about grammar when people's immortal souls are at stake?" So now he held his tongue.

There were nods of assent around the table. The first man spoke again. "You're right, of course," he said. "We must concentrate on the National Pilgrimage at the end of May. Ten thousand or more misguided Anglo-Catholics, all together at once! That gives us three months to make our preparations. If only we could get hold of a copy of their program well ahead of time, find out what they're going to do, and plan some counter-strategy . . ."

"Misguided? They're not misguided! They've deliberately chosen the path of idolatry," Gates snapped. "And unless they repent, God will punish them for it."

Bob Dexter had been uncharacteristically silent throughout the meeting. At last he spoke, and his rich, compelling baritone voice filled the room. "It's not just the National Pilgrimage, though," he said. "That only happens once each year.

Walsingham is there three hundred and sixty-five days a year, an affront to all those who love the Lord." His pale blue eyes made contact with each of the men around the table before he continued. "God has called upon Bob Dexter to make a personal sacrifice, to help to drive a stake through the heart of that popish abomination." All eyes were now on him as he made his announcement. "I have informed the PCC of my church in Richmond that Bob Dexter has accepted an invitation to become the Vicar of"—and his lip curled at the name—"St. Mary the Virgin, South Barsham, just a few miles from here, and even fewer miles from Walsingham. It is a church of long-standing popish inclinations. I will change that, and then . . ."

"Praise the Lord," whispered Noah Gates fervently. But his eyes were hard, and speculative.

Tea and biscuits were served at last, and one by one the men circulated around to Bob Dexter, to offer their congratulations on his anticipated move. "No, I haven't been there yet," he replied to a question. "I shall visit it this weekend, while I'm in the neighborhood. And I'll be instituted right after Easter."

"How did you get the job?"

He smiled modestly, drawing himself up to his full height. Bob Dexter was a tall, imposing man, still handsome at nearly fifty, with wavy ash-blond hair springing crisply from a high, domed forehead. "The former incumbent had been there for over thirty years. This time the appointment was the turn of the Martyrs' Memorial Trust. They wanted someone solid, a respected Evangelical, and they knew they could count on Bob Dexter."

Another man, white-shirted and bespectacled, joined the conversation. "You've been a wonderful spokesman for the Evangelical cause, Bob. At the General Synod last month— you were superb. The things you said to those namby-pambies who wanted to outlaw fox hunting on church property, and who called for the Church to boycott all products tested on animals . . ."

"I just told them the truth. That in Genesis 1, God gave us dominion over 'every living thing that moveth upon the earth.' You can't argue with that."

The first man added, "And the way you spoke out against the plague of homosexuality! I saw it on the news—you gave those fairies some good straight biblical teaching to think about!"

Dexter nodded. "Bob Dexter doesn't believe in pulling any punches, just to win favor with the trendies! If God said it, it's good enough for me!"

"The Church of England is full of poofters and perverts," Noah Gates pronounced. "Just look at Walsingham. I just thank the Lord that I'm not associated with a church like that."

Dexter shot him a look as the first man sprang to his defense. "It's a good thing there are men like Bob in the Church of England, Noah! Men who aren't afraid to stand up for what's right!"

Backing down, Gates amended, "The Church of England is lucky to have a man like Bob. I'm just glad I don't have to join him there, that's all. Each to his own, eh, Bob?" He laughed, an incongruously high-pitched, mirthless giggle.

Bob Dexter smiled frostily.

Before the gathering dispersed, Toby Gates found a moment to speak privately with Bob Dexter. "It's very nice to see you again, sir. How is your daughter—how is Becca?" He blushed as he asked the question. "I haven't seen her since last year's protests at Walsingham."

Dexter smiled benignly on the young man. So that was how it was, eh? Becca.

"Rebecca is very well, thank you, Toby."

"She'll be moving to South Barsham with you, sir?"

"Yes. She acts as my private secretary, you know." He

studied the young man with increased interest. Tallish, slim, a gentle face framed with soft brown curls and eyes of a curious light brown, the color of toast. Fresh skin, with the tendency to blush—but that was not unattractive in a well brought-up young man. And he was interested in Becca. That could be very useful—she could do much worse. Of course she was far too young to think of such things—only twenty—but the day would come when she'd want to marry, and he could just about bear to think of his beloved Becca married to Toby Gates. Eventually. Toby would inherit his father's printing business, and of course his Evangelical credentials were impeccable, even if he wasn't an Anglican. Dexter thought he remembered that Toby, as a university student, had been responsible for his father's Christian conversion. Yes, he decided, Toby should be encouraged. It could be the beginning of an evangelical dynasty: the union of Bob Dexter's only daughter and Noah Gates's only son. "My wife and daughter are with me this weekend," he said impulsively. "Would you like to join us for dinner at our hotel tomorrow evening?"

"Yes, sir, I'd like that very much. I should like to see Becca again." The toast-colored eyes sparkled shyly. "And Mrs. Dexter too, of course."

Bob Dexter smiled his trademarked smile, the perfect teeth with which God had blessed him maintained and enhanced by years of private dental work, provided free of charge by a grateful parishioner.

# Chapter 2

*For he shall carry nothing away with him when he dieth: neither
shall his pomp follow him.*

*Psalm 49:17*

"It was dreadful," David Middleton-Brown told Lucy Kingsley
over dinner in her South Kensington mews house, refilling her
wine glass and then his own. "It was like some sort of violation—of Lady Constance, I mean. I felt like such an intruder,
such a . . . *voyeur*. I didn't feel that I had any right to be there,
in her house. Not without her there." He stopped and took a
fortifying gulp of wine.

Lucy smiled at him. "But it's *your* house now."

"Yes, I suppose it is. Or at least it will be, when the will
is settled."

"How long is that likely to take?"

"It generally takes about a year, though with an estate of
that size it could be considerably longer. That means at least
another six months—August. She died in August, remember."

Lucy remembered very well—it had been shortly after she
and David had met. She phrased her next question carefully.
"And then what? Will you live there?"

He didn't answer directly. "Well, at least it will give me a place of my own to stay at the weekends. Daphne never complains, mind you, but sometimes I feel that I'm taking advantage of her hospitality."

No, Daphne wouldn't complain, thought Lucy. She didn't know Daphne Elford very well, but from the contact she'd had with the older woman Lucy's feminine intuition told her that Daphne was fond of David in a way she'd never admit. And David *was* taking advantage of her hospitality. Lucy wondered how Daphne felt about that—about the way he used her flat in essence as a free hotel, just a place to sleep, spending his days and evenings with another woman. "So you're not thinking of actually moving to London? Changing jobs?"

David looked at her almost shyly. He felt vaguely dissatisfied with their relationship—if you could even call it that. It wasn't that there was any actual awkwardness between them. They always talked together easily, and enjoyed the time they spent together—these weekends in London, once or twice a month. But they had never fully recaptured the warm emotional intimacy that had sprung up so naturally and so immediately between them when they'd met. It was his fault, he knew. He was the one who'd shattered the equilibrium of their relationship. And perhaps it was too late now to hope for anything else. He hesitated. "I might, I suppose. Would you like it— if I moved to London, I mean?"

She smiled at him. "Of course I would, David. It would be lovely to have you so near."

Was she only saying what she thought he wanted to hear? Uncomfortable, David looked down at his plate. He picked up his fork again, took a few bites of food, and when he finally spoke he consciously changed the subject. "This is really delicious, Lucy. What do you call it?"

"Spinach and mushroom roulade, with a white wine and cheese sauce. Do you really like it?"

"Of course. Why wouldn't I?" He raised his eyes and looked

at her again across the table. "You're the best cook I know, and everything you make is delicious."

She laughed. "Flattery will get you nowhere, young man." With both hands she pushed her hair from her face and David's heart constricted as it always did at the grace of the characteristic, unconscious gesture. Lucy Kingsley was an extremely attractive woman. Her chief glory was the nimbus of naturally curly hair which cascaded in profusion to her shoulders, hair of a shade which is generally called "strawberry blond" but which could far more accurately be described as the color of ripe apricots.

"It's just that . . ." Lucy continued, "well, I don't quite know how to tell you this." She twisted a curl around her finger, and went on in a rush. "I've stopped eating meat."

David stared at her. "Since when?"

"Since the last time I saw you, a few weeks ago."

"But . . . why?"

Lucy looked him full in the face, and spoke earnestly and deliberately. "I've come to believe that killing animals just so we can eat them is wrong: it's murder. What right do we have to do that? Are our lives worth so much more than theirs? There are so many things we can eat—delicious things— which don't involve killing, that I don't think we can justify eating meat."

Her earnestness amazed him. "But you've never felt like that before, Lucy. You've always enjoyed a bit of rare beef as much as I have! Why now? Why this sudden great conviction?"

She took a bite of the roulade before she answered. "That's a fair question. Yes, of course I've always enjoyed meat—I'll admit it." She smiled ruefully. "But I met some people recently who convinced me that I was wrong. Wrong to eat it, wrong to enjoy it."

"People? What people? How did you meet them?"

She laughed at his suspicious expression. "I met them

through my work, actually. They're involved with the British Animal Rights Coalition. They asked me to design a poster for them." She got up and left the room, returning after a moment with a poster which she put on the table beside his plate. "This is what I've done."

"BARC. Very funny," he said dryly. "But who are they? I've never heard of them."

Lucy resumed her seat. "They're new. That's why the publicity." Unconsciously she began twisting a lock of her hair again as she explained. "There have always been a lot of groups dedicated to different aspects of animal rights: anti-blood sports, anti-animal experimentation, anti-fur, anti-battery farming, anti-cruelty to animals . . ."

"Aren't they ever pro anything?"

Ignoring the jibe, she went on. "This is a new effort to bring them all together, under one umbrella, as it were." She pointed at the poster, at the gossamer umbrella sheltering a multitude of various beasts: dogs and cats, deer and foxes, chickens and cows, pheasants and grouse, badgers and hedgehogs, tigers and ermine, seals and whales and dolphins. "An umbrella of caring, protecting the helpless from indifference, from cruelty, from greed. That's what BARC aims to be."

David examined the poster with interest. Lucy's artwork was brilliant, he thought. In a total departure from her usual abstract style, she had captured just the right feeling for this fledgling organization. Whimsical without being cute, compassionate without descending to bathos, it communicated its message vividly. "It's very good," he admitted. "Much more effective than baby seals bleeding in the snow."

"Or heaps of dead dogs. Yes, I feel that the shock value in that sort of approach actually has a negative effect in the long run. People turn away from it—they don't want to know. Whereas this . . ." She paused. "But anyway, do you understand why I feel I can't eat meat any longer?"

*  *  *

Later, over brandy in the sitting room, they returned to the
subject of Lady Constance and her will. "I don't really understand why you had to go to her house today," Lucy remarked.
She was curled up on the sofa, close to the fire. "It all seems
very complicated. It's a good thing that you're a solicitor—at
least you've got some chance of understanding it all! Was it
some sort of provision in the will?"

"No, just a legal technicality. I have to inspect the property
before the will goes through probate, and formally say whether
I'll accept it or not."

She laughed bemusedly. "And are you going to accept it?"

"I should jolly well think so. It's quite a house, you know—
worth well over a million quid."

"She didn't have any family to inherit from her?" Lucy
asked.

"No one. Her husband died years ago. They never had any
children. And her brother never married. Sad."

"Very sad. But why you?"

His laugh was self-deprecating. "She liked me, for some
reason. She thought I'd appreciate her house and take good
care of it."

"I should think she did like you." Lucy smiled at him with
affection; one of the very charming things about David, she
thought, was that he never seemed to realize how attractive he
was to women. Although he could not be described as handsome in a classical sense, there was something about him . . .
Just past forty, he had retained a reasonably good figure; the
starburst of lines around his hazel eyes when he smiled was to
Lucy an engaging indication of welcome maturity, as was the
sprinkling of gray hair amongst the brown at his temples.
"And she's left it to you with no strings attached?"

At that he groaned. "One little string—one I've put off
thinking about."

"What's that?"

"She wanted me to go to Walsingham, to the Chapel of All Souls, to pray for her. Next month, on her birthday, the thirty-first of March." He grimaced. "You know how I loathe that place."

"Yes, but I've never understood why."

"Have you ever been there?"

"No, of course not. But what's so bad about it?"

"Ugh. It's so tasteless. The architecture of the Anglican Shrine Church is so nasty, and the whole place is over-commercialized, and full of such earnest people. I just can't describe how horrid it is."

"It can't be *that* bad," Lucy objected half-heartedly.

"That's what you think. You should see it." He shuddered dramatically.

"All right, I will."

"You will what?" David looked at her in surprise.

"I'll see it. I'll go with you when you go to fulfil Lady Constance's last wish."

"But why . . . ?"

Lucy smiled with satisfaction. "I've been meaning to tell you all evening. An art gallery in Norwich—the Bridewell Gallery, I don't know if you know it—is going to have an exhibition of my paintings, beginning next month. It opens the day before that, Saturday the thirtieth of March, and they want me to come up for the opening. I was going to ask you whether you'd be prepared to put me up in Wymondham for the weekend, and to escort me to the opening."

"Yes, of course. But . . ."

"That's settled, then. And on the Sunday we can go to Walsingham." She laughed at the look on his face. "Don't worry, David! You've got over six weeks to clean your house! And I promise I won't wear my gloves to look for dust."

The rest of the evening passed quickly, with lazy conversation and soft music. Over the sound of the music they could hear the wind; it had been a very cold day, and the night would be even colder. But the room was snug and cosy and dark, with the fire providing the only illumination. Sophie, Lucy's marmalade cat, for some reason much preferred David's lap to any other, and had been curled there for hours, a warm, purring ball of fur. But when the clock chimed midnight David rose with a groan. "Time to get on to Daphne's, I suppose. She'll probably be waiting up for me. At least I've got my car—it would be a long, cold walk tonight!" Lucy fetched his coat and went with him to the door, where he gave her the customary affectionate but chaste kiss on the cheek. "Good night, Lucy— thanks for the lovely meal, and a lovely evening. I'll see you tomorrow, around the usual time."

"Good night, David." She stifled a sigh as she stood at the open door, oblivious to the cold, and watched him climb into his car with a final wave. When will he realize—will he *ever* realize, she thought, that sometimes you have to take happiness where you find it? Not where you wish you could find it, or where you think it should be found, but where it is? She was wise enough to know that he must discover that for himself; it would be madness to rush him. The sigh escaped unnoticed as she bolted the door, switched off the hall light, and went up the stairs to bed.

# Chapter 3

*For they grieved him with their hill-altars: and provoked him to displeasure with their images.*

*Psalm 78:59*

It was a raw, drizzly day when the Reverend Bob Dexter paid his first visit to the parish church of St. Mary the Virgin, South Barsham, Norfolk. He went on a Sunday afternoon, when all the members of his future flock were safely at home tucking into their Sunday lunches.

The church presented a less than prepossessing aspect to him as he approached on foot, his car stowed on the grass verge opposite the Two Magpies pub. Last autumn's leaves still choked the uncut grass between the rakishly tilted gravestones in the churchyard, and the unclipped yew trees dripped dankly on his head as he passed beneath them; Bob Dexter smoothed the unwelcome drops from his wavy hair. A few stubbornly optimistic early daffodils, huddling in the shelter of the church walls, showed defiant yellow faces to the overgrown elderberry bushes.

It was a long, low building, typical in Norfolk flint. Over the years the churchyard had risen around its walls, giving it a sunken appearance. That probably meant that there would be problems with damp, he thought. The tower was at the west end, and its door, sturdy and weathered, had clearly not been opened for years. Bob Dexter approached the small north porch. Over its door was a small niche holding a plaster statue of the Virgin Mary, its paintwork faded. The outside entrance of the open porch had once been fitted with bird doors of a good quality, but the netting had now entirely disappeared, leaving only the wooden frame. Dexter pulled the doors apart and entered the porch, regarding with disdain the mildewed stone holy-water stoup.

The porch was quite small; on his right he saw a large dark-green notice board, so ancient and well-riddled with drawing pins over the years that it appeared to have been infested with wood-worm. On the top a neatly painted gold-leaf inscription read, St. Mary the Virgin, South Barsham. Diocese of Norwich, and below it the times of the Sunday Masses and Weekday Services (Saints' Days as announced; Confession by Appointment). The usual notices were posted there: a list of fees for funerals, a notification of the revision of the church electoral roll, a flower-arranging rota. A fairly new-looking notice advised, "In the event of a pastoral emergency, please contact Father Mark Judd," followed by a telephone number. That must be the curate who'd been taking the services since the old Vicar died, he decided. At the bottom of the board was a little scroll, picked out in gold paint rather than gold leaf, with the words, "Mary pray, Jesu mercy, *Ora pro nobis*," and the names "Mabel and Fred." Bob Dexter curled his lip and turned to the board on his left.

Above a large umbrella stand, its white enamel tray badly chipped, was another notice board, this one of bright blue. It boasted only one item: a poster, faded and covered in polythene, with a picture of Our Lady of Walsingham, and the inscription, "A lamp burns for this church at the Shrine of Our Lady of Walsingham." "Not for long, it doesn't," Dexter said aloud, seizing the poster by the corner and ripping it down. He immediately felt better.

The door to the church opened easily with a push. Bob Dexter frowned at the carelessness, blind trust or just plain stupidity in this part of the world; although visiting churches to admire their architectural merits was not something that interested him, on the occasions that he had been to East Anglian churches he had invariably found them unlocked, and usually deserted. That would never happen in Richmond, in London, or indeed in any civilized part of the country. Dexter told himself, not for the first time, what a sacrifice he was making on the Lord's behalf in coming to this primitive backwater.

The body of the church was down four steps. The smell hit him first—that smell peculiar to ancient country churches, a mixture of damp stone (he'd been right about the damp—he could see plaster flaking from the walls!), moldy prayer books, and stale incense. As his eyes adjusted to the gloom, he noted the finger bowl in a niche to his right, encrusted with lime scale and filled with holy water. He turned away from it to find himself confronting a large painting on wood, looking almost like a tavern sign, he thought. It was blackened with age, with varnish and with candle smoke, but he could see that it was the Virgin Mary, standing on a crescent moon, crowned with a halo of stars, rosary beads dangling from her outstretched hand. It was an offensively popish image—popish in style and tone, the repulsive subject matter entirely aside— and not even English, to his unpracticed eye. This was going to be worse than even he had imagined; again he turned, facing east.

Dexter moved to the center aisle and paused at the visitors' book which lay open on a scruffy table to his left, a blue Biro attached to it with a bit of string. He flipped through it; it was an expensive leather-bound volume which had clearly been

there for years. Its entries began some twenty years earlier and
tailed off in number as the years progressed. There hadn't been
a new entry in nearly a month, he noted. Not even the faithful
on their pilgrimages to Walsingham stopped at this church.
Beside the visitors' book were a few tracts, yellowed with
age. A pile of shabby green English Hymnals added to the
impression of neglect.

Dexter noticed that the table to the right of the center aisle
was quite a different matter. It was in fact a black oak chest,
well polished and dust-free. It contained a few recent books,
the latest issue of the parish magazine, some copies of the
diocesan newsletter, and a highly polished brass vase, cheerful
with early daffodils. How strange that the one table should be
so neglected and the other so cared for. He must remember to
ask someone about that.

The back pews were clearly reserved for the churchwardens;
their staves stood at attention like billiard cues on either side
of the aisle. Dexter marched down the center aisle. Each of the
simple stone columns appeared to have a statue—a graven
image, Bob Dexter said to himself—affixed to it. On the right
stood St. Francis of Assisi, a bird perched on his outstretched
finger, flanked by a little red sanctuary light burning on a
ledge on one side, and a tiny fish-paste pot of crocuses on the
other. The pews had been cleared around the pillar, forming
a small children's corner, furnished with miniature chairs.
Opposite St. Francis, on the north side of the church, was a
garishly painted St. George; the tatty banner behind him read
"St. George for England," and several pennants and banners,
the remnants of a long-ago Scout troop, leaned against the
column.

Even Bob Dexter recognised St. Francis and St. George,
however little he approved of them, but the next shrine he
encountered, to the east of St. Francis, baffled him totally. A
red lamp burned in front of a statue of a priest—a Roman
priest, by all appearances, in a biretta and a lace cotta. Closer

inspection of the statue revealed the name "Curé of Ars" beneath, but that was scarcely more enlightening. Someone, at least, was very fond of this particular example of idolatry: a brass bowl of fresh flowers stood beside the red lamp.

Dexter moved quickly to the front of the nave. There was no nave altar, just the pulpit on the left and a reading desk on either side. He turned to the left, past the organ—Dexter was not musical, but the organ looked a reasonable instrument—and had a look at the war memorial on the north wall. It was a large oak triptych with names on the side panels, and in the center a very realistically carved crucifix with the inscription, "Pray for the souls of the faithful departed: May they all rest in peace." This posed a dilemma; praying for the souls of the dead was an abhorrent practice, but he couldn't very well rip out the war memorial, could he? There were still people about who were sensitive about the war. A poppy wreath from last November hung on a nail at the crucifix's foot, and three older wreaths, progressively faded, leaned on the floor beneath. The British Legion standard hung on one side, and on the other was an oak-framed, faded print of a dying British Tommy in the trenches of the First World War, supported by his mate, while an enormous hovering angel waited with arms and wings outstretched to receive his soul.

Now Dexter circled around the perimeter of the church, down the north aisle, paying scant attention to the painted plaster Stations of the Cross which were affixed at regular intervals to the walls—those wouldn't be there much longer. He passed the north porch, and the obnoxious foreign painting, and at the back of the church found yet more atrocities. In the corner was a Shrine of the Legion of Mary, proudly proclaimed by a banner and decorated with ferns and spider plants. On the wall behind was one of those garishly painted white porcelain pictures—Italian, he thought it was—that always made him think of an Edwardian lavatory.

The font, with its attendant Paschal candle, was at the rear, in front of the entrance to the tower. Dexter pulled aside the felt curtain that masked the tower entrance and peered inside. The bell ropes were visible at ground level, with their striped salleys, and on the wall were the peal boards. Propped against the wall, dusty and neglected, were the seventeenth-century Ten Commandments boards. Dexter smiled. Soon, he told himself, they would be returned to their former prominence. This church could obviously do with a good dose of the Ten Commandments.

Beneath the window, on the south side of the tower, hung a very large dark painting; Dexter could just about make out a hunting scene, with a quivering saint in the foreground, being converted or something. Disgusting! Even worse was the plaster statue beneath it, Our Lady of Walsingham in full color, with little lights burning around her, and literature about the Shrine. Dexter swept the leaflets from the table and stuffed them in his pocket. And on the side wall, also with a candle burning, was a painting of King Charles the Blessed Martyr. Dexter stalked up the south aisle and peered into the south porch. It had been converted into a chantry chapel, its outside door covered by a curtain on which hung a crucifix. Dexter stepped inside and glared at the stone seat which was being used as an altar of remembrance, the six candles, the book with the names of the dead, the flowers, the prominent notice for the Walsingham Guild of All Souls. "It's a bit small," he said aloud, "but I think it would do nicely for a Sunday School. Or perhaps a book stall—for the Protestant Truth Society!"

He headed toward the chapel at the end of the south aisle, and in his concentration nearly tripped over the chair against the wall just outside. He stopped and looked furiously at the purple velvet curtain, and the little kneeler in front of the chair; he picked up the plastic-covered card on the chair's seat and scrutinized the offensive words: "A Form of Confession." His eye picked out the words, "to Blessed Mary, ever-virgin, and to all the Saints," and after an unsuccessful attempt to tear the card in two, it joined the leaflets in his pocket.

Dexter paused outside the chapel. Its wooden screen looked medieval, or at any rate quite old, with evidence of years of wood-worm, but behind the screen hung a tomato-ketchup-red velvet curtain, thus giving the impression of a closed-off room. That must have cost a bit of money! he thought. The small sign fixed to one side of the entrance read, "This is where Christ's sacramental presence is to be found. Please enter reverently," and just inside the door an oak plaque requested, "Pray for the soul of Albert Carter, whose generous gift refurnished this chapel."

Certainly a great deal of money had been spent on the chapel in recent years. It was fitted with gold carpet, and there were a dozen or so new oak chairs with red vinyl seats. A new altar had been constructed, on a plinth: it was oak, and very modern, without a frontal. Instead it had just a fair linen, albeit festooned with drippy crocheted lace, and on it was a single squat candle and a spider plant. But there were plenty of candles elsewhere in the chapel: in front of the wall safe that held the reserved sacrament, and in the wrought-iron stands in front of the pictures on the south wall. There was another Virgin, and some other saint as well. And in a very high niche, up above the modern, insipidly colored stained-glass window, was yet another statue of Our Lady. It would take a tall ladder to get that one down, thought Bob Dexter.

Only the chancel remained for his inspection. Dexter left the chapel and passed through the chancel gates, past the choir's benches and up to the High Altar. It was an old-fashioned English Altar, hung behind with royal-blue velvet curtains and surmounted by a huge central crucifix and numerous—he didn't bother to count them—tall candlesticks. They looked as though they should be worth something, as did the sanctuary lamp, which appeared to be silver. The place was truly abominable, but Dexter was beginning to see the financial possibilities. There were probably people who would be willing to pay good money for all this popish nonsense—even the statues and the pictures. If he could sell it all off, there might even be enough money to build a proper Sunday School extension.

He suddenly had the feeling that someone was watching him, and he turned slowly. On his left was a very large painted plaster statue of the Virgin, regarding him balefully with her glass eyes. In her right hand she held a scepter and a rosary, while with her left she supported a simpering child. The hand-lettered notice beneath her requested, "Mother of God, pray for us," and she was surrounded by an assortment of candlesticks, none of them lit, and a large bowl of slightly drooping flowers. Bob Dexter laughed aloud.

At that moment he became aware that he was indeed not alone in the church. There was a clattering noise coming from the area of the north porch. Vandals, come to steal his candlesticks before he could flog them off? Although the church was not locked, and theoretically everyone was as free as he to enter, already he felt proprietorial about the place. "Who's there?" he called out in his best preaching voice.

A quavery, frightened voice answered his challenge. "Gwen," it said. "Gwen Vernon."

Bob Dexter strode down through the chancel gates and confronted the figure who struggled up the center aisle, laden with a sheaf of flowers.

"I'm sorry if I frightened you," he said in a more normal tone of voice. "I just wasn't expecting anyone." He paused, then added portentously, "I'm Bob Dexter. Soon to be the shepherd of this flock."

"Oh!" squeaked the woman who faced him, nearly dropping the flowers in her shock.

Dexter smiled his trademarked smile. "My dear lady, let me help you with those. Where were you taking them?"

"In . . . in there." She indicated the chancel as he scooped the flowers out of her arms. Recovering herself, she added timidly, "My friend . . . that is, Miss Barnes, and I, we always do the flowers for Our Lady. And this morning Alice, that is, Miss Barnes, noticed that they were getting a bit, well, past their best. I hadn't noticed myself, but Alice, Miss Barnes, says I'm like that. So as soon as we'd finished our lunch she said, 'Gwen, you must go over to the church and take some fresh flowers for Our Lady.' And here I am."

Dexter decided to withhold his opinions of her devotion to Our Lady for the time being, and see what he could find out from the woman. There would be plenty of time after he'd arrived to sort out these aberrations. He put the flowers down in the chancel and regarded the woman in the murky light that filtered in through the dark Victorian east window. "There you are, Miss—or is it Mrs.?—Vernon."

"Oh, *Miss* Vernon. Thank you, Father, for your help." Dexter winced at the appellation, but Miss Vernon, her eyes already turned toward the Virgin, failed to notice.

She appeared to be in her late sixties, though her hair was no help in determining her age: she wore a wig of a most unlikely golden-blond shade, in a style that had been popular probably two decades earlier. She was quite tall, and very angular in build; her movements were jerky and she gave the impression of clumsiness. Her clothing, too, seemed to fit the image; the various garments looking as though they had been assembled at random from a jumble-sale box.

"Do you live nearby?" Dexter inquired as she went down on her knees before the statue and began sorting through the flowers.

"Oh, yes, in the village. Do you know the village? Monkey Puzzle Cottage. It's down the lane from the old blacksmith's." She looked up at him over her shoulder, adding proudly, "We have the only two monkey puzzle trees in the village. Probably the only ones in this part of the county!"

"You don't say."

She nodded solemnly, then ventured a smile.

"Have you been at this church long?" he asked.

"Yes, years and years. Ever since before old Father Lyons, God rest his soul." She sighed. "Still, times change."

"Pastor Lyons"—he couldn't bring himself to use the other term, and she didn't seem to notice—"died some months ago, didn't he?"

"Nearly a year ago. On Holy Saturday, while he was singing the Exsultet. I always thought it was such a lovely way to go." She sighed again. "Of course, it ruined the service."

Dexter frowned. What a very odd woman she was. "Was Pastor Lyons responsible for the renovations in the chapel?"

"Oh, yes. He had a legacy from old Mr. Carter. Ten thousand pounds it was, and that was a lot of money back in the sixties!" She paused, considering, then went on. "I don't mean to speak ill of the dead, mind you, but there were some who thought that the money should have been spent on other things."

"Such as?"

"Oh, like a new roof. Or having the drainage done. We do have a bit of a problem with the damp, you see."

He thought of another question. "Those tables in the back—why is one looked after and the other one so untidy?"

Miss Vernon laughed, an embarrassed deep titter. "Oh, you noticed that, did you? Old Mrs. Humphries always used to do the flowers on that table, and keep it tidy. But after she died no one else volunteered to do it. We all have our own things to look after, you see?" she added defensively, gesturing toward the Virgin.

"Well, I've kept you from your flowers long enough, Miss Vernon. Good day to you, and I'll be seeing you again soon."

"Oh, don't go yet, Father Dexter." She scrambled to her feet awkwardly. "I just wanted to . . . well, that is, Miss Barnes and I very much hope that you will come and have tea with us at Monkey Puzzle Cottage just as soon as you've settled in."

"Thank you. Mrs. Dexter and I will be happy to call on you."

"Oh! Mrs. Dexter . . ." She stared at him; St. Mary's had never had a married vicar, not within her memory anyway, and that went back a long time.

"Good afternoon, Miss Vernon." He turned and walked down the center aisle; she watched his erect back with amazement.

"Wait till I tell Alice," she whispered, half to herself and half to the Blessed Virgin Mary.

# Chapter 4

*All my delight is upon the saints, that are in the earth: and upon such as excel in virtue.*

*Psalm 16:3*

"Really, Gwen. I do think you might have told me." There were round spots of color in Alice Barnes's cheeks and her formidable bosom bounced up and down as she rubbed the cloth around and around in vigorous circles on the top of the small pedestal table.

"But, Alice, I did tell you," Gwen protested halfheartedly.

"Yes, but you didn't tell me until today. This morning. Why didn't you tell me you'd met our new priest yesterday, after it had happened?" She looked critically at the highly polished mahogany, and, satisfied, replaced the little protective mat and the telephone (giving it a swift polish for good measure), finally restoring its chintz dust cover.

Gwen gave the mantelpiece an ineffectual swipe with her duster, brushing the lusters which dangled from one of the vases so that they produced a faint, musical tinkle.

"Mind those vases," Alice said sharply. "And don't knock over the Staffordshire!" She moved briskly to the round table in the bay window at the front of the sitting room with her tin of beeswax polish, a neat, compact figure in a pastel-green twinset and a pleated skirt.

"I'm sorry, Alice, but it just went out of my head. Remember, when I got home, Babs had gone missing."

"We *thought* she'd gone missing," Alice corrected her. "But she'd just gone under my bed to chew on my slipper. Hadn't you, you naughty girl?" she addressed the King Charles spaniel which reclined in the shabby wing chair. The dog didn't move, but rolled her protruberant eyes lethargically.

"Well, anyway, I didn't remember until this morning, when you asked me to go to the bakery and get the cream cakes for Father Mark's tea. And then I thought about Father Mark, and the church, and I remembered."

"Honestly, Gwen, your memory is hopeless these days." Again Alice's bosom quaked with the effort of polishing.

"I know. I'm sorry," she said humbly.

"You *did* get the cream cakes, didn't you?"

"Yes, of course. All his favorite kinds. They're in the kitchen."

Alice stopped polishing for a moment and fixed Gwen with her bright eyes. "Why are you just standing there? You could dust the books. After all, they were *your* father's!" She paused while Gwen drifted over to the bookcase which hung above the Edwardian desk. "Describe him to me again."

"My father?"

"No, of course not! I mean Father Dexter!"

Gwen closed her eyes, remembering. "He was quite tall, and good-looking. Blond, wavy hair. Light eyes. Sort of middle-aged, I'd say. Forty-five, or fifty."

"Wearing a cassock?"

"No. A dark suit, and a grey clerical shirt."

"Not black? That's rather odd. Tell me again what he said," Alice commanded. Having finished the table, she was engaged in polishing the leaves of the waxy begonia with her cloth.

"He called me 'my dear lady,' and helped me with the

flowers. Helped me carry them up to the chancel, I mean. He didn't actually help me arrange them."

"And how did he identify himself?"

"Bob Dexter. He said that he would soon be the shepherd of the flock."

"You're sure he didn't say *Father* Dexter?"

"I don't think so."

"That's highly irregular, I must say. And what else did he say?"

Gwen took down a thick, leather-bound volume and dusted it lovingly. "He asked me some questions. About Father Lyons, and the chapel renovations, mostly."

"I wish you'd thought to invite him to tea," Alice said severely.

"Oh, but I did! Didn't I tell you?"

"No, you didn't tell me!"

"That was the most curious thing of all! I asked him to come to tea when he'd settled in, and he said that he and *Mrs.* Dexter would be very happy to call! Alice, he's married!"

Alice stopped in mid-polish, thunderstruck. "Married! I don't believe it! You must have misheard him."

"No, he definitely said Mrs. Dexter!"

There was a long moment of silence, then a look of comprehension dawned. "Gwen! He didn't actually say *his wife*, did he?"

"No . . ."

"Then Mrs. Dexter must be his mother!" Alice finished triumphantly.

Gwen sighed in relief. "Yes, of course. Why didn't I think of that? His mother must keep house for him."

"Gwen, I must say I find it most odd that you should even *think* of a priest being married! You know we've never had a married priest!"

"Sorry, Alice, I don't know why . . ."

The door opened a crack and a second dog, virtually identical to the first, padded into the room, gave a tentative look at the wing chair and, finding it already occupied, moved toward the rose-pink dralon sofa.

"Don't you dare, Nell!" Alice warned. "You know you're not allowed on the good furniture, you naughty girl!"

The dog gave her a baleful stare, and Alice noticed the remnants of something white around her mouth. "What have you been eating, Nell? It looks like . . ." She moved closer. "It looks like cream!"

"Father Mark's cream cakes!" wailed Gwen. "Oh, why did I leave them on the kitchen table!"

Father Mark Judd saw the Nottingham lace curtains at the sitting-room window twitch as he drove up; either the old dears were watching out for him, or else those dreadful dogs were on the loose again—the wing chair that seemed to be reserved for their exclusive use was not far from that window.

Monkey Puzzle Cottage was a small, double-fronted Victorian house, built of Norfolk flint, slate-roofed, and flanked by the two eponymous monkey puzzle trees. It was rather grander in detail than in scale, with mock-Tudor windows and a very elaborate front door. Father Mark, as a frequent visitor, knew that the front door was never used. He parked his car—a bequest from a grateful parishioner—in the road in front of the cottage, locked it, and walked along the small drive at the side of the house. There, alongside the house, resided a car, also never used: an aged, poison-green Mini, secure under its polythene awning. Rumor had it that the car came out once a year or so, but Father Mark had never seen the two ladies using any form of transport but their two matching black Raleigh bicycles. He judged that it would take both of them to operate the complicated crank system to raise the awning from the car. They'd told him once that the car had been bought some years ago, before Miss Vernon's retirement, when the village school had closed its doors for lack of pupils and it had been necessary for her to travel some miles to teach at the new consolidated school.

The car blocked the access to the back garden, so Father Mark's path was of necessity somewhat circuitous, around the Mini and under the pendulous, spiny limbs of the monkey puzzle tree. Fortunately it wasn't yet dark, and he reached the back door without mishap.

They were waiting for him at the door, both of them, with smiles on their faces: Miss Barnes, small and tidy and deceptively fragile-looking with her bright eyes and her fluffy white hair, and Miss Vernon, tall and angular and disheveled, bewigged as usual. The dogs were not in evidence.

"Good afternoon, ladies," he said with a smile. Father Mark Judd was an extraordinarily handsome young man, tall, well-built and muscular, with dark wavy hair falling artistically over his forehead in a widow's peak, a full-lipped mouth above a chiseled chin, and, when he smiled, devastating dimples. Miss Barnes and Miss Vernon were not well known for their susceptibility to masculine pulchritude, but he knew that they had a soft spot for him, and was aware that the dimples had had the desired effect.

"Hello, Father. Do come in," fluttered Gwen Vernon.

"Come this way," added Alice Barnes, leading him into the sitting room. It was the only room in Monkey Puzzle Cottage he'd ever been allowed to see on his regular Monday teatime visits. He imagined that most of the activity of everyday life took place elsewhere in the house; the sitting room was immaculate, and clearly used only for visitors.

Feeling immediately the chill of the room, Father Mark was glad that he had a jumper on under his cassock for additional warmth. The cottage lacked central heating, and the fire in this room seemed never to be lit. The two women were certainly dressed for the temperature, Alice Barnes in her twinset and Gwen Vernon in several woolly layers, topped by a rather moth-eaten cardigan. As he took a seat in one of the pink dralon chairs he couldn't help looking at the fireplace where, instead of a warm fire, there was a fussy pleated paper fan and a basket of fir cones.

"Are you cold, Father Mark?" Gwen asked anxiously, following his glance. "Because if you are, we could light a fire, I suppose. Or I could bring down the electric heater from my room. Or we could sit in the kitchen. It's warm in there. The Aga . . ."

"Do stop fussing, Gwen. I'm sure that Father Mark isn't as sensitive to cold as you are," Alice interposed. She turned to him. "A fire is so dirty," she apologized. "It's difficult enough to keep this room clean, without all the ash and the bother of a fire. Gwen is very cold-blooded, I'm afraid."

"Don't worry about me, Miss Vernon," he replied quickly. "I'm warmly dressed."

"You should be used to the cold. You come from the frozen north, don't you?" Alice recalled humorously. "Northumberland?"

Father Mark preferred not to be reminded of his northern working-class background. "That's right. Not that Norfolk in winter is very much warmer!" He looked around him, noting the uncharacteristically empty chair by the window, and quickly changed the subject. "Where are Babs and Nell? Not ill, are they?"

"They're in the kitchen," Gwen began.

"They've been rather naughty girls, I'm afraid," Alice interrupted, with a warning look at Gwen. She'd told her not to mention the cream cakes, but with Gwen one just never knew. "Are you ready for some tea, Father?"

He rubbed his hands together. "Oh, yes please, Miss Barnes."

"Gwen, you can help me fetch the tea things in," she commanded. It wouldn't be wise to leave Gwen alone with Father Mark—she'd probably tell him about Bob Dexter and spoil the dramatic impact of the story.

He wasn't alone long, but it was long enough to examine once again the contents of the mahogany whatnot in the corner—a few nice pieces of Victoriana, he thought—and to have another look at the large Staffordshire figures on the mantelpiece. The old dears had some lovely things. He told them as much when they returned, Alice bustling in with the tea tray and Gwen trailing behind with a cake stand. "You really do have some lovely antiques," he said, resuming his seat.

Alice's shrug was dismissive. "Nothing special. Mostly Gwen's father's old rubbish."

"They're special to *me*," Gwen said defensively.

"Of course they are," Father Mark soothed. "Family heirlooms."

Alice poured the tea through an antique silver strainer. *Proper* tea, thought Father Mark approvingly. A plume of bergamot-scented smoke wafted from the cup she handed him. "Earl Grey. How nice."

"I didn't give you any milk. You like a slice of lemon with Earl Grey, don't you?" Alice proffered a plate.

"How kind of you to remember."

"And you don't take sugar?"

"No." Having grown up on mugs of sweet tea, giving up sugar had been difficult initially, but he no longer missed it.

Gwen came forward with the cake stand. They'd been able to salvage a few of the cream cakes, and at the last minute Alice had whipped up a few scones.

"Cream cakes! My favorites! And you've made some of your delicious scones. You ladies really do spoil me. I don't deserve such treatment," Father Mark smiled modestly.

"Another cup of tea, Father?"

"That would be lovely." He held out the empty cup.

"One more scone?"

"I couldn't eat another bite."

Alice had managed, with forbidding looks, to prevent Gwen from spilling her news too soon. Now, she judged, it was time; she decided to probe in a subtle way to see how much Father Mark already knew. "You've done such marvelous work here at South Barsham, Father Mark," she began. "But whatever will you do when we get a new priest? It's not a large parish—there won't be much for you to do once we have a full-time priest again. Your appointment here was really only temporary, wasn't it?"

"Yes, but I do have my work at the Shrine," he evaded.

"That's only part time, isn't it? Saying masses for parties of pilgrims, and so forth?"

Father Mark thought for a moment before replying. "Well," he said slowly, "I'm hoping that something else will come up. I've put my name forward for . . . well, for another post. With a bit of luck . . ."

"What sort of post?" Alice was unrelenting in her curiosity.

He hesitated. "You mustn't tell anyone about this." They both nodded. "Actually, it's for quite a nice living. I can't tell you where, but it's in the gift of the Guardians of the Shrine of Our Lady of Walsingham. They have the patronage for a number of livings all over the country, you know."

"I'm *sure* you'll get it, Father Mark," Gwen asserted loyally. "After all, with your connections at the Shrine, and all you've done for them, they couldn't very well give it to anyone else, could they?"

"Well, time will tell, Miss Vernon. Time will tell."

Alice could wait no longer; she played her trump card with a flourish. "You know, do you, that our new priest has already been appointed?"

He saw no harm in sharing the little that he knew. "The Archdeacon told me last week that an appointment would be announced quite soon. That's all I know, really."

"Well." She paused significantly. "Gwen has met him!"

Father Mark sat up. "Met him?!"

"Yesterday, in church. Didn't you know that he was visiting?" Alice couldn't keep the satisfaction from her voice.

"But who is he?" Father Mark turned toward Gwen, who was nibbling nervously on a few scone crumbs.

"His name is Bob Dexter. That's what he said, anyway . . ."

The curate nearly dropped his teacup. "Bob Dexter? Not *the* Bob Dexter?"

"I don't know. I suppose so," she faltered. "But who *is* Bob Dexter?"

"Don't you know? He's one of the highest-profile Evangelicals in the Church of England! He's always shooting his mouth off in General Synod about something or another. And he's one of the loonies who organizes the protests at Walsingham every year!"

"Oh, no!" breathed Gwen and Alice in unison.

"It couldn't be," said Gwen.

"It could be," Alice countered ominously.

# Chapter 5

*He giveth snow like wool: and scattereth the hoar-frost like ashes.*
*He casteth forth his ice like morsels: who is able to abide his frost?*

*Psalm 147:16–17*

David and Lucy had had a quick meal before the concert, so it wasn't too late when he left her at her front door. "It was a marvelous concert, wasn't it? Don't you want to come in for a coffee or a brandy?" she urged.

"I'll give it a miss tonight, I think. You've convinced me that I really have been neglecting Daphne lately, and this would be a good chance for me to have a chat with her. That is, if you don't mind."

Lucy bit her lower lip, longing to put her arms around him, to kiss his generous, mobile mouth, to whisper, "Forget the coffee. Forget the brandy. Forget Daphne. I love you, David. Come up to bed with me." Was it really so impossible? People could change. After all, he had come back to her. She'd lost him for a time—the hold of the past on him had been too strong then—and he'd come back. She knew that she was important to him, that there was no one else. But he'd never given the slightest indication that he wanted anything more than a platonic relationship with her, and it wasn't worth taking the risk of losing him again. She clenched her hands at her sides. "That sounds like a good idea," was all she said. "Have a nice natter with Daphne. See you tomorrow?"

"Of course. 'Night."

He walked past the scaffolded Albert Memorial and through Kensington Gardens; though it was dark and deserted he knew his way well. He was in good spirits, partly because of Lucy and the felicity of her company, and partly with residual pleasure over an important court case he'd won the day before; he whistled a snatch of a theme from the Tchaikovsky symphony they'd just heard, his breath hanging frostily on the night air. Soon, surely, this cold weather would break and spring would make a belated appearance. The daffodils, spring's early harbingers, had struggled their way to the surface, and here and there one of them had even put forth a tentative bud, but they wouldn't be blooming for a while yet in the unsheltered park unless it warmed up. Tonight it even felt cold enough for snow, and the sky had that sort of crystalline feel that often precedes a sudden snowstorm.

Daphne. Lucy had mentioned again this evening that he'd been taking her for granted lately, and he knew that Lucy was right, but he was sure that Daphne didn't mind. They'd known each other long enough—over twenty years!—that he felt he didn't have to make excuses to her. And in spite of his neglect there was a new, or perhaps a renewed, closeness in their relationship since their holiday together last autumn. It had been a lovely holiday, exploring churches in the West Country. The weather had been glorious, the churches superb, and they'd come back from the week with their friendship almost where it had been twenty years earlier, before she'd suddenly canceled the trip they'd planned to take together. Yes, David reflected, a friendship that lasted through the vicissitudes of over twenty years must have a rather special quality. He'd try to do more to nurture it. Before he got to the flat he stopped at an off-license and bought a bottle of Daphne's favorite single-malt whisky; they could have a few drinks tonight, and a long chat.

When he emerged a few minutes later he discovered that it had indeed begun to snow; tiny ice flakes struck his upturned face like frosty pinpricks. David was exhilarated: what a splendid night it was to sit by the fire with a bottle of whisky.

Opening the door at his tap, Daphne looked surprised to see him. "I brought you a bottle," he announced, handing it to her. "And it's snowing!"

"Why, thank you, David. Do come in."

Come in? What else did she think he was going to do? Before he could reflect further on Daphne's odd turn of phrase, he was through the door and realized that she was not alone; an elderly gentleman was lumbering to his feet and stretching out his hand.

"David, you remember Cyril Fitzjames?" Daphne prompted.

"Yes, of course I do. Wing Commander, how nice to see you again." He shook the outstretched hand, dark with liver spots, and smiled into the jowled countenance.

"David, my dear boy! It's been a long time! And it's Cyril to you, not Wing Commander! We've never stood on ceremony before, have we?"

"I'm afraid I haven't been back to a service at St. Anne's since . . . well, for a long time," David admitted. "How have you been keeping?"

"Oh, very well, dear boy. Still churchwarden. Still keeping my eye on things. Still keeping this dear lady and her sacristy budget under control." He gave David an exaggerated wink with one drooping eyelid. "Of course, things at St. Anne's just haven't been the same since . . ." He sighed gustily. "Still, never mind."

David turned to Daphne. "I'm sorry, Daphne—I didn't

mean to interrupt. I didn't realize. I'll just go into the other room."

"Don't be silly. Sit down and join us."

"Actually, my boy, it's time for me to be on my way. I must be up early in the morning—Sunday, you know! Daphne, thank you so much for your hospitality, and for the pleasure of your charming company." Ever the gentleman, he took her hand and bowed.

David hadn't thought that there were very many things that could disturb the unflappable Daphne, but Cyril's courtly gesture seemed to agitate her. "Don't be so daft, Cyril," she said, coloring. "You know you're always welcome here."

"Well, I'll be shoving off. It's snowing, you say? Bad luck. Never mind. My boy, it's a real pleasure to see you again. You must come round for tea sometime when you're in town, you and Daphne." The old man struggled into his overcoat.

"I'd like that."

"We'll fix up a time, then. Cheerio."

When Cyril had gone, Daphne lost no time in fetching the glasses and opening the whisky bottle. "Sit down then, David."

He complied, choosing a seat near the fire. "Mind if I take my tie off?" Without waiting for her affirmative reply, he removed it and slung it over the back of a chair, then put his feet up. "I really do apologize for charging in like that. I hope I didn't interrupt anything important."

She scowled. "No, of course not."

"Church business?"

"Yes and no." She handed David a glass, then settled down opposite him. "Cyril . . . well, he's a lonely man. And in the last few months, since Emily's been gone, he calls round occasionally, just for someone to talk to." Cyril's hopeless attachment to the departed Vicar's wife was not a very well-kept secret in the parish. Daphne shrugged. "I don't mind. I've always been a good ear."

David raised his glass in tribute to her and smiled affectionately. Yes, Daphne had always been a good ear: undemanding,
understanding, undemonstrative Daphne. Impulsively he said,
"You're a good friend, Daphne. I don't tell you that often
enough." For the second time already that evening he saw her
blush, and wondered anew what was the impetus behind their
strange, mismatched friendship. He didn't usually give it
much thought, and it struck him now that it must appear very
strange indeed to those on the outside, to people like Lucy and
even Cyril: the plain, stout woman, never a beauty, over sixty
now, and the reasonably attractive man, no longer young himself yet twenty years her junior. But then people tended not
to understand relationships that didn't fit into neat, easily
defined categories. David didn't really understand it either,
but he valued it highly.

After a flustered moment, Daphne went on with her earlier
train of thought. "Cyril actually did have some church business
to discuss tonight—some last-minute changes in the plans for
the new Vicar's induction service."

"Oh, that's right—he's arriving quite soon, isn't he?"

"It's less than a fortnight now."

Something in her tone of voice intrigued him, and he looked
at her curiously. "Daphne, you don't sound too thrilled."

"Well . . ."

"Come on, what is it?"

"Everyone was really pleased when his appointment was
announced—he sounded like just the man we needed. But
now . . . well, I'm just not so sure, that's all."

"What's changed your mind?"

"For one thing, he's caused some real problems over this
service. The churchwardens had made all the plans, had the
orders of service printed, and everything. And then at the
last minute he's decided that some things need to be altered.
Nothing major, mind you, just a few little things, a few
matters of style . . ."

"Don't tell me he's turned out to be a raving Evangelical!" David said facetiously.

"Hardly likely," was her dry reply. "Not at St. Anne's. But I *am* beginning to wonder about his churchmanship." She paused thoughtfully, regarding the whisky in her glass. "It's beginning to appear that we might have a Modern Roman trendie on our hands."

David whistled. "Oh, boy. Lambswool ponchos, folk Masses and spider plants on the altar."

"Exactly. Of course I may be wrong—and I shall certainly give him the benefit of the doubt. But it doesn't sound good." She sighed.

"Daphne, my dear, I think you need another drink." He proceeded to pour her one.

"But the news isn't all bad," Daphne said, with a quirk of her eyebrows and an ill-concealed smile. "Have you seen the new issue of *Church Building* magazine?"

"No."

"Mine just came today." She found it under a stack of papers on the table, and riffled through it quickly till she found what she was seeking. "Look at this!"

David took it from her, and in a moment the grin on his face matched that on Daphne's. "Well, I'll be! Did you know they were doing this?" he demanded.

"Of course. But I thought it would be nice to surprise you."

The lead article, profusely illustrated with color photographs, was titled "Comper's Glories Restored in Kensington Church," and featured the work that David had supervised in the restoration of the crypt chapel at St. Anne's the previous summer.

"Read it," Daphne urged.

He skimmed through the technical details, already well-known to him, until he reached the part that said, "One of the interesting aspects of the restoration was the involvement in the project of David Middleton-Brown, a Norwich solicitor with no formal qualifications in church architecture. He over-saw the project from start to finish, displaying remarkable sensitivity and knowledge of the craft. In this case, the Law's gain is church architecture's loss; perhaps Mr. Middleton-Brown would like to consider embarking on a second career."

"Daphne! You told them all of this," he accused.

"Yes," she chuckled. "But it's all true. You really should think about doing more of that kind of thing."

"Flattery will get you . . ." David began, then, with rising apprehension, saw the speculative way that she was looking at him. "Hey, what is this all in aid of? What are you up to now, Daphne?"

She shook her head. "You know me too well. How about another drink?"

"Out with it," he ordered sternly, but he extended his glass nonetheless.

"Oh, it's just that . . . well, there's another little project that I think you might be able to help with."

David sighed and settled back in the chair. "Tell me."

"The church is St. John, North Kensington. I know the Sacristan there."

"Ah." He was unable to hide a spark of interest. "That's an E. B. Lamb church, isn't it? One of the really quirky ones?"

Daphne nodded, grinning. "I knew you wouldn't be able to resist."

"What do they want? The last time I saw that church it was in fairly dire condition. It requires a great deal more than the sort of restoration that I've had any experience with, I should think."

"Exactly. The roof is practically falling in, I'm afraid. They desperately need some expert help."

"They want an architect, then, not me," said David, with a rueful shake of his head.

"Well, no." Daphne refilled her glass again. "At least, eventually they'll need an architect, but for now . . ." She smiled to herself at David's interest; it hadn't taken much bait to hook him. "At the beginning they need some aesthetic and architectural advice—surely within your scope. But they also need some legal help. You see, it's not at all a wealthy parish, not like St. Anne's. The only way they'll be able to finance the work is by selling off the school and the church hall."

"Ah."

Daphne leaned forward. "It's important, David. The diocese wants to take the easy way out—they want to close the church, and amalgamate the parish with the one next door. They'll flog off the whole lot to some sharp property developer, and the church will be torn down."

"Not an E. B. Lamb church!" David's indignation was sharp. "That would be a crime!"

"You'll help, then?" she asked quickly.

"It will involve a lot of work, Daphne. Isn't there anyone in the parish . . . ?"

"No one. You wouldn't be stepping on any toes. No one but you could give them the kind of help they need."

Thinking aloud, he said, "They need to find a property developer who would be prepared to keep the school and the church hall standing—to convert them to offices, probably. It might mean playing several property dealers against each other, and negotiating with the charity commissioners as well. Complicated stuff."

"They trust you," she assured him. "I've told them what a good lawyer you are. They've seen the work you've done on our chapel, and . . ."

David narrowed his eyes at her. "Daphne, have you already promised my services?"

Daphne nodded, unabashed. "I knew that you'd want to be involved. It's the project of a lifetime for you!" She proffered the whisky bottle. "Here, David. I think you're the one who needs another drink now."

# Chapter 6

*For all the beasts of the forest are mine: and so are the cattle
upon a thousand hills.
I know all the fowls upon the mountains: and the wild beasts
of the field are in my sight.*

*Psalm 50:10–11*

There was nothing on the exterior of the ordinary-looking
Victorian town house on the outskirts of Norwich to distin-
guish it as the national headquarters of the British Animal
Rights Coalition. Indeed, on the ground floor, apart from the
large poster in the sitting room, there was nothing to set it
apart from a normal home. But upstairs one of the larger
bedrooms had been converted into an office, dominated by a
very sophisticated and extremely expensive computer set-up,
and the small boxroom on the first-floor landing was crammed
so full of stacks of brochures and cartons of badges and bumper
stickers that the door would scarcely open.

Often meetings were held in the office, but tonight's gathering would take place in the sitting room. There was almost a
party atmosphere in the room, with little bowls of snacks
placed strategically around on the tables. They were of course

healthy snacks—sunflower seeds and low-fat crisps and peanuts with raisins—but they were snacks nonetheless. The huge, colorful poster had pride of place tonight; it complemented rather than overwhelmed the decor, defined as it was by the modern paintings that covered the walls.

The enormous black dog in the corner didn't move when the strikingly dressed dark-haired woman entered the room, but the man on the sofa turned and gestured at the bowls of snacks.

"It's not a party, Fiona love. It's a meeting." Rhys Morgan's protest was half-hearted.

"Yes, but I think a bit of celebration is called for. I've got in some sparkling grape juice, so you can have a little toast." Fiona Crawford sat down beside him on the sofa and stroked the red hairs on his arm. "Aren't you cold in that T-shirt, darling?"

He put his arm around her. "You know I'm warm-blooded."

"Mmm. Don't I, though." She snuggled against him, and sighed. "I wish I could stay for the meeting. But I said weeks ago that I'd show up for this gallery do tonight. And if I want them all to come to the opening of the Lucy Kingsley exhibition at the end of the month . . ."

Rhys looked at the clock. "You've got the timer set on the video, have you?"

"Yes, of course. Why don't you turn the telly on now?"

With his free hand he pressed the remote control, and the television sprang to life. They'd come in on the tail end of the adverts, but within a minute or so the video clicked and began its quiet humming as *Anglia News* was announced.

Fiona watched impatiently as the newsreaders intoned the daily assortment of traffic accidents, armed robberies, and factory closures with resultant job losses. Finally they reached the features section, and she leaned forward in anticipation.

"Today in Norwich, a new national organization was officially launched: the British Animal Rights Coalition. Our reporter talked to its founder, Rhys Morgan."

Rhys appeared on the screen, looking solemn as he was confronted with a microphone.

"Mr. Morgan," said the talking head, "there are already a number of organizations devoted to animal rights. Why another one? And why is it based in Norwich? Most national organizations have their headquarters in London."

"I'll answer your second question first, I think. It's based in Norwich because that's where I live. And Norwich is actually very central for many of the activities that we're concerned about. The Norfolk countryside is full of inhumane battery farms—this county supplies most of the nation's poultry, you know. One of the largest animal research laboratories in the country is nearby. Hunting, shooting and other blood sports take place in this area on a regular basis. Cruelty to animals is not confined to the London area, I'm afraid." He paused, then continued earnestly, "And yes, there are already many organizations advocating animal rights. But they've all tended to be very narrowly focused, concentrating on one particular aspect: experimentation, blood sports, fur, and so forth. We're aiming to bring them all together, to supersede narrow interests. We see ourselves very much as an information clearing-house as well as a political pressure group." He went on in the same vein for several minutes.

In front of the screen, Rhys groaned. "I look dreadful."

Fiona gave him a fierce hug. "No you don't, my darling. You look wonderful." She watched him avidly on the screen, a stocky young man with fair, freckled skin and curly hair, thinning in front, of a shocking red hue. The angle of the camera didn't show the bald spot on top, so pronounced that it almost appeared as a tonsure. He was one of those men in whom nature seemed to compensate for hair loss on the head by supplying copious quantities elsewhere on the body, and indeed his full red beard drew attention away from his rapidly balding pate.

"Listen to this bit," he said after a while. "I think you'll be pleased."

His screen image was talking about the poster, as the camera focused on the whole, then showed each of the animals on it in close-up. "We're hoping that this poster will convey the image that we want to project, of an umbrella of caring."

"It's a very striking poster," the interviewer said. "Beautifully done. Was it done by a local artist?"

"No, it was created by Lucy Kingsley, a London-based artist. But for anyone who is interested, there will be an exhibition of her paintings opening locally on the thirtieth of March, at the Bridewell Gallery in Norwich."

"Rhys, darling!" Fiona threw her arms around him. "You've given me a plug! How marvelous!" She kissed him enthusiastically. On the screen his alter ego talked on, but soon he was being ignored by the two on the sofa. "What time are they coming?" she murmured.

"Eight."

"Oh, good. That gives us time."

"But, Fiona . . . your gallery thing."

"It starts at eight. It won't matter if I'm a few minutes late."

"But you're all dressed . . ."

"I can get all dressed again. Just shut up, Rhys, and kiss me some more."

"If you insist."

"I insist."

A few minutes later the announcer was forecasting—at long last—a break in the wintry weather for the Anglia region, but neither of them heard a word, nor did they care. They were quite warm enough already.

Gary Goldstein was the first to arrive, just after eight. He, like Rhys, wore a T-shirt emblazoned with BARC, but in his case it spanned a potbelly that should have been more decently concealed. A veteran of the golden age of protest, the 1960s, Gary looked every inch the aging American hippy that he was, with his long graying hair in a ponytail and droopy gray moustache, with his T-shirt and faded, tattered jeans. Gary's experience in causes ranging from anti-Vietnam protests to "Save the Whales" had been an invaluable help to Rhys in setting up the new organization.

"Hey, man. I caught you on the tube," he greeted Rhys. "Pretty groovy." He flopped on the sofa. "Great publicity. What strings did you pull to get that to happen?"

"As it happens, Fiona knows someone at Anglia Television. One of her regular customers at the gallery. She was telling him about the Lucy Kingsley exhibition, and showed him the poster. He was interested, and followed it up."

"She's a groovy lady, Fiona. Useful to have around, even if she didn't have all that bread!" Gary helped himself to a fistful of sunflower seeds. "Where is she?"

"She had to go out tonight. To some art thing." Rhys indicated the television. "You really thought the interview was all right?"

"Yeah. Didn't you?"

"I hope it was." Rhys sat down on the floor and began absentmindedly stroking the rough black fur of the dog, who hadn't moved for some time. The dog raised its head and licked his hand. "I thought it was very important to get across what we're all about. You know what the current perception of animal rights activists is: that they're a bunch of crazy people with their priorities all screwed up. That they go around blowing up innocent human beings out of a misplaced concern for lower life forms. I wanted to tell people that our function is largely informative. We're here to let people know what's happening to animals, and to give constructive suggestions as to what they can do about it. We're not a terrorist organization— we're people who care about animals. That's the message."

Gary nodded, looking thoughtful. "That's cool with me. But what about Maggie?"

"Maggie." He scratched the dog's ears. "We'll just have to keep Maggie under control, that's all."

"At Berkeley, no matter how committed we were to peaceful demonstrations, there was always one guy who wanted to put a bomb in the president's office. Just don't underestimate Maggie, Rhys." For him it was a long and articulate speech, but Rhys's reply was terse.

"I can handle Maggie."

"She's coming tonight?"

"Yes." It was said neutrally, but then he added with more animation, "Someone else is coming along tonight as well. Someone new."

"Yeah? Who?"

"Does the name Fielding mean anything to you?" Rhys replied elliptically.

"Only that dude on the tube. The chicken dude. With the stuffed chicken thighs."

"That's right!" he said triumphantly. "Frank Fielding of Fielding Farms! One of the biggest battery farmers in south Norfolk, star of his own television adverts."

"*He's* coming tonight?" Gary looked distinctly skeptical. "Get real, man."

"No, not him, of course. It's his son, Nicholas."

"Frank Fielding's son is coming here?"

"Yes. He saw a clip from the interview on the noon news today, and rang me this afternoon. I invited him to come along tonight."

"But why?"

Rhys smiled and proffered a bowl of crisps. "He believes in what we're doing and totally repudiates his father's way of life. But not his money, I believe," he added. "He's got a fair chunk of money, and says he has a few ideas about how we might use it."

"Holy shit!"

"Precisely."

The dog showed more animation than he had all evening when the young woman—she would not appreciate being called a girl—entered the room. He lumbered to his feet and swished his long tail; the young woman greeted the dog before speaking to either of the men. "Hello, Bleddyn. How's my favorite boy tonight?" She scratched his ears and communicated silently with him for a moment, finally raising her head and regarding the men. "So. Now we're official. BARC has been formally launched."

"That's right, Maggie," Rhys replied. "A little later we can have a toast. Fiona's bought us some sparkling grape juice. And we can watch the video of my interview, if you haven't seen it."

"How could I have seen it? You know that I just got off work." Maggie glared at him, took her coat off and threw it on a chair, then flopped down on the floor beside the dog. She, too, was wearing a T-shirt, but hers bore the name of The Green Scene, the vegetarian restaurant where she worked. "And I've just eaten, so don't bother offering me any of those crisps."

Maggie Harrison looked from Rhys to Gary, ready to begin. Everything about her spoke of a strong, uncompromising personality, from her long, straight brown hair to her determined jaw. She had round, horn-rimmed spectacles that collided with her poker-straight fringe, and she wore no makeup.

"We won't start just yet," Rhys said, then explained to her about Nicholas Fielding and his phone call.

Maggie was horrified. "Frank Fielding's son? Frank Fielding is a capitalist pig of the worst kind—one who's made his money from the dead bodies of another species. It's blood money. We should have nothing to do with his son, or his money. We'll tell Nicholas Fielding he can—"

"We'll do nothing of the sort, Maggie." Rhys spoke more severely than was his wont. "Nicholas Fielding seemed very sincere. He said that he's been thinking about all these issues for a long time, and when he saw the piece on telly he knew he had to join us. If he wants to atone for his father's sins—" The doorbell rang. "That must be Nicholas now." With a last warning look at Maggie, he went to answer the bell.

The young man whom he ushered into the room a moment later was not quite what any of them had expected. He was younger than he had sounded on the phone, certainly not yet twenty. And he looked nothing like bluff, hearty Frank Fielding, the stereotypical florid-faced farmer, known to the entire television audience of the United Kingdom for his intrusive, ubiquitous advertisements for stuffed chicken thighs. Nicholas Fielding was tall and willowy, and his chestnut-colored hair was worn in a shoulder-length bob. His features were delicate to a degree that could almost be described as pretty, and the few spots that marred his complexion were a natural condition of his extreme youth. He smiled, an open and friendly smile, and headed straight for the dog. "Hello, doggie. What's your name?"

The dog sniffed him in an interested way. "His name's Bleddyn," Maggie said grudgingly.

"Bleddyn?"

"It's Welsh for wolf," Rhys explained with a smile. "I reckon he's mostly wolfhound."

"He's your dog, then?"

"Yes."

Maggie unbent slightly, disarmed by the boy's interest in the dog. "Rhys rescued him," she explained proudly. "Someone had been using him for hunting and had mistreated him. You should have seen him—he was so skinny. But Rhys saved him, and there's nothing Bleddyn wouldn't do for Rhys."

Nicholas scratched the dog's ears as Rhys introduced him to the others. Then he spied the poster and went over to examine it. "I love this poster," he said enthusiastically. "That's what really caught my attention when I saw it on the telly. It's by Lucy Kingsley, isn't it?"

"Yes, that's right. You've heard of Lucy Kingsley?"

"Oh, yes!" Nicholas turned. "My father . . . well, I suppose you know he's very rich. Rolling in it. He's got a smart investment counselor who's got him started buying art—as an investment, you understand. My father doesn't know anything about art," he said with a condescending sneer. "But this bloke reckons that Lucy Kingsley is undervalued at the moment, and will really go through the roof in the next few years. So my father's bought several of her paintings. He doesn't much care for them—as I said, he doesn't know anything about art— but I think they're smashing. This isn't much like her usual stuff, but it's brilliant, isn't it? Have you actually met her?"

Rhys smiled at the young man's fervor. "Yes, when I commissioned the poster. Fiona, my . . . the woman I live with, owns an art gallery, and she suggested that Lucy Kingsley would be just the right person to do the poster, so we went down to London to talk to her about it. And Fiona's arranged for an exhibition of her work at the gallery, opening at the end of the month."

"What's she like?"

Rhys thought for a minute. "Youngish, sort of mid-thirties. Very pretty, very intelligent, very articulate. *And*," he added proudly, "I'm pleased to say that after I finished with her, she is now a vegetarian! I'm sure you can meet her when she comes for the opening, if you like."

Nicholas grinned back at him. "Fantastic!"

Later, after they'd watched the video and toasted their launch, they got down to business. Far from being shy in the company of those who were senior to him in age and experience, Nicholas entered into their discussions as if he had always been a member of the steering committee of BARC.

"I've been thinking about this all day," he said, "and I've got a plan."

Rhys raised an eyebrow. "Yes?"

"Well, I think I told you that I had some money." He turned to Maggie and Gary to explain. "I've been taking a year off before I go to university next September. My father thought that it would be good for me to travel, so he's given me twenty thousand pounds."

"Wow!" breathed Gary wonderingly, and even Maggie gasped a bit. Nicholas went on. "I haven't really got organized to go anywhere, so I just put it in the bank, and now there's even more. I reckon that I really should do something with it." He paused, turning back to Rhys. "I want to buy a van— a great big van. We can have it painted with BARC on the side, and have it all fitted out. Then I can spend the rest of the year doing what my father wanted: traveling!" He smiled ironically. "I can go all over the country, handing out information and making people aware of their responsibilities to animals. Raising consciousness, giving advice! Taking BARC to the nation!"

"Blood money," Maggie muttered.

"Groovy!" approved Gary.

But Rhys looked at the boy with respect. "Welcome to BARC, Nicholas," he said softly. He raised his empty glass. "To a long and happy association."

# Chapter 7

*I held my tongue, and spake nothing: I kept silence, yea, even from good words; but it was pain and grief to me.*

*Psalm 39:3*

Spring had arrived in earnest by the middle of March, and the vicarage in Richmond, surrounded by spring flowers, had never looked more beautiful than on the day the removal men were due to arrive.

Bob Dexter rose early, as was his habit, and took one last walk around the church. He'd spent much of his career at this church. No one could accuse Bob Dexter of being ambitious for promotion, he thought with self-righteous satisfaction. Twenty years at one church! Becca had been only a baby when they'd come here.

He'd been right to time his departure so that Palm Sunday had been his last appearance, he decided. It was a fitting moment to leave, at the height of the celebrations of Jesus's triumphal entry into Jerusalem, and before the somber reflections of the later part of Holy Week. It was a pity in a way that he wouldn't be there for Easter, but in one sense he felt that it would be a good opportunity for the parishioners to realize the full extent of their loss. They would miss him at Easter, and perhaps that was no bad thing.

He certainly couldn't complain about the warmth of his sendoff. The morning service had been sublime, with the stirring hymn "Ride on! Ride on in majesty!" He felt that it was particularly appropriate, almost as if the "palms and scattered garments strowed" were in part for him. In the evening they'd had a big reception in the church hall, with all sorts of tasty refreshments, and speeches of appreciation, and the presentation of the many gifts. He'd been given a beautiful leather-bound Bible and a large reproduction of Holman Hunt's *The Light of the World* to hang in his new office. There were handmade presents, too: a carved representation of *The Praying Hands* from the Men's Bible Fellowship, and from the Mothers' Union a cushion embroidered with all his favorite texts. All very satisfactory. Sad, in a way, to be leaving after so many years, but Bob Dexter felt ready to tackle the challenge that God had prepared for him.

Returning to the vicarage, he went into the kitchen for a cup of coffee and found his wife in the midst of a sea of tea chests and stacks of crockery. She looked at him with a worried frown. "I don't know if I'll have enough newspapers to wrap it all, Bob."

Dexter smiled. "The loft is full of old parish magazines. You can use those."

Elayne Dexter smiled uncertainly, not sure whether his suggestion was a serious one. Probably so: Bob Dexter was not, on the whole, given to making jokes. "All right, then."

"Any chance of a coffee?"

"Of course, Bob." She instantly stopped her packing, switched on the kettle, and selected two mugs, one of which bore the inscription "Christians aren't perfect, just forgiven," and the other "Thank God for Jesus."

Elayne Dexter had never been a great beauty, but in middle age her appearance could best be characterized as nondescript.

She had the sort of anonymous face that one could pass in the street every day, speak to in the shops, and still fail to recognize when introduced. It might be fair to say that she had lived so long in the shadow of her handsome, self-confident husband that she cast scarcely any shadow herself, but this was a situation she had long since accepted. She was the perfect Vicar's wife: stalwart of the choir, Sunday School teacher, leader of the Pathfinders, faithful member of the Mothers' Union, and head of the Women's Bible Fellowship. And she regarded Bob Dexter as only a little lower than the triune God.

"Where's Becca?" he asked. "Maybe she'd like a coffee, too."

"In your study, I think." Elayne reached for Becca's old Bunnykins mug and spooned in some instant coffee granules.

"I'll take it to her," Dexter offered. He left Elayne with her solitary mug of coffee and her packing; with a steaming mug in each hand he went up the stairs to his study and pushed the door open with his foot.

"Daddy!" Rebecca Dexter turned from his desk with a welcoming smile, and Dexter's heart turned over as it always did when he saw her. His Becca. He still couldn't believe that this exquisite creature was his daughter. It was really only recently that she'd lost her adolescent puppy fat and turned into a beautiful young woman. She had his coloring, but her blue eyes were huge and luminous, and her ash-blond hair was shiny and straight and so long that she could sit on it. He loved her hair, especially when she wore it, as now, straight down her back with just a band to hold it back from her face. That lovely face! The feature that prevented her from being a classical beauty, but paradoxically that gave her face much of its charm, was her somewhat short, slightly tiptilted nose. She wrinkled that nose now, as she smelled the coffee. "Oh, Daddy, you've brought me some coffee! You must have read my mind." She reached for the Bunnykins mug.

"Good morning, Princess. How are you?"

"Oh, fine, Daddy. I've got all of your books packed, and practically everything out of your desk."

"You don't really need to empty out the desk, you know. It's going with us." He crossed the room and looked at the array of items spread out on the desk.

She moved beside him and linked her free arm through his. "I know, but I thought it was a good opportunity to have a clear-out. I don't think you've emptied out your desk for years! And look what I found in the back of a drawer. Do you remember this, Daddy?" Rebecca pointed to a plaster paperweight, painted garishly in primary colors and bearing the imprint of a small hand.

"Of course I remember it, Princess. You made it for me for Christmas one year—it was one of the nicest presents I ever got." He smiled down at her, then looked at her searchingly. "How do you feel about leaving here, Becca? Do you mind?" Almost as if he were thinking aloud, he added, "There's nothing in the world that matters more to Bob Dexter—aside from doing the Will of God, of course—than making his Princess happy."

She shrugged. "It's a little sad. It's the only house I've ever known. There are a lot of memories in this house."

A lot of memories. "But the new vicarage is very nice," he said. "We'll settle in there quickly, I'm sure. We'll all be together, that's the important thing. And—will you be glad to be nearer to Toby Gates?"

Rebecca smiled at her father. "Toby Gates is a nice chap. I know a lot of nice chaps, Daddy."

Bob Dexter was satisfied. Becca's heart was still his.

Later in the day, while the removal men were loading their van, Elayne Dexter slipped unnoticed out of the house and went across to the church. But instead of going in, she went around the back to a secluded part of the churchyard. Sheltered by the church, she felt safe from being observed—Bob couldn't possibly see her from the vicarage, even from an upstairs window.

The tiny grave had been carefully tended; last year's grass had been kept clipped and the new spring grass, a pale vulnerable green, had only begun to poke up slender tentative shoots. Bob never came back here, never knew how much time she spent tidying this small bit of earth. Elayne removed the wilted daffodils and replaced them with fresh ones, for the last time. Next week the daffodils would be dead, and she would be far away. Bob had never asked her if she wanted to move, and even if he had, she would never have been able to tell him her real reason for wanting to stay in this place. The thought of abandoning this little grave to uncaring strangers, probably never seeing it again, was more than she could bear. Painful tears pricked her eyes and she leaned back on her heels, reading the words on the stone for the many thousandth time. The last time, she thought with a little sob. "Baby Dexter. He is with Jesus for eternity," and the dates, so long ago now—nearly eighteen years past. So few the days he'd been with her, her little Bobby. Bob had refused to have him baptized—he didn't much agree with infant baptism anyway—so he didn't have an official name, her baby. Of course he was always supposed to be Robert Dexter, after his father, during those months when they'd waited for his birth. Then when . . . things had gone wrong, Bob had forbidden her to name him. But Elayne always thought of him as Bobby, and that was how she addressed him now, as she said her farewells. "Goodbye, my darling little Bobby," she whispered through her tears. "I have to go away now, but I'll never forget you."

# Chapter 8

*When the people are gathered together: and the kingdoms also, to serve the Lord.*

*Psalm 102:22*

Bob Dexter stood in the shadows at the back of the church, as inconspicuous as is possible for a handsome man over six feet tall. From his vantage point he'd been able to observe the congregation, as well as all that went on.

There weren't many people present—no more than twenty, he judged—but that was not bad for a small rural parish, and a week night. At his Richmond church he would have had two hundred, particularly if he had been speaking, but Bob Dexter realized that different standards now applied. No doubt by next year, under his leadership, the church would be bursting at the seams. He found his mind wandering from the speaker, mentally identifying places where extra chairs could be put in next year to accommodate the overflow. Perhaps it would even be a good idea to rip the pews out; old church pews fetched a good price on the antiques market, he knew, and it would certainly give them a lot more flexibility.

Many of the congregation seemed to be elderly, Dexter observed; gray and white heads predominated. He'd bring in

young families and teenagers, the lifeblood of a parish church.
If there wasn't a Pathfinders group he'd start one right away,
and of course Elayne would take over the Sunday School.

He focused his attention again on the man in the pulpit.
The poster on the notice board had said "Holy Week talks by
Father Owen Osborne," but apart from the name Dexter had
no idea who the man was. He was a small, rather stout—even
rotund—man with a cherubic round face and a shiny bald head
wreathed with white hair. His mobile, bushy eyebrows moved
up and down rather disconcertingly to punctuate his words.
He had a cultured, Oxbridge voice, and Dexter had to admit
to himself that he could find no fault in what the man had
said. He'd been preaching from Scripture, and speaking about
Our Lord. His talk was learned rather than impassioned, but
Dexter was an educated man himself, and though it was not
his style he found the man's sermon acceptable. Perhaps this
church was not as bad as he'd thought, not as far gone in
idolatry and abominable practices.

When the address was over, he drew a bit farther back into
the shadows as the congregation trickled toward the north
porch exit. Genuflecting as they left the pews, Dexter noted
with a small shudder. He was not sufficiently well hidden,
though; Gwen Vernon, a woolly cap over her golden wig,
caught sight of him with a little squeak, and pulled Alice
Barnes in his direction, whispering frantically. Fortunately
they were among the last to leave, so he was able to escape
general attention.

"Alice, this is . . . this is . . ."

"Bob Dexter," he interposed. "And you must be Miss
Barnes. Hello, Miss Vernon. How nice to see you again."

Alice Barnes looked up at him, for once as tongue-tied as
Gwen. He certainly was an impressive-looking man; perhaps
Father Mark had been mistaken about his reputation. Finally
she spoke. "We do hope that you and—Mrs. Dexter—will
come to tea with us. As soon as possible."

Dexter considered. It might be a good thing to begin to get to know his parishioners right away. "Tomorrow?" he suggested.

The two women looked at each other and unspoken messages passed between them. It was Maundy Thursday tomorrow, and they had much to do to prepare the church for the evening service. But this was not an opportunity to be missed—to be the first in the parish to entertain the new priest. "That will be lovely," Alice said firmly. "Monkey Puzzle Cottage. Anyone can tell you where that is. Half past three, if that's convenient."

"I shall look forward to it, my dear ladies." And Dexter smiled.

A moment later he was again approached, this time by a dark-haired man in a cassock. The man was as tall as Dexter, but younger—mid-twenties, Dexter judged—and even more handsome than he in an almost film-star way. He looked Dexter in the eyes, and extended his hand. "Hello. I'm Mark Judd. I've been looking after this church in the interregnum."

Dexter took his hand, approving of the firm grip. "I'm Bob Dexter."

"Yes, I know. I've seen you on television. Welcome to South Barsham."

"Thank you. It's good to be here. I'm looking forward to beginning work."

Mark smiled. "What did you think of our little gathering tonight?"

"Quite . . . acceptable. Who was the speaker?" Dexter asked.

"Owen Osborne. He's a colleague of mine . . . at the Shrine."

Dexter stiffened. So this young man was one of *them*. He seemed pleasant enough, but clearly he'd need watching. "What do you do at the . . . at that place?"

"Oh, I take Mass for parties of pilgrims, do my turn on the rota for daily sprinklings at the Holy Well, that sort of thing."

Mark shrugged. "It's not very challenging. I much prefer parish work."

"You've been working in this parish for quite a few months, I think."

"Just about a year," Mark explained. "Father Lyons died at Easter last year. My work at the Shrine only takes up a bit of my time, so it's been good to have the parish to look after as well."

"What is the congregation like?" Dexter asked. "Was to-night's crowd . . . representative?"

Mark looked amused. "You mean, don't you, are they all so old? I'm afraid it's largely a congregation of felt bundles. Sweet old dears, most of them, but not a lot of life in the place. We don't have very many young people—though I've attracted a few recently."

Young ladies, no doubt, Dexter reflected. Unattached young ladies—or even attached ones, with looks like those. Too bad he couldn't be of any use to them: everyone knew that all the priests at Walsingham were poofs and perverts. Perhaps he'd attracted a few young men, too. That sort of thing couldn't be countenanced in his church. A Pathfinders group, that's what was needed here. Wholesome physical activity and lots of Bible study.

"You've met Miss Barnes and Miss Vernon?" Mark asked.

"Yes."

"Two lovely, devout women," he declared piously. "Always engaged in good works on behalf of the church."

"I'm having tea with them tomorrow. Perhaps you could tell me something about them," Dexter invited.

"They've lived in the village, at Monkey Puzzle Cottage, for many years. Miss Barnes was the district nurse. Miss Vernon was the teacher at the village school until it closed down. They're both retired now."

A horrible suspicion formed itself in Bob Dexter's mind. "They're not . . . unnatural, are they?"

Mark assumed a very severe and self-righteous expression. "There has been talk in the village, of course. There always is when two women live together for as many years as they have. But I think it's better not to speculate about such things, don't you?"

"Of course," Dexter said hastily, and changed the subject. "What sort of good works do they do? I know that they arrange the flowers, the ones by . . . that . . . statue in the chancel."

"Oh, Miss Vernon has been the Sunday School teacher for years. Miss Barnes cleans the silver. And now that they're retired, they devote their lives to producing and distributing religious tracts." Mark smiled blandly.

"Religious tracts!"

"Yes. They spend a great deal of time cycling around the parish, as well as neighboring parishes, and delivering their tracts to where they feel they might do the most good."

Dexter began to think that he might have been hasty in dismissing the two women as idolaters. Teaching Sunday School, and religious tracts—perhaps in them he would find allies in his battle for the souls of his congregation. It was just as well that he was having tea with them tomorrow. He could enlist their aid from the beginning.

Mark interrupted his reverie. "I must be going now. But I do hope you'll be joining us tomorrow night for our Maundy Thursday observances. I think you'll find them . . . memorable."

"Bob Dexter will be there."

# Chapter 9

*Then shall he speak unto them in his wrath: and vex them in his sore displeasure.*

*Psalm 2:5*

Elayne looked out of the window at the fresh spring morning. She was tired of unpacking, and it seemed as if the job would never be done. Bob and Becca were upstairs, sorting out his office; she'd just taken them some coffee, so she didn't think she'd be missed if she slipped out for a few minutes. She grabbed an old cardigan and let herself out the back door.

The church was only a few yards away. Elayne hadn't yet been inside, and was a bit curious after what Bob had told her about all the statues and the candles. The north porch door stood open invitingly, so she went down the steps and entered the building.

Though several of the windows were clear glass, the sunlight, so bright outside, made very little impact in here. She stood quietly for a moment as her eyes adjusted to the gloom. There were muffled voices coming from the chapel, although the red velvet curtain screened it from view, and she moved toward the voices, looking with amazement at each of the statues as she passed.

Elayne was light on her feet, and the occupants of the chapel were engrossed in what they were doing, so her arrival went unnoticed. The scene before her in the chapel was so unfamiliar that it took her a moment to assimilate what was happening. Two elderly women—from Bob's description she recognized them as Gwen Vernon and Alice Barnes—were in the process of creating a garden, right there in the chapel. There were bunches of daffodils, and frothy sprays of golden forsythia, and all manner of greenery, and the two women were arranging them with great care in front of the altar. Interspersed among the flora were a number of very large candlesticks; on the altar was a decorated box made of some sort of metal, its hinged door standing open. And high above the altar, in a little niche on the wall, she noticed a statue of a woman holding a baby. The draping of her garments, carved skilfully in stone, emphasized the fluid curve of her body as she leaned slightly, compensating for the weight of the child.

Elayne didn't understand it, but recognized that it was very beautiful. Something about the loving care with which the women handled the foliage made her think about that lonely grave—its daffodils would now be wilting—and tears sprang to her eyes. Elayne swallowed hard. She *mustn't* cry over Bobby. Not now. She moved forward and the women turned.

"I'm . . . I'm so sorry to bother you," she said softly, "but could you tell me what you're doing?"

The two women looked at her, then at each other. A lone stranger in the church—not likely that she was a tourist. Could she be . . . ?

Sensing their thoughts, she added, "I'm sorry. I should introduce myself. I'm Elayne Dexter."

Gwen allowed herself a small glance of triumph at Alice—clearly *not* his mother after all!—as she scrambled to her feet. But Alice was the first to reach Elayne, with her hand outstretched. "Welcome to St. Mary's, Mrs. Dexter. I'm Alice Barnes."

"I thought that you must be. Bob has mentioned you, and Miss Vernon. How do you do?"

The formalities out of the way, they turned their attention to the flower-bedecked altar plinth. "Why are you doing this?" Elayne repeated.

"It's the Garden of Repose," Alice replied. "For the Vigil tonight."

"I'm afraid I don't understand. Would you mind explaining it to me?"

"The Garden of Gethsemane, where Jesus spent the night in prayer—" Gwen began, but Alice interrupted.

"I'm sure that Mrs. Dexter knows about the Garden of Gethsemane." She turned to Elayne. "We create the Garden of Repose in here, and tonight at the Maundy Thursday service the procession will end up here. With Our Lady looking on." She pointed at the statue high up in the niche. "The Host will be put in the tabernacle"—she indicated the box on the altar— "to represent Christ in the garden, and people will stay throughout the night in prayer, in preparation for Good Friday tomorrow. We don't stay *all* night," she added practically. "There's a rota. People come in for an hour or so at a time. But there will be someone here at all times. You're welcome to come if you like. It's really lovely with only the candles for light."

Elayne gazed at the garden, so beautiful but so alien. "I'd like to see it, but I—I don't think Bob would want me to," she replied doubtfully.

In the end, Bob went to tea at Monkey Puzzle Cottage on his own. Elayne had intended to accompany him, but when it was time to leave she was in the midst of preparing a casserole to put in the oven for their evening meal. "Can't you wait until I've finished with this?" she asked.

"I'm afraid not. They said half past three, and Bob Dexter is not in the habit of being late."

"Oh, all right. I suppose you'd better go on without me, then. Or why don't you take Becca?"

"Becca is arranging my books on the shelves in my office. I'll just have to go by myself." He sighed a martyr's sigh as he took his keys from his pocket.

"Are you going in the car, then? It's not far, is it?"

Dexter glared at his wife. "Of course it's not far," he explained to her in a patronizing voice. "Nothing in the village is far. But I have something heavy to take with me. This morning when I was unpacking my papers I found a huge box of Noah Gates's tracts—you know, those ones he did called 'Jesus: the only way to God.' That curate told me last night that Miss Barnes and Miss Vernon produce and distribute their own tracts, so I thought I'd take them some of Noah's. Perhaps they can take some of them round at the same time."

Elayne looked doubtful. Somehow from what she'd seen of Miss Barnes and Miss Vernon, she didn't think they'd be very interested in Noah Gates's tracts. But Bob seemed to know what he was talking about, so she held her tongue.

As Dexter stowed the box in the passenger seat, he took one of the tracts out and looked at it approvingly, then put it in his pocket to show the ladies. So often these leaflets were poorly printed and badly presented, but Noah knew how to do things properly. He always said, "If you can't give your best to Jesus, who can you give it to?" And so they were of a very high quality, printed on glossy paper.

Now that he was living in the neighborhood, Dexter thought, he ought to pay a call on Noah and see if there might be any way he could be of help to him. Perhaps he could write a few tracts, something that they could distribute to the misguided at Walsingham. Next week he might have time for a trip to Fakenham.

The visit to Monkey Puzzle Cottage did not have a propitious beginning, had Dexter believed in such superstitious

nonsense as portents. He took the wrong turning by the Two
Magpies, and soon found himself out of the village. By the
time he had corrected the error, and located the cottage, he
knew that he would not be on time.

Dexter spotted the monkey puzzle trees and pulled his car
up on the verge. The lace curtains twitched, then parted as he
approached the front door, and frantic gestures indicated that
he was to go around to his left. Dexter scowled as he fought
his way around the house, past the car and under the monkey
puzzle tree, finally arriving at the back door. Uncivilized,
that's what it was. Why on earth couldn't they open the front
door?

Amongst the greetings, Gwen Vernon fluttered with apologies. "I'm so sorry, Father. We don't use the front door. A
nuisance, I know. But there's such a draft . . ." She indicated
the ancient thick velvet curtain that hung across the inside of
the front door.

Dexter forced a smile. "I quite understand." In a moment
he found himself in the sitting room, ensconced on the dralon
sofa in the seat of honor. No sooner had he sat down than
the door was pushed open and two dogs appeared, eager to
investigate the intruder. They snuffled round his trouser legs
with enthusiasm while Dexter sat stiffly.

"Babs! Nell! You mustn't bother Father," Gwen protested
halfheartedly, then added, "You don't mind, do you, Father?"

He forced a smile to take the sting out of his words. "I don't
like dogs," he admitted.

"Out, girls!" Alice ordered, and the dogs obeyed grudgingly. She followed them to shut them in the kitchen.

Dexter smiled again at Gwen, a bit more convincingly. "So,
Miss Vernon—may I call you Gwen?"

It seemed a bit precipitate, if not actually improper—Father
Mark *always* called her Miss Vernon—but she nodded.

"It's a very pretty name," he added ingratiatingly. "Gwen-
dolyn, is it?"

"Actually, it's short for Guinevere," she explained. "My father was the foremost authority of his generation on Tennyson. *Idylls of the King*, you know." She indicated the bookshelf over the desk. "Those are his books. And his desk. He was a very noted academic. At Cambridge."

Alice reentered the room. "Oh, Gwen. You're not on about your father again, are you? I'm sure that Father Dexter isn't interested."

Gwen shot her a hurt look and subsided into one of the chairs.

"Gwen was just telling me about her name," Dexter said easily. "And you, Alice—were you named for Alice in Wonderland, then?" He smiled again.

Alice looked shocked. "I should think not. I was named for my godmother."

Gwen leaned forward. "And what shall we call you?" she asked shyly. "Father Bob or Father Dexter? We call Father Mark Father Mark, but we always called Father Lyons Father Lyons, if you understand what I mean."

Dexter drew back, controlling his expression. "You may call me Bob," he said with forced heartiness. "Or if that seems too disrespectful, 'Pastor' will do."

Alice and Gwen looked at one another. Neither could bring herself to look at Bob Dexter.

It went from bad to worse. Over tea, Gwen mentioned Elayne. "We were expecting Mrs. Dexter to be with you," she said.

"She was tied up at home and couldn't get away," Dexter explained.

"But she told us this morning that she'd be coming."

"This morning? You saw Elayne this morning?"

"Why, yes. We met her in church. We were working on the Garden of Repose, and she . . ." Gwen tailed off as she saw the expression on Dexter's face.

"Elayne didn't tell me she'd been in church this morning."
His voice was quiet and flat.

"Gwen . . ." Alice said warningly.

"Oh, dear. Well, I'm sure I didn't mean any harm . . ."

Alice jumped in and changed the subject abruptly. "We
know that you won't be instituted until next week, and that
you're not officially our Vicar until then, but Gwen and I were
wondering if you would be willing to hear our confessions
tomorrow morning—we like to make our confessions on Good
Friday before the Three Hours."

"Certainly not," he said, far too forcefully. The very idea
filled him with horror. Even if he had believed in such popish
nonsense, he couldn't imagine a bigger waste of time than
listening to saintly old women bleating about their imagined
sins. And if their sins were real—if, indeed, Miss Barnes and
Miss Vernon enjoyed carnal knowledge of each other—he most
assuredly did not want to know about it. It didn't bear thinking about.

"But it's a Sacrament of the Church!" Alice reminded him
sharply.

"Perhaps Father Mark . . ." Gwen interposed.

"Yes," he said. "I think you should ask him."

Father Mark's name came up again a few minutes later. "I was
told by—that young curate, Mark, that you ladies produced
religious tracts," Dexter probed. "Do you have some sort of a
printing press?"

Alice and Gwen exchanged glances. "I don't know what
Father Mark told you, but perhaps he's given you the wrong
idea," Alice replied at last, cautiously. "I wouldn't exactly call
them religious tracts."

"We don't have a printing press. We do them by hand,"
explained Gwen. "I do the calligraphy and Alice does the
illustrations. Decorations, really."

"And you distribute them in the parish?"

"Well, yes, and beyond. We go round once a week on our bicycles with them. As far as we can get on our bicycles." Gwen smiled tentatively. Perhaps if she kept on talking he wouldn't ask to see them, and a crisis could be averted.

"Do you think I might see?"

Again the women looked at each other. "Well, we work in the dining room," Gwen replied elliptically. "That's where we work."

Dexter rose to his feet. "Please lead the way. I'd quite like to see what you do."

There was nothing for it. Alice shot Gwen a look of reproach, as though she might have stopped it, and crossed the hall to the dining room with Gwen and Dexter behind her.

It was a small room with a red Turkey carpet, dominated by a very large round rosewood table. Crowded around the table were five chairs, and a rosewood chiffonier was backed against one wall. Dexter noticed immediately the large print of Our Lady of Walsingham hanging on the wall, and his face stiffened into disapproval even before, with a half-hearted gesture, Gwen indicated the array of hand-lettered prayer cards spread out all over the table. Dexter picked one up. "Hail to thee, O Queen of Heaven," he read with mounting fury. Queen of Heaven! "Ladies, I'm afraid this just won't do!"

Alice pressed her lips together, and Gwen crossed her arms across her narrow chest.

The battle lines were drawn.

# Chapter 10

*They made a calf in Horeb: and worshipped the molten image.*
                                            *Psalm 106:19*

Bob Dexter attended the Maundy Thursday service at St. Mary's as a guest; since his institution and installation as Vicar would not take place until the following Monday, he had no official right to be there. He arrived shortly after the service began, and sat by himself in the back pew.

Elayne had wanted to come with him, but he'd insisted that she stay at home and continue with the unpacking. He'd been rather cross with Elayne: his discovery that she'd been in the church that morning without telling him was most disturbing. But he'd believed her explanation that she'd merely forgotten to mention it, and had let her off with a warning about her faulty memory. She'd been suitably penitent, and had meekly accepted his edict that she remain at home that evening.

There was a fairly full church tonight, he noted—more people than on Wednesday evening. The sense of anticipation was almost as heavy in the air as the smell of the incense, which Dexter found overpoweringly noxious. Although he had not intended to draw attention to himself, he was unable to stifle a rather ostentatious cough as the Gospel procession brought the incense out into the nave of the church, and several people looked at him curiously.

The service began as a normal communion service. But after Owen Osborne's brief meditation (Dexter wouldn't dignify so short a talk by calling it a sermon) on the Upper Room, strange things began to happen. Osborne and the curate, Mark Judd, tied towels around their waists and moved out into the center aisle, followed by servers with basins and ewers. The two clergymen knelt beside the people seated on either side of the aisle, Osborne on the left and Judd on the right, and carefully washed the bare feet of each, dried them carefully with the towels, then moved on to the people behind. This was done in total silence, and was repeated until twelve parishioners had been so treated.

The rest of the service followed its normal course, but at the conclusion, instead of the blessing and dismissal, there were signs of other unusual events. Dexter sat up straight and watched very carefully as the servers mobilized and Owen Osborne took the lidded, pierced silver pot which held the incense and swung it by its chain toward the chalice that had been left on the altar. One of the servers put a piece of cloth around Osborne's shoulders, and with the edges of it the clergyman lifted the chalice from the altar.

The man with the large processional cross turned toward the congregation and moved out into the aisle, flanked by the two acolytes with their candles. But the young man with the incense walked backwards, swinging it at the chalice which was reverently borne in Osborne's outstretched hands. As the procession passed along the aisle the members of the congregation knelt, their faces averted. They sang quietly, "Of the glorious Body telling," and over the sound of their song could be heard the chink of the chains of the swinging thurible. The procession turned and went along the back of the church, right past Dexter, who choked violently at the proximity of the incense, puffing out in clouds and wreathing Osborne's head in smoke. The old man's face seemed transfigured as he gazed at the chalice which he bore before him, and Dexter could see the same awed, adoring look on the faces of the congregation. "Therefore we, before him bending, this great Sacrament revere," they sang in unison plainsong, joining on the end of the procession until the entire congregation was moving, following the procession around the side of the church to the chapel.

Fascinated in spite of himself, Dexter followed at the rear. As he entered the chapel he saw the artificially created garden, now lit only by candles, with all the people gathered around. At the end of the song Osborne moved up to the altar and put the chalice into the metal box which stood open to receive it, then took the incense and swung it repeatedly. Finally he knelt down before the altar and quietly read out Psalm 22: "My God, my God, look upon me; why hast thou forsaken me: and art so far from my health, and from the words of my complaint?" At the end of the Psalm he rose and left quickly; the congregation melted away without a word, and Dexter found himself standing alone in the chapel, staring with horror at the idolatrous abomination.

"Worshipping a piece of bread!" he thundered. "I've never seen anything so . . . so shocking in my entire life!" His eyes blazed in a white face.

Elayne busied herself in making him coffee. "I'm sure they don't look at it that way," she suggested. "I asked Miss Barnes about it. About the tabernacle—that's what they call that box. She said that the wafer represents Christ's presence. They're worshipping Jesus, not the wafer."

"Nonsense!"

"But Bob—"

"Elayne, you know nothing about this! You weren't there— I was! And you can believe me when I tell you that it was absolutely disgusting! It was like the Israelites in the wilderness, worshiping the Golden Calf! Bowing and scraping to an idol . . ." He shuddered dramatically. "God will punish them for it. You can mark my words."

She handed him the "Thank God for Jesus" mug. "But if they think—"

"I don't care what they think!" he shouted. "Right is right, and wrong is wrong, and God has sent Bob Dexter to this place to teach these people the difference!"

"But—"

He turned on his wife with fury. "Stop contradicting me, woman! And I absolutely forbid you to talk to those hateful women ever again! Do you understand me?"

She cast her eyes down. "Yes, Bob."

"Only four more days, and then I'll show them! They'll learn soon enough that Bob Dexter will not abide their ungodly behavior!" He slammed the mug down on the counter with such force that it shattered; Elayne looked in horror at the shards of pottery, the set white face of her husband, and the outstretched hand, dripping bright red blood.

# Chapter 11

*For in the time of trouble he shall hide me in his tabernacle: yea, in the secret place of his dwelling shall he hide me, and set me upon a rock of stone.*

*Psalm 27:5*

The house was very quiet. Lying awake, Elayne could hear the regular ticking of the bedside clock, and her husband's measured breathing. Bob Dexter always slept deeply; in years gone by he'd never been the one to rise in the middle of the night to minister to an ailing Becca. After a long while Elayne eased out of bed, shivering suddenly in the chill of the room. Bob did not stir. She found her discarded clothing on the chair— Bob always berated her when she failed to hang her clothes in the wardrobe as soon as she took them off—and dressed quickly and quietly. Her shoes, too, were easily found in the dark, and the old cardigan that she wore for extra warmth. In a moment, Bob Dexter was alone in the bedroom, and Elayne crept down the stairs and let herself out of the house.

The church was a dark shape in the night, with only a very faint light filtering through the windows of the chapel. But the north porch door was open, and Elayne found her way easily.

She caught her breath at the sight before her in the chapel. There were only two people there, kneeling silently and motionlessly before the altar. The Garden of Repose was indeed beautiful; the flowers, so vibrantly colorful by day, seemed curiously muted and transformed in the light of the flickering candles. The tabernacle glinted gold, reflecting the flames. And high above in the shadows, the ancient statue smiled radiantly and lovingly at the child in her arms, her beautiful face illuminated softly by the candlelight.

Bob Dexter had a longstanding commitment to lead a youth retreat over the Easter weekend, so he'd planned to leave the house early on Friday morning.

Becca was up early, too, to make him his breakfast, and she looked with horror at his bandage-swathed hand. "Daddy, you can't possibly drive with your hand like that," she insisted. So she hurriedly packed a case and went with him, as his chauffeur; when Elayne woke a bit later, she was alone in the house.

She found a terse note on the bedside table to inform her of the fact. "Becca has gone with me to the retreat. We will be back on Sunday evening."

It was not often that Elayne was completely alone. The cup of tea that had been left with the note was quite cold, so after a few minutes she got up and went downstairs to make a fresh pot. She washed up Bob's and Becca's breakfast dishes, which had been left on the kitchen table, then went back upstairs and luxuriated in a hot bath for nearly an hour.

"Idle hands are the Devil's workshop," she'd heard Bob Dexter say often enough, so Elayne thought hard about what to do next. The unpacking had been entirely accomplished, and everything was in its place. There was not much point in baking hot cross buns with no one to eat them, and there was no church fête on the horizon for which she could busy herself making jams or knitting loo-roll covers. On Good Friday the village shops would probably be shut, so there wasn't even the opportunity to spend some time poking around their unfamiliar shelves on the pretext of needing a light bulb or a packet of sugar. She would have loved to read a book—a forbidden pleasure when Bob Dexter was around—but she knew that there was nothing interesting in the house, and she had not yet discovered the whereabouts of the nearest public library.

She could write a letter, Elayne decided at last. She wished there were someone in Richmond whom she could write to, but Bob had always discouraged her from getting too close to anyone in the congregation—showing favoritism, he called it—so she had not a single friend to show for the last twenty years of her life. She couldn't very well write to her sister, she thought. She and her only sister had been very close when they were young, but her sister had married a country doctor, a supremely secular man with whom Bob Dexter had nothing in common and in whose company he was most uncomfortable. So now their contact was sporadic at best; Dexter had always had the very good excuse of not being able to get away at Christmas or weekends, and Elayne saw her sister very rarely. They always wrote to each other at Christmas, general letters full of the children's latest accomplishments, but she didn't know what she could say to her sister now.

Elayne did write occasionally—once or twice a month, perhaps—to her mother, though the reply was rarely more than a brief, breathless phone call. She never had the feeling that her mother needed or even appreciated her letters, so busy was she with her friends and her social activities. Since Elayne's father had died, shortly after his retirement, his widow had made a new life for herself in the south coast town where they'd retired and her family was no longer the center of her life. Elayne decided to write to her now, to tell her about the move and to describe their new surroundings. She found some writing paper in the bureau in the sitting room and settled down with pen in hand.

When the letter had been signed, addressed and stamped,

she decided she might as well walk into the village and post it immediately, though it would not arrive until after the long Easter weekend. The post was generally collected only once on Good Friday, but perhaps she had not yet missed that noon collection. She looked at her watch: a quarter to twelve.

On her way into the village, Elayne passed several people who seemed to be heading for the church, and realized that there would probably be a service beginning at noon. Why not go? she thought. There was nothing better to do, and at least it would pass the time.

The church was very somber, with none of the candlelit magic of the night before. The high altar had been stripped down to the bare wood, and the only cross visible was made of wood rather than of precious metal. Elayne chose a seat near the rear.

The service started at twelve o'clock with a familiar Good Friday hymn, and Elayne joined in with her pure soprano voice. A few people turned around to locate the source of the abnormally tuneful singing but she was oblivious to their stares. After the hymn, a rotund man in a black chasuble mounted the steps of the pulpit and fixed his gaze on the congregation. He looked not in the least impressive to Elayne, who was used to Bob's commanding presence in the pulpit, but as he began to speak she was immediately captivated by the quality of his voice, which was cultured and melodious; only after a few minutes did she really begin to listen to what he was saying.

Owen Osborne talked about the Pietà, the representation of the Virgin with the dead body of her son. He began with an historical perspective, explaining that the image had first appeared in Byzantine art, and that it had been popularized by the *Revelations* of St. Bridget of Sweden. Then his voice dropped and became more personal; Elayne found herself straining to hear his words. He spoke of the Virgin as a mother of a son, a mother who had given birth as any other mother,

who had held her infant son in her arms, nourished him
with her own milk, sung him to sleep, and loved him. And
then . . . years later she had once again held him in her arms,
the Savior of the world, who had given up his life so that
all men—every mother's son, and daughter too—might be
reconciled to God. At what point, he asked, did that mother
know what awaited her son? When she cradled his infant body
in her arms, did she have foreknowledge of that other terrible
embrace? Was her joy in his birth mingled with the pain of
knowing his fate? He invited the congregation to go into the
chapel after the service to contemplate the statue of the Virgin
with her child, and to meditate upon it. "Say your rosaries,
and think of that mother. Try to see that statue as a Pietà—
for that mother with her baby was holding, as well, in a very
real way, the body of her dead son, for that moment and for
eternity."

The service went on for a long time after that. There were
more hymns, two more talks, and at one point most of the
congregation went up into the chancel to kneel at the foot of
a cross, and to kiss it. Bob would have hated that, Elayne
thought with detachment. But most of what happened after
Owen Osborne left the pulpit the first time was a blur to her.
She sat completely still, not singing, not listening—thinking
only of that mother holding her baby, holding her dead son.
Bobby, she thought. Bobby.

She escaped during the singing of the final hymn, and
walked around aimlessly for a while. Finally, inexorably, she
was drawn back into the church, and into the chapel. Miss
Barnes and Miss Vernon were kneeling there, rosary beads in
their hands. Elayne stood for what seemed an hour, gazing at
the statue in the niche. That lovely serene face, so full of love:
was it also full of pain?

At last Alice completed her prayers, and pulled herself to
her feet while Gwen finished. Elayne approached her tentatively; she was not surprised, after what Bob had told her about

yesterday, that Alice regarded her with suspicion. "I'm . . .
I'm so sorry to bother you, Miss Barnes," she began, indicating
the rosary beads in Alice's hands, "but do you think . . . could
you teach me to do that?" Elayne looked up again at the statue;
she was sure that the Virgin was smiling at her.

# Chapter 12

*Lord, thou knowest all my desire: and my groaning is not hid
from thee.*

*Psalm 38:9*

Shopping in a busy market-town like Wymondham was difficult on any Saturday in the year; on the Saturday before Easter
it was complete madness even to attempt such a thing. But
David Middleton-Brown had very little choice on this particular day: the following Friday Lucy would be arriving, so this
was his last chance to prepare for her visit.

He'd arisen quite early to get a start on cleaning the house.
It had been all very well for Lucy to say, when she'd invited
herself to stay, that he'd have more than six weeks to do the
cleaning, but in the intervening time he'd spent all of his
weekends in London. The task that he'd embarked upon of
trying to save St. John's, literally to keep the roof from falling
in, had necessitated a number of meetings with church officials
and various property developers. Not that he'd minded that,
of course—the work was fascinating, if time-consuming, and
he'd enjoyed the opportunity it had given him to spend more
time with Lucy. Fortunately, the negotiations had now reached
a point at which he could conduct them largely at a distance,

by post and by phone. For by now his house was in a deplorable state, and his larder was even worse; this weekend of cleaning and shopping was in the way of a frantic last-ditch effort.

Mid-morning he took a break from the cleaning. Thinking that he'd have too many purchases to carry home comfortably, he got the car out, though the supermarket was only a short distance from home.

In the end it was hopeless. The car park of Somerfield, the huge supermarket on the edge of town, was absolutely jammed with cars, people, and white shopping trolleys, and David gave up in disgust. Instead, he drove into the town, down Market Street past the Elizabethan market hall. The town car parks were completely full, so he ended up in Church Street, in front of the Abbey church, where he could usually be sure of a place on the street.

The Abbey, with its striking double towers, looked beautiful in the spring sunshine, and David's spirits lifted as they invariably did when he saw it. It would be nice to spend Easter here, in the church that he loved.

He locked the car with care; it was a new (for him) automobile, a second-hand Volvo which he'd bought a few weeks ago. The weekly trips to London had at last taken their toll on his venerable Morris, a vehicle that had served him well during years of commuting the short distance from Wymondham into Norwich, and he'd parted from it with some regret.

Automatically, his steps turned up the path that led to the church. The Abbey Church of St. Mary and St. Thomas of Canterbury had been on the site since 1107, first as a priory, then as an abbey, and finally as a parish church. David had first visited it as a young boy on a school trip; that visit had been the beginning of a life-long love affair with this church in particular, expanding eventually to include the love of church architecture and furnishings that was his chief avocational interest. He occasionally wished, in a reflective moment, that he had followed his heart to a career somewhere in that field, rather than giving in to his mother's pressure and opting for the safer and more secure alternative of the law. As it happened, the law had been a good choice; David made an excellent solicitor, with his incisive mind and solid instincts. Nevertheless the Church was still his first love, but—*Church Building* magazine's prompting aside—he knew that it was too late now to make a change.

The majestic tones of the organ met David at the door, and he recalled that the organist was engaged in a series of recitals in which he would play the complete organ works of Bach. Anxious not to disrupt the recital, he moved quietly up the wide north aisle of the church, which was in fact the Lady Chapel, lit a few candles before the exquisite painted and gilded statue of Our Lady, and said a prayer.

The church was in the curious state of disarray that exists between the somber commemorations of Good Friday and the explosion of joy at the Resurrection. The altar frontals had not yet been changed, but several women were hard at work arranging the Easter flowers, great sheaves of snow-white lilies overhanging the pedestals. Tonight would be the Easter Vigil, with the Paschal Candle, the pure beauty of the Exsultet, and finally the joyous, heart-stopping cry of "The Lord is risen! He is risen indeed! Alleluia!" David found himself looking forward to it with anticipation.

Anticipation was hardly the operative word as he walked back toward Market Street. The street, like the supermarket car park, was thronged with people. You'd think, David reflected, that the shops were closing down for the next six months, rather than for just two days.

There was an old-fashioned butcher's shop at the foot of Market Street. David paused and looked in its window longingly. No meat for next weekend. It really was too bad, he thought, that Lucy had given up eating meat. What could he cook for her? He would have done a lovely boeuf bourguignonne, but now he just didn't know. Lucy wouldn't care for this shop at all, he thought, with its deeply scarred, blood-stained chopping block, the careless heaps of innards, bones and feathers in the window, and the faint stench of meat near its best-before date. Being totally honest with himself, he had to admit that it was less than appealing, but for David familiarity had great charm, and it was with regret that he passed it by and headed up the street toward the health-food shop.

David had lived in Wymondham most of his life, with the exception of the ten or twelve years during which he'd been away at university, then working in London and Brighton. When his father had died, about ten years ago, he'd found a job at a firm in nearby Norwich and returned home to look after his mother, until her death the previous spring. In all of his years in Wymondham he'd never before darkened the door of the health-food shop, but today David was desperate. In its window was displayed an array of healthy-looking baked goods, replete with wholemeal flour and devoid of undesirable additives. And probably devoid of taste, he said to himself glumly. The shelves were full of things he'd never heard of—pulses and grains and protein substitutes. He looked in the refrigerated case at the tofu, and at the unappetizing brown items labelled "pinto pie" and "aduki shepherd's pie." He smiled to himself, then, at his own lack of adventurous spirit: he realized that he had a lot to learn. It was like a foreign language, one that Lucy would have to teach him some day. But Lucy was not here, and now was not the time.

He'd just have to leave it a few days, he decided, going home at last empty-handed. He'd have to stop at Somerfield one evening next week—they were open until eight, so he could go on his way home from work on Tuesday or Wednesday. That would give him time to think, to plan.

The next two days passed quickly for David, in a flurry of cleaning and church-going. On Sunday night he went to bed early, exhausted by his labors.

In the middle of the night he awoke with a start. Pleasure, embarrassment, and astonishment struggled in his mind as he tried to make sense of what had just happened to him.

She had come to him in his dream, here to this bed: Lucy, her face as radiant as her hair in the preternaturally bright moonlight that had streamed through his window. She had smiled at him, gravely and questioningly. Without conscious thought, almost without volition, he had held out his arms to her and she had come to him, into his bed, without a word. And then . . . His face was hot in the dark as he remembered the vividness of their passion. And he lay awake for hours afterwards, reliving the dream, reconstructing the whole of their relationship, trying to understand what it all meant.

David had known for a very long while that he loved Lucy, in his own way. But there had never before been a sexual dimension to his feelings for her—given his past history, he had frankly not imagined that there ever would, or even could, be. Now, however, he could scarcely deny what had happened, and somehow that changed everything. He loved her, and he wanted her: it was most disturbing. His love for her had been taken for granted, the sort of thing one didn't actually have to *do* anything about, and that had suited him very well; the sudden and unexpected introduction of this unfamiliar element into what had become a relatively comfortable, or at least predictable, relationship confused and frightened him. How could he go on as if nothing had changed? Those regular weekends in London—an art gallery or a concert, a meal together, the brotherly kiss on the cheek—what would happen now? How could he cope?

And on Friday she was coming to stay.

# Chapter 13

*Blessed is the man, whom thou choosest, and receivest unto thee: he shall dwell in thy court, and shall be satisfied with the pleasures of thy house, even of thy holy temple.*

*Psalm 65:4*

Becca Dexter's weekend on the retreat with her father had been spent primarily in Bible study; on Monday morning she felt the need for some fresh air. She announced her intention to her mother over a late breakfast. "I think I'll walk into the village, Mum. Do you need anything?"

Elayne frowned, thinking. "Today's a bank holiday. The shops won't be open, will they?"

"I don't know. They might be."

"I could do with a loaf of bread, if the bakery or that other little shop are open."

"Right, Mum. Anything else?"

"I don't think so, dear. Tomorrow I shall have to do a big shop in Fakenham." Elayne looked uncertainly at the remains of the loaf of bread, deliberating whether or not there was enough left for her to have a piece of toast, and finally decided against it. If Becca couldn't get any more bread today, it would be wanted for Bob's breakfast tomorrow. "Doesn't your father need you this morning?"

"No, he said I could have the day off. He's got some things to do to get ready for the Institution tonight. He's going to Fakenham, I think." Becca finished her tea. "I'll be off then, Mum. I'll see you in a bit." Elayne watched her go, then started the washing up.

It was a beautiful spring day, so mild that Becca's lightweight jumper was warm enough without a jacket. The kind of day, she thought, when anything could happen. She had a great sense of anticipation as she walked along the lane, past the church, and into the village, looking with interest at everything around her. She'd never lived in the country before—never even spent much time outside the Greater London area. But this was her new home, and she was eager to become a part of it.

The village pub, the Two Magpies, looked a nice spot, she thought. It was most picturesque, with its half-timbering and its thatch, and the creeper around the door. Daddy wasn't much of a one for drinking, to say the least, but perhaps he'd bring her here some evening for a soft drink. It would be a good way to meet some of the non–church-going residents of his parish, she'd tell him.

South Barsham was a middling-sized village, with several shops to its credit. There was a butcher's shop, a bakery, a post office-cum-grocery-cum-petrol station, and even a shop that sold clothing, though the things displayed in its window were not promising: some utilitarian-looking garb for men, children's school uniforms for the local comprehensive, and one or two ladies' garments that appeared several decades out of fashion. There was also a bank, open three mornings a week, and incongruously, the old school-house had been converted into a very posh restaurant with a French chef, nightly drawing crowds of *Good Food Guide* devotees from Norwich and even farther afield.

But on this Easter Monday morning, nothing looked open. Becca stopped in front of the bakery and peered at the "closed" sign which hung on the door.

"Oh, they're not closed, are they?" a voice spoke at her side. Becca turned to see a tall elderly woman in a golden wig, her face creased with dismay.

"I'm afraid so. The sign says they won't be open until tomorrow. The bank holiday."

"Oh, dear! I'd forgotten about the bank holiday!"

Becca smiled at the woman. "It's not the end of the world, is it?"

"Alice will be very upset if I come home without the cream cakes!"

"Surely she won't blame you, if the bakery's not open?" Becca said sensibly.

"Oh, you don't know Alice," the woman replied darkly. Nell and Babs, secure on their leads, whimpered as if in agreement.

"What lovely dogs!" Becca exclaimed, bending down to stroke them. "What are their names?"

"This one's Nell, and that one is Babs," said the woman, mollified slightly. "And I'm Gwen Vernon. Miss Vernon," she added, looking with interest at the friendly young woman. The girl's face was completely obscured by a curtain of very long blond hair as she crouched over the dogs, but Gwen could see that she was tall and extremely pretty.

Becca stood and offered her hand. "It's nice to meet you, Miss Vernon. I'm Rebecca Dexter, but everyone calls me Becca. I'm new in the village—you probably know that! My father is the new Vicar."

Flustered, Gwen swapped the dog leads to her left hand with difficulty and shook the girl's hand. "I've met your father," she said. "And your mother . . ." As soon as she'd said it, she wondered if perhaps she'd betrayed something, but the girl's face retained its friendly, interested smile.

"How nice! And now you've met me, so you know us all!"

"Yes . . ." Gwen was at a loss for words.

"And who is Alice?" Becca asked in her open way. "The person who will blame you for the bakery being closed?"

"Oh, Alice. Miss Barnes. She, that is, we, live in the village, at Monkey Puzzle Cottage."

"What a fun name for a house!"

"We have two monkey puzzle trees. The only ones in the village," Gwen explained with pride.

"I don't think I've ever seen a monkey puzzle tree! What do they look like?"

"Oh, they're splendid. Very exotic, I always think. You must come and see them some time."

"I'd love to!" Becca replied quickly. "I could come today, and meet Miss Barnes as well! I've got the day off, you see."

"Oh, well, yes," Gwen fluttered. "You must come—for tea. Though of course we won't have any cream cakes. If you don't mind . . ."

Becca laughed. "I don't mind. Cream cakes are bad for my figure, anyway!" she said diplomatically; Becca, after a plump adolescence, could now eat anything she wanted without gaining an ounce. "I'll look forward to seeing you later, then. And you, too, Nell and Babs!"

Bob Dexter's chief priority for the day was the preparation of the church for the evening's ceremonies of Institution and Induction. Since he as yet had no official position at the church, he could not actually remove anything from it—all the offensive statues and pictures had to remain in place, at least until tomorrow, when he would well and truly be in charge. But he could certainly do his best to minimize them, and to draw attention elsewhere.

He'd been on the phone early to Noah Gates, and Noah had agreed to meet him at Gates of Heaven on that holiday as a special favor.

When Dexter arrived, on the dot of ten o'clock as arranged, both Noah and Toby Gates were waiting for him in the reception area. "Thank you for coming, Noah," he greeted him. "And Toby, too. How nice to see you. Bob Dexter doesn't forget a favor."

"You said that it was important?" The shorter man looked up at him, a mixture of curiosity and impatience in his small black eyes.

"A matter of utmost urgency," he replied solemnly. "Something must be done about the church."

"Your church?" Gates asked.

"That's just the problem. It's not my church—*yet*. Not until tonight, when the Archdeacon hands over the keys." Dexter paused. "It's bad, Noah," he said, shaking his head sorrowfully. "Very bad. Much worse than I'd even imagined. The idols! The images! Appalling!"

Gates was practical. "So what can you do, Bob? And how can I help?"

"Posters!"

"Posters?" echoed Toby.

"Yes, posters. I want the biggest and the best posters you've got, Noah. I want to plaster the church with posters, cover the statues with them. Posters that will make people think, make people realize that Bob Dexter means business!"

Gates nodded with grudging admiration. "I can help you there, Bob."

An hour later, they'd been through all the posters that Gates of Heaven had in stock. Dexter had selected a number of different designs, many with biblical texts and others with punchy sayings such as, JESUS IS LORD or GOD SAID IT, I BELIEVE IT, THAT SETTLES IT.

"These should do the job nicely." Dexter smiled, well pleased. "Tonight Bob Dexter shall confront them with the Word of God!"

"And tomorrow . . ." said Noah Gates.

"Tomorrow I shall begin. Every bit of popery in that church shall be removed."

"Won't that be a very big job, sir?" asked Toby.

"Yes, indeed. But Bob Dexter never shirks a challenge, young man. If necessary, I shall do it single-handed."

"If you need some help . . . that is, if you think another pair of hands might be useful," Toby offered diffidently, "I could come."

Dexter consider the offer. "Thank you very much indeed, Toby," he said at last. "Yes, you might be very helpful. After all," he added, with uncharacteristic self-deprecation, "Bob Dexter isn't as young as he used to be."

The church was packed, Dexter noted with satisfaction as he waited for the procession to begin. Practically every seat was filled. It would appear that everyone in the village had come to see their new Vicar take possession of his benefice. But instead of an expectant hush, there was a buzzing like a nest of angry wasps as the congregation regarded the posters which bedecked the church. "Not even fit for a primary school," Alice muttered furiously to Gwen.

Dexter wore his charcoal-gray business suit with a paler gray clerical shirt; it was not necessary, he thought, for him to show off by dressing up. But the visiting clergy of the Deanery, two abreast at the beginning of the procession, were not all so restrained. Many of the clergy associated with Walsingham had come—just to flaunt themselves in his face, he was sure—and they were in full regalia, even to their birettas. How dare they? thought Bob Dexter. But starting tomorrow, he'd show them. He'd wipe the smile off that curate Mark Judd's face.

As he passed, Dexter smiled at Becca, standing in the front row of the nave with her mother, singing the first hymn. Becca was looking exceptionally lovely tonight, he thought, with her hair loose down her back in a shining curtain. Her eyes were shining too—with pride in him, Dexter told himself. And how proud he was of her, his beautiful daughter.

He was not the only one to notice Becca that night. With Mark Judd was another young priest, Stephen Thorncroft. A friend and colleague of Mark, as one of the part-time assistants at the Shrine of Our Lady of Walsingham, Stephen Thorncroft also served as Vicar of a neighboring parish. Although he could not begin to compete with the startling good looks with which Mark had been blessed, Stephen was a handsome young man in a scholarly sort of way, with fair hair, a long ascetic face, and a sensitive mouth; his gray eyes were intelligent behind gold-rimmed spectacles.

Stephen first saw Becca as he rose from his seat in the choir stalls to sing the Gradual hymn; in that instant he felt as if the breath had been knocked out of him entirely. Singing was out of the question, but when he finally felt able to speak, he leaned toward Mark and whispered under cover of the hymn. "Who is she?"

"Who?"

Stephen inclined his head. "That incredible creature in the front row."

"Oh, that's Dexter's daughter," Mark murmured with a smile.

"Dexter's daughter? You're joking!"

"No joke, my friend."

"But she's . . . she's . . ."

"Quite a stunner, wouldn't you say? If you like the type."

Stephen closed his eyes, then opened them again. She was still there. "Do you think I could meet her? Later, at the reception?"

Mark was amused. "I'm sure you could. But if you're smart, you'll stay away from her. With that one, you'd get Daddy in the bargain. And I don't think you'd want that."

Stephen sighed, a sigh of despair mingled with joy. "This is serious, Mark," he whispered at last. "I'm in love."

# Chapter 14

*My zeal hath even consumed me: because mine enemies have*
*forgotten thy words.*

*Psalm 119:139*

It was raining when Tuesday dawned, but a bit of spring rain
was not enough to dampen Bob Dexter's enthusiasm for the
task that faced him. He was up very early, and had already
begun when Toby Gates arrived at the church just after
nine.

Toby had not seen St. Mary's, or anything quite like it,
before; he looked with amazement at the statues and the candles. "Good morning, young man," Bob Dexter greeted him
cheerfully, peering out of the south porch.

"Good morning, sir. This really is . . . quite something,
isn't it?"

"Isn't it? But it won't be by the end of the day, I can assure
you." Dexter joined Toby at the back of the church.

"Whatever are you going to do with all this stuff?"

"Temporarily, anyway, we're going to move it all to the
south porch." He gestured toward the little room he'd just
left. "I've been clearing it out to make room. It can all be
stored in there until I'm able to dispose of it."

"Well, I'm ready to get to work, Reverend Dexter."

"Good man," he said approvingly.

Mid-morning, Becca dashed over from the vicarage with coffee for the laborers.

"It's really raining!" she announced, shaking the droplets from her hair. "I hope the coffee isn't too watered down!"

"Becca, Princess, how thoughtful!" Dexter came to her immediately, kissed her cheek, and took a mug from the tray that she carried.

"Hello, Becca," Toby said with a shy smile.

"Oh, hi, Toby. Coffee? Sugar?"

"Yes, thanks. No, no sugar."

Becca dropped into a pew and sipped her own coffee. "You've really made progress, haven't you?"

Dexter surveyed the church. All of the statues from the nave had been removed and stored. St. Francis was gone, and St. George, and the curious priest, as well as Our Lady of Walsingham. Gone, too, was the painting of King Charles the Martyr, and the gruesome hunting scene, and the popish picture of the Virgin standing on the crescent moon. "Quite an improvement for two hours' work, wouldn't you say?"

"What else have you got to do?" Becca questioned. "It looks like you've just about finished."

"We've got to take those Stations of the Cross off the wall—that may be a bit tricky. And the English altar up in the chancel has to be dismantled. It's a good thing I've got Toby here—that's definitely a two-man job!" Dexter smiled at the tongue-tied young man, who blushed.

"What will you put there instead?" she wanted to know.

"For the moment, we'll leave the plain altar table there. We'll just take down the corner posts and the hangings." Dexter looked toward the east end of the church. "What I'd like to do, of course, is to get a nice modern communion table for the nave. Up there, in front of the screen," he gestured.

"What about that statue in the chapel?" Toby asked. "Are we going to take that down today?"

Dexter frowned. "I don't think we can. It's up very high, and I haven't seen a ladder around here that's tall enough. It may have to wait for another day."

"And what will you do with all the things you've removed? You're not just throwing them away, are you?" asked Becca.

"Ah! That, Princess, is how Bob Dexter plans to finance all the changes in this place!" Dexter put a hand on her shoulder. "There's quite a market for all this nonsense, if you know the right people. When I've sold it all, I'll be able to afford some proper carpet for this place, and a sound reinforcement system, and some new, bright lighting—maybe even a new Sunday School room in the chapel!"

"But who will buy it? You don't know any of those people—the right people, Daddy."

Dexter gave a short laugh. "But I know a man who does!" He squeezed her shoulder. "Last night, at the reception after the service, I had a word with that young curate chap, Mark Judd. He's not really a bad fellow, for one of that Walsingham lot. I told him what I wanted to do, and he said that he could help me to find the right buyers. Quite decent of him, really."

"Yes . . . I don't think the Walsingham priests are necessarily all bad, Daddy." Becca looked thoughtful.

Dexter suddenly remembered that while he'd been talking with Mark Judd last night, Becca had been having an animated conversation with a blond young man in a cassock—another of those Walsingham priests. That wouldn't do. "Toby," he said abruptly, "You will be staying for lunch, won't you? I'm sure that Becca will be glad of the chance for a nice chat."

"Why, yes, thank you, sir. My father doesn't expect me back at Gates of Heaven until this afternoon." Toby smiled at Dexter, then at Becca. "And I was wondering if you would like to come out with me for a meal tomorrow evening," he added to Becca, then turned back to Dexter. "That is, if it's quite all right with you, sir."

"Yes, of course." Dexter nodded approvingly; the boy was quick on the uptake.

"I'd love to, Toby," said Becca with a smile.

For David, Monday night had been even worse than Sunday night. At least he'd had a few hours of sleep before his dream on Sunday; on Monday night sleep had eluded him entirely. He'd tossed and turned, worried and fretted in the narrow bed he'd slept in for years.

The idea came to him in the early hours of the morning—perhaps he'd get a new bed. He told himself that his sleeplessness could be cured by this simple expedient. His old bed was just knackered, that was all—a new, more comfortable one would make all the difference. And why should he replace it with another single bed, just because his mother had thought it more suitable? A double bed, with more room to spread out, would undoubtedly be much more conducive to a good night's sleep.

So David told himself. It had nothing at all to do with Lucy, or with her imminent visit. There was no chance that she'd be sharing his bed, after all. She'd never given him any indication that she was interested in him in that way. No, that wasn't quite true—once, a long time ago, she'd wanted him to stay the night with her. But he hadn't realized it, and a lot had happened between them since then: he'd asked her to marry him, and then immediately changed his mind, and she'd said that she wouldn't marry him anyway. It had taken a long time after that for their relationship to be restored, or perhaps reconstituted to the platonic friendship they now shared. No, it had nothing to do with Lucy.

Nonetheless, he felt acutely uncomfortable, and even embarrassed, when he went into the bed shop during his lunch hour on Tuesday.

The young man who served him was accommodating and helpful, but David, who had never bought a bed before, found the whole experience trying in the extreme. It was with relief that he left the shop at last, having made his choice and received assurance that delivery would be made on Wednesday evening.

# Chapter 15

*Them that are meek shall he guide in judgment: and such as are gentle, them shall he learn his way.*

*Psalm 25:8*

"Now remember, Toby, Becca is a working girl, even if she does work at home," Bob Dexter said with a smile. "Not too late, please."

"Of course, sir. I have to work tomorrow myself."

"Bye, Daddy. See you later." Becca kissed her father on the cheek.

"I'll wait up for you. Have fun, both of you. And do drive carefully, Toby," he added. He stood at the door and watched their departure.

"I thought we'd go into Norwich for a meal, if that's all right with you," Toby said, opening the car door for Becca. "I know a rather nice place there."

"Sounds great," she smiled. "I haven't been to Norwich yet."

"It's a vegetarian restaurant. I hope that's okay."

"Yes, of course. I didn't know that you were a vegetarian, Toby."

"I'm not, not really. But . . . well, it's just one of the

things that's been bothering me lately. Eating meat, I mean. Cruelty. Cruelty to animals, cruelty to each other. There's too much of it in this world, Becca."

"Why don't you tell me what's been bothering you? I'm a good listener," Becca invited.

"Do you mean it, Becca? I *would* like to talk." His look of gratitude startled her with its intensity.

"Of course."

"Somehow I feel that you'll understand."

So the journey into Norwich went by quickly, with a great deal of earnest conversation. The Green Scene lived up to its name; it looked like a small forest, with its green-painted walls and myriad plants in hanging baskets dangling over the diners' heads. The tables and chairs were varnished pine, simple and blocky, and there were no tablecloths.

Toby led Becca to a table in the corner; the laminated menus were on the table. "It's not licensed," he apologized. "So we can't have any wine."

"Oh, that's all right. We never have it at home. Daddy doesn't really believe in drinking, you know. I'm surprised that you do."

Toby flushed guiltily. "My father doesn't believe in it at all, of course—you know how strict he is. But once in a while, when I'm not with him . . . Well, I don't think a little glass of wine every now and then will do you any harm," he finished defensively.

"No, I'm sure it won't," she soothed.

"Mineral water, then?"

"Yes, that's fine, Toby."

The waitress, dressed in a Green Scene T-shirt and jeans, appeared to take their order. She regarded them fiercely through round horn-rimmed spectacles beneath a straight fringe of brown hair. "What would you like?"

"Mineral water for now. I'm afraid we haven't had a chance

to look at the menu," Toby apologized. "If you could give us a few more minutes . . ."

"All right," she said ungraciously, stalking away.

Becca smiled, amused, and picked up the menu. "What do you recommend?"

"The ratatouille pancakes are good. And I've had the bulgar chili—that's nice, if you like something a bit more spicy."

The waitress returned with a bottle of mineral water and two glasses. "Have you decided yet?"

Toby looked across the table. "Becca?"

"Um . . . Oh, I think I'll have the ratatouille pancakes."

"Make that two," Toby added.

"Right," said the waitress. "With salad?"

"Yes, please." When she'd departed, Toby sat tense for a moment, then settled back in his chair. "Anyway, Becca, as I was saying . . ."

The waitress returned. "We're out of pancakes," she announced. She folded her arms across her thin body and peered out from under her fringe. "So what would you like?"

Becca looked again at the menu. "Oh, I don't know. Nut cutlets?"

"The nut cutlets are very nice," the waitress commented in an almost friendly voice. "I recommend them."

"All right," Becca agreed. "But with vegetables, I think, rather than salad."

"And I'll try the vegetable curry," Toby decided.

"With rice." It was a statement rather than a question.

"Yes."

The young woman brought them cutlery, wrapped in bright green paper napkins; Toby waited till she'd gone before he began again. "As I was saying, Becca, it's all become very difficult for me. You know how strong my faith has been. You know that I helped to bring my father to Jesus, and that our lives have been built around the faith. But now—I just don't know any more. I *want* to believe it all, but it doesn't make

sense to me anymore. It's just not as simple as my father—
*your* father, too—would like to make it seem."

"I'm not sure that I understand," she said with a small
frown.

"For my father, and your father, it's all so black and white.
Things are right, or things are wrong. You believe something,
or you don't. You go to heaven, or you go to hell."

"Yes . . ."

"But life just isn't like that! It's not black and white! There
are so many shades of gray, Becca . . ." Toby stared down at
the table, frowning. "So many shades of gray . . ." He looked
at her again, his light brown eyes shining, almost as if with
unshed tears. "Isn't it possible to believe in a God of love,
without all the other stuff that goes with it? Without the
judgment, and the narrow restrictions? Telling people how to
live their lives? *Their* lives, Becca." His voice shook. "Doesn't
everyone have the right to live their life as they think best?
And the way other people worship—who are *we* to say that
it's wrong?"

"Love," Becca said. "Yes, I see."

He smiled at her, suddenly radiant. "Yes, I knew that you'd
understand." He reached across the table for her hand, and
gave it a squeeze.

They talked all through the meal, and through their pudding
and their coffee. At last, reluctantly, Toby looked at his watch.
"I mustn't keep you out any longer," he said with real regret.
"Or your father won't let you come out with me again."

"Well, it's been a lovely evening, Toby."

He took her hand again. "You have no idea how much it's
meant to me, Becca, talking to you like this." He looked into
her eyes earnestly. "You're the only person I've ever been able
to be totally honest with. I feel so . . . so free now."

The waitress slapped their bill on the table. "You can pay
at the desk on your way out," she announced.

Toby sighed and got up, then helped Becca out of her chair. As he paid the bill, she studied a large poster near the door. "Look, Toby. Isn't this poster smashing?"

"British Animal Rights Coalition," he read. "What a good idea. I think I saw something about them on television a few weeks ago."

The waitress came around from behind the till. "You're welcome to join us any time," she said with real warmth. "Shall I take your names for our mailing list?"

# Chapter 16

*Have I not remembered thee in my bed: and thought upon thee when I was waking?*

Psalm 63:7

"Mr. Middleton-Brown?" the blond girl said hesitantly, looking at the paper in her hand. "You gave me this letter to type two days ago, on Tuesday. I typed it for you—it's been signed and posted." If it had been anyone but Mr. Middleton-Brown, she wouldn't have dared mention it: Karen, the youngest and newest typist at the firm, the lowest of the low. For anyone else, she would have retyped the letter, without a word. But Mr. Middleton-Brown wasn't like the rest of the solicitors, who treated the typists and secretaries like so many pieces of furniture. Mr. Middleton-Brown was different—he was nice. He always had a kind word for everyone and made a point of speaking to the girls by name, treating them like real people.

David looked absently and perplexedly at the paper she'd handed back to him. "So I did, Karen. So I did. Well then, never mind." He went up the stairs to his office and shut the door behind him.

Karen sat for a minute with a puzzled frown. "I don't know what's the matter with Mr. Middleton-Brown," she said to the woman who was passing by with a stack of papers. "He just hasn't been himself lately."

Nan perched on the edge of Karen's desk and leaned toward her confidentially. "What's he done now?"

"He just gave me a letter to type that I'd already done, earlier in the week. That's not like him. And . . . oh, I don't know. He just seems so absent-minded. Almost like he doesn't even see you when he's talking to you. And he's been drinking ever so much tea. And keeping his office door shut."

Nan smiled knowingly. Her position at the firm was a difficult one to define: she'd begun to work there several years ago, completely untrained and unqualified, after her youngest child started school. She'd begun as a general dogsbody, making cups of tea and running the photocopying machine. But her enthusiasm for the job and her natural abilities, along with her down-to-earth common sense, meant that before long she was being asked to do all sorts of things, and she had now become an indispensable fixture at the firm of Goodacre and Whitehouse. Everyone liked Nan, with her infectious smile, her curly brown hair, and her generous figure; even the solicitors knew her by name. "Do you know what I think?" she said. "I think that Mr. Middleton-Brown is in love! It's that time of year, you know."

Karen's large brown eyes widened. "In love! But he's . . . he's so old!"

Nan laughed, realizing, as one who was over thirty herself, how differently things appeared to those under eighteen. "He's barely over forty. I suppose that must seem old to you—you're only a baby. But take it from me: there are a lot of women who think Mr. Middleton-Brown is very attractive indeed."

Karen shook her head, confronting an unbridgeable generation gap. "If you say so. Oh, I know he's awfully sweet, but . . . Do you think he's attractive?"

"Oh, very. Not that I'm looking, mind you. My Charlie

keeps me happy." She chuckled at the thought of her stolid farmer husband, the only man she'd ever wanted.

"But what makes you think he's in love?" Karen repeated.

"Oh, I know about these things." Nan leaned closer. "You said yourself he's been absentminded and dreamy."

"Yes . . ."

"When I took him up his tea a bit ago, he was sitting in his chair, staring off into space, with the daftest smile on his face. I don't think he even knew I was there. I know a man in love when I see one."

"But . . . who? Who's he in love with? Anyone we know?"

"That's the question, isn't it? Who's the lucky woman?" Nan paused dramatically, and looked over her shoulder to make sure she wasn't overheard. "Do you know anyone called Lucy?" Karen shook her head. "Well, yesterday after he'd gone to lunch, I went up to his office to collect his dirty cups—as you say, he's been drinking tea by the gallon—and just happened to catch sight of his desk blotter. He'd written 'Lucy' all over it!"

"But that's the sort of thing my brother would do—and he's only sixteen!"

Nan chuckled again. "Well, that's the thing about men in love. They're all alike—it doesn't matter how old they are!"

Karen selected and absently contemplated a strand of her fine, limp hair, then began chewing the end of it. Her mother deplored this unconscious nervous habit, but haranguing had not cured her of it. "I don't know very much about Mr. Middleton-Brown. Has he ever been married?"

"No, I don't think he ever had much of a chance. He lived with his mum—took care of her, you know—till she died last year. She was a right old so-and-so, his mum. Made his life a real misery, I shouldn't wonder."

"Did you ever meet her?"

"Oh, I *saw* her once or twice, at the office Christmas do.

But she wouldn't have spoken to me—I wasn't grand enough for her. She only talked to the solicitors. A real snob, she was. And he's such a nice man, too." Nan turned quickly at the sound of footsteps on the stairs.

"Nan, would you mind doing me a favor?" David asked. "You know that French restaurant, the newish one?"

"Oh, yes. My Charlie took me there for a real slap-up meal on our anniversary last year. A *romantic* meal," she added slyly, with a significant look at Karen. "Candlelight, soft music . . ."

"And it was good, was it? I just wondered if you'd mind ringing up and booking me a table for Saturday night? About eight o'clock, I should think. For two." He added as an afterthought, "And could you check to make sure they do vegetarian food?"

"Of course, Mr. Middleton-Brown."

"Thanks, Nan." He turned and was halfway up the stairs again, before adding over his shoulder, "Oh, and would you mind bringing me another cup of tea?"

"Right away." She grinned triumphantly at Karen as soon as he was out of sight and earshot. "What did I tell you?"

A few minutes later, David sipped the latest cup of tea distractedly. There was a pile of work on his desk—letters, telephone messages, and briefs, all requiring his urgent attention—but he was unable to concentrate on any of it.

The new bed had arrived the previous evening, and it had made some difference, or perhaps his exhaustion had just caught up with him at last—he'd finally slept a bit last night, dreaming again of Lucy. In the dream he had seen her face so clearly, had recognized all the features of the woman he loved.

But what disturbed him so profoundly now was that he was unable to picture her face in his mind, and the harder he tried, the more elusive her image became. He could remember each of her individual features, but they refused to coalesce in his mind into the whole of Lucy. They remained disparate, frag-mented, tantalizingly close to being captured. The closest he'd come to picturing her, consciously, had been on the fringes of sleep. And sometimes, when he wasn't trying so hard, she was *almost* there, at the edge of his mind, waiting for him to glimpse her. David closed his eyes in frustration. Would he even recognize her when he saw her? he wondered fancifully. Tomorrow. Not long now. Tomorrow he'd see her.

# Chapter 17

*Man being in honor hath no understanding: but is compared
unto the beasts that perish.*

*Psalm 49:20*

The new BARC van, purchased with Nicholas Fielding's
money, would be a great asset when it arrived, but until
that day, Rhys Morgan's estate wagon would have to do. On
Thursday evening it was stretched nearly to the limit of its
capacity, with Rhys and Maggie in the front, Gary and Nicholas in the back seat, and Bleddyn in the rear with the brochures
and the display units.

They'd been making a presentation about BARC that evening, at a meeting of a north Norfolk Deanery Synod. With
debates raging on a national level about hunting on church-
owned land, many churchmen were beginning to consider their
responsibility toward other forms of created life; Rhys had
found the invitation to speak tonight a hopeful sign of a new
openness in the church.

It had gone reasonably well, he thought. Or at least it would
have, had Bob Dexter not felt that he had to make a mark at
his first meeting in the Deanery. "Just our luck," he remarked
ruefully. "That clown Dexter only arrived this week."

"He was a real pain in the ass," Maggie stated. "All that 'dominion over all living things' crap. What a speciesist."

"But at least some of the others were listening to us," Nicholas said eagerly. "And asking some very intelligent questions."

"Yeah, that guy who asked about cruelty-free products—that was pretty groovy," Gary added. "He seemed really interested."

"He was one of the Walsingham crowd, wasn't he?" asked Rhys.

"Yeah."

"I really think we ought to go to that National Pilgrimage this year," Maggie put in. "We could protest against the killing of foxes on Walsingham-owned land."

"Burn candles for the dead foxes?" Nicholas suggested humorously. "That would be a laugh."

"Huh." Maggie glowered in the dark. "That's not funny. I did that once. We were having this vigil for the dead foxes, with candles. My friend and I were standing by this woman in a fur coat, and we started, you know, kind of flicking drops of wax onto her coat. And do you know what the bitch said to us?"

"What?"

"She said she didn't care—she was rich enough to buy another one, and we were only encouraging the fur trade!" She scowled; her glasses slid down her nose, and she stabbed them back into place with a finger.

They all contemplated man's inhumanity to other species in silence for a moment.

"Would you mind dropping me off at home?" Nicholas requested as they neared Norwich. "It's not far out of the way."

"Fielding Farms?" Maggie spat. "You want us to actually go to Fielding Farms?"

"Sorry. I didn't think."

"It's all right," Rhys said quickly. "We can take you. I don't think it will contaminate us to enter its portals."

Nicholas hesitated. "Maybe . . . do you think you could come in for a coffee? My father's not home tonight, so you wouldn't have to see him."

"I could use a coffee," Rhys accepted.

"Well, *I* won't go in," Maggie said heatedly. "You can leave me in the car, if you're going in *that* place."

Rhys refused to be intimidated. "Very well, Maggie. Stay in the car, if you like. I'm going in."

"I'll keep Maggie company," Gary offered.

"Suit yourselves." They could tell that he was angry, but no one was willing to back down.

When Rhys and Nicholas had disappeared into the large farm house, taking Bleddyn with them, Maggie and Gary were silent for a moment. "It makes me sick, the way everything has to be done to please that spoiled brat," Maggie said at last, quietly but with intensity. "Just because he's got money, I suppose."

"Oh, he's not such a bad guy." Gary stroked his moustache thoughtfully. "And he *is* only a kid. When I was his age—"

"Yes, I know." Maggie's voice was venomous. "Berkeley. The glory days. Sit-ins in the president's office, burning of draft cards. Life will never be quite so exciting again, will it, Gary?"

"Well, all right, you don't have to get nasty." He retreated into a hurt silence; Maggie slumped in the front seat.

After a few minutes she sat up suddenly. "This place is like a bloody concentration camp! It really gives me the creeps! We ought to *do* something, Gary. Something to leave our mark on Fielding Farms."

"Like what?"

She leaned over the back of the seat and regarded him with scorn. "Don't you have any backbone? Any imagination?"

Stung, he thought aloud, "Well, we could always paint

something—some slogans or something—on the sides of the buildings. If we had any paint, that is."

"That's not much good, is it? We don't have any paint."

"Well, if we did . . ."

"But we don't," she stated.

"I don't know, Maggie. Rhys wouldn't like it if we—"

"I don't bloody care if Rhys likes it or not. He's not the only one in this organization, you know."

"But he *did* start it. And it's his money—"

"The hell it is! It's Fiona's money! Just because she's so bloody besotted with him, and lets him spend her money however he likes—"

"Cool it, Maggie. I know that *you're* a liberated woman, and would never let a man tell *you* what to do, but—"

"That's it!" she interrupted him excitedly. "That's it, Gary! Liberation!"

"What? What are you talking about?"

"Liberation!" She pounded on the seat. "Gary, you and I are going to liberate the chickens of Fielding Farm! Right now! Come on!" Maggie jumped out of the car and ran toward the meanly proportioned buildings where Fielding's chickens lived in cramped misery before giving up their lives and their thighs. "Liberation!" she called out softly into the spring night, as Gary followed her with trepidation and a kind of excitement. And just beyond, in the spring night, the foxes waited patiently.

# Chapter 18

*I am feeble, and sore smitten: I have roared for the very disquietness of my heart.*

*Psalm 38:8*

The timing of Lucy's train had been planned so that David could collect her at the station after he finished work, but as it happened, he went home to Wymondham at midday. He hadn't accomplished a great deal that morning—all week, for that matter—and was worrying about the things that needed to be done at home. At last he could stand it no longer; he told Nan, who was filling in as she usually did during the receptionist's lunch hour, that he wasn't feeling well, and escaped before she could ask any questions.

There were the *pots de crème* to be made, for one thing. And the last-minute cleaning and dusting. He prepared all the ingredients for that night's mushroom stroganoff, put the champagne in the fridge, ironed his mother's best damask tablecloth and laid the dining-room table. He polished the heavy silver candlesticks, then drove quickly into town to buy new candles and an armload of fresh flowers. Some of them he arranged for the dining-room table, but there were enough left for a few discreet bouquets around the house. The last, choicest blooms he reserved for a small nosegay which he put in the guest room, on the table beside the bed.

David walked around the house, trying to forget that he'd lived there almost all his life, trying to see it as a stranger— as Lucy—might see it. An ordinary, 1930s semi-detached house, a bit on the small side. His parents had bought it when they'd married, late in life for both of them it had been, after the war. From that house his father had traveled into Wymondham every day for over thirty years, to his job at the bank, first on foot, then by bicycle, and latterly in a car. In that house his mother had sat, day after day, year after year, managing and manipulating the lives and psyches of her husband and her only child. To that house David had been brought at birth, had lived in it as a child, as an adolescent; to it he had returned a grown man, after his father's sudden death. It was so difficult to see it with fresh eyes; he was so used to every inch of it, every crack in the wallpaper, every creak of the floorboards. An ordinary house. Two reception rooms on the ground floor, the estate agents would say: the dining room, though small, was just about acceptable; there was some good furniture, and David had had some say in its decoration. He'd always hated the sitting room, where his mother had spent much of her time and which had reflected her rather pedestrian tastes, and last autumn he'd completely redecorated it. It was not a large room, but it was now comfortable and tasteful. There was the kitchen, fitted not very recently and laid out inefficiently, and a minute loo. A narrow entrance hall, carpeted, and a straight stairway. Three bedrooms upstairs: Mother's room, the largest, at the back of the house, still untouched nearly ten months after her death. David's room, in the middle. And the small guest room at the front, fragrant now with the flowers. A poky bathroom with ugly turquoise fixtures. A steep staircase, leading to the attic room under the eaves, the room that had once been his only escape from Mother . . .

How would it all look to Lucy? Her house was so much of a unity, and so perfectly mirrored her serene personality.

He remembered that he'd not yet put fresh towels in the bathroom, and while he was there he decided to give the washbasin a last polish. Then he returned to the dining room for a final check. Yes, it looked fine. The grandfather clock in the corner chimed and David looked at it, aghast. Six o'clock already! Damn! He was going to be late for her train.

It was only nine miles from Wymondham into Norwich, nine miles of uninteresting, scrubby terrain via the straight, flat A11 duel carriageway. But David didn't spare a thought, as he might have done, for how this landscape might look to Lucy. He was far too involved in his frantic calculations as to how fast he might travel and how soon he might arrive at Norwich station. The station was on the east side of the city, on the outskirts, but extremely inconvenient for access from Wymondham, particularly with Norwich's complex one-way system. And as soon as he reached the ring road, David found himself in the middle of rush-hour traffic. There was nothing to do but sit and fume, and look for his chances to weave through the traffic, all the while keeping his eye on the clock.

He was just about at the river by 6:35, the time her train was due to arrive. With any luck, he thought, the train would be late—they so often were. When he finally reached the station he was nearly ten minutes late by the clock in the car. What an inauspicious beginning for the weekend, he thought, furious with himself.

She was waiting for him in the station. There was an instant of shocked recognition: yes, *that's* what she looks like, he thought with satisfaction. Lucy.

She saw him at the same time, and came to him, smiling. "Hello, David."

He wanted to kiss her, but took her case instead. "I'm so sorry I'm late, Lucy. The traffic . . ."

"That's all right. I thought that you might get held up in

traffic, this time of day. I was quite happy waiting. I knew you'd get here eventually."

"But I wanted to be here when you got off the train." His voice was heavy with disappointment. "Wouldn't you know it! Any other time, British Rail would be running half an hour late! Just my luck they're on time for once."

She laughed at his self-deprecating scowl. "Never mind, David."

He steered her out of the door and toward the car. "Did you have a good journey?"

"Oh, fine. It was a very fast train—it left London at five, and only made one stop, at Ipswich."

"Did you manage to get some tea in the restaurant car?"

"There wasn't a restaurant, only a buffet car—and their tea is pretty vile. Those bags with the milk already in them, you know."

"Ugh." His mother had instilled in him a strong prejudice against tea bags in any form. "Well, if it's not too late for you, you can have some tea when we get—home." He stowed her case in the boot and turned to face her, smiling at last. "I'm so glad you've come," he said simply.

The mushroom stroganoff had been delicious, and Lucy had complimented him on the *pots de crème*. Now they sat lingering over their coffee.

David regarded her across the table. He couldn't believe how *right* it seemed for her to be here with him. He needn't have worried that she'd be critical about the house, or out of place here; she seemed entirely at home, relaxed and happy. As she talked about the last-minute plans for the exhibition's opening, and all the frantic phone calls she'd received from Fiona at the gallery, he reached across the table and took her hand. After a while she laced her fingers with his and they sat like that for a very long time, saying little but smiling at each other contentedly. David knew that he was behaving like a lovesick adolescent, but for this one evening at least he was perfectly happy, and not in the least self-conscious.

At last Lucy sighed with regret, disengaged her hand gently, pushed her hair back from her face, and rose from the table. "I think we'd better tackle the washing-up, David. It's getting late, and tomorrow is going to be a big day."

After the washing-up, accomplished with much shared laughter, he showed her up to the guest room. She automatically proffered her cheek for his kiss, but he surprised her; with a finger under her chin he turned her face toward him, and for a moment his lips lingered on hers, softly and shyly. Then he moved away quickly to the door, where he turned. "Lucy . . ."

She looked at him searchingly. "Yes?"

"I . . . I'm glad you've come."

"David . . ."

"Yes?"

She paused. "Good night."

"Damn," he said to himself under his breath. "Damn, damn, damn." Why was he such a coward? Why hadn't he . . . ? Damn.

He could hear her in the room next door, moving around quietly for a few minutes, making her preparations for bed. And then . . . nothing.

The sheets were cold as he slid between them, but his body burned with longing. She was under the same roof, in the next room even, with only one thin wall between them. He couldn't bear it—to have her so near that if he strained his ears he could almost believe that he could hear her measured breathing. Oh, Lucy . . .

Perhaps she would come to him, as she had in his dream.

He lay awake for hours, his body tense and his mind in turmoil.

But she didn't come.

Of course she didn't.

On the other side of the wall Lucy lay, very still but very much awake. She had a great deal to think about: David had changed toward her—she wasn't sure why, or how. Perhaps it was just having her on his own turf that had caused him to see her in a different light, she speculated. Whatever the cause, she welcomed it. Tonight it had almost seemed that they were on the brink of something, of a major shift in their relationship. And his kiss, so different from the ones he'd given her before, had confirmed it. But why hadn't she had the courage to take it further? Why hadn't he? She wished desperately that she were on the other side of that wall tonight, sleeping content in his arms, replete with loving. She would only be here two nights, and one of them had been wasted already.

What awakened him, finally, was the smell of freshly brewed coffee. David opened one eye and looked at the clock. It was almost eleven o'clock. He groaned in disbelief; they were due at the gallery by twelve. Once he'd fallen asleep, near dawn, his exhausted body must finally have sought refuge in the deep sleep it had craved for nearly a week. David reached for his dressing gown.

Lucy looked pointedly at the clock as he came into the kitchen. "I was beginning to think I'd have to send out a search party! Do you always sleep so late?" She was unable to keep a faint tinge of irritation from her voice.

"No," he answered shortly. "I'm sorry."

"Well, have some coffee—that will get you going—and some hot croissants."

"Oh, where did the croissants come from?"

"I was up early, and walked into town. I got them at the bakery."

"They smell lovely." He sat down at the kitchen table and took the mug of coffee from her. "Thanks, Lucy. Did you sleep well?"

She hesitated, then smiled. "To tell you the truth, the traffic kept me awake for quite a while last night, and woke me early this morning."

"Oh, I'm sorry. That room is probably the worst one in the house for traffic noise. The house isn't that far from the main road, and being in the front of the house . . ."

"Never mind. I enjoyed my walk around Wymondham this morning. It's a lovely town, isn't it?"

"I'd like to show it to you in detail, when there's time."

She looked at the clock again, frowning slightly. "There certainly isn't time now, David. How long will it take us to get to the gallery?"

He noticed then that Lucy was dressed and ready to go. Suddenly he felt quite self-conscious, unshaven and in his dressing gown. He wouldn't blame her if she were annoyed with him, oversleeping like that on her big day. "Not long," he assured her, gulping down the rest of his coffee. "I'll go and get ready right now."

# Chapter 19

*The words of his mouth were softer than butter, having war in his heart: his words were smoother than oil, and yet be they very swords.*

*Psalm 55:22*

Saturday was a particularly busy day in Norwich as well as in Wymondham, and of course they were running late. "Where will you park the car?" Lucy asked, chewing on her lower lip; it was the most anxious he'd ever seen her, David reflected.

"I can put it in the car park behind my offices," he thought aloud. "It's not very far from the gallery. But it would probably be best if I dropped you at the top of Bridewell Alley. The gallery's only a few yards down the hill. Then I'll park, and catch up with you there."

"Good." She looked around her, then, as they wound through the narrow, crowded streets of Norwich. "I had no idea that Norwich was so hilly. Or so picturesque."

"Yes, it's a real medieval city."

"It's nice to see you in your own setting, David. Now I'll be able to imagine your day-to-day life."

\* \* \*

The Bridewell Gallery was already jammed with people when David arrived. He glimpsed Lucy, surrounded by a crowd; she waved at him but he was unable to fight his way through to her. Instead, he circled around the gallery, examining her paintings and eavesdropping with interest on the comments that were being made. She'd shown him most of the paintings that were on display, weeks ago in her London studio; she'd even asked his advice about which ones to send, so he felt as though he were encountering old friends. The paintings were very good indeed, and they were being quite well received, if the overheard comments were anything to go by. Some of them were already marked SOLD; Lucy would be pleased.

He'd just managed to grab a glass of wine from a passing waiter when a strikingly well-dressed, attractive woman came up to him and peered at his face. "David?" she said. "It *is* you. David Middleton-Brown!"

It was a situation from a nightmare. David prided himself on never forgetting a face, but this woman was a total stranger to him. She was possibly about Lucy's age, and very pretty, with skillfully cut wispy black hair framing her face, a face that was dominated by eyes as green as a cat's; her skin was milky white and unlined, and she was dressed in a flowing garment that had clearly come from the showroom of some famous designer. He stalled for time. "Oh, hello."

"Whatever are you doing here, David? You've never been in the gallery before, have you? At least not since I've owned it. I know that you live around here somewhere, that you work in Norwich—I've been thinking for a long time that I'd probably run into you one day. I really should have rung you."

"Um . . ." She'd called him by name, and seemed to know all about him, so clearly he should know her. But he really was at a total loss, and the woman suddenly realized it.

She laughed. "You don't know who I am, do you?"

"I'm so sorry . . ."

"Fiona Crawford. I know it's been a few years, but have I changed so much?"

He stared at her as the light dawned. Fiona Crawford. His old friend Graham's ex-wife. He hadn't seen her in over ten years, since he'd left Brighton, where he and Graham had worked together. But the amazing thing was that in the intervening years, Fiona Crawford had seemingly grown younger rather than older. She'd always been an attractive woman, he remembered, but in a very tailored, almost severe, way: she'd worn her black hair pulled back in an austere knot at the nape of her neck, had masked those amazing cat's eyes with spectacles, and had always dressed in conservative suits, expensive but timelessly unfashionable. The perfect solicitor's wife, he'd always thought her. Well, she was a solicitor's wife no longer, and here she was before him, exhibiting a fey prettiness that belied her years. "Fiona!" he said at last. "Yes, you've changed!"

"For the better, I hope." She laughed again.

"Oh, yes. Your hair . . . and the glasses?"

"Contact lenses. They make quite a difference, don't they?"

He couldn't help staring, but she took it in good humor. "So what are you doing in Norwich, Fiona?"

"I live here now. Didn't Graham tell you about the divorce?"

He'd seen Graham last summer, on a quick trip to Brighton. "Yes, but I didn't know . . ."

"I've been here about six months. I'd always wanted to run an art gallery, and this one was for sale." Fiona waved her hand in a proprietorial way. "I love it. And this exhibition is my first big event. It's going to be quite a success, don't you think?"

"It already is. You've done very well, Fiona."

She smiled, delighted. "And I've got a new man in my life," she confided candidly. "You must come round to dinner one night, and meet him—we can catch up on things." Fiona had always been a good hostess, David remembered, and had often kindly included him in family gatherings on holidays and other special occasions. She had also been an inveterate matchmaker, he recalled. He wondered if she still was, then noticed that she was looking speculatively at him. "You aren't married yet, are you, David?"

"No," he replied, amused.

"Ah." She seemed to be thinking for a moment. "Are you by any chance free this evening, David? I was planning to invite Lucy Kingsley for dinner tonight. You could meet her. Would you like that?"

He hated to sacrifice their evening at the French restaurant, but the ironic humor of the situation appealed to him. "Yes, that would be nice."

"I'll introduce you to her right now!" And Fiona passed like magic through the crowd surrounding Lucy, dragging David in her wake.

"Lucy," she said, "I'd like you to meet an old friend of mine. David Middleton-Brown."

Lucy turned; he caught her eye and winked. She smiled at him solemnly. "Hello, Mr. Middleton-Brown. How nice to meet you."

"And you, Miss Kingsley. I must tell you that I admire your paintings very much."

"Why, thank you."

"Lucy," put in Fiona, "I've been planning to ask you if you'd like to join me and Rhys for dinner tonight, after the opening. Rhys would like to see you again. And David has agreed to join us as well."

Lucy smiled again. "Well . . ."

"Oh," Fiona said suddenly, crestfallen. "I just remembered that you said you'd be staying with a friend for the weekend. Perhaps you'd planned to spend the evening with her . . ."

"Him, actually," Lucy corrected.

"Oh," Fiona looked devastated, seeing her spur-of-the-moment matchmaking coming apart at the seams.

"But I'm sure he won't mind," Lucy assured her. "Will you, David?"

Fiona looked back and forth between them, baffled; they both burst out laughing and she suddenly saw the joke. "Oh," she said. "You two know each other!" She joined in the laughter.

"Yes," said David at last, exchanging a meaningful smile with Lucy. "Yes, we know each other."

He scarcely saw Lucy after that. Naturally enough, it seemed that everyone in the gallery wanted to see her, to talk to her. A long-haired young man had attached himself to her, following her around with slavish devotion, and there were so many others. Eventually David found a quiet corner where he could drink his wine in peace and observe the goings-on with a sort of detached humor.

After a while a young woman glided over to his solitary corner and raised a glass of wine in greeting. To describe her merely as a young woman with abundant hair and long legs would be to do her a grave injustice. She was surely one of the most breathtakingly beautiful women David had ever seen, with the sort of perfect face that appears on the covers of high-fashion magazines. The abundant hair was tawny blond, worn in a frothy mane, and the long legs were clad in black fishnet tights. In between was a body that David, who admittedly was no judge of such things, would have called perfectly proportioned, resplendent in a black dress that was so low at the top and so high at the bottom that it seemed in imminent danger of meeting in the middle. He regarded her with something akin to awe.

However, when she spoke the powerful illusion of worldly

sophistication was immediately dispelled. "Hi-yah," she said, in a breathless mid-western American twang. "I'm Tiffani. Tiffani with an *i*," she added, giggling. "Who're you?"

"David Middleton-Brown. A pleasure to meet you, Miss . . ."

"Tiffani. Just call me Tiffani. Everybody does. It's funny, the way you English people like to be so formal. We don't stand on ceremony where I come from, ya know, Davey."

He winced. "And where is that?"

"Indiana. Beanblossom, Indiana."

David wasn't entirely sure she wasn't making that up, but decided that it wasn't the sort of thing one would invent. "Beanblossom?"

"Yeah. So I'm a stranger here in London, England." She giggled. "Except I'm not in London, am I? I'm in Nor-wich. Talk to me, Davey. I just love to listen to you English people talk."

He was acutely uncomfortable already; now he virtually froze. But she didn't seem to notice. Tiffani carried on. "I guess you're wondering what I'm doing here at this wing-ding, huh? I'm here with my boyfriend Geoffy—he's into art, ya know. But I don't really know much about art, and I don't know anyone here but Geoffy, and he's got other people to talk to, so I was feeling a little lonesome, ya know, and I saw you standing in the corner looking lonesome too, and thought that we could at least be lonesome together, ya know?"

"I'm amazed that a woman who looks like you do could ever be lonely," David said frankly, raising his eyebrows. "I should think that the men would be queuing up."

Tiffani shrugged philosophically. "You'd be surprised, Da-vey. I think that a lot of men are, ya know . . . *intimidated* by beautiful women. At least that's what Geoffy says."

David nodded; that seemed all the response that was neces-sary. "I guess you're wondering how I happen to be in England at all," she went on. "Well, that's a long story, but we've got all afternoon, don't we, Davey?" And she launched into a tale that took her from Beanblossom Queen to Hollywood and a modeling career, to meeting the fabled Geoffy and this visit with him to his native land. Today's appearance at the opening was apparently coupled with a visit to Geoffy's nephew, who lived somewhere nearby.

"Yesterday we were visiting Geoffy's nephew. He's a, ya know, kind of a minister. He lives in this big fancy place with all these other minister-guys."

David was not particularly interested in Geoffy's nephew, but at least this was a conversation of sorts. "What is he like, Geoffy's nephew?" he asked idly.

"Oh, kind of cute, I guess. If you like that kind of guy." Tiffani giggled. "But, ya know, not my type. I like older men." She looked at David through her lashes and moistened her red lips with her tongue.

With unusual perspicacity, he got her drift. Panic-stricken, he babbled on. "You say he lives in a fancy place. What is it like?"

She shrugged, bored with any conversation that didn't revolve around herself. "Big. Old. Rich. You know, really fancy, with lots of neat old stuff around. Geoffy really liked all the pictures on the wall—he spent the longest time looking at them, at every one!"

"Well, that's not too surprising, is it, if he's interested in art?"

"Yeah, but these pictures were really gross! Not like, ya know, Rembrandt or anything. One of them was a lady with her, ya know, boobs on a plate!" She giggled again, coyly. "And there was one of some animal getting its, ya know, guts ripped out—totally yukky. And some guy with his head chopped off. I mean, gross!" Tiffani rolled her eyes.

A waiter approached. "Would you like some more wine?" David asked her.

"Oh, yeah! Look—mine's all gone!"

He put the empties on the waiter's tray and took two full glasses.

"Thanks, Davey! Cheers!" She sipped the wine daintily and looked at him through her lashes. "So, Davey. I've told you about me. Now you tell me why, ya know, you're here, all by your lonesome, standing in the corner. A nice, handsome man like you!"

Once again he felt hot, and not in a pleasant way. He knew that he sounded awkward and stuffy as he replied. "I don't really know many people here. I'm here because of Lucy Kingsley. Miss Kingsley and I, that is, we . . . She's staying with me this weekend . . ."

Tiffani burst into peals of laughter. "Oh, I see! How funny! You and Lucy Kingsley, and me and Geoffy!"

David didn't see the humor at all; he smiled politely.

"And you and me here in the corner, Davey! Oh, Geoffy will just die!"

"Who *is* this Geoffy?" he asked at last, when she'd calmed down.

"Why, Geoffrey Pickering, of course!" She turned incredulous eyes on him. "I thought you knew!"

"*The* Geoffrey Pickering? *Dr.* Geoffrey Pickering?"

"Yeah, sure. Look, he's over there talking to your Lucy Kingsley!"

Sure enough, Lucy was deep in conversation with surely the best-known man in the art world, Dr. Geoffrey Pickering. His face was familiar to anyone who watched television, for in addition to the several series in which he'd popularized art for the masses, he appeared regularly on news programs whenever comment was required on any issue relevant to art. He was even a regular guest on several intellectual quiz programs.

Dr. Geoffrey Pickering: art historian, media figure, citizen of the world. David regarded him curiously, here in the flesh. If anything, he was even more handsome in person than on screen: although he must have been nearly sixty, he was tall and well built, and possessed of film-star good looks, with swept-back silver hair and piercing blue eyes. He was very tanned, from the California sun; David knew that he had a home in California, as well as one in London and one in Italy. In keeping with his carefully cultivated persona he was dressed in impeccable English tweeds, clearly from Savile Row; David wondered idly if he wore tweeds even in the heat of Southern California. He could just as easily imagine him in a pastel shirt, unbuttoned to the navel, with multiple silver chains nestled among silver chest hairs.

He was no mere poseur, though; the man undoubtedly knew about art. David was convinced of that after the most recent BBC series, twelve comprehensive programs on "The Art of Italy." But informative though the series had been, David hadn't made it beyond the program on the Renaissance. He found Pickering's manner profoundly irritating—condescending, arrogant, pretentious—and he usually tried to avoid seeing him on television whenever possible. Without knowing anything of him but what he'd seen on the screen, David thoroughly disliked the man with a sort of unreasoning prejudice. To be confronted with him in person—and the man was talking to Lucy, besides!—was really quite irksome.

"Isn't he cute?" Tiffani said fondly. It was vacuous, even for her.

"Cute?"

"Yeah. He's really just a big teddy bear. Don'tcha think?"

More like a grizzly bear, with teeth, David reflected. *I wouldn't like to get in his way.* All that smooth sophistication aside . . .

"Did you see his TV shows? The ones on Italy?"

"Some of them."

"They were good, weren't they?" Tiffani lowered her voice. "He's hoping that they'll get him his 'K'. You know."

"Knighthood. Yes. Very likely, I should think." Yes, David could see him as *Sir* Geoffrey Pickering.

"He wants it real bad," she confided. She giggled. "I didn't know what he meant, when he told me he wanted a 'K'. I gave him a kiss!"

David smiled, amused in spite of himself. But he was less than amused to see Tiffani beckoning the great man over to their corner, when she'd caught his eye. "You must meet Geoffy," she declared.

Geoffrey Pickering sauntered over, one sardonic silver eyebrow raised questioningly. "What is it, darling?"

"Geoffy, sweetie-pie, you must meet Davey. Davey Middle-something. Isn't it just the funniest thing! I was talking to him, and found out that he and Lucy Kingsley are, ya know . . ."

Pickering turned to David with an appraising look that managed to be highly offensive as well. His voice was silky. "So . . . you're Lucy's latest! My, my. Congratulations are in order, I suppose. I was just talking to her, but she didn't mention that she'd acquired a new lover." He extended his hand as his eyes traveled from David's head to his feet.

David ignored the scrutiny as well as the outstretched hand and replied, with as much civility as he could manage, "I don't see that it's any of your business, quite frankly. I don't know how you know Miss Kingsley, but her private life is surely—"

Pickering's hearty laugh cut across David's words. "Know Lucy Kingsley? How naughty of her not to have told you! *Know* her? I've known her in the biblical sense!" He paused and looked David squarely in the eye, scarcely concealing his amusement. "Of course I know Lucy Kingsley. My dear chap, I used to be married to her!"

# Chapter 20

*O God, the heathen are come into thine inheritance: thy holy*
*temple have they defiled, and made Jerusalem an heap of*
*stones.*

*Psalm 79:1*

Although they didn't generally leave it so late, Alice and Gwen
had been away all week, and Saturday afternoon was their first
opportunity to do their flowers for Our Lady.

It was about three o'clock when they entered the church.
They'd heard no intimation of the drastic changes that had
taken place in the church since they'd been there for the Institution on Monday night. The posters had been bad enough, but
this was desecration. Their first reaction on entering, naturally
enough, was shock. Gwen sat down heavily in the back pew
and burst into tears; Alice was made of sterner stuff, but even
she reached in her pocket for her handkerchief.

"Oh, our church! Our beautiful church!" Gwen wailed,
inconsolable. "That monster! He's . . . he's *violated* our
church!"

A figure in a black cassock glided out of the south porch,
concern on his face. "Ladies!"

"Father Mark!" Alice demanded. "What is the meaning of this . . . this *outrage?*"

"Miss Barnes. Miss Vernon. I'm so sorry that you had to learn about it like this. I wanted to tell you myself, to prepare you for the shock." His voice was soothing, sorrowful, as he patted Gwen's shoulder.

Gwen raised a tear-stained face. "Why didn't you stop him?" she sobbed.

"He had no right!" Alice added fiercely.

"Unfortunately, my dear ladies, he had every right." Mark sat down next to Gwen and took her hand. "He has the freehold now. That means he can do whatever he likes."

"But what has he done with it all?" Alice wanted to know. "All of our beautiful statues? The pictures, the Stations of the Cross, the candles—where are they?"

Mark indicated the south porch. "In there. It's all in there."

"What will he do with it now?" Gwen's voice trembled. "Isn't there anything we can do?"

Shaking his head, Mark looked grave. "He's going to sell it all, I'm afraid. Every bit of it."

"But who will buy it?" Alice asked.

"I can't stop him from selling it, ladies," Mark explained. "But what I *can* do is to make sure that it all goes to good homes, so to speak, where it will be loved as we've loved it here. I've told him that I'd help him to find buyers for everything."

"And he's accepted your help?"

"Yes. He needs my help—he doesn't know any of the right people himself."

"So what will you do, Father Mark?" Gwen squeezed his hand and he returned the pressure, comfortingly.

"I'm making a list now. Some of the things may be worth a lot of money—I'll get professional help to sort those out. Then I'll circulate a list to the people who would be interested in the rest, the things that have sentimental value for all of us."

"You *are* good, Father Mark."

He smiled, then frowned thoughtfully. "There's just one thing that really worries me, though. The monstrance."

Alice looked at him sharply. "The monstrance?"

"Yes. Father Dexter seems to have a special hatred for it, for what it represents. He says that Benediction is the tool of the Devil."

"That evil man!"

"He says that no matter what it's worth—and I frankly don't think it's worth all that much—he won't sell it. He wants to destroy it. He wants to break it up himself. He says he never wants it used again, by anybody."

"Oh!" breathed Gwen. "The monstrance! How dreadful! How can we stop him?"

"We could take it," Alice said slowly. "If we hid it where he'd never find it . . ."

Father Mark nodded. "I can't encourage you, of course. That wouldn't be proper. But if you *did* take the monstrance, and confessed it to me, I would give you absolution. In fact, I would have to say that it wasn't a sin."

Gwen and Alice looked at each other.

There was no point staying in the church—no statue of Our Lady to do the flowers for. "Won't you come home with us for a cup of tea, Father Mark?" Alice asked persuasively.

"I believe that we could all use a good cup of tea right now," he agreed.

Settled a short while later in the sitting room of Monkey Puzzle Cottage, Father Mark tried to take their minds off the terrible desecration of their church. "You've been away, I believe?"

"Yes," said Gwen. "We've been to stay with Alice's nephew, south of Norwich."

"School holidays," Alice explained. "My nephew's wife works—so many women do these days, even married women, who don't need to—and they like us to come during the school holidays, to give them a hand with the children."

"But we're always back for Sunday," Gwen added. "At least . . ." Her face crumbled again. "Now, I don't know . . ."

"Pull yourself together, Gwen," Alice ordered. "It doesn't do any good to feel sorry for yourself. We must think of a plan of action."

"And Father Mark!" Gwen exclaimed. "We've been awfully selfish. This is all terrible for us, but what about *you*? What are you going to do now? Have you heard anything about that other living that you've applied for?"

The young priest smiled, but they could see that it took some effort. "Yes," he said at last. "I . . . I didn't get it. I just heard."

Gwen was indignant. "Didn't get it? But that's terrible! After all you've done for them at Walsingham! They've given it to someone else?"

His hand gripped his teacup. "Yes." He forced a laugh. "But at least they've kept it in the family, so to speak. They've given the living to my friend Stephen Thorncroft. He'll be taking it up in the summer."

"Oh, Father Mark! I'm so sorry! Whatever will you do now?" Gwen's face was creased with misery.

"Just try even harder for the next one that comes along," he replied lightly. "And in the meantime, I'll continue with my part-time work at the Shrine, and of course continue to enjoy the company and the hospitality of my good friends here in South Barsham."

"You're *always* welcome here, Father Mark. You know that," Alice assured him. Gwen nodded violently in agreement.

He smiled at them with gratitude. "Thank you, ladies. That means a great deal to me."

"If only Father Dexter would go. Then you could be here permanently," Gwen said plaintively.

"I don't think he's going anywhere, Miss Vernon." Mark shook his head.

"He's *got* to go!" Alice announced. "How do we get rid of him?"

"As I said before, he's got the freehold. That means that the church, the churchyard and the vicarage belong to him, for as long as he wants to stay. Unless he wants to leave, there are only three ways to get rid of an incumbent—" Mark paused significantly. "Neglect of duty—"

"That doesn't seem likely," Alice muttered.

"Or gross immorality—"

"Not him." Gwen shook her head.

"Or . . . death."

"Oh," said Gwen.

"Ah," said Alice.

# Chapter 21

*Thinkest thou that I will eat bulls' flesh: and drink the blood
of goats?*

*Psalm 50:13*

"Just fancy you knowing Fiona Crawford," Lucy said later, in
the car on the way to Fiona's house. "Small world."

"Yes, but I honestly didn't recognize her. She's changed so
much, Lucy." David shook his head. "She used to be . . .
almost dowdy. Smart, but very staid, very matronly. She always struck me as a model wife—devoted to her children and
all that."

"She has children, then? I didn't realize."

"Oh, yes, two. They're almost grown, actually. James is at
university, and Sarah—I think she's in her last year at some
boarding school."

"She's never said much to me about her ex-husband. What's
he like?" she asked, curious.

"Oh, Graham. He's a nice chap," David replied shortly.
The one thing he did *not* wish to discuss at the moment
was ex-husbands; he didn't trust himself on the subject. That
horrible man! He'd been suggestive, offensive, downright
rude. How could Lucy ever have . . . ? David couldn't bear

even to think of it—of Lucy in that vile man's arms. "And what is this Rhys like?" he asked.

"I think I'll let you judge that for yourself. He's probably not . . . quite what you'd expect."

"Hm. That's intriguing."

"But Fiona's mad about him."

"Really?"

"Absolutely head-over-heels, from what I've seen. It's funny." Lucy looked out of the window, smiling to herself. "Love, that is. You just never know what attracts people to each other. Sometimes the unlikeliest people get together, and people on the outside can never understand why. You can see why the ancients attributed it to Cupid's arrows—sometimes it seems as arbitrary, as random, as that."

This, too, was treading on dangerous ground. David couldn't think of a more unlikely pair than Lucy and that appalling Geoffrey Pickering, yet once she'd cared for him enough to marry him. He scowled, casting his mind around for a less painful subject on more or less the same theme. "You seemed to have an admirer this afternoon—that young man with the long hair who followed you around like a little puppy-dog. Who was he?"

"Nicholas Fielding, you mean?" Lucy laughed. "He was really quite sweet. One of Rhys's animal rights converts, apparently."

"What was he doing there?"

"Oh, he's quite a fan of mine, it would seem. As I say, he was quite sweet. And he bought a painting!"

"Come in, Lucy. And David. Any trouble finding the house?" Fiona greeted them.

"None at all."

"I'll never forgive you two for the trick you played on me." Fiona turned, laughing, and led them into the sitting room. "Rhys, darling, you'll never believe what they did to me. This is David," she added. "And Lucy you know. David, I'd like you to meet Rhys Morgan."

Lucy was right: Rhys Morgan was not at all what he would have expected. He was shorter than Fiona, for one thing, and not particularly attractive, with his thinning carroty hair. He certainly wasn't a fashionable dresser—he was wearing a T-shirt, jeans and trainers. David contrasted him mentally with Graham. Graham was tall, and good-looking in a boyish sort of way; he'd always had nice clothes, and he wore them well. Rhys couldn't have been more different. And of course there was the little matter of the difference in their ages . . .

Rhys shook his hand with a pleasant smile. "I hope you don't mind dogs." He indicated the huge black animal which wagged its tail tentatively at the newcomers. "He may be big, but he's a real softie." David noted that his voice was pleasant, with a hint of a Welsh lilt.

"Have you fixed us something nice for dinner, darling?" Fiona asked, putting her arms around him.

"Definitely, my love. I've had the kitchen to myself all day, you know."

"You didn't come to the gallery this afternoon?" David enquired.

Rhys shrugged. "Not my scene, I'm afraid. Can you imagine me in this kit among all those nobs? And I never go anywhere without Bleddyn." The dog wagged his tail at the mention of his name.

"Rhys is the head of the British Animal Rights Coalition," Fiona said proudly, pointing to his T-shirt. "He founded it."

"I look forward to hearing all about your work."

Rhys grinned, and for the next hour or so took him at his word.

David found Rhys intelligent and articulate, but by any standards it was a long evening. Dinner was a trial for David. The first course—seaweed soup—was bad enough, but the main course was stir-fried tofu and vegetables. David struggled through it somehow, even without the assistance of wine to dull the pain; Rhys made it clear that alcohol was never served in their home.

David found it difficult, too, to deal with his embarrassment at the open affection between Fiona and Rhys. In short, they were unable to keep their hands off one another, even during the meal. Perhaps he was only jealous, he reflected self-mockingly, but it hardly seemed proper.

At last it was time for coffee. Fiona, tearing herself away from Rhys, asked David for his help in the kitchen.

"I'm surprised that you drink coffee," he remarked, rising at her bidding. "Isn't caffeine a stimulant, like alcohol?"

"Yes," Rhys admitted. "But it's my one vice. Apart from Fiona, that is!" In response, she stroked his head as she passed him, and he grinned at her.

Fiona deliberately closed the door of the kitchen, and turned to face David. "Well?" she demanded. "What do you think?"

"Very nice," he said feebly. "I can't say that I've ever had tofu before, but—"

"Not the meal, silly! Rhys! What do you think of him? Isn't he wonderful?"

"He's very nice, Fiona. I'm glad that you've found someone who makes you so happy."

She smiled, as if at something unseen over David's shoulder. "Oh, it's not just happy, David. It's so much more than that. For the first time in my life, I feel . . . complete. Alive. I never knew what I was missing with Graham. I loved Graham, in a certain way, but this is *different*." She focused her eyes on David at last, looked at him intently. "Do you understand what I mean?"

"Yes, I think so."

"And in bed," she went on candidly, without embarrassment, "I just can't tell you how good it is. I can't get enough of him. We can't get enough of each other." She looked away again. "Oh, I know that he's over ten years younger than I am—nearly fifteen years, in fact. But that doesn't matter, David. It doesn't matter at all. It may seem strange to other people, but I don't care. All that matters is that I love him, and he loves me."

She touched David's hand, and fixed him again with her cat's eyes. "I don't really know why I'm telling you all this, David. But I wanted you to know. When you love someone as much as I love Rhys, you just can't let anything stand in your way."

"Yes," he said thoughtfully. "Yes, Fiona. I understand."

Fiona smiled at him in a knowing way. "You love Lucy, don't you?"

"Yes," he replied unwillingly.

"Does she know it? Have you ever told her so?"

"No."

"You must tell her!" Fiona said forcefully. "For God's sake, David, tell her!" She paused, putting a hand on his arm for emphasis. "Better yet, *do* something about it! Tonight!"

# Chapter 22

*My heart was hot within me, and while I was thus musing the*
*fire kindled: and at the last I spake with my tongue . . .*
                                                    *Psalm 39:4*

"Stir-fried tofu!" David shuddered, safely in the car. "It was
revolting, Lucy."

She smiled at him affectionately. "If it was that bad, why
did you have seconds?"

"I had to be polite, didn't I? But I couldn't look at you—
you read my mind too well."

Lucy laughed. "Not always. And what did you think of
Rhys?"

"Oh, he's nice enough, for a fanatic: no meat, no alcohol!"

"No leather," she added. "But I wouldn't really call him
a fanatic. He's quite reasonable about his beliefs. He's just
committed, that's all. He's an idealist."

"Well, I still don't understand what she sees in him."

"What did I tell you?" she smiled.

"He's nothing at all to look at."

"Not my type," Lucy agreed.

"But she's crazy about him."

"Besotted."

"It made me a bit . . . uncomfortable, the way they kept touching each other," David admitted.

"I think it's rather sweet."

"But they're not teenagers!"

"No."

"And don't you think it's a bit strange?" he asked. "Him being so much younger, I mean?"

"What's so strange about it?" Lucy challenged him.

"Well, usually . . ."

She frowned. "I don't understand why that's such a big issue. If it were the other way around—if he were that much older—no one would think anything of it. Just look at that bimbo that you were talking to today."

"Tiffani."

"Tiffani?" she echoed, raising an amused eyebrow.

"Tiffani. With an *i*," David confirmed.

"I'll bet she dots the *i* with a little happy face," Lucy speculated with a wicked smile. "Assuming she can write, that is. Anyway, she must be nearly forty years younger than Geoffrey Pickering."

Geoffrey. She'd brought the subject up, so he could ignore it no longer. "Geoffrey Pickering," he said quietly. "I talked to him today. Or more accurately, he talked to me. Why didn't you tell me that you'd been married to him?"

"But I did, David. Ages ago. Don't you remember? I told you about my marriage, and about . . . about the other two lovers I've had. I haven't kept anything from you."

"You told me that you'd been married to someone named Geoffrey. You didn't say that it was Geoffrey Pickering."

"I didn't think it was that important."

"But I thought . . . I just assumed that Kingsley was your married name!"

"Good heavens, no. I told you that the marriage only lasted a few months. I went back to my own name as soon as I'd divorced him."

David absorbed all this in silence for a moment, his eyes
on the road, but his brain was clamorous with unanswered
questions.

"I just assumed, when you said that you'd met Geoffrey at
art school, that he was your age—another student. Pickering
must be nearly sixty!"

"Oh, he was one of my teachers. Art history. He wasn't
so grand in those days." She turned to face him, sensing
his tension. "Why are you upset? I didn't lie to you, David.
I told you about my marriage, months ago. It's ancient
history. Today was the first time I'd seen Geoffrey since the
divorce."

"I just don't understand," he said at last. "He's so . . .
objectionable. He's pompous, overbearing, pretentious . . ."

"Yes, isn't he?" she laughed.

"Was he like that when you married him?"

"Oh, not so bad, of course. The years have intensified his
negative qualities."

"But how could you have . . . ?"

"I was young, David. Only eighteen. I've told you all this
before." She spoke quietly, twisting a lock of hair around her
finger. "I was escaping from my churchy upbringing. He was
sophisticated, worldly. He knew about wine, about good food,
about art, music, the theater—about the world that I wanted
to be a part of. I was naive enough to think that that was the
way to achieve it."

"But . . . did you love him?" The words were torn out of
him, painfully.

"Oh, no, not really. I convinced myself that I did, of course.
I was fascinated by him, and by what he had to offer."

"But you married him," David stated miserably. He
wouldn't look at Lucy. They were having their first real row,
and now of all times. He knew that he was being unreasonable,
but he couldn't help the way he felt.

"Yes, I married him. It was a big mistake, and it was a

long time ago—half a lifetime ago, David. What difference does it make? Why does it matter?" she challenged.

Now was not the time to tell her, here in a moving car, and these were not the circumstances he would have chosen. But he had no choice. "Don't you know why it matters? It matters because I love you, Lucy. I love you with all my heart." The words sounded so clichéd, so trite to his ears; embarrassed, he stared straight ahead at the road. If he had turned his head, he would have seen her smile.

In a few minutes they were home, out of the car, in the house. Now that it had been said, a detached sensation of unreality descended on David: it was as though this were happening to someone else, or perhaps occurring in a dream.

"Would you like a drink?" he heard himself asking. "Brandy?"

"No, thanks. I'd rather go to bed," Lucy replied with an enigmatic smile.

Could she mean . . . ? Surely not, he thought. Confused, David listened to himself babbling. "Yes, I suppose you're tired. It's been quite a full day. And if you didn't sleep well last night . . . I'm sorry about that. Sorry about the traffic noise. Mother's room is quieter. You can sleep there tonight, if you like."

Lucy held her breath as she considered how to respond. David's declaration of love gave her the courage—indeed, gave her the right—to make the next move. She came very close to him and put her hands on his shoulders. "And where would *you* like me to sleep tonight, my love?" she asked softly.

His heart flip-flopped. Almost unwillingly, he replied, "In my room. In my bed. With me."

"I'd rather hoped you'd say that," she murmured, moving even closer and lifting her face to be kissed.

# Chapter 23

*Then shall I teach thy ways unto the wicked: and sinners shall
be converted unto thee.*

*Psalm 51:13*

It was very quiet in the vicarage on Saturday evening. Bob
Dexter had been in his study for most of the day, working on
his sermon for the next morning, and Becca was in her room.
Elayne, finishing the washing-up from their evening meal,
kept her eye on the kitchen clock nervously.

Eight o'clock. She went upstairs to check on her family—
to make sure that she wouldn't be missed for a while.

Becca's bedroom door was closed; she wouldn't bother her.
The door to Bob's study was ajar so she tapped softly. "Yes?"
he demanded.

"Can I get you anything, Bob? Some coffee?"

"No. I wish you wouldn't interrupt my train of thought,
Elayne! This sermon is very important! It will set the tone for
Bob Dexter's entire ministry in this place!"

"Sorry . . ."

"I'll let you know if I want anything." His voice was irri-
tated, dismissive; she tiptoed away without another word.

The church key, handed over to Dexter with such ceremony by the Archdeacon on Monday night, was kept on a hook near the back door. Elayne slipped it in her pocket and was gone, pulling the door shut quietly behind her.

Alice, with a key of her own, was already waiting for her in the church.

"Hello, Miss Barnes," Elayne greeted her shyly. "It's very nice of you to come out like this."

"Not at all," Alice protested gruffly.

"Miss Vernon hasn't come?"

"No. Gwen stayed home with Nell and Babs. They were feeling a bit unsettled after their trip in the car this afternoon. They have very delicate constitutions, you know."

"Those are your dogs?" Elayne asked. "Becca mentioned that you had dogs. They're girls, are they?"

Alice sniffed. "Of course. Male dogs are so . . . vulgar, don't you think?"

"Are they? I don't know. I've never had a dog." Elayne looked regretful. "Bob hates dogs. He'd never let me have one."

Alice forebore to say what she thought of Bob. It wasn't his wife's fault that the man was so wicked, she reflected—the poor woman was to be pitied rather than blamed. Instead she asked, "Well, have you got it?"

"Yes." Elayne put her hand in her pocket. "It's not a very nice one," she apologized. "But it was the best that I could find in Fakenham."

With a dismissive snort, Alice took it from her. "No, it's not very nice. Plastic. You should have mother-of-pearl, or pink quartz. And it should have double links, so it doesn't break. We must take you to the Shrine shop one day to get a proper one. But this will do for now. Shall we get started?"

"Can we go in the chapel?" Elayne requested hesitantly. "Where . . . she . . . is?"

"Of course." Alice marched to the chapel, Elayne following

behind. "Now," she said. "Kneel down, and repeat after me: 'Hail Mary, full of grace . . .' "

Bob Dexter looked up from his sermon. He'd been working so hard that the words were beginning to blur together in front of his eyes; he decided that he could use a break, and a cup of coffee. "Elayne!" he called, peremptorily. There was no reply. "Elayne!" he repeated. After a moment he frowned and went to investigate.

"Elayne!" he called again at the top of the stairs. When there was still no answer, he pushed Becca's door open without knocking. She was sprawled on the bed, reading a magazine; her Bible lay unopened beside her. "Becca, do you know where your mother is?"

Becca looked up, smiling a bit guiltily as she closed the magazine. She was ready for bed in a pink nightgown, her hair in a plait over her shoulder, and she looked very young. "No, Daddy. I haven't seen her since supper."

"She was up here bothering me a little while ago, but now she doesn't answer me."

"Why did you want her?"

"I was ready for a break, for some coffee."

Becca jumped up. "I'll make you some coffee, Daddy."

"That's very sweet of you, Princess." He followed her downstairs with a fond smile.

"How is the sermon coming along, Daddy?"

"Oh, very well. I want it to be something that will make them all sit up and take notice, you know."

"I'm sure they will."

"My text," he expanded, "is from the Psalms: 'Are your minds set upon righteousness, O ye congregation: and do ye judge the thing that is right, O ye sons of men?' "

Becca filled the kettle and found his "Christians aren't perfect, just forgiven" mug. "Why don't you tell me about it, Daddy?"

He beamed. "Well, Becca, when I finish with them tomorrow morning, they'll know that Bob Dexter is in charge. I can guarantee that. I shall ruthlessly expose their idolatrous practices as hateful to Almighty God. I shall have them—" He broke off as the back door opened and Elayne slipped in. She started guiltily as she realized that she was not alone. "Where have you been?" Dexter asked in a hard, quiet voice. When she didn't answer immediately, he repeated in a shout, "Where have you been, woman?"

Elayne thought quickly. "Oh, I . . . I just went over to the church for a moment. I was in the kitchen, and thought I saw a light on in the chapel. I thought I ought to go over and investigate . . ." It sounded lame, even to her own ears, but Dexter accepted it.

"Why didn't you tell me?" he demanded. "It might have been someone dangerous—someone who'd broken in to steal the silver!"

"You didn't want to be disturbed," she reminded him diffidently. "It didn't occur to me that there could be any danger. I just thought that perhaps someone had left a light on by mistake—someone who'd been there earlier, or something . . ."

"And who was it?"

"Oh, just . . . just that Miss Barnes. Saying her prayers." That, at least, was not an outright lie, Elayne justified to herself.

"It won't do, having people wandering around the church at all hours," he stated, glowering. "And it's not necessary! You can pray to God just as well in your own home as in a church!" Dexter stroked his upper lip. "Tomorrow I shall insist that anyone who has a key to the church must give it up. I'll have them all back, on the spot. And I'll be sure that I get one from Miss Barnes!"

# Chapter 24

*I was glad when they said unto me: We will go into the house of the Lord.*

*Psalm 122:1*

"Good Lord, Lucy! Look at the time!" David stared at the bedside clock, dismayed. "The Mass at Walsingham starts at half past eleven! It's after ten already."

She opened her eyes reluctantly; like the previous night, if for different reasons, it had not been a night for sound sleep. "How long will it take us to get there?"

"It's not a good road. Only two lanes, and very winding," he explained, groping on the floor for his dressing gown. "But there won't be much traffic on a Sunday morning, and if the weather conditions are good—I suppose we can do it in under forty-five minutes. Maybe less." He sank back against the pillows. "Five more minutes in bed, then?" he suggested hopefully.

"I'm afraid not, darling," Lucy smiled, snuggling up nonetheless for one last kiss. "I don't want you getting us killed— not today, anyway. We can always come back later, you know."

\* \* \*

Somehow they made it to Walsingham on time. They spoke very little on the way: it took all of David's concentration to keep his eyes on the road. He was abundantly, astonishingly happy, happier than he'd seen since . . . since Brighton. That thought cast a slight shadow on his happiness, and brought with it the need for confession: he wanted no secrets between them now.

"There are things that you don't know about me," he began.

"Not now," Lucy interrupted gently, her face turned toward him, ignoring the fresh, tender-green spring morning. "Not today. Some time we'll have to talk about it, but not today."

"But if you knew . . ."

"No," she said. "None of it matters. Not now. Not today."

When they reached the narrow, cobbled streets of Walsingham, she turned her attention out of the window at last. "What a quaint place! What's so horrible about it, David?"

"Oh, wait until you see the Shrine. Then you'll know. Or take a look at these shops."

It was not yet the high season for pilgrimage, so the streets were relatively free of people. Walsingham was a picturesque village, rich with history. It was nearly a thousand years ago, in the year 1061, that a woman named Richeldis had had a vision in this place: a vision of the Virgin Mary, instructing her to build a replica of the house in Nazareth where the Annunciation had taken place. A Holy Well sprang forth on the spot, the house was built—by miraculous means, the legend said—and for several hundred years this shrine had been a center for pilgrimage, in England second only to Canterbury. A large abbey had also been established, primarily to care for the thousands of pilgrims to the shrine. Henry VIII had of course seen to it that the shrine was destroyed, along with the abbey, at the Dissolution; ironically, he had several times been to Walsingham as a supplicant pilgrim, praying that his wife Catherine of Aragon might conceive a son.

In the twentieth century, after lying in ruins for nearly 400 years, Walsingham experienced a rebirth. A Roman Catholic shrine was established at the Slipper Chapel outside the village, where pilgrims had once left their shoes so that they might walk the last mile barefoot. And in the 1930s, the Anglo-Catholic Vicar of Walsingham built the Anglican Shrine church, with a new "Holy House" built to the dimensions of the medieval one, surrounded by fifteen chapels.

The main street of the village was narrow, with ancient buildings crowding the pavement on either side; most of them were now profitably engaged in selling souvenirs: postcards, cheap medals, rosaries, painted statues, icons, prayer cards, and even bottles for water from the Holy Well, which the Anglicans now claimed inside their shrine.

"Yes," said Lucy, looking at the shopfronts. "I'm beginning to see what you mean. A bit tacky, isn't it?"

David nodded. "Here's the Abbey, on the right." All that was visible from the street was a tall, protective stone wall. "And the pump, on the left. That's where the protesters congregate, at the National Pilgrimage." He pulled into a large car park, nearly deserted. "And now we'd better fly. It's twenty-five minutes past eleven." Taking her hand, he guided her quickly down another narrow street and through a door. "We'll take a short cut through the pilgrim's hospice, instead of going through the Shrine church," he explained. In a moment they were in a large garden.

The Chapel of All Souls was a freestanding building in the garden, behind the Shrine church. David and Lucy found seats just before the priest, a plump elderly man, waddled to the altar.

"Well, thank goodness that's over," David smiled. The Mass had ended, he'd said his prayers for Lady Constance, and they were once again out in the sunshine.

"Do you have to come every year?" asked Lucy, knowing that in spite of his protestations he undoubtedly would.

"I think she would have liked me to. On her birthday, and

on her year's mind—the anniversary of her death—which is the Feast of the Assumption. We'll see. I'm not making any promises at this point." He shook his head, but he continued to smile.

"Can we go into the Shrine church now?"

"The weather's so nice—why don't we walk around the garden first? Look, here's this horrible sepulcher."

Lucy peered inside the black bunkerlike object; inside was a near life-sized replica of Jesus in the tomb, grotesquely gory. "Ugh. Why didn't you warn me?"

"You need to experience Walsingham in all its awfulness. How about these Stations of the Cross?"

They were large, and garishly painted, fixed at intervals around the perimeter of the garden. "What's that big thing in the middle?" she asked.

"It's an outdoor altar. They can do Masses outdoors, and at the National Pilgrimage they give Benediction from there," David explained.

As they walked around, they gradually became aware that they were being watched. A young fair-haired priest, tall and handsome in a black cassock, seemed to be staring at them. After a moment he approached with hesitation.

"Excuse me," he said diffidently. "Aren't you Lucy Kingsley?"

"Yes . . ." She scrutinized the man; he didn't look familiar. Perhaps he'd been at the gallery yesterday, out of his clerical garb, she decided.

The priest smiled in relief. "I thought so. You probably don't remember me. I'm Stephen Thorncroft—you were married to my Uncle Geoffrey."

"Stephen!" Lucy exclaimed, delighted. "Of course I remember you! You were at the wedding—you must have only been eight or ten at the time!"

"That's right."

"You've grown up!" Impulsively, she embraced him. "But

how did you recognize me, Stephen? It was such a long time ago."

He smiled at her. "I may have grown up, but you haven't changed very much at all. You made quite a big impression on me, you see! You looked like a fairy-tale princess that day— I thought that you were the most beautiful thing I'd ever seen." He was slightly embarrassed but sincere.

"Flatterer!" Lucy laughed.

"No, I mean it. And you talked to me that day, too— remember?"

"Yes, at the reception," she recalled.

"We sat in the corner and talked for the longest time. You didn't treat me like a child—you talked to me as though I were a grown-up. That really impressed me."

Lucy smiled at him, remembering. "I didn't feel much like a grown-up myself that day," she explained. "I was really nervous, and hardly knew anyone there. You were non-threatening. I enjoyed talking to you."

David stood off to the side, feeling totally superfluous. How ironic, he thought, that on this of all days, when all he wanted was to be alone with Lucy, it should be her odious ex-husband's nephew who should intrude.

Stephen continued, "So, what have you been doing with yourself for the last . . . oh, it must be seventeen or eighteen years!"

"Something like that. It's a long story. Painting, mostly."

"I was sorry when . . . well, you know. When . . ."

"When Geoffrey and I were divorced? I should never have married him, Stephen. I was just too young. I didn't know what I was doing."

"I'm sure that Uncle Geoffrey's not an easy person to live with."

"That's true," Lucy agreed.

"He was married and divorced twice after you, you know."

"Yes, I'd heard that."

"And for the last few years—" Stephen smiled wryly. "Well, he's stopped bothering with the formalities. He was here to see me a few days ago with . . . a most extraordinary young woman."

Lucy bit her lip and tried to keep a straight face. "Oh, really?"

"Yes. She was very young. American. And she had the most unlikely name: Tiffani."

"With an *i*," David muttered humorously under his breath; they didn't hear him.

"And you?" Stephen asked hesitantly. "Have you remarried?"

As Lucy shook her head, David interposed, "Not yet."

"Oh, I'm so sorry," she said quickly. "I've been very rude. Stephen, this is . . . the man in my life. David Middleton-Brown."

Stephen appraised David as they shook hands. "Lucky man," he said.

"Yes, I know." David put a proprietorial arm around Lucy.

"Could I invite the two of you to come for a drink?" Stephen asked. "At the College? I wish I could ask you to stay for lunch, but they don't cater for any extras, I'm afraid."

"Yes, that would be very nice, wouldn't it, David?"

"I wouldn't say no to a sherry," he admitted.

This must be the place Tiffani had told him about, David realized as they entered the dining room. But it was far from the baronial hall that she had described to him, however inarticulately. It was in fact a converted medieval tithe barn—a cowshed, he said to himself with scorn. The furnishings were on a large scale, but they all appeared to David's expert eye to be not quite right in one way or another: a knob missing here, or a handle there, spoke of discarded, rejected, second-best furniture, probably given or bequeathed to the College by those who had no further use for it. And the paintings on the walls were truly hideous—mainly bad copies of seventeenth-century Italian religious paintings, the worst that the Counter-reformation had to offer. He recognized one that Tiffani had described so colorfully, a simpering St. Agnes proffering her bell-like breasts on a platter. There was a large and murky Assumption of the Virgin, and a copy of a Caravaggio, the original of which hung in the National Gallery: Salome receiving the head of John the Baptist, his mouth open in shock and his stump bleeding onto the silver platter. Charming subject matter for a dining room, David reflected. At one narrow end of the room stood a large sideboard with an almost matching pair of candelabra on either end; above it hung the other painting that Tiffani had mentioned, the conversion of St. Hubert with a hunting scene in the background, dogs viciously ripping the flesh of a stag. The massive sideboard with the huge painting above, placed as it was, could almost have been an altar, David mused humorously: an altar to food.

The oblong table which filled the center of the room was long and solid, though none of the chairs surrounding it matched it or each other. "I see that you've taken Dr. Grantley's admonitions to heart," David remarked with a smile.

Stephen laughed. "Yes, he hated round dining tables, didn't he?"

"I believe that he said that a round dinner table was 'the most abominable article that ever was invented.' "

"That's absolutely right," confirmed the elderly priest who had celebrated Mass earlier, joining them. He raised his eyebrows, perched like furry caterpillars above his deepset eyes. " 'Democratic and parvenue,' wasn't it? Used by 'dissenters and calico-printers'? I like a man who knows his Trollope." The old man's voice was mellifluous, but his cassock was theadbare and bore marks that looked suspiciously like gravy stains, and when he smiled his teeth were uneven and none too clean.

Stephen introduced them to Father Owen Osborne, who then drifted off in search of a drink, but they were shortly joined by another young priest, darkly handsome. "This is Father Mark Judd, my colleague and friend."

Mark Judd smiled charmingly, his straight white teeth a great deal more attractive then Father Osborne's. "This is certainly your week for visitors, Stephen. Your uncle with his . . . friend . . . on Friday, and another two today!"

Stephen nodded as he supplied them with sherry. "Mark really hit it off with Uncle Geoffrey," he explained to Lucy. "Uncle Geoffrey's going to help him with something."

"Geoffrey being helpful? That doesn't sound very likely." Lucy rolled her eyes, pushing her hair back from her forehead with a graceful gesture. "What's in it for him?"

"I appealed to his professional pride," Mark laughed. "And his curiosity. He was looking at the paintings in here, and I told him about all the ones we're trying to flog off at the church where I've been working. I said that we desperately needed some expert advice about valuation, and where to go to get the best prices. He offered to come and have a look, and give his opinion."

"Mark has been looking after a parish during a long interregnum," Stephen explained. "Now the new incumbent is having a clear-out."

"To say the very least!" Mark amplified. "It was quite a spiky place, in an old-fashioned sort of way. And the new Vicar is none other than Bob Dexter, Mister Evangelical."

"*The* Bob Dexter?" David asked in surprise.

"You've heard of him?"

"Of course. He is, as you say, Mister Evangelical. He seems to be in some sort of competition with Tony Higton as to which one can write the most letters to the *Church Times*, and give more speeches at General Synod! But what on earth is he doing here? I thought that he was very well established in the

London area, with a real power base there. Why would he come to rural Norfolk?"

"I think he probably thought it would be a challenge, to be right on the doorstep of Walsingham, so to speak," Mark speculated. "He's always been very active in the protests, you know."

"Ah." David nodded. "What is he like? Is he as frightful as he comes across in his letters and on television?"

"Every bit," confirmed Mark. "He's inflexible, arrogant, and dogmatic. Ruthless, and without a sense of humor. But he has a great deal of personal charisma, somehow. And I have to admit to a certain amount of admiration for someone who's willing to stand up for his beliefs the way he does. And for someone who's prepared to do whatever is necessary to get what he wants—or what he thinks God wants." He paused, glancing provocatively at Stephen. "*And,*" he added, "anyone with a daughter that pretty can't be all bad, eh, Stephen?"

Stephen's fair skin was flushed. "I don't know what Becca has to do with it."

"Ah, so we're on a first-name basis with the beautiful Becca, are we?" Mark teased. Stephen bit his lip, looking extremely uncomfortable, and Mark went on to Lucy and David, "Stephen's in love, you see. With Bob Dexter's daughter."

Lucy looked interested. "What's she like, Stephen?"

"A vision of loveliness, isn't that right, Stephen?" Mark put in.

Stephen finally spoke, with some asperity. "It's all very well for you to joke about it, Mark, but Becca is . . . well, she's just . . . Becca. It doesn't matter who her father is."

"It may not matter to you, but I can assure you that it matters to Bob Dexter. I don't think he'd be very amused at the thought of his beloved daughter . . . consorting . . . with a Walsingham priest!" Mark said, laughing.

Amused? He probably wouldn't believe it, David thought.

Walsingham priests were not exactly well known for their pursuit of women. But apparently Geoffrey Pickering's nephew was an exception to the rule.

"My intentions toward Becca are honorable," Stephen protested. "I know that I haven't known her very long, but . . . well, don't you believe in love at first sight?" he appealed to Lucy.

"It can happen," she agreed. "But I do think you ought to be careful, Stephen. Don't rush into anything."

"I won't," he said. "But I've been appointed to a new living, starting in the summer, and I'll be leaving Walsingham, so I have to make the most of the time I've still got here."

David nodded approvingly.

There were signs that lunch was imminent. "We'd better be on our way, Lucy," David suggested. "These reverend gentlemen will be wanting their lunch, and we mustn't detain them."

# Chapter 25

*For thy servant David's sake: turn not away the presence of thine Anointed.*

*Psalm 132:10*

Bob Dexter stood at the church door, greeting his departing parishioners. Most of them bore rather stunned looks on their faces. His sermon had been a great success, he told himself; he'd hit them right between the eyes with the Word of God. They were obviously not used to hearing the Word of God. And of course they were all still reeling from the drastic alterations in the church. Dexter had a good memory for faces, and as he'd met most of the congregation on Monday night, he was able to greet the majority of them by name, thus putting them at even more of a disadvantage. It was most satisfactory.

Alice Barnes attempted to slip out, ungreeted, behind an amply proportioned worshiper, but Bob Dexter was too quick for her; his arm shot out and seized her before she could escape. "Miss Barnes."

Cornered, she retaliated as best she could. "Good morning, *Father* Dexter."

He glared at her. "Miss Barnes. You heard what I said in

the notices, about the keys. I believe that you possess a key to the church. I would like it back, please. We can't have unauthorized people wandering about in here all the time."

Her bosom heaved. "Unauthorized! I like that! After all I've done for this church . . ."

"Nevertheless, Miss Barnes, I will have your key back. Right now. You have it with you?"

She was unable to lie. From between her breasts she drew forth a cord, the sort on which scouts wear their whistles; on it dangled the key in question. With all the dignity she could muster, she pulled it over her head and slapped it into Bob Dexter's outstretched hand. She pursed her lips together, gave him a venomous look, and stalked away without a word.

Bob Dexter smiled.

"Aren't we going to look at the Shrine now?" Lucy asked.

"I just can't cope with it at the moment," said David, leading her back to the car. "I need some lunch first."

"Where will we eat?"

"I always keep a copy of the *Good Food Guide* in the glove box for emergencies like this," he explained. He soon retrieved the well-thumbed volume and sat in the car for a look. "South Barsham," he suggested after a moment. "The Old School-house. It sounds quite good, and it's very near here. They do vegetarian meals, it says."

"Lovely," she agreed.

Within a quarter of an hour they were sipping another sherry in the building where Gwen Vernon had spent so many years attempting to impart knowledge to largely unreceptive young minds. With Lucy across the table from him, and the prospect of a good meal, David was in very good humor.

"Well," he said. "Imagine running into 'Geoffy's nephew' like that. Small world."

"Stephen's a nice chap, isn't he?"

"Not bad," he admitted. "For Walsingham. And for Geoffrey. How on earth did a nephew of his end up in Holy Orders? Geoffrey doesn't seem exactly like the religious type."

"Oh, he's not. None of the family are, in fact. It must have been quite an act of courage—of rebellion, I suppose—for Stephen to go against the family like that and enter the priesthood."

"He must have had a strong sense of vocation."

"Funny, isn't it? I remember him as a very bright, sensitive boy. And to run into him now, all these years later . . ."

The waitress appeared to take their order. David gave it, then added, "And a bottle of champagne, please."

"Champagne? Isn't that pushing the boat out a bit, David? And you do have to drive home."

"I'll be careful," he promised. "But we do have something to celebrate today. Us."

Eventually, by the time they'd finished their meal, the champagne gave him the courage to say what he wanted to say. "Lucy," he began. "I think we need to talk about our future."

"Is that really necessary?" she replied quietly. "Can't we just be happy in the present for now?"

He should have read the signs and stopped, but he rushed on, heedless. "But it's important to get this settled—to know where we're going. I want to marry you, Lucy. As soon as possible. Say that you'll marry me."

She looked at his hands, his gentle hands with the badly bitten fingernails; she couldn't bear to look at his face. The silence stretched out painfully; at last she said, so softly that he wasn't sure he'd heard her, "No."

"What?"

"No," she repeated, a little more loudly, then at last raised her eyes to his stricken face. "I wish you hadn't asked. I wish you could have just left it . . ."

"But why not, Lucy? I thought . . . I thought that you loved me. You said . . . Last night . . ."

"I *do* love you. You must know that. But love isn't everything. It's not always enough. There are other factors . . ."

"Such as?"

Lucy took a deep breath and attempted to put their discussion on a rational, non-emotive level. "Well, David, for one thing, there's the logistics of it all. You live in Wymondham, I live in London. One or the other of us would have to uproot . . ."

"I don't mind," he said eagerly, relieved to see such an easy way out. "I'll move to London. I could find a job in London without much problem."

She shook her head. "All these things take a lot of thought. You can't just change jobs overnight, because . . ."

David had a sudden, painful thought. "I suppose I wasn't good enough in bed," he ruminated bitterly. "Did I disappoint you, Lucy?"

"Can you seriously ask that?"

"Then why?" He looked down at his clenched hands. "Is it because of . . . my past? What happened before I met you?"

"No," she said honestly. "The past is the past. I don't know the details—they don't really matter. I have a past, too, you know. If you say that you love me now . . ."

"I *do*. You must know that I do."

She met his eyes. "It's just too soon, David. That's all. We've been lovers for less than twenty-four hours. Don't you think we need a little more time to adjust?"

"Then you're not saying that you want to break it off? To never see me again?"

She laughed aloud. "Of course not! Is that what you thought?"

He nodded miserably.

"I have no intention of breaking it off," Lucy assured him. "Quite the contrary. I just want to give it a bit more time. Don't you understand?"

"But I'm sure!" he insisted. "Aren't you?"

"Don't you see, my love?" she said gently. "It's not a question of being sure. I'm sure that I love you. But there's no hurry. If it's going to last, why then, it *will* last, whether we're married or not. And if not . . . well, isn't it better not to rush into anything permanent?"

"But you married Geoffrey . . ."

"Exactly. That's my point. It didn't last, wouldn't have lasted no matter what. I was silly and immature. I thought that if I didn't grab him immediately, he'd change his mind, or find someone else."

"I don't want *you* to find someone else," David admitted wretchedly.

"And you think that being married will keep that from happening?" Lucy laughed again, reaching for his hand. "I can assure you, my darling, that I'm not looking for anyone else. And if *you're* going to start looking elsewhere . . ."

"Of course I'm not!" David was stung. "Is that what you think? That this is just a phase I'm going through, and that eventually I'll go back to . . ."

"No, David. I don't think that at all. But if . . . well, as I said, we haven't had much time together, to test our commitment."

"I know that I want to spend the rest of my life with you," David stated stubbornly, desperately. "I'm not going to change my mind like I did . . . the last time."

She squeezed his hand. "I'm not saying that I'll never marry you—just that I think we must take our time. Let's give it a year, David darling. We can spend the weekends together, see how it works. And then . . . well, we'll see. If you still want me by then, that is!" she added with a smile.

David sighed. It would have to do.

However, he was far from happy. After lunch he declined once again to visit the Shrine and drove straight back to Wymondham in near silence.

Lucy, too, was silent for most of the drive, thinking about

what had gone wrong. The last thing she'd wanted to do was to hurt David. She wished fervently that he hadn't pressed the issue of marriage. She didn't really blame him for being upset—it was only natural, she supposed, that he should think of marriage as the next logical step in their relationship, and should take her refusal as a personal rejection. Lucy realized that the problem was with her: the disastrous failure of her first marriage had scarred her very deeply, and made her excessively cautious about making such a commitment again. She even questioned, in her own mind, the viability of the institution; she'd seen so many unhappy people in so many miserable marriages. Even her best friend Emily Neville, who enjoyed what was widely considered a "perfect marriage," was not without problems; last summer she had briefly but dramatically left her cleric-husband, the beautiful and gifted Gabriel, in circumstances and for reasons that Lucy had never really understood. But whatever her own hang-ups, marriage was evidently very important to David, who was, she knew, a most conventional man. Lucy determined that she'd try to keep an open mind, and to make it up to him as best she could. She didn't want to lose him, of that she was certain.

# Chapter 26

*I have hated them that hold of superstitious vanities: and my trust hath been in the Lord.*

*Psalm 31:7*

"Becca, darling," Bob Dexter said over lunch on Monday. "I've got to go out this afternoon. There's a meeting at Gates of Heaven, a 'MISSION: Walsingham' meeting. Have you got enough to keep you busy for a few hours?"

"I've done all your letters already," she replied. "And I'm up-to-date on the filing. I was wondering," she added hesitantly, looking at her father through lowered lashes, "if you'd mind if I had an hour or two off? Miss Barnes and Miss Vernon have asked me to tea."

Dexter frowned. "I'd really rather you didn't. I don't like you spending time with those women. They're not suitable company for you. You should be spending your free time with people around your own age, and people who think the same way we do—someone like Toby Gates, for instance."

Becca chewed her lip. "Please, Daddy? They're harmless, really. And they mean well." She bestowed on her father the smile that always got her what she wanted.

"Well . . ." Stroking his chin, he considered. She was right, he supposed. What harm could it do?

"I'm seeing Toby tomorrow night," Becca added in propitiation.

"Oh, all right, Princess," he conceded, patting her arm; he was rewarded with a fleeting look of such intense gratitude that he thought he must have imagined it. "But mind you're back in plenty of time for family prayers before supper."

This time Bob Dexter took care that he was not the last one to arrive at Gates of Heaven; in fact, only Noah Gates and his son were in the board room when Dexter entered. The room was dominated by the huge fluorescent "MISSION: Walsingham" banner behind Noah Gates's seat at the head of the table.

"Good afternoon, Noah." Gates acknowledged the greeting with a nod. "Toby! How nice to see you again!"

"Hello, sir," Toby replied, surprised and gratified by the warmth in Dexter's voice.

"I understand that you're seeing Becca again tomorrow night." Dexter clapped the young man on the shoulder with a smile.

"Yes, sir. I thought that we might go back to the restaurant where we ate last week."

"So this is becoming a regular thing! Be careful, young man, or you'll be stealing my Becca's heart away from her old dad." Dexter's smile was no longer altogether genial.

Toby flushed painfully. "I can assure you, sir . . ." he stammered.

"Don't worry, my boy." Dexter waved his hand as he took a seat at the end of the table opposite Noah Gates. "It's good for Becca to get out, especially with someone I can trust. I *can* trust you, can't I, Toby?"

"Of course you can trust my son," Noah Gates interposed in a steely voice. "I've brought him up properly. He knows right from wrong. Are you suggesting otherwise?"

"Not at all, Noah. Not at all. But a father can't be too careful, can he?" Bob Dexter raised his eyebrows and regarded father and son with a bland smile.

Soon the other members of the "MISSION: Walsingham" steering committee had assembled, uniform in their white shirts and displaying their identical white-bread smiles, and it was time to begin the meeting. From the outset, it did not go according to Noah Gates's unwritten agenda.

"Now that we're all here," he began, "there are a few things—"

"Don't you think," Bob Dexter asked from the other end of the table, "that we should open with prayer? Commit our enterprise to the Lord?"

"Yes, of course . . ."

With a smooth movement, Dexter rose to his feet. "Dear Lord Jesus," he began in his sonorous baritone preacher-voice, before anyone else had a chance to react, "we gather here today in Your name, to seek Your will. We know that You will guide us, for we have called upon You. In Your Holy Scriptures You have promised us that he who seeks will surely find, and You have given us Your Holy Spirit in our hearts as a token of Your favor."

His voice dropped, then gradually rose as he continued. "O Lord, You know that there are many who dwell in darkness. Their eyes are blinded by superstitious vanities. They call upon Your name, but they see You not. Help us, O Jesus, to help them. Give us the words to say, and the methods to reach them, so that they might be saved for all eternity, and escape from the everlasting damnation to which they have condemned themselves by their idolatrous practices. Help us, Jesus, to love the sinners even as we hate their sin. Give us wisdom, give us courage. And prepare their hearts even now to receive Your holy words, that they might see the error of their ways and turn to You. Make us Your instruments, O Jesus, so that all might follow You, and dwell one day with us in Your eternal kingdom." For a fraction of a second, Dexter's eyes opened and flickered over the bowed heads around the table. "Guide us this day, and ever more. In the name of Jesus, Amen.

"And now," said Bob Dexter, smoothly. "I'd like to tell you all a few of my experiences in dealing with the members of my parish. It could be helpful in trying to understand the Walsingham mentality." All eyes swiveled to the far end of the table.

Noah Gates had lost control of the meeting, once and for all.

# Chapter 27

*And I said, O that I had wings like a dove: for then would I*
*flee away, and be at rest.*

*Psalm 55:6*

David was up early on Friday, and off to his offices. He had a
great deal of work to get through that day, and he intended
leaving as early as possible that afternoon for London and Lucy;
the week without her had seemed interminable, and he could
hardly wait to see her again. At this hour there was little traffic
on the A11—nothing to require his attention, and take his
thoughts from Lucy. Once in Norwich, he threaded his way
through the complicated one-way system and parked his car
in the small private car park behind Princes Street, a narrow,
picturesque street of converted Georgian houses, one of which
held his offices. Early as he was, he let himself in with his
key—not something that happened very often, he thought
wryly—then, as he always did, automatically and unconsciously, he checked his tie in the mirror just inside the front
door. But this time, something about the tie caught his attention, and he frowned. It was the one that his mother had given
him for Christmas, the year before she died. He'd never liked

it. Why had he worn it today, today when he was going to see Lucy? He made a mental note to change it before he left for London—to throw it away, even.

He was not the first one in the offices, David found as he passed through the typists' room. A girl was sitting at a typewriter—a small, childish-looking blond girl, Karen. But she wasn't typing, and there was something different about her appearance. David, who was fairly observant, realized that it was her hair. It was fine-textured blond hair: the last time he remembered seeing her it had fallen limply to her shoulders; now it was a bit shorter and had been permed into a thousand tiny corkscrews. She glanced around. "Good morning, Mr. Middleton-Brown," she whispered over her shoulder.

"Karen?" he said tentatively. "Your hair . . ."

"I've had a perm."

"Very nice, too." He stopped as she swiveled in her chair and turned her face up to him; her brown eyes were swimming with unshed tears. "Why, Karen, what's the matter?"

"Oh, Mr. Middleton-Brown!" She ended on a half-sob. "I'm sorry . . . I don't want to trouble you . . ."

Oh, Lord, he thought, now what? But he conquered his impulse to flee and sat down on her desk, leaning toward her. He felt that he should take her hand, to reassure and comfort her, but decided at the last minute that she might interpret it the wrong way. "Karen, tell me what's wrong. Is it the job? Are we giving you too much work? Is that why you're here so early?"

Looking away, she shook her head and the multitudinous corkscrews bobbed madly, but it was a moment before she spoke. "No, it's not that. I just needed . . . to get away from my family, to be alone for a little while."

"Would it help to talk about it?" He paused. "That is, if you don't mind talking to an old man like me."

She smiled a watery smile, and David realized with a fairly unpleasant pang that she *did* think of him as an old man, and he needn't have worried about her misinterpreting his kindly gesture. She *was* very young, after all—perhaps not even eighteen; he was probably older than her father. He took her hand. It was a very small hand, and cold; the tiny nails were cut short, for typing, and the pale pink polish on them was chipped. He gave it a reassuring squeeze and she returned the pressure gratefully. "Come on—tell me what's wrong. Boyfriend trouble?"

Again she shook her head, but this time she met his eyes. "I saw a program on the telly last night," she whispered at last, and one of the tears in her brimming eyes squeezed out and ran down her cheek. "It was about animals. About the awful things that they do to them." She gulped. "There were these baby seals. They hit them with clubs. The men. There was blood—all over the snow. Oh, it was horrible. And badgers. The dogs—they ripped them apart." One by one the tears escaped. "I couldn't sleep at all last night. And now . . . I just don't know what to do. How can people be so cruel? To poor little helpless animals, who never did them any harm? Oh, Mr. Middleton-Brown, what can I do? What can anyone do?" Her soft, full lower lip trembled, and her babyish face looked as though it were ready to dissolve in tears.

Although it was clearly a rhetorical question, and she didn't really expect him to have any answers, David felt that he had to say something. For a moment he looked at her helplessly, then inspiration struck. "Karen, there are other people who feel the same way. Other people who love animals, and want to help them. I know someone that you could talk to." She was still clinging to his hand, but with his free hand he felt in his pocket for his diary. He'd send her to see Rhys Morgan— maybe she'd enjoy his blooming tofu.

"Darling, you've got to talk to Daphne."

"Hmm?" Though it was quite late on Saturday morning, David was barely awake.

"You've got to talk to Daphne," Lucy repeated, nuzzling his neck.

He opened his eyes. "Daphne?"

"Daphne. You've got to tell her. About us."

He reached for her, but she wriggled out of his grasp. "David, this is serious. You have to talk to her."

"Daphne. Yes, I know. Later. There's no hurry." He reached for her again.

She resisted him. "David! Listen to me!"

"Yes, I heard you. I have to talk to Daphne," he acknowledged reluctantly.

"You're putting it off, aren't you?"

"I just don't see the great rush. She's not going anywhere."

"That's just it," Lucy emphasized. "She's *not* going anywhere. She's probably sitting around her flat, waiting for you to show up."

"Surely that's a bit dramatic?"

Lucy shook her head. David had evidently never realized how fond Daphne was of him, though to her, an outsider, it was manifestly apparent. It would probably do no good to explain it to him at this late stage. "When was the last time you spoke to her?" she contented herself with asking.

"A few weeks ago," he shrugged. "Last weekend you came to Wymondham, the weekend before—Easter weekend—I stayed home, you remember, so it would have been the week before that, when I was last in London, meeting with those property developers."

"And did she know that you wouldn't be staying with her this weekend?"

"No, of course not. It's not the sort of thing I'd want to put in a letter, is it?" he defended himself. " 'I'm sorry that I'll no longer be requiring your spare room—I've had a better offer?' But I never told her I *would* be staying with her this weekend."

"Darling, I'm sure she's wondering. She was probably expecting you last night."

"I always drop her a line when I'm coming," David protested. "So she wouldn't have been expecting me. Come here, Lucy love. Surely it can wait a few more minutes! I'll go to see her this afternoon."

"All right, if you promise." Mollified, she allowed herself to be drawn into his arms.

Daphne was out when David arrived at her flat, just before teatime, but he let himself in with the key she'd insisted he keep for just such occasions. He browsed on her bookshelves, selected a promising-looking volume about ecclesiastical embroidery in the nineteenth century, and made himself comfortable on her shabby, over-stuffed sofa. He quickly became engrossed, and looked up abstractedly as she entered. "Oh, hello, Daphne. Hope you don't mind me making myself at home."

She looked surprised to see him. "Of course not, David. You know you're always welcome here," she said. "Tea?" She was already on her way to the kitchen to fill the kettle.

"Yes, but you don't have to wait on me," David protested, as he had done so many times before. Reluctantly, he put the book down and followed her to the tiny kitchen.

"Just go back in the other room and sit down," Daphne ordered. "There's not enough room in here for both of us. I'll be out in a tick."

He obeyed her, resuming his seat on the sofa. But instead of picking the book up, he began to think about what he might say to her. Lucy was right—he *had* been putting it off, and had even avoided thinking about it. This wasn't going to be easy. But he and Daphne had weathered worse storms in their long friendship. And he didn't think that Daphne had any objections to Lucy. Undoubtedly, though, it would mean a major change in their relationship, logistically if nothing else: no longer would he be calling upon her hospitality, using her spare room on frequent weekend visits. There would be no more holidays together, no more cosy late-night chats over a bottle of whisky. He hoped that she wouldn't mind too much.

Daphne interrupted his reverie as she eased the tea tray on to the table and sat down. "David, I have to talk to you," she said brusquely, running her hands through her bluntly cut gray hair.

He sat up in surprise. "There's something I have to talk to *you* about."

"Don't interrupt me." Daphne had put on her half-moon reading glasses, and she looked at him now over the tops of them, pursing her mouth wryly. "This is difficult enough as it is. Just let me say what I have to say."

"All right." He sat very still, trying to think what it might be.

Daphne took a deep breath, and plunged in. "I wanted you to be the first to know. I'm going to be married."

"Married?" He stared at her, thunderstruck.

She laughed self-consciously. "Yes, I know it must seem hard to believe."

"But . . . but . . . who?"

Daphne didn't look at him as she replied. "Cyril. Cyril Fitzjames."

He sat silently for a moment, struggling to absorb this knowledge. "Cyril."

"Yes. I . . . we . . ." She twisted her hands together in her lap. "David, it's not easy to explain. There are reasons . . ."

"You don't owe me any explanations," he said quickly. "Cyril is a nice chap. If you love him . . ."

She looked squarely at David for a moment, then looked away. "It's rather more complicated than that."

"What do you mean?"

She busied herself pouring the tea as she explained. "The

new Vicar of St. Anne's. You know that it's been a difficult adjustment for me—for a lot of people."

"Yes . . ."

"It's his first parish—he's very young. He's been insistent from the beginning on getting his own way. Cyril says that he's a spoiled brat."

"There must be more to it than that." David found it hard to understand; he was unable to imagine anyone who couldn't get on with Daphne. She was always willing to give the benefit of the doubt, to see things from the other side.

Daphne shot him a look over her spectacles. "His churchmanship is very different from Gabriel's, from mine. Gabriel and I were on the same wavelength. This new chap . . . well, it's been difficult, as I say."

"MRP," David encouraged her.

"Modern Roman Practice. Yes." She handed him a cup of tea, made just as he liked it.

"Better than a 'clap hands for Jesus' Evangelical, I should have thought."

"Only just, if you can believe it. We haven't really got on very well, the new Vicar and I. And now . . . well," Daphne paused, sighed, "I'm being given the push."

David stared, aghast. "Your job?"

"Yes. He doesn't really need a Sacristan. And if he did . . ." She smiled ruefully. "But our differences are irrelevant. He doesn't need a Sacristan. He's getting rid of all the lovely old vestments, the altar hangings . . . It's just like you said before he came. Lambswool ponchos, and spider plants on the altar."

"The silver?" he asked fearfully.

"Most of it has scarcely been out of the safe since he arrived. He uses those great fat stumpy candles, a pair of them on one side of the altar to balance the spider plants. No candlesticks, of course. And he prefers pottery chalices—against all hygiene considerations, as well as against all taste."

"And your flat . . . ?"

"The flat goes with the job, of course."

David looked at her searchingly. "And so you're marrying Cyril."

"Yes." Again she was unable to meet his eyes. "He has asked me to marry him. He's been lonely ever since his wife died, nearly fifteen years ago. As long as Emily was around, he could keep himself occupied following her about, but since she and Gabriel left St. Anne's, even though she's still in London . . . well, he's been spending more and more time here. Dropping by, just to talk. We get on well."

"But *marriage*, Daphne! It's such a big step! It will mean a lot of changes in your life. Are you sure it's what you really want?"

She looked into her teacup. "I believe that we can be happy," she answered at last. "Things *do* change, David. Life changes, whether you want it to or not. It might not be exactly what I would have wanted," she added softly, then rushed on, "but it's what I've been given. A chance at happiness, from an unexpected direction. And I mean to make the best of it." She raised her eyes to his at last, almost defiantly.

David expelled a deep breath. "Well," he said after a moment, "I certainly hope you're right about this. And I wish you all the best," he added warmly.

"Thanks, David." She grinned at him then, relieved that it was out in the open. "And now—what is it that you wanted to talk to me about?"

While he was away, Lucy had prepared a simple but delicious supper for them, and he'd picked up a bottle of wine on his way back. Daphne's startling announcement was the main topic of conversation during the meal.

"So I needn't have worried about telling her about us," David concluded ruefully.

"She took it well?"

"It was a bit of an anticlimax after *her* news." He shook his head. "I still can't believe it. Daphne, getting married for the first time at her age. There's hope for me yet!"

Lucy ignored the provocation. "Well," she said, "it fits in nicely with an idea I had while you were away. I was thinking that it would be good for us to give a dinner party. We could have it in honor of Daphne and Cyril."

"A dinner party? Here?"

"Of course here." She smiled at him almost shyly. "I thought that it would be nice for us to entertain as a couple. To let people—our friends—get used to the idea of us being together."

"What a marvelous idea!" He returned her smile as he pictured the scene: Lucy's dining room, silver glinting in candlelight, wine sparkling, delicious food, scintillating conversation . . . "But who else would we invite?"

Considering, she pushed her hair from her face. "I suppose we could invite Emily and Gabriel. If we gave them plenty of advance notice, that is—since he's become Archdeacon, the Angel Gabriel's diary is rather full! I suppose," she added, laughing, "that I should more properly say the Venerable Angel Gabriel!"

David didn't laugh. "Yes . . ."

She looked at his reluctant face in surprise. "You don't seem keen, darling! I thought that you liked Emily."

"Yes, I like Emily very much."

"Then what's the problem? Oh, I know that the Angel Gabriel can be a bit hard to take at times, but—" Lucy studied him intently as he averted his face. "What is it, David?"

"I've tried to tell you this before but you wouldn't let me," he said defensively. "You must know that I loved someone else . . . once. Before."

"I had rather guessed that." She smiled, and squeezed his hand reassuringly across the table. "I don't even think I get any prizes for guessing that it was a man. I don't mind, darling. Honestly, I don't. But why . . . ?"

David still wouldn't look at her. "It was . . . it was Gabriel."

"Oh." She sounded surprised, he thought, and less than pleased. "Gabriel."

"He was the only one. Ever. It was a long time ago," he added quickly. "Long before I met you. Before he met Emily, even. When I . . . we . . . lived in Brighton. He hurt me, and . . . it took me a long while to get over it. Years." It was very important that he make her understand, so he chose his words carefully. "It was unresolved—that was the problem. I never knew why . . . it had ended so suddenly, and I just couldn't let go. But now—now it's over. Completely. I've moved on. You're everything to me now, Lucy. Do you understand?"

She nodded, her eyes meeting his. She understood. At last, she understood a great deal.

# Chapter 28

*Behold, how good and joyful a thing it is: brethren, to dwell together in unity!*

*Psalm 133:1*

If the BARC meetings got much bigger than this, Rhys reflected, they'd have to start looking for new premises. The capacity of his office on the first floor of the house was just about stretched to its limits with the eight people—and one large dog—who were there on this Saturday evening in the middle of April.

BARC was growing by leaps and bounds, thought Rhys: three new converts. He studied them with interest in the few moments of preliminary chitchat before the meeting got down to business. Karen, the tiny, childish-looking blonde with the ridiculous corkscrew curls, was sitting in a chair, her hands folded in her lap, looking withdrawn and miserable. Maggie had been at her already—she'd laid into her about the perm, accused her of aiding and abetting animal testing, being an accessory after the fact to the murder of innocent laboratory animals. The girl hadn't known how to defend herself, and her tender heart had been horrified by her own sins of ignorance. Rhys would have to try to compensate somehow for Maggie's bluntness, try to make Karen feel better. She was such a vulnerable-looking little thing, no match at all for Maggie.

The other pair were interesting. They'd come together, and they shared a clean-cut wholesomeness, though the girl, Becca, was a real beauty. Sitting close together on the small sofa, they were both very smartly clad; Toby actually wore a white shirt and a tie under his jumper. Such sartorial splendor was a novelty in what had always been—apart from Fiona's stylish elegance—a casually dressed group. They seemed odd candidates for BARC—what had brought them here? he wondered. Idealism, like himself? Tender-hearted sentimentality, like Karen? Certainly not dyed-in-the-wool activism, like Maggie or Gary. Perhaps it was youthful rebellion against parental values and authority, like Nicholas; it had not escaped Rhys's notice that Becca's surname was Dexter, though he hoped that Maggie had not made the connection. Or perhaps, he thought, catching Fiona's eye as she smiled at him, it was simpler than that: perhaps it was love. Perhaps they just wanted an excuse to be together. Becca Dexter had that indefinable sparkle of a woman in love, unless his imagination was running riot. And that color in Toby's cheeks—certainly the room wasn't that warm . . .

Nicholas, sprawled on the floor stroking Bleddyn, grinned at Rhys in anticipation: this was going to be his big night. Maggie was pointedly ignoring Nicholas, talking instead to Gary. At last Rhys judged that it was time to begin.

After he'd officially welcomed the newcomers, Rhys turned to Nicholas. "I think you have something to tell us," he invited.

The boy jumped up with alacrity, his long hair flopping. He spun around to face the assembled group and announced, "The new van has arrived!"

"Huh." Maggie looked bored. "I thought it was going to be something important," she muttered to Gary.

Nicholas ignored her. "It's parked not far away. We can all go and look at it, if you'd like," he suggested.

"At the end of the meeting," Rhys amended. "First we need to talk about what we're going to do with it. I must say," he added, "that I've seen it, and it's a splendid vehicle. We owe Nicholas a great deal of thanks for his generosity in providing it."

Maggie studied her fingernails. Karen looked up and dared to open her mouth. "Could I ask, what is it for?" she piped timidly.

"I'm sorry. Karen, and Becca and Toby, you don't know about the van. Nicholas has purchased it, and had it all fitted out so that we can take it around the countryside. BARC, as you all know," he amplified, "is primarily an educational organization. We're in business to inform people about animals, and remind people of our responsibilities to them. This van will be a great help to us in doing that. It's distinctive-looking—our logo is painted on the side. And it has space in it for all our brochures, and informational bumf. It's even big enough to sleep in, and it has basic kitchen facilities. The idea is that someone—Nicholas, probably"—the young man grinned and nodded—"will drive the van around and disseminate the information wherever and however possible. He'll be able to go anywhere in the country, really, and be gone for days at a time."

"Sounds like a great idea," Toby ventured shyly.

"A waste of money," Maggie grumbled, but Rhys silenced her with a stern look.

"We think so. We'd like to try it out fairly close to home at first, so that several of us can go along and learn the ropes. I think that it would be good if we all knew how to drive it, and so forth."

"Let's face it, man—there's a lot of educating to be done around here," Gary agreed in a rare outburst of verbiage. "With all the battery farms," he looked apologetically at Nicholas, "and the testing labs, and the hunting and shooting that goes on."

Karen's lip trembled. "The seals," she whispered. "The baby seals."

Maggie looked at her scornfully. "No one's killing seals off Blakeney Point."

For once, Karen refused to be intimidated into silence. "Well, bunnies, then. And poor little foxes."

Casting her eyes up to heaven in disbelief, Maggie shrugged expressively. "Where do you find these people, Rhys?"

"That's quite enough from you, Maggie. We're very happy to have Karen with us." His voice was sharp; since Maggie's ill-advised "liberation" of the Fielding Farm's chickens he had little patience with her histrionics.

"So where are we going with the van?" Nicholas interposed quickly. "Any ideas?"

"Well," Becca spoke for the first time, "if you're looking for somewhere around here, not too far . . ."

"Yes?" Rhys encouraged.

"There's a big field near my father's church," she offered naively, without thinking of the consequences. "There would be plenty of space to park the van, and even to camp out if the weather was nice . . ."

Toby looked at her with some surprise; he didn't think it was the sort of enterprise that Bob Dexter would be very keen to support. But Becca seemed able to talk her father into just about anything, he'd discovered. If anyone could get around Bob Dexter, it was Becca.

"That sounds like a very good idea," approved Rhys. "In a few weeks' time the weather ought to be warm enough for camping. We could *all* go, then—or those of us that were willing and able. A trial run. The first week of May, do you think?"

"Sounds great!" Nicholas enthused. "And now—how about going out and having a look?"

# Chapter 29

*Hearken, o daughter, and consider, incline thine ear: forget also thine own people, and thy father's house.*

*Psalm 45:11*

Contrary to the expectations of Alice Barnes and Gwen Vernon, the world had not come to an end with the arrival of Bob Dexter in South Barsham. Indeed, over a month into the new regime, life at St. Mary's had settled down into a routine which, though different, was tolerable. Alice and Gwen found that there were even compensations for the presence of the odious Bob Dexter: they had quickly come to love Elayne, and Becca was a delight. It gave them perverse pleasure to spend as much time as they could with the two Dexter women, knowing that Bob Dexter would certainly not approve—if he knew.

The consuming worry of their lives, at the moment, was the monstrance. Sooner or later he was going to discover that it was missing, and then there would, so to speak, be hell to pay.

It had been easy enough to take it, even without their church key. Father Mark had kept his key—Bob Dexter had never thought to demand its return—and he hadn't asked any awkward questions when they'd asked to borrow it. "Certainly, ladies," he'd said with a bland smile. "I know that I can trust you with it."

"I told you we shouldn't have taken it," Gwen moaned as they were tidying the sitting room, one Saturday morning near the end of April.

"No, you didn't!" Alice snapped. "Don't give me that! You were in favor of taking it!"

"But he's going to find out!" Nervously she tugged on a lock of her golden wig, setting it slightly askew.

"Not if we don't tell him anything. Remember, Gwen, if he asks! We don't know anything!"

"But . . ."

"But nothing, Gwen. He can't prove a thing." Alice pursed her lips together and folded her arms across her chest. "He can't prove a thing," she repeated doggedly.

"But what if he comes here? What if he gets a search warrant and searches the house?" Gwen chewed on her lower lip.

"Clergymen don't get search warrants!" Alice glared at her with scorn. "He's not a policeman, Gwen!"

"But if he came here . . . I really think we need to get it out of the house, Alice. I'm sure he'd find it here, if he came . . ." Her eyes went involuntarily to the old wing-backed chair, the one used only by the dogs, where the monstrance was concealed beneath the lumpy seat cushion.

"You mean you'd give it away," Alice glowered. "Yes, you probably would at that. You're no good at keeping secrets, Gwen. No good at all."

"That's not true! I'd just feel better about it if it were . . . somewhere else," she protested faintly.

"Where else could we put it?" demanded Alice.

"Could we give it to someone else?" Gwen suggested.

"I'm not implicating Father Mark in this! He knows nothing about it! It wouldn't be right to involve him."

"Not Father Mark. How about . . . how about Elayne?"

"Oh, don't be ridiculous!" Alice barked. "You want to give it to Bob Dexter's wife, to hide in his own house?" She pounded furiously on the cushions of the pink dralon sofa, fluffing them up.

"But Alice, don't you see? That's the one place he'd never think to look! In his own house!"

Alice stopped fluffing the cushions, and looked thoughtful. "You might just be right, Gwen. We wouldn't want to involve Becca, of course"—her face softened at the mention of Becca's name—"but Elayne . . ."

"That's another reason why we need to get it out of this house," Gwen pointed out. "Becca. We wouldn't want her to find it. And she's coming this afternoon to stay with Babs and Nell. While we're out delivering prayer cards. She might . . ."

"Yes, I *know* that Becca is coming this afternoon, Gwen. You don't have to tell me." Alice moved on to the chair cushions. "But surely she'll stay in the kitchen. She usually does. It's nice and cosy in there, by the Aga. There's no reason for her to come into the sitting room."

"You never know," Gwen muttered.

Becca regularly had Saturday, as well as Sunday, off from working for her father, so she didn't have to ask his permission to go, or even inform him where she was going. Not that he'd really be able to object, she told herself—what harm could he find in looking after a couple of dogs? The ladies had a long way to go on their bicycles. It took them several hours, and they couldn't really leave Babs and Nell on their own that long. Daddy didn't like Miss Barnes and Miss Vernon, and didn't like her seeing them, but he wouldn't stop her from going. If only he knew . . .

Becca spent a long time getting ready. She'd washed her hair in the morning and had let it dry naturally—it took a long time to dry but it looked nicer, and felt softer, when she didn't have to use the hair dryer on it. She experimented with pulling it back, and with putting it up on top of her head, but decided in the end to leave it loose, cascading down her back in a shimmering silvery veil. *He* liked it that way—liked to stroke it while he kissed her. She was glad, now, that Daddy had never let her cut her hair.

She'd had a bath as well, and now she slipped out of her dressing gown and into her new underclothes. She'd bought them one day in Norwich, when Daddy had gone in to visit the Christian bookshop. Mere wisps of pink silk they were, a far cry from the utilitarian Marks & Spencer's cotton that she usually wore. In them she *felt* different, even after she'd covered them with her outer clothing. She felt like a woman, not a girl. A woman going to meet her lover.

Becca didn't ordinarily wear much makeup—she didn't need to—but today she enhanced her own coloring with a hint of blusher, and emphasized her wide eyes with a touch of pale blue shadow and a little mascara. The lipstick she would do without—it wouldn't stay in place long, anyway. As soon as the women were safely gone . . .

As luck would have it, she ran into her mother on the stairs. "You're going out?" Elayne asked.

"Yes, to Monkey Puzzle Cottage. To look after the dogs."

Elayne observed her with mild curiosity. "You look a bit dressed up for dog-sitting."

Becca laughed. "Not really. I might go out later."

"With Toby?"

It was an innocent question, but Becca started guiltily. "Um, maybe. I'm not sure."

Elayne smiled, and patted her daughter's shoulder. "Well, dear, have a nice time."

A nice time.

When Becca returned home, several hours later, she was glad that her parents were nowhere in sight. She hurried to her room and closed the door, then examined her face closely in her dressing-table mirror.

She *must* look different. She was convinced of that: if they saw her now, they would know. They would know that she was no longer a little girl, but a real woman. Strangely, though, the mirror revealed no change. Her lips felt bruised with kissing, but they looked quite normal. Her eyes were bright—though not unusually so. There was perhaps a slight flush in her cheeks, but nothing her parents were likely to notice.

Her whole body sang with joy, but no one looking at her would know that. She smiled at herself in the mirror, remembering the feel of his arms around her, his body pressed to hers . . . To be on the safe side, she showered quickly then changed back into her Marks & Spencer's cotton undies; she was certain that she moved differently in the silk ones. A last quick check in the mirror revealed nothing amiss. Reassured, she went down to join her parents for dinner. Although she knew otherwise, to them she would still be their little Becca.

# Chapter 30

*I have declared thy righteousness in the great congregation: lo,
I will not refrain my lips, O Lord, and that thou knowest.
I have not hid thy righteousness within my heart: my talk hath
been of thy truth, and of thy salvation.*

*Psalm 40:11–12*

And Bob Dexter saw everything that he had made, and, behold, it was very good.

Or so he thought to himself on a Thursday afternoon in early May as he inspected the changes he had wrought in St. Mary's Church. He was meant to be meeting Mark Judd in the church that afternoon to review the progress of the sale of the church furnishings. Mark was a bit late, to his annoyance: why couldn't other people be on time, as he always was? It could be done—he was living proof of that—and it showed such wanton inconsideration for others to be late. Bob Dexter's time was valuable: he didn't squander it, and didn't appreciate others squandering it for him. So he filled the minutes while he waited, surveying the new and improved St. Mary's Church.

He could scarcely remember it as it had been, dark and dim and uninviting. Now it was much brighter—the fluorescent striplights attached to the ancient pillars guaranteed that—

and very much more welcoming. The walls had been given a coat of emulsion—magnolia, not quite so sterile as white would have been. And the red bricks and encaustic tiles of the nave floor had been covered with beige carpet-tiles. Much lighter, he thought approvingly, and it would be so much warmer in the winter than the cold brick. The organist might complain that the acoustics had been deadened, but that seemed a small price to pay for the increase in comfort.

The pews had been removed, of course: they had been far too limiting as far as use of the space was concerned, and their dark wood had contributed largely to the oppressive gloom of the church. In their place was an array of new chairs, made of a light-colored composite material; Bob Dexter preferred not to call it plastic—that sounded too common.

The new nave communion table was a beauty, he reflected. It was also of a low-maintenance composite material, intended to look like wood but resembling no wood ever seen. It was semicircular in shape, and held a large arrangement of showy spring flowers, only slightly wilted by Thursday. No candle-sticks, of course. It was quite large, and completely blocked the entrance to the chancel, which was no problem since the chancel was no longer used.

St. Mary's pulpit was ancient, the remainder of an eigh-teenth-century three-decker which had been cut down so that only the pulpit part was left. It, too, had received a coat of magnolia paint. That was only a temporary measure, though; eventually Dexter intended to replace it with a new one, more prominent as befitted the place where the Word of God was proclaimed. But that was something that would have to wait until all the furnishings had been sold and the money was in hand. Dexter stalked impatiently to the south porch and contemplated the things that were left. All of the statues had gone, even the Curé of Ars, sold to Mark Judd's idolatrous friends and colleagues. The riddel posts and other bits of the English altar were against the wall: why hadn't that been sold?

The huge painting was there, sold but awaiting collection. And there were still a few assorted cheap candlesticks, brass flower vases, and miscellaneous tat. The one thing that was *not* there, and which had been nagging at Dexter's mind for some time, was the monstrance. As far as he'd been able to tell from Mark Judd's lists, it had not been sold, but he certainly hadn't been able to find it. That was one reason why he was particularly anxious to see Mark today.

For he had decided upon the monstrance as his ritual sacrifice. Several weeks ago in a conversation with Noah Gates, Noah had made it clear that in his opinion, if Dexter were ideologically pure, he would have destroyed the offensive contents of the church rather than sell them and thus perpetuate their ungodly use. Dexter had bridled at the implication. It was all very well for Noah to feel that way, but Noah was a man of great wealth and could afford to make gestures like that. He, Bob Dexter, had to be a steward of what God had provided—the only means to fund the changes that were necessary to make St. Mary's into a church that was worthy of God. But the monstrance: that was expendable. Mark's enquiries had revealed that it was made of plated base metal and worth very little in monetary terms. And its usage, so totally contrary to Scripture, was hateful to Bob Dexter. When he located the monstrance, he would destroy it. Then no one else could ever use it.

Dexter went down the south aisle and into the chapel. Here, too, his plans had been carried out to great effect. The gold carpet had stayed, of course, and the tomato-ketchup curtain, but very little else: the chapel was now a Sunday School room. Some of the posters of Bible verses which he'd obtained from Noah Gates for the Institution ceremony had been relocated to the walls of the chapel, and had now been joined by the children's own efforts, crudely crayoned representations of Bible stories. It must have been the Good Shepherd last week, he thought, or perhaps it was the Lost Sheep—there was a proliferation of cotton wool stuck in blobs to the papers, all with little stick legs. But there, on the floor at the back—yes! Dexter ground his teeth and reached the spot in a few long strides. On the floor was a fresh nosegay of tender spring flowers, their blossoms still dewy. He swept them up and crushed them in his fist, then glared up with hatred at the serenely smiling Virgin. *Someone* was continuing in their idolatry, in spite of his best efforts to stamp it out. Every day, without fail, they were here—a little bunch of flowers, lovingly picked and carefully placed. With prayers and devotion, no doubt, he thought furiously. He'd never found the guilty person, despite his vigilance. He'd suspected at first that it was Miss Barnes and/or Miss Vernon, but when confronted they'd denied it, and at any rate he knew very well that they no longer had a key to the church. That was the puzzling thing about it: the flowers appeared at odd times of the day, sometimes when the church had been locked. As far as Bob Dexter knew, no one had a key. Well, one day he'd catch them in the act, he reflected, and then . . .

He looked up again at the Virgin. Her inaccessible niche had thus far protected her from the fate that her fellows had suffered. She had to go, he decided at that moment. Immediately. That would stop all this nonsense with the flowers. Anyway, that niche would be just the spot to put a speaker for the new sound reinforcement system, due to be installed within the next month. He was so deep in his plans that he started at a sudden noise in the church, then realized that Mark Judd had arrived at last.

He was hard put to conceal his irritation at the young man's lateness, though Mark was full of apologies. "It was a pilgrim party at the Shrine," he explained. "One of the women was taken ill. I had to locate the chap in charge of the tour group . . ."

Dexter refrained from saying that Walsingham had that effect on a lot of people, himself included. "Never mind," he said shortly. "Now, about the furnishings." He led the young priest to the south porch. "I'd like an update on the status of the sale."

Mark found his lists and consulted them. "Well, as you see, we've cleared most of it."

"This picture is taking up a great deal of space. It's going soon? It's been sold, hasn't it?"

"Oh, yes," Mark assured him. "Dr. Pickering has bought it. It just hasn't been convenient for him to collect it. But I'll give him a ring and hurry him along, if you like."

"Yes, please," Dexter asserted firmly. "And the English altar?"

"I have a possible buyer for that. Someone is coming to have a look at it this weekend, I believe."

"Good. What about the other bits?"

Mark looked at the assorted odds and ends, then scanned down the list. "No luck with the rest, I'm afraid. It *is* rather the dregs. But I'll keep trying."

Dexter paused for a moment, then asked abruptly, "What about the monstrance? Do you know where it is?"

"The monstrance?" Mark furrowed his brow. "Isn't it here?"

"No, it is not here," Dexter snapped. "I'm not in the habit of employing one, certainly, but I *do* know what a monstrance looks like, and it is *not* here."

Mark examined the heap of candlesticks and vases more closely. "I'm sure I haven't sold it. I wonder where it could be?"

"You're sure that you don't know where it is?"

"No. Come to think of it, I haven't seen it for several weeks." The young priest shook his head in a puzzled way. "Still, it isn't worth very much. No one would have nicked it for its value. I suppose it's bound to turn up."

"I wonder." Bob Dexter glowered thoughtfully. After a minute he went on. "Now, the other thing. It's time for that last statue to come down. It's stayed there far too long as it is. I want it down by the weekend."

"How do you aim to get it down? Will you hire someone to do it?"

"I'd like to do it myself," he replied with a chilly smile. "It would give Bob Dexter great satisfaction. But I'll need a very tall ladder. Do you know where I might be able to borrow one?"

Mark considered. "I think so. I seem to remember that one of the parishioners . . ."

"Tomorrow, if possible," Bob Dexter emphasized.

"I'll see what I can do," Mark promised. "Leave it with me, won't you?"

"Thank you."

Hesitating slightly, Mark went on. "About that . . . other matter." Dexter watched him inquiringly as he drew an envelope from his cassock pocket. "I believe that this is what you wanted."

"Ah." Dexter took the envelope and pocketed it, unopened. "Thank you, Mark. I'm very grateful. And I must tell you that Pimlico is looking very promising. I may have some news for you quite soon." He smiled, adding, "Bob Dexter always remembers a favor. And you've done me more than one, young man."

# Chapter 31

*But now they break down all the carved work thereof: with axes and hammers.*

*Psalm 74:7*

At breakfast on the last morning of his life, Bob Dexter had a sudden thought. "Elayne," he said as he raised a piece of toast to his mouth, "has anyone been around asking to borrow the church key?"

His wife darted a quick look at him, then frowned. "No, Bob. Not that I know of. Perhaps when I was out, Becca might have—"

Becca was tucking into her cornflakes. "No, Daddy," she put in promptly. "No one's ever asked me for the church key."

"Oh, there were those tourists, about a fortnight ago," Elayne amended. "But I didn't give them the key, I let them in myself. They didn't stay long—they said it was nothing like the description in their guidebook." She turned enquiringly to Bob. "Why, dear? Is something missing?"

"Well, yes. The monstrance." He paused, waiting for her to ask what a monstrance was—there was no reason why she should know—but Elayne merely poured him another cup of tea. "And that's not all," Dexter went on. "Someone has been sneaking in at odd times, leaving flowers under that statue."

Elayne turned to top up the teapot with fresh boiling water from the kettle. "Oh, really?"

"Yes. I just wondered if you might have given the key to someone. Perhaps you've forgotten, Elayne. Try to think now—it's important. Someone from the congregation, say Miss Barnes?"

She kept her back turned and began running hot water into the sink for the washing-up. "No," she insisted. "I would have remembered."

"But if someone keeps coming in, Daddy," reasoned Becca, "they would have to borrow it more than once."

"Not necessarily. Not if they took it and had a copy made." Dexter took a sip of his tea. "It's the only explanation that makes sense."

"Maybe you should have the lock changed," Becca suggested.

"I shall do better than that." Dexter dabbed at his mouth with a satisfied expression. "I'm taking the statue down. Today."

A handful of cutlery clattered in the sink. "Today?" asked Elayne.

"Today. As soon as I can get a ladder. This nonsense has gone on long enough. Far too long, in fact."

"And . . . what will you do with it?" she queried faintly. "With the statue?"

"I've made my mind up," asserted Bob Dexter. "When I get that statue down, I'll take a hammer to it. Before the day is over, I'll see it in a million pieces."

He had not yet finished his breakfast when the doorbell went. "I'll get it, Daddy," Becca volunteered cheerily. She returned a moment later, looking unsettled. "It's Stephen Thorncroft, Daddy."

"Stephen Thorncroft?"

"You know," Becca explained nervously. "That Walsingham priest . . ."

"I *know* who he is, Becca! What on earth does he want at this time of the morning?"

"He said he'd like a word with you."

"Well, bring him in." Dexter frowned, then amended, "No, don't bring him in here. Take him up to my office—I'll see him there when I've finished my tea. He can wait a few minutes."

Just the few precious moments that he'd spent in Becca's company, waiting for Bob Dexter, left Stephen feeling distinctly weak. His heart was pounding and his hands were clammy, though the knowledge that her father could appear at any moment constrained him from saying any of the things that he wanted to say to her in their short time together. His emotional turmoil put him at a distinct disadvantage when Dexter finally arrived; he was terrified of betraying his feelings to Becca's father.

"Yes? What can I do for you?" Dexter made an effort at cordiality, but he was clearly impatient.

Stephen looked out of the window, toward the long, low bulk of the church, and took a deep breath. He *must* not think about Becca. When he turned back to Dexter, he had regained some measure of self-control. "It's about the statue," he said. "The Virgin and Child."

"What about the statue?"

"Mark tells me that you're planning to remove it today."

"Yes, that's right." Dexter nodded.

"Well, I was wondering . . . that is, I would be interested in buying it from you."

"It's not for sale," Dexter stated firmly.

"You mean you've already sold it?"

"I mean that it's not for sale," he repeated.

"But what are you going to do with it? You're not going to keep it?"

Dexter raised his eyebrows. "It's not really your affair, young man. The statue is my property." Stephen flushed, and Dexter went on with satisfaction, "But since you've asked, I shall tell you. I intend to destroy it. With my own two hands. It is a Graven Image, forbidden by the Ten Commandments."

Stephen gasped. "But surely you wouldn't—"

"Surely I would." He narrowed his eyes. "And now, if that's all . . . I have quite a busy day ahead of me." He began walking toward the door.

"But . . . but . . . you can't!" Stephen didn't move.

Dexter turned. "Why not?" he asked pleasantly.

To Stephen, as an Anglo-Catholic, the statue represented the continuity between the Anglican Church and its Catholic past, and affirmed the validity of his Orders, so its symbolic importance to him was great. But he knew Dexter couldn't possibly understand unless he put it in monetary terms. "It's a very valuable statue! It's medieval—worth a great deal of money!"

For a fraction of a second, Dexter wavered. If he really could get a lot of money for it . . . But he must stay firm; Noah would be proud of his adherence to principle, and since he didn't have the monstrance to destroy . . . He imagined his own feeling of satisfaction, pounding the hated idol into dust, and knew that that was worth any amount of money that the young priest—or anyone else—could offer. "No. Bob Dexter's mind is made up."

"Please think about it," Stephen pleaded. "Don't do anything right away. Have it valued, if you like. I'll pay the market price."

"Good day, Reverend Thorncroft," Dexter said firmly, guiding him to the door. "I'll see you out myself—there's no need to bother my daughter again."

Becca! Cold terror touched Stephen's heart. Surely Dexter didn't know, *couldn't* know . . .

# Chapter 32

*Thou makest him to have dominion of the works of thy hands:*
*and thou hast put all things in subjection under his feet;*
*All sheep and oxen: yea, and the beasts of the field;*
*The fowls of the air, and the fishes of the sea: and whatsoever*
*walketh through the paths of the seas.*

*Psalm 8:6–8*

Bob Dexter spent the morning dictating letters to Becca. If she was more distracted than usual, he didn't notice; there was a great deal of work to be done in the three weeks or so before the Walsingham National Pilgrimage and his mind was focused on that. He'd taken much of the burden off Noah's shoulders by offering to keep in touch with the key volunteers around the country, and to coordinate their plans. There was a lot to think about: many of the volunteers would be coming from great distances, and would need accommodation in the homes of local Christians. And of course he had to keep track of who might have an extra seat or two in their van, and who might need a lift. Noah was busy enough printing up the tracts to hand out to the misguided pilgrims; Dexter congratulated himself that his own gift for organization had helped to free Noah from the drudgery of all these details. One day, he thought, he'd get himself a computer; that would be a great help in the administration of "MISSION: Walsingham." In the meantime he had to make do with a comprehensive card index and his own very good memory.

They worked through lunch—he was too busy to take the time out to go downstairs for a family lunch, so Elayne brought up a plate of sandwiches and some coffee for them to consume while they worked. But mid-afternoon he looked out of the window to a most curious sight: a bright blue van with the inscription BARC on the side, parked in the field by the side of the church. A huge black dog capered in the field, and several scruffily dressed young people seemed to be setting up tents. Those young crackpots who had made such fools of themselves at the Deanery Synod meeting back in March! He frowned and stopped abruptly in mid-letter. "That's enough for now, Becca. You can start typing. I'm going out for a few minutes."

Subsequent events in Becca's life had pushed BARC to the back of her mind; she had completely forgotten that today was the day for them to arrive for their camping weekend, and had consequently not mentioned the matter to her father. From where she was sitting she couldn't see them, and merely replied, "Fine, Daddy."

"Elayne!" he called as he went down the stairs. There was no reply. Impatiently Bob Dexter left the house and stalked the short distance to the field where the van was parked. The bearded red-haired chap had seemed to be in charge, he recalled, or perhaps it was the mouthy girl with the stringy brown hair.

It was the red-haired chap who popped his head out of a tent with a cheerful grin. "Good afternoon, Reverend Dexter."

"What exactly do you think that you're doing on my land?" Dexter challenged.

"Camping!" Rhys waved his arm at the tents and smiled. "Just what it looks like, in fact."

"This is private property, you know!"

Rhys crawled out of the tent and stood up. With his small stature, he was no match for Bob Dexter, who towered over him. But Maggie, who was throwing a stick for Bleddyn, quickly came to his side. "Rhys, is this Holy Joe hassling you?" she demanded.

Rhys shook his head. "It seems we have a small misunderstanding."

"There's no misunderstanding. You are on my land, and you have no right to be here," stated Dexter. "If you leave now, I'm willing to say no more about it," he added magnanimously.

"Just a minute, mate!" Maggie's eyes glittered dangerously behind her spectacles. "We were invited to come here!"

"Invited? Don't be ridiculous! Bob Dexter didn't invite you!"

"Reverend Dexter." Rhys's voice was quiet but firm. "It was your daughter who invited us. Becca."

"Becca?" He took a step backwards, stunned. "I don't believe it!"

Maggie shot Rhys an aggrieved look as the penny dropped and she realized who the girl at the meeting was, then turned her fury on Dexter. "It's true all right, you disgusting pig! And if I'd known she was *your* daughter, I would never have agreed to come here! I would never have allowed her and her boyfriend to come to our meeting! She must be a stupid cow if she's *your* daughter. I heard the ridiculous things you said at that meeting. All that crap about man having dominion over all living things! You're an ignorant cretin!"

Dexter stared at her, his mouth open. How dared she! No one had ever talked to him like that. "Young woman," he said at last, "as a Christian, I will ignore your insults to Bob Dexter personally. But to insult my daughter, and to insult the Word of God—"

Gary ambled up at that moment, wearing a beaded Indian headband round his forehead. "Hey man! What's happening?"

They ignored him; Maggie and Dexter glared at each other, breathing heavily. "There's some bad vibes coming down here. Come on, guys, be cool," Gary pleaded.

"It's too late for that, I'm afraid," Rhys said. "It's clear that we're not welcome here, so I think we'd better be on our way. There's some common ground not far away where we could—"

"No!" Maggie spat, bristling with hostility. "We're not going anywhere until I've told this fascist carnivore a thing or two."

It was Bleddyn's turn to investigate the newcomer. The dog loped up, waving his plumed tail back and forth in greeting. Dexter turned and, before anyone realized what was happening, administered a vicious kick to the dog's ribs. Bleddyn yelped in pain and went down.

"You bloody bastard!" screamed Maggie, going to her knees beside the dog. "You've hurt him!" Bleddyn struggled to get up, but fell back whimpering. "You've broken his ribs!"

"You should keep your vicious dog from attacking innocent people," Dexter said self-righteously. "Dangerous animals like that ought to be put down."

"He was only saying hello." Rhys's voice was choked with emotion and his fair skin was scarlet under its freckles.

"He attacked me," insisted Dexter.

Maggie lifted her face from crooning over the dog and looked up at Dexter with pure, murderous hatred. "He should have killed you, you monster. Now why don't you just sod off!"

# Chapter 33

*Confounded be all they that worship carved images, and that delight in vain gods: worship him, all ye gods.*

*Psalm 97:7*

Bob Dexter was aware, even as he was engaged in his confrontation with Maggie and Rhys, that the church door was slightly ajar; he knew that it had been locked that morning. He determined, as he left them bent over the injured dog, to investigate. Perhaps it was his lucky day, and he'd catch the phantom flower-leaver in the act.

He entered the church quietly, almost stealthily, and crept to the chapel. Yes! There was someone there, kneeling beneath the statue. It was a woman—he could tell that much, though her back was to him and her head was bowed. He could just make out the little bunch of flowers on the floor in front of her. Dexter moved into the chapel silently, standing at the back for a moment as he savored his triumph. He had her at last, this vexatious person who had so disturbed him with her illegal devotion to an inanimate idol. She couldn't escape from him now. He listened carefully; in the silent church he could hear the click of the rosary beads in her hands as well as her quiet voice repeating, "Hail Mary, full of grace . . ."

When he could stand the hateful words no longer he strode forward. "Stop it!" he ordered. "Stop it this minute!"

The woman turned, with the frozen, panic-stricken face of a rabbit caught transfixed in the glare of a car's headlamps. It was his wife.

"Elayne!" was all he could say for a moment, and then, "What on earth . . . !"

In the interminable-seeming seconds of silence that followed, the stark terror on Elayne's face melted into a calmness drawn from some unknown source. "Bob."

"Is this your idea of a joke, Elayne?"

She considered the question unsmilingly. "No, it's not a joke."

"What do you think you're doing?" he demanded. His tone of voice, condescending scorn mingled with distaste, was one that he used often with her, usually to good effect.

"I'm praying."

"To that piece of stone?"

"If that's what you choose to call her."

Elayne got up from her knees then, and her husband came toward her, not to help her but to tear the rosary from her hand. He threw it on the floor with contempt, then stepped on it deliberately, grinding the plastic beads under his heel. He folded his arms across his chest and regarded her with lingering amazement. "Why, Elayne? Why are you doing this? I thought that you were a good Christian woman. I thought that you loved Jesus."

"Oh, I do. He's up there, too, you know." She pointed to the child in the Virgin's arms.

"Blasphemy!" he cried. Swiftly, without stopping to think, Bob Dexter struck his wife across the face.

He had never hit her before; his weapons tended to be psychological and verbal rather than physical. The blow startled her, but as she took a step back from him, touching her stinging cheek, her strength seemed intensified rather than diminished. "Do you want to know why?" she asked softly.

He nodded, too horrified to speak.

"It's because of the baby. Because of Bobby."

"Don't call him that." Dexter's voice grated harshly. "He didn't have a name."

"Of course he had a name. You just wouldn't let me use it. His name was Bobby."

"No." Dexter turned away. "I don't want to talk about it. It's not healthy to dwell on the past."

"He was our son, Bob. You can't just pretend he didn't exist."

"He wasn't a baby. He was a . . . thing."

Elayne raised her voice at last; each word was enunciated clearly and painfully. "He . . . was . . . a . . . person! A person, Bob! A creation of God, given to us through our love for each other!"

"No."

"Yes, Bob!" She clasped her hands together and spoke passionately. "That's the whole problem, isn't it? You just can't accept that God could make a mistake. No, Bobby wasn't perfect. But he was our son! And I loved him! I love him still!" The last sentence caught on a sob; she turned and gazed up at the statue. "*She* understands," Elayne whispered. "*She* understands what it's like to lose a son. I could talk to her about it. I could never talk to you, Bob. You didn't want to talk about it—you never wanted to talk about it. You forgot about him, put the whole episode out of your mind as soon as you could. You had Becca, after all. It was always Becca, wasn't it? I don't think you ever really wanted another baby—Becca was all you needed. But the hurt never stopped for me. And when I had to leave Richmond, leave Bobby's grave behind . . . I found *her*. She understands my pain." She went to her husband and knelt at his feet. "Please, Bob," she pleaded through her tears. "Please don't destroy her. She means so much to me . . ."

He whirled around and regarded her with disgust; it was as though he hadn't heard a word of her tearful confession. "Get up, woman!" he ordered. "And get out of my sight! You make me sick! I've given you a good home. I've given you everything that a wife could want. I've been to you as God to the Church, just as He commanded in Holy Scripture. And this is how you repay me? This is what you call obedience? You've betrayed me, woman! Get out of my sight!"

# Chapter 34

*For we consume away in thy displeasure: and are afraid at thy
wrathful indignation.
Thou hast set our misdeeds before thee: and our secret sins in the
light of thy countenance.*

*Psalm 90:7—8*

Bob Dexter had never been much for walking; now he got in
his car and drove around the narrow country lanes for a long
time—he didn't know how long. Eventually he found himself
back in South Barsham, and on impulse turned down the lane
by the old blacksmith's and bumped along until he reached
Monkey Puzzle Cottage.

There were no heralding barks from Babs and Nell, and no
foreshortened muzzles pressed to the sitting room window; no
twitches of the lace curtains, either, and Bob Dexter concluded
that the women must be out walking the dogs. He decided to
wait, sitting in the car rather than on the pink dralon sofa
which, improbably, rested under the spiny limbs of the monkey puzzle tree, as if to offer a resting place for weary passers-
by. But Dexter was not curious by nature, and didn't even
spare a thought for this incongruous sight.

Sure enough, after a while they came up the lane, the two ugly spaniels trotting ahead of the two elderly spinsters. Alice Barnes strode purposefully, her arms swinging rhythmically at her sides, while Gwen Vernon seemed somehow to trail in her wake, all fluttering garments and flapping arms.

Gwen saw his car first. She clutched frantically at Alice's arm. "He's here!" she hissed. "I knew that he'd come!"

Alice spoke to her through clenched teeth. "Leave this to me, Gwen. Don't say anything. This may just be a pastoral visit! Anyway, if he looks, he won't find a thing. So don't worry!" She marched up to the car and tapped on the window with her house key. "What can we do for you, *Father* Dexter?"

He opened the door and got out. "I'd like a word with the two of you, if it's not too much trouble. May I come in?"

"Yes, of course." He followed Alice around the side of the house, past the sofa, the monkey puzzle tree and the polythene-tented automobile; Gwen and the dogs brought up the rear.

They were obnoxious dogs, he thought, but at least they had the good sense to give Bob Dexter a wide berth. Once in the house, Babs and Nell nosed open the sitting-room door and disappeared, presumably to fight for possession of their favorite dilapidated chair. Alice led the human members of the party into the kitchen; Bob Dexter no longer merited being entertained in the sitting room, which was reserved for honored and welcome guests.

He'd never been in the kitchen before. It was small, as were all the rooms in the tiny cottage, and was dominated by the huge Aga, which on this warm day threw off an uncomfortable amount of heat. In the winter it would keep this room cosily warm, in contrast to the chilly sitting room; it was no wonder that the women spent much of their time here, sitting in the spindle-backed chairs with the worn flowered cushions.

Gwen automatically went to the kettle. "Would you like some tea?" she offered. Alice glared at her, but Dexter nodded. Gwen fussed about getting down the tea caddy, and the old brown pot. No silver pot today, and no good china cups. No cream cakes, either—in fact, she wouldn't even offer him any biscuits, not even custard creams.

Alice remained standing; it would be a bad move, she thought, to let him sit down and make himself comfortable. The sooner they could get rid of him, the better. "Well?" she asked after a moment. "To what do we owe the honor of this visit?"

Although she deliberately kept her tone of voice neutral, the irony was not lost on Bob Dexter. "I wanted to ask you about something," he said, matching her neutral tone. "As you know, we've been selling the surplus church furnishings."

Alice raised her eyebrows in acknowledgment, and Gwen nodded lugubriously.

Dexter pulled out a chair and sat down; after a moment Alice gave up and followed suit. "The sale has been going rather well. The trouble is, there's one item missing from the inventory. The monstrance. I wondered if you ladies knew anything about that."

Gwen looked alarmed, and Alice shot her a warning glance. This was going to be difficult—how could she answer truthfully without giving them away? "Is that tea nearly ready, Gwen?" Alice asked, playing for time and attempting to distract Gwen.

"Not quite." Gwen was grateful for the opportunity to turn away, fiddling with the sugar and the milk.

Father Mark had said that to take the monstrance—steal was not the word—in order to preserve it from destruction would not be a sin. That must mean that to lie—ever so slightly—to protect it would likewise not be classified as a sin. Unfortunate though it may be, that seemed the only way.

"Do you know where the monstrance is?" Dexter repeated.

Now that was a different question from the one he'd asked before, Alice realized gratefully. Perhaps she wouldn't have to lie. "No," she replied firmly. "I don't know where it is."

They'd given it to Elayne a few days earlier, so presumably it was somewhere in the vicarage, but she didn't know that for sure.

"You haven't seen it, then?"

"Not recently," she answered. That was just about true, depending on your definition of recent.

Gwen hovered behind his chair, grimacing. Dexter turned impatiently; she gave the tea another stir and poured it out. "Milk, Father? Sugar?"

"Just milk. And for goodness' sake stop calling me Father!"

For once Alice was grateful for Gwen's dithering; it had got her out of a line of questioning that was becoming more dangerous by the minute. But the respite was only temporary. After a few sips of his tea, Bob Dexter continued his interrogation.

"Let me ask you one more time, Miss Barnes. Did you or Miss Vernon take the monstrance from the church?"

Ah. Praying that Gwen would not betray her, Alice took a deep breath and said calmly, "No."

"You're sure?" he pressed.

"Yes."

"Then I won't take up any more of your time," he said, drinking down the rest of his tea and standing up.

At the door he paused. "I'm bound to tell you, Miss Barnes, that I don't believe you. I think that you took it, and that it's somewhere in this house."

Her bosom quivered with indignation. "Are you calling me a liar, *Father* Dexter?"

"I think that you're being economical with the truth, Miss Barnes."

"The monstrance is *not* in this house!"

He looked at her shrewdly, then looked at Gwen cowering behind her. "Miss Vernon. Could I have a word with you? In private?"

"I don't believe that's necessary," Alice snapped.

"I'll be the judge of that. Miss Vernon, would you step outside with me, please?"

With a frantic look at Alice, Gwen followed him; her instinct to obey a priest, however unworthy he was, was too strong to overcome. He closed the door firmly in Alice's face and led Gwen out to where the sofa sat forlornly under the monkey puzzle tree.

"Sit down, Miss Vernon." Gwen complied; neither one seemed to find their surreal seating arrangements at all worthy of mention. "Now. I'll ask you the same question that I put to Miss Barnes. Do you know where the monstrance is?"

Gwen sighed gustily in relief. "No," she replied quickly. "I don't know where it is."

"You're sure?"

"Yes." She wouldn't meet his eyes.

Dexter studied her nervous demeanor. "Are you willing to swear that on the Holy Bible?"

Gulping, Gwen nodded.

"All right, then." He paused. "There's one other thing, Miss Vernon."

She stuck her thin legs out in front of her and studied the ladder on her stockings. "What's that?"

"I believe that you've been seeing quite a bit of my daughter lately. She's been spending a lot of time here, looking after your dogs and so forth. I don't think that's a very good idea, do you?"

He was unprepared for the vehemence of her response. Gwen Vernon jumped up and clasped her hands together; her voice shook. "If that's what you're worried about . . . well, you don't have to worry about it anymore. Your daughter is not welcome in this house!"

"What?" Dexter stared at her in disbelief: his Becca not welcome?

She compressed her lips and swallowed hard. "I promised Alice that I wouldn't say anything to you," she gulped.

"About what? Tell me, Miss Vernon! If it concerns my daughter, I have a right to know."

Gwen couldn't contain herself. "Your daughter! That Jezebel! That harlot!" She waved her hands in the air in agitation. "A scarlet woman! Is that how you've brought her up? We trusted her! We trusted her in our home, with our dogs! And how did she repay our trust?"

Dexter remained rooted to the sofa, incapable of making a sound.

"Betrayal! Violation!" Gwen wailed. "On that very sofa! Our beautiful dralon sofa, unclean!"

"Don't be ludicrous, woman!" Dexter bellowed at last. "It's Becca we're talking about, not some . . . some floozy." The woman was obviously quite round the bend, he thought scornfully but with relief.

"Becca! We trusted her," Gwen repeated, dirgelike. "No better than she should be. Disgusting! On our sofa! While we were away! We have proof!"

"Proof? What kind of proof could you possibly have?"

Gwen drew herself up to her full height with a shuddering sigh. Her hysteria had departed suddenly and she spoke with a kind of embarrassed dignity. "I couldn't possibly tell you. Nell found it. Dogs do have a regrettable nose for disgusting things, I'm afraid."

"What . . . ?"

"Anyway, we've asked her. She's admitted it. And she's not even sorry!" Gwen turned and started back toward the house. "Your daughter is not welcome in this house," she repeated over her shoulder. "Now perhaps you'd better go, Father Dexter."

# Chapter 35

*But if his children forsake my law: and walk not in my
judgments;*
*If they break my statutes, and keep not my commandments: I
will visit their offenses with the rod, and their sin with
scourges.*

*Psalm 89:31–32*

Bob Dexter had no memory of getting in his car and driving
home. His chest felt as if it were in an iron vise; he wondered,
remotely, if he were having a heart attack. His Becca—NO.
It couldn't be true. It couldn't *possibly* be true. Not his Becca,
his lovely Princess. The woman was mad. Yes, she was mad.
Or spiteful, trying to hurt him. Saying the one thing that
could break his heart. Not his Becca. Not that. He could bear
just about anything but that.

The vicarage was quiet when he arrived at home—no sign
of Elayne. But Elayne was of no importance. Becca was the
only one who mattered.

Becca heard him come in. "Daddy, is that you?" she called
out from her room. "Mark Judd rang. He said to tell you that
he'd found a ladder for you."

He was as white as a sheet, Becca thought, when he opened

the door of her room. That gave her a presentiment of disaster, but her concern was for him. "Daddy! You look terrible! Whatever is the matter? Is it Mum? Has something happened to Mum?"

"Becca!" He came to her, took her hands in his. "I've just been to Monkey Puzzle Cottage. Miss Vernon told me something—something about you. Something terrible. I know that it can't be true, Princess. Tell me that it's not true." He thought then that she would look at him blankly, ask what it was, and then it would be all right. He would know that it wasn't true.

Becca sighed. There was no point in lying about it. "Yes, Daddy, it's true," she said as gently as she could.

His cry of pain was so terrible that she shrank from him; he turned even whiter than before. "He forced you, then!" Dexter gasped in agony. "He . . . he raped you! Oh, Becca, my darling girl! I'll kill him!" he vowed.

"No, Daddy, it wasn't like that," Becca said softly. "He didn't force me. I wanted to. I love him."

Dexter gasped and recoiled; his color went rapidly from white to crimson to purple. "Whore!" he bellowed. "Harlot! Trollop!"

Becca shook her head. "Daddy, try to understand! I love him! He loves me. It's only natural that we should . . ."

"Natural? It's against God's laws! Fornication! I brought you up to believe in Jesus, to follow the Word of God—" He struggled for breath. "That a daughter of mine should deliberately turn her back on God and choose the path of wickedness—"

"Please, Daddy, be reasonable—"

"Reasonable? When my daughter commits fornication and thinks it's all right because she loves him? He talked you into it, didn't he?" He gripped her shoulders. "Who is he, Becca? Who is this man that you love more than Jesus, more than Bob Dexter? Who is he?"

Becca pulled away, frightened by the look in his eyes. "I won't tell you."

"You won't tell me? I'm your father, Rebecca. You belong to me. You *will* tell me."

"I *don't* belong to you," she contradicted. "I love you, Daddy, but I don't belong to you. I'm a person in my own right, a grown-up person, and I have to do what I think is right, not what you tell me to do."

For the second time that day, Bob Dexter raised his hand in violence to a member of his family. His hand caught Becca on the cheek, and she cried out in surprise as much as in hurt. He was unmoved. His eyes narrowed. "It's Toby Gates, isn't it?" he demanded. Becca shook her head, tears in her eyes. "You're trying to protect him! But it won't work." He took the key from her door. "I'll just go and have a little word with Mr. Toby Gates. You can stay here and think over what you've done . . ." Dexter locked the door from outside.

"No, Daddy!" she cried through the door. "It's not Toby! Toby and I are just friends! Don't you understand, Daddy? Toby is gay!"

Toby. Gay. Of course. No wonder he'd protested so sincerely that his intentions were honorable—he wasn't man enough for them to be otherwise. So it wasn't Toby. But he had to get away from Becca for now, had to forget the terrible pain of her betrayal. Becca wasn't going anywhere. He could deal with her later.

His mind was unable to cope with the thought of Becca—her defilement, her violation. Violation! The word pounded in his brain. But she'd asked for it, welcomed it. It was too much to bear; his thoughts turned to Noah Gates. Noah Holier-than-Thou Gates, who had dared to pass judgment on Bob Dexter for not being pure enough in his convictions. And Noah Gates, Mister Christianity, founder and head of "MISSION: Walsingham," had a son who was a pervert, a sodomite! Noah obviously didn't know, or he wouldn't dare to hold his head up in public, wouldn't be able, in all conscience, to continue at the helm of "MISSION: Walsingham."

Bob decided, then, to drive to Fakenham, to Gates of Heaven, and have it out with Noah there and then. He looked at his watch. Amazingly enough, though the morning seemed like a lifetime ago, it was not yet six o'clock.

The interview with Noah had been stormy; Dexter hadn't expected it to be otherwise. Noah hadn't taken the news well. He'd denied it at first, blustered around a bit; at last he'd called Toby in and put the question to him. Toby had admitted it, and Noah could deny it no longer. The boy had cried— Dexter curled his lip in contempt, driving back home some time later. And he'd always liked the toadying little queer: it showed that even Bob Dexter could be wrong about people. That reflection reminded him of Becca, and how she'd deceived him. Becca. She was no better than a harlot, a strumpet! Pretending to be such a good girl and all the while . . . So it was with hardened anger that he returned to the vicarage.

There was still no sign of Elayne—all for the best, he thought. He unlocked Becca's door and went in. She was curled up on her bed; she raised her head to look at him, and he gasped in horror. Her hair! Becca's beautiful hair! Her head was roughly shorn, almost naked, and on the dressing table was the mute evidence of the crime, a pair of nail scissors and a heap of shining silver-gilt tresses.

Her eyes were red-rimmed, but her voice was firm. "Hello, Daddy."

"Becca! What have you done?" he cried.

"I've cut my hair," she said. "It's *my* hair. I'm my own person. You don't own me."

"No!" he shouted. "No!" His desire to hurt her, to strike back at her, was overpowering. He removed his belt and wielded it over her; at last he had the satisfaction of seeing her cower. "Now," he ordered, "you'll tell me the name of the man who dishonored you!"

"No, Daddy, please! Please don't hit me!"

He held her down and brought the belt down across her back. "Tell me!" he screamed. "Tell me!"

Terrified, Becca knew that she had to give him an answer or he would surely kill her. "It's Stephen," she whimpered. "Stephen Thorncroft."

Bob Dexter's body was not found until the next morning. It was Mark Judd who found him, when he brought the prospective buyer of the English altar into the church to inspect the merchandise. He was lying where he'd fallen at the foot of the ladder, twisted in such a contorted position that Mark knew immediately that he was dead.

At first it was thought that he'd lost his balance and fallen, alone in the church the night before, and had died, immediately or in protracted agony, of internal injuries. But the autopsy results were clear: he might have fallen from the ladder, but he had died of injuries to the head, inflicted deliberately and at close range with an unidentified blunt instrument.

There was a witness to the murder, for murder it surely was. But she, secure as ever in her ancient niche, cradled her child, smiled serenely, and said nothing.

PART TWO

# Chapter 36

*In the time of my trouble I will call upon thee: for thou hearest me.*

*Psalm 86:7*

When, on Tuesday, May 14, Stephen Thorncroft was arrested on suspicion of murdering Bob Dexter eleven days earlier, he was offered the customary one phone call. Asserting his innocence, he waived the right until the following day, when it was clear that he was going to be charged.

He rang his uncle Geoffrey, who was by great good luck at his home in London. A short time later, Geoffrey picked up the phone and dialed Lucy's number, obtained through directory enquiries.

Lucy was painting in her studio on that Wednesday morning. Wednesday was the day when she customarily attended the weekly lunchtime organ recital at St. Anne's Church, Kensington Gardens, so she was a bit rushed, trying to finish the painting before it was time to go. She frowned when the phone went, but was too conscientious to leave it unanswered. It might be important. It might even be David: although he had a well-known aversion to the telephone, he'd begun ringing her occasionally, and last weekend was the first one they hadn't spent together since their relationship had altered so drastically. David was very much a creature for routine, she'd discovered, and this break in the pattern of their lives, the result of a family christening she'd had to attend in Shropshire, had disturbed him. Their new routine had been established very quickly: long-seeming, lonely weeks apart, and weekends together in London that passed all too swiftly. David usually came as early as he could get away from work on Friday, and left as late as he dared on Sunday night, although once or twice he'd been unable to tear himself away and had stayed until very early on Monday morning.

It wasn't David, she realized with regret as she picked the phone up, but it took her a moment to recognize who it was.

"Lucy," said the voice on the other end, "it's the man who used to share your bed."

"Who?"

"Oh, forgive me, my dear. I suppose there have been so many that you've begun to lose track."

"Geoffrey!"

He laughed. "Right the first time. Congratulations."

"What do you want?" She was puzzled; he hadn't rung her in years.

"I crave a boon, my dear ex-wife. In other words, I need to ask a favor of you."

"I might have known. Why should I do you a favor?"

"I reckon you owe me one. After all, I allowed you to divorce me, didn't I?"

"Only because it suited you as well."

"Well, for old times' sake, then."

"That's fairly dodgy ground, Geoffrey. As you should know. Tell me what the favor is."

"You know my nephew Stephen."

"Yes, Stephen Thorncroft. He's a nice chap," she admitted unwillingly. "I ran into him not long ago."

"So he told me. You see, Lucy, the thing is—" Geoffrey

paused for dramatic effect. "Stephen's been arrested. He's being charged with the murder of Bob Dexter."

"What!" Lucy gasped. Of course she knew about Dexter's murder: as a minor media figure, and a clergyman at that, murdered under somewhat spectacular and gruesome circumstances, he had gained more press in death than he had in life. But Stephen Thorncroft's name had never appeared in the newspaper reports of the case, and she'd had no idea that any arrest was imminent. "But how . . . how can I help?"

"You will help, then?"

"If I can," she promised. "I like Stephen."

"I hoped you'd feel that way. He rang me a few minutes ago from the police station. He's still in shock, poor lad—says he didn't do it, of course. When they started questioning him he said he didn't need a lawyer because he was innocent. Now, though, of course he must have a solicitor. He didn't even know of one, but remembered that you'd told him that your new boyfriend, what's-his-name, was a solicitor."

"David," she supplied automatically.

"That's right. David. He used his one phone call to ring me, to see if I could get on to you and have you contact your bloke. A bit around the houses, I know, but it was all he could think of at the time."

"Don't you know any solicitors?" she asked. "High-powered chaps?"

"Yes, I offered to find him a London lawyer. But he said he wanted your boyfriend. Said he liked him, and that he was located close by. He's in police custody in Fakenham, but apparently he's being taken to Norwich to appear before the magistrates."

"David practices in Norwich."

"Is he any good? As a lawyer, I mean?" Geoffrey asked. "A bit provincial, I would have thought."

"David is a very good solicitor," she defended loyally. "I'm sure he is."

Geoffrey sounded amused. "And you're not a bit biased, of course."

"Well, perhaps just a bit." Lucy laughed at herself. "But I'm sure he's excellent."

"You'll ask him, then?"

"Yes. Not for you, mind you," she added pointedly. "For Stephen."

That jibe could not go unanswered. "Is he any good in bed, by the way?" Geoffrey asked with spite.

"What?"

"I just wondered," he said silkily. "You *are* sleeping with him, aren't you?"

"I don't see that my relationship with David is any concern of yours," Lucy retorted, ice in her voice.

Geoffrey laughed. "Perhaps you're not sleeping with him." Pure malice underlay his words. "I thought you'd grown up, that's all. I didn't realize that you were still the same girl who wouldn't go to bed with me till I'd married you. But I suppose if that hard-to-get act worked for you once, it might work again. Of course you're not as young and innocent as you were then . . ."

"You bastard," she said softly, putting down the phone.

Lucy sat for a few minutes, simmering with fury, before she felt sufficiently self-controlled to ring David's offices. Nan was answering the phone this morning, filling in while the receptionist was on sick leave. "Goodacre and Whitehouse," she said pleasantly.

"Could I please speak to David Middleton-Brown?"

"I'm sorry, but Mr. Middleton-Brown is in court this morning. Can I ask him to return your call later? He'll be in his office this afternoon."

Lucy sighed in vexation, looking at her watch. There was no time to waste. "Could you please tell him that Lucy rang?"

Lucy, thought Nan with interest. The beloved Lucy. "He has your number?"

"Oh, yes." She looked at her watch again, and thought quickly. In a couple of hours or so she could be in Norwich. "Never mind," she contradicted herself. "Tell him not to ring. Tell him I'm coming—I'll be there as soon as possible."

"Yes, certainly, I'll tell him."

Nan told him as soon as he came in after lunch.

"Any messages?" David asked automatically at the reception desk.

"Yes." She watched him covertly. "Someone named Lucy rang."

He smiled, oblivious to Nan's scrutiny. "Does she want me to ring her back?"

"Well, at first she said yes, but then she said she would be coming instead."

"Coming? Here?"

"That's what she said. She said she'd be here as soon as possible."

"Thanks, Nan!" he beamed. Nan watched with amusement as he virtually bounced up the stairs to his office. "You'll let me know when she arrives?" he turned back to ask.

"Of course, Mr. Middleton-Brown. Immediately," she added with a knowing smile.

The intercom buzzed, interrupting the work he was concentrating on only sporadically. "Mr. Middleton-Brown, your visitor has arrived."

He bounded down the stairs. "Lucy!" Under the avid gaze of Nan, as well as one or two clients and another solicitor returning late from lunch, he had to content himself with squeezing her hand, and kissing her cheek. He took her case. "What a marvelous surprise! How did you find this place?"

"I took a taxi from the station," she explained as he led her up the stairs. Once they'd reached the privacy of his office, he kissed her enthusiastically and at length.

Finally she pulled away from him with regret, breathless. "That's all very well, my love, but that's not why I'm here."

His scowl was only half feigned. "You disappoint me. I was hoping that you'd seen the light—that after the weekend without me you'd realized you couldn't live apart from me for another minute, and had come to tell me that you'd marry me right away."

She laughed at his downcast face. "Oh, darling. We don't have time to go into that at the moment. This is a matter of life and death."

In a few minutes she had told him everything she knew about the urgent errand on which she'd come, wisely editing her rendition of Geoffrey's phone call. He listened without interrupting until she'd finished, a frown creasing his brow.

"But why did he ask for me?" he wondered.

"Because he liked you, that day we met him, and because you're so close."

David shook his head. "But I'm not the right bloke at all for him."

"Why not?" she demanded. "You're a good solicitor, aren't you?"

"Yes, I suppose so. But it's not my line at all, Lucy," he protested. "I'm a country solicitor. Wills, divorces, minor lawsuits, that sort of thing. Traffic violations, maybe. Not crime. Not murder. He needs someone who's experienced in criminal law. I'm sure that his uncle could get him fixed up with someone . . ."

"He wants *you*," Lucy insisted.

"I don't know."

"I have faith in you, David darling." She put her arms around him.

"It's very difficult for me to concentrate when you do things like that," he warned.

"Just say yes, then."

He scowled. "It just goes against the grain to do anything for that detestable Geoffrey."

"Yes, he *is* detestable," she agreed with feeling. "Don't do it for Geoffrey. Do it for Stephen. Do it for me," she amended slyly.

"If you put it that way . . ."

"Thank you, darling. And I'll help you, all that I can. I think that we could make a pretty good team, don't you?"

"That's what I keep telling you. Will you stay for a few days, then?"

Lucy nodded. "I took Sophie to Emily's on my way to the train. So I can stay at least through the weekend. Maybe longer."

"That sounds like a bribe if ever I heard one. Clearly unethical."

"What are you going to do about it?" she teased.

"That, Lucy love, will have to wait till later," was his rueful reply as he disengaged himself. "At the moment, I think I'd better get to Fakenham and see my client, if I can, before he's charged."

Lucy waited in the car while David went into the police station. He was back sooner than she'd expected, frowning as he got in.

"Didn't you see him?"

"Yes." He fastened his seat belt. "But not for as long as I would have liked. They'd charged him already. They're in a hurry to take him to Norwich this afternoon, to the prison."

"To Norwich? That's what Geoffrey said. But why?"

"With a serious charge like murder, they don't want to keep him here locally. He'll go before the mags in Norwich in the morning."

"How did he seem?" Lucy asked with concern. "Is he all right?"

They were coming out of Fakenham; David stepped on the accelerator. "He seems fine. A bit pale and subdued. A bit shaken up, understandably enough. But he's a bloody fool."

"What do you mean?"

"He wouldn't see a solicitor when they pulled him in. He was innocent, he said. He didn't need a solicitor." He scowled.

"He *is* innocent." It was a statement, not a question. "He must be."

"That has nothing to do with it. God only knows what he's said to those cops. I really feel at a disadvantage, coming into it at this stage."

"Well, what did he tell you?" Lucy wanted to know.

"That he'd rowed with Dexter on the day he was killed. Over some statue, apparently. Dexter had cleared the church out, except for this one statue that was too high for him to reach without a tall ladder. He'd made his mind up to get rid of it. Stephen offered to buy it, he says. He says it's medieval, valuable. But Dexter said he wanted to destroy it, that it was a graven image." For a moment the connoisseur of church furnishings took over from the lawyer and David shook his head. "Some of these Evangelical types are beyond belief."

"So when was this row with Dexter?"

"In the morning. But then . . ." David scowled again. "He went back and had another row with him later. When Dexter was in the church, actually in the process of getting the statue down. But he didn't tell the police at first. That's where he was so bloody stupid. He didn't tell them he'd seen Dexter again, not until someone else who was interviewed said that they'd seen him come out of the church that evening. Then he had to admit it. But it looked very bad."

"Was the second row over the statue again?"

"That's what he says. But I don't find it very convincing,

and apparently neither do the police. I think he's hiding something."

Lucy thought for a moment, twisting a lock of hair around her finger. "Remember what that other priest, his friend—his name was Mark, wasn't it—said about Dexter's daughter? He was teasing Stephen about her. Stephen seemed quite smitten. Could they have rowed over her? Protective papa, and all that? The hated Walsingham influence?"

David took his eyes off the road for an instant. "Lucy, you're brilliant! Now *that* makes sense!"

"*Cherchez la femme*," she laughed.

"I'll put it to him the next time I see him. If he's being chivalrous and trying to protect her . . ."

"When will you see him again?"

"Tomorrow, in court. I'm hoping they'll let me have some time with him after he's remanded."

Lucy regarded him seriously. "What evidence have they got against him? Is it only circumstantial? That he rowed with Dexter twice, and lied to them about the second row? Or is there anything concrete?"

"I'm not really sure at this point. He was the last person known to see Bob Dexter alive. He lied about it, or at least withheld the truth. But they must have more to go on than that. They must think they've got a damned good case against him or they wouldn't have charged him."

"How can you find out?"

David bit his thumbnail. "I think I'll have a little chat with the sergeant at the police station. It just so happens that I handled his divorce for him a few years ago. I got him off a lot more lightly than he deserved—he owes me a favor. Sergeant Spring is a bit dim, but he's never been averse to a chat over a pint. I'm sure he could fill me in on a few things. Perhaps I'll have a word with him tomorrow."

"What are you—we—going to do now?"

He looked at the dashboard clock. "Go home, I should think. Why? Did you have something in mind?"

Lucy smiled. "I'm sure I can think of something."

"If you can't, I can." David didn't actually break the speed limit, but he was back to Wymondham in near-record time.

# Chapter 37

*Thou hast put away mine acquaintance far from me: and made
me to be abhorred of them.*
*I am so fast in prison: that I cannot get forth.*

Psalm 88:7–8

The press loved it, of course: the pale, serious, bespectacled
young man in the dog collar remanded in custody for the
murder of a fellow clergyman. But it was all over very quickly,
and Stephen Thorncroft was taken to Norwich Prison to await
Her Majesty's pleasure.

Leaving the courtroom, David caught the eye of Sergeant
Spring, who grinned in recognition. "I know it's a bit early
now, but could I buy you a drink some time?" David asked
casually. "I can come to Fakenham, if you like."

The sergeant looked at his watch. "As a matter of fact,
mate, I'm off duty this afternoon. Meet you half way?"

"Right." They agreed on a pub on the road that ran the
twenty-odd miles between Norwich and Fakenham, near the
wildlife park. "See you later, then."

It was several hours before David was able to see Stephen at
Norwich Prison. When, at last, he was ushered into the

barren interview room, it was a very different young man
from the Stephen he'd previously encountered that he saw
sitting before him. Stephen retained his dog collar, but instead
of his cassock he was wearing a plain black clerical shirt and
ordinary trousers. Somehow without his cassock he seemed
stripped of his very identity, and David knew that Stephen
felt it too. "Are they treating you well?" he asked after an
awkward pause.

"Oh, yes." Stephen smiled wanly. "So far, anyway. No
rubber hosepipes yet."

David sat down on the other side of the narrow, scarred
table. "Stephen," he began, "I'm not going to lie to you.
You're in a lot of trouble."

"I'm beginning to realize that." He gave a short, almost
bitter laugh. "I was naive enough to believe that innocence
was some kind of protection. But I can see that I was wrong."
He looked down at his hands, clasped before him on the table.

David was silent for a moment until the young man looked
up and met his eyes. "I still don't know very much about your
case," he said quietly. "I've been given a copy of your statement, which I've read, and I know what you told me yesterday.
I intend to find out as much as I can from the police. But I
can't help you, Stephen, if you won't help yourself. You must
tell me the truth, or I can't do anything for you."

Stephen looked away. "I don't know what you mean."

"I think you do." David paused. "When you went back to
the church that night, and rowed with Dexter the second time,
it wasn't over the statue, was it?"

Stephen's eyes flickered behind his spectacles but he said
nothing.

"It was over Dexter's daughter," David rapped out.

The young man started. "How did you know?"

David's smile was without amusement. "It was a good guess.
That day we first met—you as much as admitted that you were

in love with her. And I got the feeling that he didn't know, and wouldn't be too thrilled if he did."

"And you remembered that. How clever of you."

David spoke with some asperity. "I'm trying to help you. What do you think you can possibly accomplish by lying to me? Now. Tell me. What exactly did you row about?"

Stephen sighed. "It was about Becca, of course. I didn't think the police really needed to know that. And I don't think that the details are important . . ."

"Tell me." David's voice was uncompromising.

Reluctantly the young man began. "He . . . found out . . . that I . . . that we . . . you know."

"How did he find out?"

Stephen's eyes flickered again. "From Becca. She told him. I think he . . . oh, I don't know. He must have forced it out of her. He was a bastard," he added with real passion.

"So you rowed."

"Yes."

"And then what? You just left? Walked out of the church?"

"Yes."

David studied him for a moment. There was still something not quite right in the story. "And that's all? You're telling me everything?"

"Yes." But Stephen wouldn't look at him.

Sergeant John Spring was already standing by the bar with a half-empty glass when David arrived, a bit late after his interview with Stephen. Spring was out of uniform, and had clearly put the time waiting to good use by chatting up the barmaid, with some success; she was smiling at him with great favor. The sergeant was a solidly built, youngish man with the sort of looks that David had always assumed women liked: close-cropped dark hair, wide blue eyes, and a trim brown moustache adorning a round, open face. As he smiled at the barmaid, his lips parted to reveal very even, very shiny white teeth. He saw David. "A drink for my friend, sweetheart," he said to the barmaid. "What will you have, mate?"

"I'm supposed to be buying," David demurred.

"You can get the next round."

"Whisky, please."

She bent down for a glass, taking her time so that the sergeant could get the full picture. Spring grinned appreciatively as he paid for the whisky, then carried the glasses to a table in the corner. "Did you get a look at those knockers?" he asked, not bothering to lower his voice.

"Hard to miss them," David admitted.

"Not bad. Not bad at all." He leered at her from a distance for a moment, then raised his glass. "Cheers, mate." He drank deeply. "You married yet, Dave?"

"No," was the terse reply.

"Good thinking. Still playing the field, eh, mate?" He winked.

David shrugged noncommittally.

"Me, I got married again after that divorce that you took care of for me. Not much choice, if you know what I mean." He winked again. "Bit of a shotgun wedding. Still, I can't really complain. The wife doesn't cramp my style, if you know what I mean. She has her life, and I have mine."

Yes, thought David, she probably has an exciting life looking after his kids, washing and ironing his uniforms, and cooking his meals, while he . . . No woman in Norfolk seemed to be safe from his charms; David recalled the way he'd ogled a young girl who'd come into the station the previous afternoon to report a stolen bicycle. Although he would hope that Lucy would be immune to the man's attractions, which were purely of a physical nature, unhampered by any mental agility, David was glad that she had chosen to remain in the car yesterday, and that she was safe at home in Wymondham this afternoon.

If he had his way, she and Sergeant Spring would never have the opportunity to meet.

They both knew why they were there, and after the small talk was dispensed with they got down to business over the second round of drinks.

"I really don't know very much about this Dexter business," David began. "As you know, I came into it quite late. I wondered what you might be able to tell me. Strictly unofficially, of course, Sergeant."

"Call me John," the policeman grinned. "After all, we're old buddies, aren't we? I'll give it to you straight, Dave. Your young bloke is in a hell of a lot of hot water."

"What have you got on him? Just the fact that he rowed with Dexter? I'll admit that doesn't look good, especially since he didn't tell you at first about the second row . . ."

John Spring chuckled. "No way. Just between you and me, Dave, your bloke wasn't the only one who rowed with Dexter that day. Not by a long shot."

"Really?" David said with interest. "Who else?"

"His wife, for one. And his daughter." Spring's eyes lit up and he digressed for a moment. "That daughter of his, Rebecca her name is. Now *there's* a dish for you. Big blue eyes, blond hair, and what a body! You wouldn't have to pay me to hit the hay with *her!*"

Could the man think of nothing else? "Did he row with anyone else?" David prompted after a moment of the sergeant's silent, reminiscent lust.

"Oh, yes. There were a couple of old bags from the church, Barnes and Vernon their names were. He went to their house and had it out with them. Accused them of stealing something from the church, apparently. And then there were some animal rights nuts who were camping on his land. He tried to run them off, and he hurt their dog. They weren't very happy, to

say the least. It was them, by the way, that put the finger on
your man. They'd moved on, away from the church like Dexter
asked them to, but they came back later that night. They saw
Thorncroft coming out of the church."

David had an inspiration. "They weren't by any chance a
group called BARC?"

"Yeah, that's it. Funny sort of name, isn't it? BARC, like
a dog. I wonder if they meant it to be funny?" Spring picked
up his empty glass and looked at it quizzically.

"You need another drink, John."

"I wouldn't say no, if you're still buying." He looked over
at the bar, and in a moment the barmaid came to their table.
"Another round, sweetheart," he announced, scrutinizing the
legs that had hitherto been concealed behind the bar. He did
not find them wanting, in a short black skirt and black fishnet
tights. When she'd brought the drinks a moment later he
picked up the pound coins that David had left on the table
and insinuated them into her pocket, his hand lingering on
her thigh. "Keep the change, sweetheart."

She smiled down at him. "Ta."

"And ta to you, Dave." Spring saluted him with the foamy
pint of bitter. "Now. What else did you want to know?"

"Dexter seems to have been quite busy that day. Any other
rows?"

"Not that we know of, mate." He regarded David over the
foam as he drank.

David sipped his whisky. "Why did he row with his wife
and daughter?"

"The wife, it was something about the bloomin' statue,
apparently. The daughter, I'm not sure. She wouldn't really
say, was pretty upset about the whole thing. I think she must
have had a boyfriend that the old man didn't know about, and
he found out, and cut up rough about it. She didn't kill him,
so I didn't want to press her. Well, I *did* want to press her,
but . . ." he amended with a leer.

"How do you know she didn't kill him?" David interrupted quickly.

"Her mum says that she was in her room all evening, all night. The girl never went out. Anyway, a sweet young thing like that—she wasn't going to whack her dad on the head with an iron bar, no matter what he did to her."

"So he was killed with an iron bar? You know that for sure?"

Spring nodded. "Didn't I tell you that? That's what really nailed Thorncroft. We found the murder weapon last week. His prints are on it. Along with Dexter's blood."

David stared. "What?" Stephen hadn't seen fit to mention this little detail to him, and it would be next week before he would have another chance to talk to him, and ask for his explanation. Silently he cursed his client.

"Yes, there's no doubt about it, mate."

"Well, what exactly was the murder weapon? And where did you find it?"

Scratching his head, Spring tried to explain. "We found out from Thorncroft—when he finally admitted he'd been there that night—that Dexter was using some sort of a crowbar to pry this statue out. There wasn't any crowbar there when the body was found. We sealed the church, of course. And last week we found it in a little room off the side of the church. The scene-of-the-crime blokes had overlooked it at first because it was part of an altar, they said. I don't really understand—it looks like an iron bar to me. But the young bloke who's in charge there now—Judd, his name is—said that it fitted on to the altar and you hang something from it. Can't really picture it, myself."

David's eyes lit up. "An English altar! It has posts on the four corners, and between the posts are iron bars to hold the curtains at the back and sides."

"That's it." Spring nodded in satisfaction and tipped his glass back; it was nearly empty again.

"So he was killed with one of the bars from the English

altar." David smiled in spite of himself. "There's something rather fitting about that. He would have hated it."

"Forensics found blood on it, and tissue. He was killed with it, all right. And your bloke's fingerprints were there, too. I *might* be able to slip you a copy of the forensic report, Dave." He looked meaningfully at his empty glass.

On temporary receptionist duty at Goodacre and Whitehouse, Nan had been too busy to engage in much gossip or, as she preferred to think of it, exchange of interesting information. But even a busy receptionist was entitled to a cup of tea in the afternoon, so she took her tea into the typists' room and hovered over Karen's typewriter. "You missed her yesterday," she began. "Mr. Middleton-Brown's lady-friend. Lucy. She was here."

Karen raised her head from her typewriter. "Really?"

"She rang in the morning for him, when he was in court. Said to tell him she'd be coming. And sure enough, she turned up right after lunch."

"Oh! So you saw her."

Nan grinned. "Yes."

"What's she like?"

Nan's powers of observation were acute, and she imparted the description with relish. "A few years younger than him. Maybe thirty-five. Tallish, slim. Really pretty, with long curly blondish-red hair. Nicely spoken. Very stylish, in a Laura Ashley sort of way." Her eyes sparkled. "They make ever such a handsome couple. Mad about each other, they are. Bonkers. I could tell."

"Where *is* Mr. Middleton-Brown?" Karen asked with a frown. "I haven't seen him all day."

Nan laughed. "If I didn't know better, I'd think he was off skiving with his Lucy. But he had to go to court this morning, and said he might not be back till much later." She drank down the last of her tea. "I suppose I'd better get back to the reception desk. Jacquie only took it over for a few minutes so I could have my tea."

She'd been back at the reception desk for just a few minutes when David returned, only slightly the worse for an afternoon of drinking in the course of duty. "Any messages, Nan?"

"A few, Mr. Middleton-Brown. Nothing really important."

"Good." He leaned over the desk. "Listen, Nan. I'm going to have to clear my diary as much as possible for the next week or so. Would you be able to make some phone calls and cancel some of my appointments? See if someone else can take on some of the routine things?"

"Of course, Mr. Middleton-Brown," she replied readily, but she looked at him with curiosity. *Was* he going to skive off with his Lucy?

"It's the Bob Dexter murder," he confided. "I've agreed to represent the young man who's been charged. It's going to take a lot of my time."

"Oh!" Now he really had her attention. "Stephen Thorncroft!"

"You've been following the case, I see," David smiled.

"Well, yes. As a matter of fact," she confided, "I have a sort of special interest in it."

"Why is that, Nan?"

"It's my husband's auntie. The one who visited us after Easter, remember? I told you about her—about how I could work that week, because she was there to keep an eye on the kids while they were off school." David nodded, and she went on. "Well, she actually knew that Bob Dexter. She lived in his parish, went to his church. Charlie's auntie is a real religious sort," she added. "Anyway, the police even questioned her about him. After it happened, I mean. She'd had a row with him the day he was done in, and that made her a suspect!" Nan concluded with relish.

David tried to conceal his excitement. "Do you think you could arrange for me to talk with her?" he requested.

"No problem," Nan agreed, smiling. "I'm sure she'd be happy to have a chat with you, Mr. Middleton-Brown. When would you want to see her?"

"As soon as possible. Saturday?"

"I'll give her a ring." Nan reached for a pencil and wrote down the address. "Miss Alice Barnes, Monkey Puzzle Cottage, South Barsham," she said as she wrote. "She lives with her friend, Miss Vernon."

Lucy, too, had had a busy day. She had walked into the Wymondham town center, and had spent some time at the public library, housed picturesquely in the fifteenth-century chapel of St. Thomas à Becket. There she had looked up and photocopied all the newspaper reports of the Dexter murder and the subsequent investigations. It had been covered extensively in the local Norfolk papers, as well as in the nationals, so the task had taken several hours. She'd also been to the shops and had returned home with the ingredients for a special supper.

Coming home to an empty house was one of the most difficult adjustments David had been forced to make when his mother died—he hated it. But it was with distinctly mixed feelings that he returned home that evening, opening the door to be met by delicious cooking smells. On the one hand, it was marvelous beyond words to have Lucy there. But the joy was tempered by the knowledge that it was only temporary, only an aberration in their routine. He wanted her there always, every day.

"Something smells wonderful," he greeted her, coming into the kitchen.

"Hungry?"

"Starving," he confessed, adding sheepishly, "I only had

time to grab a bag of crisps and a Kit Kat for lunch. How about you?"

"I had a jacket potato at the Green Dragon."

"Mm. They do a lovely bacon roll."

Lucy wrinkled her nose in distaste. "You can't tempt me with that, I'm afraid. Anyway, I've been busy. I've got some things for you. From the library."

"And I've got a lot to tell you." He kissed the top of her head as she bent over the cooker. "It's good to be home, Lucy."

Over supper David told her about his difficult interview with Stephen. She listened thoughtfully. "Poor chap," she said at last. "It must be dreadful for him."

"I think that actually being in prison has hit him rather hard. He's finally realized that it's not a game."

"And all this business about Becca Dexter. There's something a bit odd about that, even though he admitted that she'd been the cause of the row."

"Yes," David agreed. "*She* didn't say anything about it to the police."

"Who's protecting whom?" Lucy mused. "He was obviously trying to protect her for some reason. Does he know something that would implicate her? And did she keep quiet to protect *him*?" She twisted a curl abstractedly. "And what did you learn from your policeman-friend?"

"He's no friend of mine," David grimaced. "A former client, but not a friend."

"Why? What's the matter with him?"

David scowled. "He's a real ladies' man. Macho to the hilt. And thick as two short planks. But I did learn quite a lot from him." He related the conversation to her.

"BARC!" she exclaimed at that point in the narrative. "How extraordinary! But whatever were they doing there?"

"Yes, an odd coincidence," he agreed. "They were camping,

apparently just there on an information-disseminating mission. But they were Stephen's undoing." He went on to explain, and then told her about the evidence of the fingerprints.

When he finished, Lucy again looked thoughtful. "There are a few things that just don't add up," she said.

"Such as?"

"Well, we're back to the business of Becca, for one thing. What *is* her story? I'd dearly love to have a chat with Becca Dexter."

"Hm. I don't know how that could be managed."

Lucy smiled. "We'll see. Then there's Mrs. Dexter. Your friend said that she'd rowed with her husband over the statue. Does that make sense to you?"

"Well . . ." David furrowed his brow. "No, not really. Why would she care about the statue? Presumably she's a good Evangelical like her husband."

"Precisely," she nodded. "Then there's the matter of BARC. Why did they come back to the church that night, when they saw Stephen? What were they up to?"

David looked thoughtful. "Go on."

"And the oddest thing of all is about this iron rod, the bit of the English altar that was used to bash his head in."

"What's odd about that? Aside from the fact that Stephen didn't bother to tell me that his prints were on it?" David fulminated.

"How did the police find out that Dexter had been using an iron rod as a crowbar to remove the statue?"

"Spring said that Stephen told them," David repeated. "After it came out that he'd been there that evening."

"And they didn't have any other way of knowing that? No one else mentioned the iron rod?"

"No . . ."

"So why would Stephen have told them, if he'd used it to kill Dexter? Why would he have mentioned it at all?" she finished triumphantly.

David regarded her with admiration. "I'm glad you're on my side. Have you ever thought about a legal career?"

She laughed. "Well, what's our next step, darling?"

He told her then about Nan's connections in South Barsham, and his intention to visit Monkey Puzzle Cottage on Saturday. "But that's marvelous!" she said. "Couldn't be better! You'll have those old ladies eating out of your hand, if I know you, David Middleton-Brown!"

He shook his head self-deprecatingly. "Tomorrow, though . . ."

"I think that I should talk to Fiona," Lucy declared. "Perhaps she'd be able to shed some light on BARC's involvement."

"That's good! And I could have a word with Karen, our typist. She's got involved with them as well."

"I'll go into Norwich with you tomorrow," she decided. "I'll drop into the gallery, and perhaps suggest lunch to Fiona. Make it seem rather casual, if possible."

"I've got plenty of paperwork to do at the office. All the newspaper reports to sift through. And maybe John Spring will come up with something for me."

"And on Saturday," Lucy announced, "we shall visit the scene of the crime!"

# Chapter 38

*He bringeth forth grass for the cattle: and green herb for the
service of men;*
*That he may bring food out of the earth, and wine that maketh
glad the heart of man: and oil to make him a cheerful
countenance, and bread to strengthen man's heart.*

*Psalm 104:14–15*

Fiona Crawford was busy with a serious customer, so Lucy
browsed around the gallery until Fiona was free. Eventually
she caught her eye.

"Lucy!" Fiona approached her with surprise. "Whatever are
you doing in Norwich?"

"I'm staying with David," Lucy admitted truthfully.

Fiona regarded her with a knowing smile. "Ah. I see. Of
course."

Presumably he'd taken her advice, then, she thought with
satisfaction. Lucy looked happy, there was no doubt of that.

"I thought I'd drop in and see how you were."

"How nice!" Fiona looked at her deceptively simple, extremely expensive gold watch. "Listen, it's almost lunchtime.
Are you free for lunch, or are you meeting David?"

"He's really tied up today, so I'm free. I'd hoped you'd be able to join me," Lucy confessed.

"Great. If you can wait just a few minutes . . ."

There were no other customers, so in short order Fiona retrieved her handbag from the back room and flipped over the sign on the door to read "closed." "Where would you like to go? Any ideas?"

"I don't know Norwich at all," Lucy demurred. "I'll have to leave it up to you. Vegetarian, of course," she added. "Is there anything good around here?"

Fiona hesitated. "We really ought to go to the Green Scene, I suppose. But . . . well, it's good enough, but I find the fare a bit spartan. And—" She looked guilty. "It doesn't have a license. Rhys doesn't believe in drinking alcohol, as you know, but I do like a glass of wine with my lunch now and again. What Rhys doesn't know . . ."

"Can't hurt him," Lucy finished sympathetically.

"Let's go to Mange Tout. It's not completely vegetarian, but they always have a choice of vegetarian dishes, and they do some lovely salads. And the sweets . . ."

"Sounds perfect," Lucy agreed.

They'd walked the short distance to Mange Tout, climbed the stairs to the first-floor restaurant, found a table, and ordered their salads before they had much of a chance to talk. Raising her glass of white wine cheerily, Fiona began, "So, how is David?"

"Oh, he's very well."

"And how are . . . things . . . between you?"

"Good," said Lucy with a little smile. "Very good." Fiona waited for more, but it was not forthcoming. She had not known Lucy long enough—or intimately enough—to learn that, although she was an excellent listener, with a real gift for drawing people out, Lucy very rarely talked about herself.

She was not in the least ashamed of her relationship with David, but she felt that it was, and should remain, private—something for the two of them that concerned no one else. Not even her family knew about David: during the last weekend, spent among them, she hadn't mentioned him at all, and not entirely because she feared her clergyman-father's disapproval of a union unblessed by Mother Church through the Sacrament of Holy Matrimony. It was simply no one else's business.

"And Rhys? He's well?"

Fiona glowed at the introduction of her favorite topic of conversation. "Oh, yes! He's alarmingly healthy. He's been enjoying the warm weather, of course. He goes out running every morning, and it makes such a difference when the weather is good."

"How is BARC doing? Have they been gaining members?"

"Yes, it's growing all the time. Rhys reckons that it's a cause whose time has come. Everywhere they go, they meet such a good response, such interest. They've got a new van, you know. That's going to make quite a difference to them." She went on in the same vein until their salads arrived.

"Oh, this looks lovely," Lucy said. She wasn't sure how to introduce the topic of Bob Dexter's murder in an unobtrusive way, but in the end she didn't have to.

"They ran into a spot of trouble a fortnight ago," Fiona confided, taking a quick sip of her wine. "BARC, that is."

"Really?"

"They almost found themselves in the middle of a murder," she elaborated with relish. Encouraged by Lucy's interested look, she went on. "I wasn't actually with them at the time, and neither was Rhys," she admitted. "We were back at the van."

"What happened?"

"Well, they'd taken the van and parked it in a village, by a church. And who do you think made them leave?" She paused for effect. "Bob Dexter! The chap who got his head bashed in—the very same day!"

"So they left?"

"They didn't go far, just to some common land nearby where they could set up the tents. I joined them later, after the gallery closed."

"Somehow I can't imagine you sleeping in a tent," Lucy couldn't help interrupting, looking bemusedly at the other woman's designer dress.

Fiona laughed. "Ludicrous, isn't it? It shows you what love can do! I just can't bear for Rhys to be away from me, for even one night," she confided sheepishly. "I hated it, but I went. Don't get me wrong," she added. "I believe in BARC, and like to support them—I'm even going to Walsingham with them, to the National Pilgrimage, at the end of the month!"

"And what happened later?" Lucy prompted, bringing her back to the subject. "They went back?"

"Yes. It was Maggie's idea—she goes a bit over the top sometimes. She thought that they should go back and stick some bills up on the church notice boards—some BARC posters, that sort of thing. As a protest, to let Dexter know that he hadn't really won. He'd hurt Bleddyn, you see. He kicked him. Maggie was livid, and so was Rhys."

"Is he all right now?" Lucy asked with concern.

"Yes, still a bit sore, I think. Poor thing—one of his ribs was cracked. But he's on the mend."

Lucy paused as she considered her next question. "So who went back to the church? Maggie?"

"And the other two. Gary and Nicholas. You've met Nicholas, remember? And Gary is our resident American hippy."

"Not Rhys?"

"No. Rhys didn't think it was a very good idea, and he wanted to stay with Bleddyn. And me."

"But he let them go?"

Fiona smiled whimsically. "Yes. It seemed like a good chance . . . for us to be alone. While they were away, we made love in the van." Her face assumed a far-away look, remembering; Lucy finally had to prompt her to continue.

"But what happened to them?"

"Oh, they came back. Before we were quite finished, as a matter of fact," Fiona added in her forthright away. "They'd stuck up a few posters on the big notice board outside the church, but then they were frightened away by this chap leaving, in a great rush. They didn't know that Dexter was actually in the church. But apparently the chap had just killed him, and came out in a real state."

"They actually saw Stephen Thorncroft come out of the church?"

"They didn't know who he was then, of course, but they saw a young priest. They described him quite clearly."

Lucy chose her words with care. "So none of them . . . actually went in the church."

"No. At least they said not."

"Did they tell anyone what they'd seen?"

"They told *us*, of course. But they didn't know that Dexter was dead, so they didn't realize that what they'd seen was important. Not until much later, anyway."

"Then they went to the police?"

Fiona laughed. "Not a chance. Maggie's allergic to the police, I think. Gary, too—they've had too many unpleasant run-ins with what they call the fuzz. Rhys told them, later, when we'd found out about the murder, that they should go. But he couldn't force them."

"But the police found out?" Lucy asked carefully.

"Yes. It was the posters, of course. They traced them through the posters."

"Of course."

A young waiter interrupted them. "Would you ladies like any sweets, or coffee?"

Fiona looked at her watch. "Oh, blast! Look at the time, Lucy! We've been sitting here nattering away . . . I've got to get back and reopen the gallery!"

"I didn't really learn that much from her," Lucy explained to David later, in the car on the way home to Wymondham. "She wasn't actually there at the church at all, and Rhys didn't go with them in the evening when they saw Stephen." She told him, quickly, what she'd found out. "So apparently your typist Karen wasn't with them," she added. "Did you have a chance to talk to her about it?"

"Yes, I did. When they went to South Barsham on Friday afternoon, she was working. She'd planned to join them later, after work. But no one thought to phone her, to tell her they'd moved."

"Did she go anyway? She has a car?"

"Yes, she runs a little red Mini—she recently passed her driving test, I think. She went, but when she got to the church, and found that they were gone, she went back home."

"Hmm." Lucy looked out the window thoughtfully. "She didn't see them at all, then? And didn't see Stephen?"

"No."

"Did the police question her about it?"

David laughed. "No, thank God. She was terrified enough talking to me—she would have had a nervous breakdown if she'd had to talk to the police! She's a funny, nervous little thing. She sat there with these great brown eyes on me, like some frightened rabbit, and it was 'Yes, Mr. Middleton-Brown' and 'No, Mr. Middleton-Brown.' " He mimicked her faint, tremulous whisper.

"I wonder why the police didn't interview her? After all, she was at the scene of the crime at around the relevant time."

"I don't suppose her name ever came up. She wasn't with the others, and none of them probably even gave her a thought afterwards, or knew that she'd come."

Lucy turned to face him. "Are you sure she didn't see *any-thing*? Is *she* sure?"

"I don't know," he admitted. "I only asked her if she'd seen the others, or Stephen. Like I said, it was damned hard work getting anything out of her at all," he added defensively.

"I wonder . . ." Lucy was lost in thought for the remainder of the journey home.

# Chapter 39

*He hath graven and digged up a pit: and is fallen himself into
the destruction that he made for other.*

*Psalm 7:16*

They called in at the church first; they'd left plenty of time to
allow them to explore it at their leisure. Fortunately, it was
unlocked—the policy of keeping St. Mary's locked up had
died with Bob Dexter.

David had brought his Pevsner, of course, and that was
helpful for the exterior architectural detail, but once inside it
was useless. He stood at the back and looked around with
amazement.

"I've been in this church before, on a church crawl—a long
time ago, admittedly. But I don't believe it's the same place!"

"What was it like before?" Lucy wanted to know.

"Very dark. Completely over-the-top with statues and bits
of tat, but rather charming in a tacky sort of way. I mean,
how many churches have you ever seen with a shrine to King
Charles the Blessed Martyr?"

"Probably none," she admitted. "Is there one here?"

"There *was*. I very much doubt that it's survived the depre-
dations of the Reverend Bob Dexter. Not much else has."

"What about the famous statue? The one he was trying to get down?"

"Ah." David looked around. "I don't see it. Perhaps it's in the chapel."

"In here?" Lucy peered into the south porch. "No. There just seems to be some bits and pieces in here."

He looked over her shoulder. "That's the English altar, presumably minus the lethal side bar. The chapel is at the east end, beyond that red curtain."

In a moment they were gazing up at the statue in its little medieval niche. "It's lovely," David declared. "A very rare survival. It would be a crime to destroy something like that."

"But another crime took place instead," said Lucy slowly. "The hunter became the hunted."

Lucy remained behind in the church while David drove the short distance to Monkey Puzzle Cottage. He would have liked to have her along, for moral support, but she quite reasonably argued that the two old women were more likely to open up to one person on his own; David did seem to have a gift for hitting just the right note with older women, Lucy stated, and didn't need her help.

Turning down the lane by the old blacksmith's, he found the house without difficulty, spotting it instantly where it lurked between the two monkey puzzle trees. David shivered involuntarily; he had a very strong, virtually phobic loathing for monkey puzzle trees. To him they seemed utterly evil, and he was sure that they were possessed of malevolent souls which would eternally haunt anyone who cut them down. He tried to avert his eyes from the long, tentacle-like branches which held the little house in an unholy embrace, but realized with horror that he would have to walk under one to gain entrance to the cottage; Nan had alerted him to go to the back door.

The day, though warm, was wet, and the monkey puzzles

dripped with rain. David scuttled quickly between the mummified car and the sodden pink sofa which sat forlornly beneath the tree, breathing a sigh of relief as he reached the back of the house.

They were waiting for him at the back door: a short, capable-looking woman with fluffy white hair and a capacious bosom, with her taller, gaunt-faced companion hovering behind. "I'm Alice Barnes," she announced before David had a chance to speak. "You must be the gentleman that Charlie's wife said was coming."

"David Middleton-Brown." He tried not to wince at the firmness of her grip on his hand. "It's very kind of you to see me."

"My friend Gwen Vernon," she introduced as an afterthought, leading them into the sitting room. Gwen bobbed in acknowledgment.

David took in the room with interest in a few seconds of appraisal. It was a tiny room, and seemed crowded with Victorian antiques—the desk against the wall, the table in the window, the whatnot in the corner, stuffed to bursting with rare and not-so-rare bits of Victoriana. The decorative items, too, were Victorian, from the shell pictures, the silhouettes and the insipid watercolors on the walls to the large Staffordshire figurines and the blue glass vases with their dangling lusters which adorned the mantelpiece, flanking the mahogany clock. Oddly out of keeping was the new carpet, garishly colorful with abstract, blobby flowers, and the brace of rose-pink dralon chairs on either side of the fireplace. David, invited to sit down, chose for himself the upholstered wing chair which reposed between them, exceedingly shabby but, he recognized, a very good piece of furniture in spite of its dilapidated condition.

"Tea?" Alice offered.

"I don't want to put you to any trouble."

"It's no trouble," she asserted.

"Then thank you, Miss Barnes."

Everything must have been in readiness, and the kettle on the boil, for she was only gone for a moment, during which time Gwen fluttered silently to alight on one of the pink chairs, and to smile at him nervously.

The two dogs followed Alice into the room with baleful looks at the interloper who had usurped their chair. "Babs, Nell, back to the kitchen!" Alice ordered, but they ignored her and lay down on the floor at Gwen's feet. Alice poured the tea from the silver pot and proffered a cake stand laden with cream cakes.

David felt at something of a disadvantage, burdened with a fragile teacup and a plate of things he really ought not to eat, flanked on either side by the women. He swiveled his head back and forth between them as he spoke.

"Nan told you why I wanted to talk to you?" he began, after sipping some tea, nibbling on an eclair, and making the appropriate noises of appreciation.

"About Father Thorncroft, she said," Alice responded. "You're representing him, I understand?"

"Yes, that's right."

"But we don't really *know* Father Thorncroft," Gwen piped.

Forestalled, Alice frowned in annoyance. "We don't really know Father Thorncroft," she repeated. "We've met him, of course, at Walsingham. We know Father Mark very well, of course," she emphasised with pride, "and Father Thorncroft is a friend of his. I don't know how we can help you."

"We've already talked to the police," said Gwen. "We've told them everything we know."

David nodded. "Yes. I don't expect you to tell me anything about Stephen Thorncroft. But," he smiled at them ingratiatingly, "you can be a great help to me nonetheless. I think you're just the right people to fill me in on life in South

Barsham, especially at the church. You must know everyone in the village . . ."

"Yes," admitted Alice with some pride. "We've been here for donkey's years, you know."

"And everyone in the church."

"Of course."

"So you see, Miss Barnes, Miss Vernon—I really do need your help." He smiled again, pleadingly this time.

"Well," said Alice. "I'm sure if there's any way we can help you, we'll be more than happy to. Won't we, Gwen?" Gwen nodded fervently.

David took another bite of his eclair, careful lest the cream that squished out from the sides should disengage itself and fall into his lap. "I've been to the church," he said, "and I must say that I find it absolutely appalling. I've never seen such a ghastly mess!"

"Oh, yes!" Gwen breathed. "He wrecked it, our beautiful church! Violated it!" She closed her eyes, remembering it as it used to be, and a pair of desolate tears squeezed out from their corners. "You should have seen it!"

"It's beyond belief that such a thing could be allowed to happen," Alice added, her bosom quivering with indignation. "In just a few weeks—all of it gone! The statues, the paintings—everything!"

"But what did he *do* with it?" David asked.

"Scattered to the four winds!" Gwen announced melodramatically, waving her arms in demonstration and nearly upsetting her teacup.

Alice glared at her, but only said, "He flogged it all off. Every bit of it."

"Father Mark assures us that most of it has gone to good homes," Gwen added, "but still . . ."

"Bob Dexter," Alice pronounced firmly, "was a very wicked man. And I'm not sorry that he's dead."

"Oh, Alice!" squeaked Gwen. "That's a sin!"

"If it is, I shall confess it to Father Mark. He'll absolve me," she stated.

"You didn't get along with Father Dexter, then?" David asked innocently.

Alice snorted. "You can say that again."

"And he hated to be called 'Father,'" Gwen added.

David had managed to convey, without actually saying it in so many words, that he was One of Them in the matter of churchmanship; unconsciously they had warmed to him. Now he shook his head. "I really don't know how you put up with it as well as you did," he sympathized.

Alice nodded briskly. "It wasn't easy. But Christian charity, you know . . ."

"How did he treat his family, do you know?"

"He was foul to his wife," Alice said without hesitation.

"Poor, dear Elayne," sighed Gwen.

"If you ask me, Elayne Dexter was a saint to put up with that man the way she did," added Alice.

David found it difficult to conceal his surprise; he hadn't expected to find even a remnant of sympathy for any member of the Dexter family in this household.

"You . . . approve of Mrs. Dexter, then?"

Improbably, Alice's face softened. "Elayne is a pet. She deserved better from life than that nasty, brutal man. Still, she's free of him now."

"Of course, *he* never knew that we were friends with Elayne," Gwen confided, almost proudly. "He wouldn't have allowed it."

"And the daughter? Becca?"

Alice clamped her lips together and frowned; Gwen's face puckered. David rushed ahead to reassure them. "You don't have to be afraid of betraying a secret. I know that she and Stephen Thorncroft were . . . seeing each other."

A startled glance passed quickly between the women. "Oh, you know that, do you?" said Alice.

"Yes. Father Stephen told me himself."

"Oh, did he?" Alice paused. "More tea, Mr. Middleton-Brown?"

David knew from Sergeant Spring that the two women had quarreled with Bob Dexter on the day of his death, but it was only after considerable quantities of tea, cream cakes and reassuring small talk that he felt secure enough to ask them about it.

They'd already told their story to the police, so the retelling of it was fairly painless, and quite polished. Alice did most of the talking.

"He stormed in here and accused us of stealing!" she said with indignation. "He said we'd taken the monstrance, and were hiding it here! And he wouldn't even believe us when we denied it! He took Gwen outside and harassed her on her own! She was almost in tears, poor Gwen." Gwen nodded in confirmation.

"So the monstrance had gone missing from the church?" David asked.

"That's right."

"Did you have any idea where it might have gone?"

They looked at each other uneasily. "Well . . ." Alice suddenly decided to come clean with this very nice young man who was, after all, trying to help poor innocent Father Thorncroft. "Well, as a matter of fact, we *did* know where it was, but it *wasn't* here."

Relieved of the burden of lying, Gwen became voluble. "We *told* him it wasn't here, and that was the truth! But he wouldn't believe us! He just kept badgering us, asking us if we'd taken it, if we knew where it was."

"And where was it?" David asked with real curiosity.

Gwen smirked in remembrance at their cleverness. "It was right under his nose, at the vicarage! Dear Elayne was hiding it."

When he got back to the church, Lucy wasn't there. Assuming that she must have gone off for a walk around the village, David spent a few minutes examining the scene of the murder. He closed his eyes and tried to imagine it—in the darkness or semi-darkness, Dexter up on the ladder, working away with his improvised crowbar. Apparently quite a few people knew he'd be here that evening, engaged in that task. Had one of them been in the darkened church, waiting their chance to shake the ladder, then to strike the stunned Dexter with the iron bar which had fallen with him? Or had he indeed fallen unaided, and someone later had taken the opportunity to render him permanently unconscious with the means that was to hand? There was something about the setup here that wasn't quite right, but David couldn't pinpoint it.

Lucy came in with a poorly concealed smile. "Darling, you'll never guess where I've been!"

"Surprise me."

"I've been having tea at the vicarage!"

"The vicarage!"

She beamed. "Yes. I was sitting in here, doing what you're doing now—trying to picture the murder, and imagine how it happened. A woman came in—she didn't see me. She went up and put some flowers under the statue, and knelt down to pray."

"Elayne Dexter."

"How did you know?"

David grinned. "I've been busy, too. I've just found out that Elayne Dexter was a secret, if recent, Anglo-Catholic convert, with a particular love for that statue."

She sighed. "You've stolen my thunder."

"Well, go on," he urged.

"I thought, naturally, that she was putting flowers on the spot where her husband had died, in his memory. But of course that wasn't the way of it at all. We started talking, and she invited me to have a cup of tea with her at the vicarage." Lucy pushed her hair away from her face with a thoughtful look. "David, that poor woman. He must have been absolutely frightful to live with. Authoritarian, humorless . . ."

"What is *she* like?" he wanted to know.

"Oh, she's lovely. I don't mean to look at—she's rather washed-out, if you know what I mean. But she has such a sweet nature. Very shy, and downtrodden. But I think she's beginning to come out of it a bit, now that he's no longer around to tell her how hopeless she is."

"You liked her, then."

"Very much," Lucy confirmed. "We really hit it off. She talked to me as if we were old friends."

"You always were a good listener. Tell me everything," he urged, sitting down on the plinth below the statue.

She sat down beside David and turned to face him. "Well, she told me all about the row they had had that afternoon. I don't think they ever rowed much—it was one of those marriages where things go on under the surface, but not much is ever said. As I said, she was quite thoroughly under his thumb, and was never allowed to express her own opinions. I don't suppose it ever occurred to him that she had any, apart from those she shared with him." Lucy didn't try to conceal her dislike of the late Bob Dexter.

"Was the row about the statue, then? Like John Spring told me?"

She nodded, and went on to relate Elayne's story in all its pathos. "The thing that John Spring didn't tell you, because he didn't know," she finished, "was that Elayne went back to the church later, in the evening, to talk to him."

"What?"

"Yes. She wanted to make a last plea for the statue, and"—

she paused for dramatic effect—"to tell him that she intended to leave him."

"Leave him!"

"Apparently she'd spent much of the afternoon talking with Miss Barnes and Miss Vernon at Monkey Puzzle Cottage, and they'd convinced her that it was the only thing to do, for her own sanity. They said they'd support her, help her. So she decided to tell him while her courage was fresh."

David shook his head. "They never told me that she'd been there that afternoon."

"No, I don't suppose they would have." Lucy nodded sagely.

"But when? Dexter was there in the afternoon, and she wasn't there then."

"It must have been after he left. At first, after their row, she walked around the countryside for a long time, then went to Monkey Puzzle Cottage. From there she went straight to the church, she says."

"And what happened? They quarreled again, I assume?"

"Well, not really. She said that he was very cold to her, very dismissive. He didn't believe that she'd leave him. He was up on the ladder and wouldn't even come down to talk to her. Just told her to go away and leave him alone."

"So she went?"

"That's what she says," Lucy confirmed. "She went back to the vicarage and spent the rest of the evening with Becca."

David chewed on a nail abstractedly, then suddenly turned to her. "Becca! Did you talk to Becca?"

"No," said Lucy slowly. "She wasn't there. I wish I could have talked to her. There are a lot of things I'd like to ask Becca." He looked at her, inquiring, but she merely shook her head. "There's something about this situation with Becca that still doesn't add up."

"You don't suspect Becca of killing her father, do you?"

"No. Elayne confirmed that Becca was at home all evening, from the time she'd left Dexter alive in the church."

"And you don't think she'd lie to protect her daughter?"

Lucy twisted a lock of hair thoughtfully. "Perhaps. I don't know. I just wish I could talk to Becca."

David took both Lucy's hands and looked at her earnestly. "Lucy love, I want to ask you something. Think carefully before you answer. I know that you like Elayne Dexter, that you find her sympathetic and believable. I know that you think her husband was an unmitigated schweppes. But do you think it's possible that she killed him?"

Lucy took her time considering his question. "No," she said at last. "No, I don't think so."

"Why not?"

"Well, she loved him. In spite of everything, she loved him." Her nose wrinkled with distaste. "She could never have put up with him for nearly twenty-five years if she didn't. I know that I couldn't have put up with him for five minutes!"

David laughed. "That doesn't necessarily exclude her! Quite the reverse, I should have thought. Don't you know that 'each man kills the thing he loves'?"

Lucy smiled wryly. "Perhaps."

"She had a motive—you must admit that. And she had the opportunity, and no alibi."

Closing her eyes, Lucy spoke with deliberation. "But she told me that she'd been to the church. She hadn't told the police that, and no one saw her. If she'd killed him—why blow her own alibi? Why tell me she'd been to the church? Why not just say she'd gone straight home to the vicarage and spent the evening with her daughter? No, David," she said. "I don't believe that Elayne Dexter murdered her husband."

# Chapter 40

*Which refuseth to hear the voice of the charmer: charm he never so wisely.*

*Psalm 58:5*

David and Lucy took a day off on Sunday, attending Mass at Wymondham Abbey in the morning. After lunch at home they went off in the car, in the opposite direction from Walsingham and South Barsham. They ended up in Suffolk, at Southwold and Blytheburgh, on a church-crawl, as David began to impart his love for and knowledge of churches to Lucy.

On Monday morning it was back to work as usual, at least for David. Lucy was beginning to say that perhaps it was time for her to think about returning to London, that possibly she had done as much as she could to help him with the case, and of course he was protesting strenuously. That morning, however, she was still in Wymondham, and it was with great regret that he left her drowsing in bed, the tea that he had made for her cooling on the bedside table.

Nan had been relieved of her temporary receptionist duties, so it was mid-morning before David saw her, when she brought a cup of tea to his office. "Good morning, Nan," he smiled. "Thanks."

"So," she said, "how did you get on with Charlie's Auntie Alice and her friend? They're a funny old pair, aren't they?"

David shook his head bemusedly. "They were very sweet, but definitely eccentric. I can't say I've been to too many houses that provide a sofa outdoors!"

"What do you mean?"

"Isn't that a regular feature? Under the monkey puzzle tree, the one by the drive. There's a very waterlogged pink sofa."

Nan looked puzzled. "Not pink dralon, is it?"

"Yes, I think so. It was really too wet to tell. But there were definitely two pink dralon chairs in the sitting room, so it probably matched them. An odd place to put your sofa, don't you think?" he asked flippantly.

"I don't understand it," she said slowly. "That sofa is their pride and joy. They bought it, along with the chairs and the new carpet, with the money that Auntie Alice was given when she retired a few years back. Why would they put it outside? Unless they've both really gone bonkers, that is?"

Why indeed? thought David. "Anyway, Nan, thanks for arranging my visit. It was most helpful, and they couldn't have been nicer."

"I'm glad," she confessed. "To tell you the truth, Mr. Middleton-Brown, I wasn't sure how they'd take to you. They don't usually go much for men. Aside from my Charlie, who's family, and all those priests, that is. They do love their priests." She left, shutting the door behind her. David sat still for a moment, his eyes staring ahead at nothing in particular but his brain in high gear. After a moment he picked up the phone, too excited to worry about his resistance to using the instrument, and dialed his number in Wymondham.

It rang quite a few times before Lucy answered. She responded tentatively with the number. "Lucy!" he said. "It's me."

"Oh, hello, darling. You sound agitated."

"I *am* agitated. I thought you weren't going to answer. Where were you?"

"I was packing my case. I thought that perhaps I'd go back to London this evening, if you could take me to the train. I've got a few commissions that I should be getting on with, you know. I haven't had a brush in my hand for over a week!"

"No!" he said urgently. "You can't go, Lucy! Something's come up. I need your help."

"You know I'll do whatever I can."

He paused. "I feel really silly asking you this," he confessed sheepishly. "I ought to know this already, but can you drive a car?"

Lucy laughed. "Of course I can drive a car. I grew up in the country, remember."

"Good girl. Well, then, I'll be there in a quarter of an hour or twenty minutes, and I'll tell you then what I need you to do."

He was back at his office in less than an hour, dropped off by Lucy as she embarked on her errand in his car. A few minutes later, the receptionist put through a call. "Dave?" said the voice on the other end of the phone. "It's John. John Spring."

"Hello, John. Have you got something for me?"

"As a matter of fact I do, mate. I've got to come into Norwich this afternoon to deliver some papers to the prison. So if you've got a photocopier, and a bottle of whisky and a couple of glasses . . . I've got something that might interest you."

"How soon can you be here?" David asked, his eye on the clock. He didn't know how long Lucy's errand would take, but he didn't want Spring around when she returned.

"Oh, in an hour or so. You in a hurry or something?"

"Well, it's just that . . . I've got a few appointments later this afternoon."

"I'll be there as soon as I can," Spring promised.

He was as good as his word; Nan had scarcely returned
from buying the whisky when he arrived at Goodacre and
Whitehouse. Although he knew perfectly well how to get up
the stairs to David's office, he lingered at the reception desk
for a word with the pretty receptionist. "Sergeant Spring to
see you," she buzzed David.

"Send him up. He knows the way." In order to save time,
he had the whisky bottle open and was pouring generous
measures into the two glasses when Spring entered.

"Dave! A man of his word!" Spring accepted the glass with
a grin. "Cheers, mate!" He sat down in the chair that was
provided for clients and made himself comfortable. "So, how's
things, Dave?"

"Oh, fine."

"Did you have a good weekend?"

"Not bad," David said noncommittally. "You?"

Spring smiled what David had come to recognize as his
lecherous smile. "Smashing! I told the wife that I was on
duty—that one works every time. A policeman's lot may not
be a happy one, but there are certain advantages, if you know
what I mean! Remember that lovely little barmaid at that pub?
The one with the great knockers?" David nodded. "Well, she
had the weekend off. Need I say more?" he leered. "Or should
I say, *we* had it off? Ha, ha." He laughed uproariously at his
own wit.

David smiled weakly, looking at the clock out of the corner
of his eye.

Half an hour, a number of salacious stories, and several glasses
of whisky later, David was looking openly and pointedly at
the clock. He still didn't have the reports that Spring had
promised, and the policeman was showing no signs of handing
them over and clearing out. "Did you say you had to go to the
prison?" he asked at last. "Will they be expecting you?"

"Oh, no hurry, Dave. Just sometime this afternoon is all.

It's nice to have a bit of time off the hook, have a little laugh and a drink or two with a friend, isn't it?" He leaned back in the chair and took an appreciative sip of the whisky. "This is a good tipple, mate. You know your Scotch, I'll say that for you. Makes me think of a little lassie I once knew . . ."

David stifled a sigh. As soon as he could interrupt, he said, "You brought something with you? Shall I buzz Nan and see if the photocopier is free?"

Reluctantly Spring curtailed his erotic reminiscences. "Here, Dave." He pulled out a sheaf of papers. "The forensic report—it's a bit long and tedious, but if you want to have a look at it . . ."

"Thanks, John." He buzzed Nan on the intercom and within a moment she was there to collect the papers for photocopying.

John Spring appraised her with interest. Over thirty, he thought, but not bad for it, and sometimes those mature women were the hottest thing going. "Hello, sweetheart," he offered as an opening gambit, waving the papers with a winning leer. "I think I've got what you want."

"I doubt that," she said coolly. David watched with amusement as she took the papers from Spring, clearly unimpressed. "I'll be back in a few minutes," she told David, ignoring the policeman.

Spring accepted defeat with equanimity; he didn't very often cast his net in vain, but there were plenty of fish in the sea, and there was no use wasting time with one that didn't want to be caught—it was her loss, after all. He was about to top up his glass when Nan returned; with relief David took the papers from her, restored the originals to Spring, and screwed the lid back on the bottle, as seemingly oblivious to Spring's disappointment as Spring was to his impatience. "No time for another drink?" the policeman suggested.

If Spring wasn't out of here soon, he was bound to encounter Lucy. "Why don't you take the bottle with you, John?" David handed it to him with a smile.

"That's decent of you, Dave. Ta very much." David escorted
him firmly out of his office and down the stairs to the reception
area; Spring's head swiveled from side to side, in the vain hope
of catching sight of a stray secretary. But the only female in
sight was a client in the reception area, a wrinkled specimen
who must have been at least eighty. Then, of course, there was
the receptionist, a pert and pretty girl with, David knew, a
very large and very possessive boyfriend. It would almost be
worth it to let Spring chat her up and see what would happen,
he thought. But he couldn't take the chance. Lucy should have
been here by now—she'd surely be here any minute.

"Thank you for the report, John," he said at the door. "I'll
be in touch. Perhaps we could meet again for a drink, later in
the week—at that pub on the A1067?"

Mollified, Spring nodded, tucking the whisky bottle firmly
under his arm. "You're on, Dave. What say I give you a ring
on Friday?"

David went to find Nan then, to make sure that she hadn't
been offended by Spring's heavy-handed overtures. He needn't
have worried. "I've run into his sort before," she assured him.
"Fancies himself, doesn't he? Thinks he's God's gift."

"But women fall down at his feet all the time, Nan! I've
seen it happen! He just crooks his little finger, and women
come running!"

She tried to look serious and dignified, but was unable to
suppress a chuckle. "Mr. Middleton-Brown, I should think
that you'd give me credit for more sense than to be taken in
by a wally like that. He's not a patch on my Charlie. Or on
you either, for that matter, if you don't mind me saying so."

"Me? You've got to be joking!" David shook his head.
"Sometimes, Nan, I think that I'll never understand women."

Lucy arrived a few minutes later; she went straight up to his
office, barely containing her excitement.

"David!" she greeted him. "You're absolutely brilliant!" She collapsed into the chair so recently vacated by John Spring.

"Tell me," he said eagerly. "Tell me what happened."

"Let me catch my breath." Lucy looked around suspiciously. "This room smells like a distillery," she observed. "What have you been doing in here?"

"Never mind that. Tell me!"

She smiled. "You were right, of course. Right that there was something distinctly odd about the sofa. And right in thinking that they would never have told you—they would have been far too embarrassed to tell a man."

"But they told *you*."

"They told me everything. I'm a woman, you see."

"I had rather noticed that." He raised his eyebrows.

Lucy scowled humorously. "Very funny, darling."

"So they told you . . ." he encouraged, leaning forward.

"That Becca Dexter had defiled their sofa. They were terribly upset about it—felt that they'd been betrayed by her, when they'd trusted her in their house. They couldn't bear to keep the sofa, when it had been violated, as they said, by Becca's vile lust."

"But what about *him*? What about Stephen Thorncroft? It takes two, doesn't it?" David asked indignantly.

Lucy nodded. "But he's a priest, you see. That puts him in a different category altogether. It means that he's by nature pure—not really a man at all. Something of a neutered, sexless creature, they seem to think. So she must have corrupted him, tempted him, lured him to his doom."

"They came right out and told you all this?"

"Well, not in so many words, of course. There was a great deal of waffling about, talk of 'a man of the cloth'—not even naming any names. But it was fairly clear what they meant."

"I'm curious," he said, "about how they found out? Surely Becca wouldn't have told them?"

She laughed. "It was the dogs. They found 'the evidence,' I was told. Quite a picture, isn't it?"

David couldn't suppress a snort of amusement. "I can just see one of those nasty little creatures presenting 'the evidence' to a horrified mistress!"

"Apparently after that they confronted Becca, and she admitted her perfidy. Wasn't even sorry, they told me. They were scandalized, and told her never to darken their door again."

David leaned back in his chair. "Well, it explains a great deal, doesn't it? The mystery of the cast-off sofa is solved!" He paused as he thought through what Lucy had told him. "The question, now, I suppose, is whether or not Bob Dexter knew about it? Could he have found out? They certainly wouldn't have told him, would they?"

"He *did* know," Lucy confirmed with satisfaction. "They told him that afternoon, the day he was murdered. Apparently he got poor Miss Vernon so upset with his questions about the monstrance that, when he mentioned Becca, she just blurted it out. Bob Dexter knew, all right."

"Ah." David leaned forward again. "Then the real wonder is, Lucy love, that Bob Dexter didn't kill Stephen Thorncroft!"

Before they left the offices, Lucy took advantage of the opportunity to have a few words with Karen.

As before, the girl appeared terrified, but Lucy's calm and matter-of-fact manner soon reassured her. "Karen," she said, "I just want to ask you one question."

"All right, Miss Kingsley."

"You can call me Lucy," she smiled. " 'Miss Kingsley' makes me feel very old!"

The girl returned her smile tentatively. "All right . . . Lucy."

"I know that Mr. Middleton-Brown has asked you whether

you saw any of your friends from BARC that night, or whether you saw the young priest, and you said that you didn't. What I want to ask you, Karen, is this: did you see *anyone at all* near the church, or coming out of the church, that night? Think carefully, Karen—it could be very important."

"Why . . . yes," the young girl replied. "I saw two old women. One was short, and the other one was taller. They came out of the church, and got onto their bicycles and rode off. They didn't see me."

They opened a bottle of champagne with their dinner that night, feeling that at last they were beginning to make progress. "I almost forgot," David said when they were halfway through the meal. "John Spring came by this afternoon with the forensics report. Hence the smell of the distillery in my office. I had to bribe him with a bottle of whisky, and I thought he was going to sit there and drink the whole thing. I had a hell of a time getting rid of him."

"He must have left just before I arrived."

"Yes."

Lucy's voice was teasing. "What a shame. I'd like to meet this paragon of manhood sometime. Or are you afraid that he'd sweep me off my feet?"

"Don't be ridiculous," said David stiffly, refusing to meet her eyes.

She had evidently struck a raw nerve, she realized with a pang—he must still be quite insecure about their relationship. "Let's have a look, then," she urged, sensibly changing the subject. "At the forensics report."

"Not now. Surely it can wait till later?" he said plaintively. "Or tomorrow? I fancied an early night tonight. The champagne makes me . . ."

"Not a chance, darling." She was unyielding, and after a moment he went and got it from his briefcase, flipping it across the table to her.

She studied it in silence for some minutes, turning the pages over one by one and digesting the official prose. "Have you looked at this?" she asked at last.

"No, I didn't have a chance to. He left right before you got back from Monkey Puzzle Cottage."

"So you don't know what it says."

He could sense her excitement, and he knew her well enough to know that there must be good basis for that excitement. "Is there something interesting? Something that will help our case?"

Lucy looked at him over the papers, smiling. "I'm not a lawyer, and I don't pretend to understand all this gobbledegook. It's clear that Stephen's prints were on the murder weapon, just like John Spring told you. But unless I'm very much mistaken, this indicates that they were *on the same end* as Bob Dexter's blood! Tell me, will you, how he managed that one?"

Much later, after they'd talked about it all for hours, after they'd made love, just as they were about to fall asleep, David whispered in Lucy's ear. "Did I ever tell you, Lucy?"

"What's that, darling?" she murmured sleepily.

"Did I ever tell you that I hate monkey puzzle trees?"

# Chapter 41

*O deliver me, for I am helpless and poor: and my heart is wounded within me.*

*Psalm 109:21*

For the second day in a row, Lucy parked David's car outside Monkey Puzzle Cottage, hoping that the women would be at home and would be willing to see her. After Karen's revelation yesterday, she thought that they had a question or two to answer.

She'd got on well with the women on the previous day, and it had been comparatively easy to obtain the information she'd sought. But this, she thought, might be a little more difficult. They'd obviously been deliberately concealing their visit to the church on the evening of Dexter's murder. What did they have to hide? Were they protecting someone else, or was it something altogether more sinister?

Lucy had endeared herself to them on her first visit by admiring their handiwork: their lovingly created prayer cards. They were probably working on them now, as they had been yesterday when she came; the curtains in the room to the right of the front door twitched as she pulled up. By the time she got to the back door, they were waiting for her.

"I'm so sorry to bother you again," she apologized with her sweetest smile. "But there's something else I need to ask you about."

"Come in, Miss Kingsley." Alice beckoned her inside with something only just approaching warmth. She and Gwen had agreed, after Lucy's visit yesterday, that Miss Kingsley really was quite a superior sort of young woman—after all, she'd told them that her father was a priest!—and she seemed quite well suited to that nice Mr. Middleton-Brown. But two visits in as many days was perhaps a little excessive. Then Lucy handed Alice a bunch of flowers, and Alice warmed to her.

Babs and Nell sniffed around Lucy's feet; she bent to scratch their ears and murmur a friendly greeting. Alice unbent a bit more. "Come into the sitting room. Or would you like to come into the kitchen, perhaps? We were just going to have our morning coffee."

"The kitchen would be lovely," Lucy agreed. It was cosy in the kitchen—much more conducive to the sort of conversation she had in mind than the chilly, sterile sitting room.

Efficiently, Alice made the coffee while Gwen took a stab at arranging the flowers in a vase. Lucy sat down at the table. "I was wondering," she said, "if I might buy some of your prayer cards from you, to take back to my church in London. The quality of them is so professional—I think they'd go down a treat at St. Anne's."

Gwen whirled around. "Oh! That would be wonderful, wouldn't it, Alice?"

Alice smiled, showing her teeth. "I believe that could be arranged, Miss Kingsley."

"Do you think that your father's church might like some of them, too?" Gwen suggested somewhat daringly, suddenly envisioning a whole industry developing.

Lucy didn't bother to explain that her father had recently left the parish ministry for a cathedral canonry. "Oh, yes, I should think so. That is, if you can spare them. I know how much time goes into them. Surely you can't produce that many."

"Well, we *are* retired," Alice explained. "We have a lot of time to devote to them. Especially since . . . well, things may change now, of course, but there wasn't much for us to do at St. Mary's when Father Dexter was there."

That gave Lucy an opening. As Alice handed her a cup of coffee, she said hesitantly, "Actually, I need to ask you a question about Father Dexter. You were so kind to talk to me yesterday. But something has come up since I talked to you."

Alice looked at her sharply. "Yes, Miss Kingsley?"

"You know that I've been helping Mr. Middleton-Brown with his case by talking to people," she began diffidently. Alice nodded with impatience. "Well, yesterday afternoon I spoke to . . . someone . . . who'd been near the church on the night of Father Dexter's murder. She said that she'd seen two women come out of the church, and go off on bicycles." She furrowed her brow, looking puzzled. "From the description, they sounded like you. But I don't understand—you didn't go to the church that night, did you?"

Alice made a hissing noise as Gwen gasped; they looked at each other and for a long moment there was silence. Lucy was conscious of the clock ticking.

"Have you . . . mentioned this to anyone else?" Alice asked at last. "The police?"

"No. Only Mr. Middleton-Brown."

"Yes," said Alice firmly, making up her mind. "Yes, we were there." Gwen uttered a strangled sigh.

Lucy looked back and forth between them but said nothing. After a moment Alice continued. "We didn't say anything to the police because we didn't think it was important. He was alive when we got there, up on the ladder. He was still alive when we left him, of course."

"But . . . why?" Lucy asked. "Why did you go there?"

Gwen sighed again. "Elayne," she moaned. "Dear Elayne."

"Elayne was so upset when she left us," Alice explained. "She'd decided to tell him that she was going to leave him."

"Of course," Gwen exulted, "she didn't have to leave him, did she? And now she can go to the National Pilgrimage with us, and—"

"Don't be so silly, Gwen," Alice snapped. She turned back to Lucy. "We were worried about Elayne. Worried that he'd bully her, make her change her mind. So we decided to go and give her some moral support when she talked to him. When we got to the church, though, she'd already come and gone. She'd taken the shortcut across the fields, walking, and we had to go the long way on our bikes, so we missed her."

"What did he say to you?"

"He just told us to go away. He said that his family affairs were none of our business, and that we were to stay away from Elayne."

"So we went," Gwen added. "He was up on the ladder, prying away at the statue with that bar, and he wouldn't even come down to talk to us."

"And you went straight home? You didn't go looking for Elayne?" Lucy asked.

"Yes," said Gwen.

"No," said Alice. They looked at each other. "That is," Alice amplified, "yes, we went straight home. No, we didn't go looking for Elayne." She paused. "We thought that she'd probably gone home to talk to Becca about . . . you know. We didn't want to bother her then."

Lucy frowned as she realized the implications of what Alice had just said. "She went home to talk to Becca? Did Elayne know about Becca?"

Again Alice and Gwen exchanged glances. "Yes," said Alice. "Yes, Elayne knew. We had to tell her, you see. Because Gwen," she shot her a venomous look, "had told *him*. We didn't know *what* he'd do to Becca. We thought her mother ought to know, in case she had to protect her from *him*."

"We didn't approve of what Becca had done, of course," Gwen added self-righteously. "There are no excuses for that kind of wanton behavior. But her father—well, he'd already proved that he was a violent man, when he hit Elayne that day. The *beast*," she frowned. "The *brute*. We didn't want him to *hurt* Becca."

"Then why did you tell him?" Alice rounded on her sharply. Gwen subsided into contrite silence.

"And how did Elayne take it when you told her about Becca and Father Stephen?" Lucy wanted to know.

"Elayne thought that it was Toby Gates," Gwen muttered.

Alice ignored her and gave Lucy a long, appraising look. Once again she made up her mind. "Miss Kingsley," she said slowly, "I don't know why you and Mr. Middleton-Brown think that it was Father Stephen that Becca . . . lured into the sins of the flesh. That she corrupted on our sofa. We certainly never told you that. We never told anyone who it was—it was far too upsetting." She sighed. "It wasn't Father Stephen, Miss Kingsley. Becca told us. It was our own dear Father Mark."

It was about time for her to have a little chat with Becca Dexter, Lucy decided when she was finally able to get away from Monkey Puzzle Cottage. She tried to sort out the implications of what she'd learned as she drove to the vicarage. Becca had apparently lied to *everyone*. Why?

Elayne opened the door with a welcoming smile. "Lucy! What a nice surprise! Come in. I was just about to make myself a sandwich for lunch. You can join me—Becca's out."

"Becca's out?" Lucy tried to conceal her disappointment as she followed Elayne to the kitchen.

"She went out a short time ago. I don't know when she'll be back."

Elayne seemed genuinely pleased to see her. She must be a very lonely person, Lucy thought with compassion, and not just since her husband's death. Had she ever really had anyone to confide in? No wonder she'd so appreciated the attentions of the women at Monkey Puzzle Cottage, and had so opened up to Lucy herself.

Getting the bread out of the bin, Elayne asked, "You're vegetarian, didn't you say? Is cheese all right? Cheese and pickle?"

"Fine, thanks," Lucy smiled, taking a seat. She watched as Elayne efficiently made the sandwiches and brought them to the table.

"How nice of you to drop by! What are you doing back in South Barsham? Is your solicitor-friend still making enquiries?"

"I've just been talking to Miss Barnes and Miss Vernon," Lucy replied carefully; she didn't want to say too much until she'd spoken to Becca. "Did you know that they'd followed you to the church . . . that night?" Lucy tried to be delicate when dealing with the subject of her husband's murder; in spite of everything she must have some unresolved feelings about him.

"The night that Bob died?" Elayne said. "No, I didn't know that. How did you find out? Did they tell you?"

"Not at first. But someone saw them, and now they've admitted it. They wanted to back you up, it seems. In case there was trouble, or you lost your nerve."

Elayne smiled. "They really are dears, those two. They've been so supportive." She sighed. "I don't know what I'd do without them—I've never been very good at coping on my own."

"It looks to me like you're doing very well," Lucy said sincerely.

They both jumped as the front door slammed. "Becca?" said Elayne with concern.

In a moment she stood framed in the kitchen door, a tall young woman with cropped blond hair. She might have been pretty, Lucy surmised, but at the moment it was impossible to tell: her face was blotchy-red and swollen, and her eyes were overflowing with tears and smudged with mascara. She held a soggy tissue over her mouth; from behind it she choked, "Oh, Mummy!"

Elayne went to her quickly, leading the unresisting girl to sit at the table. For a moment she stood beside her daughter, stroking her hair comfortingly and making soothing noises while Becca sobbed painfully. Both seemed oblivious to the outsider in the kitchen; Lucy felt that perhaps the least conspicuous thing to do was to remain where she was.

"What is it, Becca, darling?" her mother said gently. "What's the matter?"

The girl raised her tear-stained face. "Oh, Mummy, I want to die! He doesn't love me! Mark doesn't love me!"

Elayne hid her surprise quite well. "Tell me, darling," she urged.

Gradually, in a gulping voice interrupted frequently with sobs, the story came out. Lucy, an eavesdropper, an interloper, sat quietly and listened to the whole sad tale. As Lucy related it later to her own lover, the girl had been inexperienced and innocent, kept so deliberately by her overprotective and possessive father. She'd met the young priest at Monkey Puzzle Cottage on her first visit there, right after their move to South Barsham: he always went there for tea on a Monday, it seemed. A romantic at heart, and very vulnerable, she'd fallen desperately in love with the ravishingly handsome young man, so different from her father in his beliefs, yet somehow like him in his strength of character. Their romance, conducted of necessity in secret, had taken the predictable course, from tentative kisses and timid embraces up to the ultimate consummation on the pink dralon sofa in Monkey Puzzle Cottage. The next step, particularly for a conventional girl like Becca Dexter, had to be marriage. Didn't it? But today, when she'd timidly suggested marriage to her lover, he had laughed. Laughed!

He'd said, Becca related broken-heartedly, that he'd never marry her. She was a sweet girl, and all that, but that was as far as it went. He didn't love her, never had loved her.

When the tale had been told, and the girl sobbed on in her mother's arms, Lucy found that her fists were clenched in anger. She, too, wanted to reach out and stroke the cropped silver-gilt head, to tell her that it didn't matter, that no man was worth the pain she'd suffered.

Elayne and Becca had both accepted Lucy's presence as somehow natural, sensing perhaps her deep sympathy, and so she stayed on. After the initial storm was over, Elayne put the kettle on, and they sat around the table nursing mugs of strong tea.

"I just wish you'd told me sooner, Becca," Elayne said after a while. "Not that I could have done anything, but I wish you'd trusted me with the truth. That night when I came back here, after Alice and Gwen had told me—You never said that it was Mark Judd. You let me think that it was . . . someone else."

Becca squeezed her mother's hand; since Bob Dexter's death they had become much closer than they'd ever been before. "I couldn't, Mummy. Surely you see that. Not when I thought . . ." She caught on a sob.

"There, there, lovey. You thought that I'd tell your father. And he . . ." Elayne stopped at the enormity of the thought. "Your father," she repeated. "Who did your father think that it was?"

"Oh, Mummy, I feel so terrible about this," she whispered. "I lied to Daddy. I told him . . . I told him that it was Stephen Thorncroft! I had to! He would have killed me if I hadn't told him something, and I was so afraid for Mark—so afraid that Daddy would hurt him. I didn't know that Stephen would go to the church that night. I don't know what Daddy said to him, what he said to Daddy. All I know is that Daddy's dead, and somehow it's my fault. Oh, Mummy—I've been so frightened!"

Lucy stared at her, appalled. Without volition, she said, "You told your father that Stephen Thorncroft was your lover?"

Becca turned to her. "Yes," she whispered. "And then . . . then when Daddy . . . died—I didn't know what to do."

"Even when Stephen was arrested . . ."

"It was too late then," Becca cried, anguished. "It would have only looked worse for him if I'd told the police what I'd told Daddy!"

"Yes, but if you'd told them the truth . . ."

"I couldn't have told them the truth!" she sobbed. "What if Mark . . . ?"

"You thought that Mark might be involved in your father's death," Lucy surmised; her voice was compassionate.

The girl nodded miserably. "But he couldn't have been," she said after a moment. "I know that now. Daddy didn't know that we . . . were lovers. And I found out something else when I was going through Daddy's files last week. Daddy was trying to help Mark find a new job, in London—Pimlico, I think. He'd written some letters on Mark's behalf, using his London contacts. Daddy liked Mark, was trying to help him. There was no reason . . . why Mark . . ." At the thought of the young man, so beloved but no longer hers, Becca dissolved in tears again.

Later, of course, back in Wymondham, Lucy told David all about it. Although it was in many ways a breakthrough in the case, she was very subdued, displaying none of the excitement that she'd shown the day before, and seemed withdrawn into her own thoughts.

David put his arms around her. "You really feel sorry for her, don't you?" he said gently. He felt her resistance.

"Yes. I can't believe the way he treated her. Seducing her,

and then . . . It happens all the time, I know, but . . ." Lucy's voice was bitter; she pulled away from David. "The bastard!"

"Steady on, Lucy! It's not my fault! I'm not Mark Judd!"

"No, but you're a man," she said flatly.

He looked at her, feeling absolutely helpless in the face of such logic. "I'm sorry."

With a rush of tenderness, she realized how unfair she was being, and flung herself into his arms.

# Chapter 42

*Yea, even mine own familiar friend, whom I trusted: who did also eat of my bread, hath laid great wait for me.*

*Psalm 41:9*

It was as well, thought David, that he had arranged to see his client at Norwich Prison on Wednesday. He had a few matters to discuss with him.

He found Stephen looking even more wan and colorless than the week before. Prison life was no picnic, David knew, but the conditions for a prisoner on remand were luxurious in comparison with what would be in store for the young man if he were actually convicted of murder.

"What's new?" Stephen greeted him with a peaky smile.

David sat down; he wasn't really in the mood for smiling, or for small talk. "Quite a lot, actually." He folded his hands on the table in front of him. "Are you ready to start telling me the truth for a change?"

"What about?" Stephen frowned defensively.

"Well, for one thing, about how the hell your fingerprints got on the murder weapon! A little detail that you hadn't bothered to mention to me!"

Stephen squirmed in his chair. "Oh, that."

"Yes, that." David glowered furiously.

"Well . . ." Stephen hesitated, then in a rush the story came out. "I told you that we'd quarreled about Becca. I went to the church to try to get him to change his mind about destroying the statue—I'd managed to get some money together by passing the hat round amongst the priests at Walsingham, and I wanted to offer it to him. When he saw me, he went mad—I've never seen anyone so angry. He said that I . . . that I'd dishonored his daughter. He said that he'd kill me for what I'd done to her. He came down off the ladder, swinging that iron bar at me." He looked earnestly at David. "I believe he would have killed me, too. But I grabbed the end of the bar, and pulled it out of his hands. It caught him off balance, and he fell. I threw the bar away, to the side, and then I left. And that is the truth," he concluded emphatically.

David met his eyes. "And you didn't get any help for him?"

"He wasn't badly hurt—I'm convinced of that. Just a bit stunned—had the breath knocked out of him, that's all. At that point I just wanted to get away. He would have killed me," he repeated, his gray eyes troubled. "Of course I feel badly about it. You don't have to reproach me. I've reproached myself every hour of every day since it happened. I should have gone for help. Perhaps he'd be alive today if I had. I'll always have that on my conscience."

For a moment David was silent. It spoke well for the young priest that he was more concerned about his spiritual culpability than he was about the incriminating nature of the evidence against him. "The police thought that the fingerprints, and the fact that you wouldn't tell them how they'd got on the murder weapon, was rather damning evidence against you," he said at last. "I must tell you, though, that I don't think it will stand up in court." Stephen raised his head, and David went on, "You see, I've had a copy of the forensic report. And it shows that your prints are on the same end of the iron bar as Dexter's blood."

Stephen was quick to grasp the implication. "I see. Are there any prints on the other end, then?" For a moment he was almost animated.

David regarded him shrewdly. "That's the other interesting thing about it. There aren't any other prints, except a few smudgy ones of Dexter's on the same end as yours. That means that . . . whoever . . . hit him with that bar wiped it clean afterwards—at least the end that they'd held."

"I see," repeated Stephen, thoughtfully.

"The other thing that I have to tell you is that Lucy has been talking to Becca Dexter. She's learned a few things that I find extremely interesting."

"Oh?" Stephen's face was a picture: wariness at betraying too much struggled with a strong desire to hear something—anything—about his beloved. The wariness prevailed; he said no more.

"You and Becca were never lovers," David stated quietly.

The young man looked resolutely at his folded hands; his knuckles were white. "No."

David slammed his fist down on the table. "Then why the bloody hell did you tell me that you were?"

Stephen sighed. "I didn't . . . exactly . . . tell you that we were. I only let you think it. I only said that Dexter thought . . . that that was why . . ."

"But why? Why not tell me the truth?" he demanded with controlled fury. "As I keep saying, I'm trying to help you! And you continue to lie to me, to conceal the truth!"

"Because I love her!" the priest said with quiet passion. "Don't you understand? I love her! If she'd told him that . . . that we were lovers, she must have had a good reason. Don't you see? I didn't tell him that it wasn't true, and I didn't tell you, because she wouldn't have wanted me to!" He fixed David with his gray eyes, pleading for understanding. "Of course it wasn't true. I never laid a finger on Becca. I've scarcely ever even spoken to her—I've worshiped her from afar. I've adored her since the moment I laid eyes on her. Don't you see?"

"So you were protecting her," David said. "From what, I wonder? Did you know—or suspect—that she was involved somehow in her father's death?"

"Of course not!" Stephen rapped out too quickly.

"Or was it her real lover, your friend Mark Judd, that you were protecting?"

Stephen gasped; in an instant all the residual color drained from his face. When he tried to speak, his voice came out in a nearly soundless croak. "What?"

He didn't know, realized David with a real stirring of compassion. Stephen didn't know about Becca and Mark. Poor chap. He softened his voice. "Becca told Lucy everything. She and Mark had . . . made love . . . at Monkey Puzzle Cottage, while the ladies were away. But they found out, and told Bob Dexter. She told her father that it was you, just to buy herself a little time, and to protect Mark." He added, "She felt very badly that you'd been implicated. But at first she was too frightened to speak out, and when you were arrested she thought it was too late to tell the truth—that it would have looked even worse for you if she had."

David wasn't sure whether Stephen had even heard him. The young man blinked rapidly behind his spectacles, as though he were fighting back tears, and his tongue moistened lips that had gone suddenly dry. "Mark," he said.

"You didn't know." It was more a statement than a question.

Slowly, Stephen shook his head. "No, I didn't know." His voice came out in an anguished whisper. "Of course I didn't know." He clenched his fists. "I should have, I suppose. He hinted about it, but I ignored him—I didn't want to know. Couldn't have borne it." He closed his eyes. "Once or twice—there were long blond hairs on his cassock. They could only have been Becca's. But . . . oh, Becca!" he lamented. David said nothing; after a moment he sensed a glint of anger joining the shock and sorrow in the young priest's demeanor. "Why?" Stephen demanded. "Why did Mark do it? When he knew how much I loved her? He was my friend . . ." Stephen Thorncroft buried his head in his hands.

"But did you just leave it at that?" Lucy queried a few hours later. "Didn't you tell him that Mark had . . . dumped her?"

David put an arm around her and drew her head on to his shoulder. "I wasn't sure what to do," he admitted. "Whether he'd be happier—or at least less miserable—to think that Becca was happy. After all, he's gone to great lengths to protect her, to safeguard her happiness. I thought that perhaps he'd feel even worse if he knew that it was all for nothing, that *her* heart was broken as well."

"So what did you do?"

"In the end I told him. Of course it hurt him to think of Becca suffering. But, Lucy, I think—I think that it gave him a bit of hope. Something to hold on to. A reason to fight. I think it was the right thing to do."

"I think so, too." He stroked her hair, and for a moment they were both silent, thinking of the wretched young man in Norwich Prison that night. "So," said Lucy after a while, "where do we go from here?"

"I'm not sure," David admitted.

"Stephen didn't kill Bob Dexter," Lucy stated.

"No."

"But someone did."

"Yes . . ."

"Who could have done it, darling?"

David spoke slowly, choosing his words with care. "It's not up to you to find that out, Lucy. It's not even up to me. My job ends with demonstrating Stephen Thorncroft's innocence. I think that at the next remand hearing, or at least by the committal, I'll be able to present enough evidence to have him released. The police . . ."

"I suppose you think your dim friend Sergeant Spring is going to find out!"

She had a point, thought David. His energies did seem to be directed largely elsewhere. "Well . . ."

She pulled away from him in excitement. "Get me some paper, David, and a pencil!"

He located his briefcase and complied quizzically. In a moment Lucy had settled down at the table, wielding the pencil with an artist's competence. "We're going to reconstruct what happened that day," she explained. "First of all, Dexter had a series of rows. Stephen was first?"

"Must have been," David confirmed. "He was at the vicarage just after breakfast."

Lucy made some notes, writing Stephen's name at the top of the page. "And then?"

He considered. "As far as we know, it was a quiet morning after that. BARC must have been next, in the afternoon."

"Right. BARC. Maggie, Rhys, and Bleddyn. From there Dexter went straight to the church, where he quarreled with Elayne?"

"Yes, that's right. Then he drove around, and ended up at Monkey Puzzle Cottage. That must have been about tea-time."

She scribbled away. "And he wouldn't have wasted any time after that getting back to the vicarage, to confront Becca."

"I should have thought it was a wonder he didn't run down someone on the road in his haste," David agreed.

"Then what?" she asked, lifting the pencil.

"I'm not sure," he said slowly.

"Well, when did he go to the church? To take the statue down?"

David frowned. "It must have been right after that."

Lucy looked pensive. "Well, let's think about who went to

the church, and when. Perhaps that will clarify things. Do we
know what time Bob Dexter died?"

David consulted his papers. "Some time between seven and
ten, the autopsy said. He'd had a cup of tea at Monkey Puzzle
Cottage, and the stomach contents . . ."

She wrinkled her nose. "That's not very helpful. That
doesn't exclude anyone, does it?"

"No, and it doesn't help that everyone is so indefinite about
times."

"Well, what *do* we know?" Lucy chewed on the pencil
rubber. "We know that Stephen left Bob Dexter alive some
time after seven." She turned over the page and made some
notes. "And that Maggie Harrison and the other BARC members saw Stephen leave the church."

"We know that Karen saw Miss Barnes and Miss Vernon
leaving the church, earlier than that," David contributed.
"And that Elayne had been there even earlier."

Lucy scribbled quickly, then regarded her notes. "So, the
chronology looks like this: Elayne was there first, followed
shortly by Miss Barnes and Miss Vernon."

"And then Stephen."

"And then . . ." Lucy lifted her eyes and regarded him
gravely. "And then, someone else."

"But who?"

Abstractedly she gnawed on the pencil. "Everyone agrees
that Becca didn't go to the church that night," she offered.

"But can we be sure of that?" David wanted to know.

"Not if her mother was prepared to lie for her. And I'm not
so sure that she wouldn't." She frowned. "How about Mark
Judd?"

David looked through the stack of police reports. "No indication that he was anywhere in the vicinity that evening,
apparently."

"But is there any proof that he wasn't? Does he have an
alibi?"

"Slow down, Lucy love. Mark Judd doesn't need an alibi—
he didn't have any motive, if he was expecting Dexter to help
him get a plum job in London. Especially since Dexter didn't
have a clue about him and Becca."

"Too bad," said Lucy. "After what he did to Becca, it would
have been nice . . ."

David laughed. "I agree that he's a bastard, Lucy, but that
doesn't make him a murderer!"

"No, I suppose not," she admitted with regret. "But who
. . . unless one of the BARC people went into the church."
She grabbed David's arm in mounting excitement. "Listen!
We only have Fiona's word that they didn't go in!"

"Well, we know that she and Rhys didn't. They weren't
even at the church."

"No, they can give each other a perfect alibi," she smiled.
"But what about Maggie? She might have left the men. She
might have gone in on her own, as soon as Stephen left. If she
saw Dexter lying there, the man who'd hurt Bleddyn, and the
iron bar right to hand . . ."

"Possible," David admitted. "We could certainly look into
that."

"Or," Lucy mused, twisting a curl around her finger, "or,
we could be on completely the wrong track. It could be someone else altogether. Someone we don't even know about. Someone . . ." A name nagged at the corner of her mind, a name
mentioned by someone within the last day or two. An unfamiliar name, but a name with some significance . . . If only she
could remember.

She sat up suddenly. "Walsingham!" she said.

"Walsingham?"

"Next Monday is the National Pilgrimage!"

"Is it?" David asked. "Yes, I suppose you're right—it's the
bank holiday, isn't it?"

"I think," she said, "that the answer lies at Walsingham.
They'll all be there, don't you see?"

"What do you mean?"

She ticked them off on her fingers with excitement. "Elayne is going with Miss Barnes and Miss Vernon. And all of the BARC people—Fiona told me that they were going, presumably to hand out their information. So that's Rhys, Fiona, Maggie, Karen, Nicholas, and the hippy bloke. And Mark Judd, certainly."

"Becca?"

"Probably not," she admitted. "Although she's gone in other years, with the protesters. That's another group—all of Bob Dexter's Evangelical friends. They'll all be there."

"Without Bob Dexter."

"Yes. And there's one other person who won't be there."

"Stephen Thorncroft," David supplied.

Lucy nodded thoughtfully. "If there's one thing that's clear in my mind, David, it's that Walsingham is the place to be this weekend. And I intend to be there!"

# Chapter 43

*Lord, remember David: and all his trouble . . .*

*Psalm 132:1*

David sat in the corner of the pub on Friday evening, staring glumly into his drink. John Spring was late, very late—David was already on his second whisky.

He was thinking miserably about Lucy, and about their discussion on Wednesday night. In vain he'd tried to persuade her that Walsingham was absolutely the last place on earth that any sane person would want to be on National Pilgrimage weekend. He personally tried to avoid Walsingham whenever possible, but to go this weekend would be insanity. Lucy, though, was convinced that only at Walsingham would they learn who had killed Bob Dexter, and she'd been unshakably determined to go. Worse yet, she wanted to go for the whole weekend. Wasting no time, that very evening she'd rung up Owen Osborne, who was in some way involved in the administration of the Shrine. Needless to say, the pilgrim hospice was completely booked for the weekend—David had of course told her that it would be. But that blasted Osborne had been kindly disposed toward her, in spite of the fact that she was a woman, and had managed to pull a few strings and book her into the unused half of a twin room; she would be sharing with a single lady from a parish pilgrimage party. There would be no room for David, even if he'd been inclined to go. What's more, she had left for London early the next morning, to get herself sorted out before the weekend, she said. She'd been away from home for more than a week already, and needed to see to a few things.

So on this Friday night David was alone, without much more than a trace of his usual self-deprecating good humor, and feeling extremely sorry for himself. He took a sip of his drink and sighed. Why was she being so stubborn? Why wouldn't she listen to him?

John Spring bounded in with a grin on his face. "Sorry I'm late, mate! I got detained, if you know what I mean!" he winked broadly; David was very much afraid that he knew exactly what he meant, and hoped that he'd be spared the details.

"Can I get you a drink?" he asked quickly.

"Ta. A pint of the usual." Spring craned his neck with interest as David went to the bar for the beer, but to his disappointment the pretty, compliant barmaid was nowhere in sight. In her place, pulling his pint, was a thick-set, muscular man with a tattoo. Bad luck. Still, he thought, ever philosophical about such things, he couldn't complain, not after what had just happened to detain him.

David returned with the beer and they chatted inconsequentially for a while. He was, after all, not spared the details of Spring's latest amorous adventure, or indeed of several others within what seemed to David an astonishingly short space of time. When did the man find time to work, he wondered? How had he ever made sergeant?

After a while he switched off, merely making appropriate noises at what he judged were the proper points in the narrative. He couldn't bear to think about sex. Not with Lucy in London, and him here. He looked at his watch surreptitiously.

Nearly half-past nine. On an ordinary Friday night, he thought, they'd be finished eating by now. Maybe even finished with the washing-up. Maybe even in bed. Damn Walsingham, he thought. Damn and blast it.

For a moment he wasn't sure whether he'd imagined it, whether it was a reflection of his own thoughts. Through the fog of his lugubrious musings, he thought that John Spring had mentioned Walsingham. "What did you say?"

"I said that it was going to be a bad weekend, with all that lot at Walsingham." Spring made a rueful face. "Just my luck to pull duty."

"Duty?" David asked, his interest caught at last. "What sort of duty?"

"You know," Spring explained patiently. "It's this National Pilgrimage lark. Happens every year, this time. But the last few years it's been nasty, with all those protesters getting hot under the collar."

"Nasty?"

"They shout around a lot, and wave their Bibles. We're out in force, of course, to keep it from getting any worse." He lowered his voice. "This year we've had a tip that it might get violent. As I said, just my luck to be on duty this weekend. I'll be there all three days, just to keep an eye on things." Spring laughed, looking at his nearly empty glass. "Not that there's much to keep an eye on, mind you, Dave," he added. "Not as far as women go, anyway. The Anglo-Catholics are all damned ugly, and the Evangelicals are even worse—all those miserable holy women! I tell you, Dave, a pretty woman would stand out a mile in that crowd!"

# Chapter 44

*Thy statutes have been my songs: in the house of my pilgrimage.*
*Psalm 119:54*

It was nearly two hours from Liverpool Street to Norwich by train, so Lucy must have had quite an early start from home to be arriving at 11:25, David thought as he waited for her on the platform. When he'd been so upset about her going to Walsingham, on the Wednesday night, she'd declared her intention to get there, if necessary, without his help—she was perfectly capable, she'd said, of taking a coach from Norwich to Walsingham. But that was out of the question, as far as he was concerned; he would collect her at the station and drive her to Walsingham, he'd insisted. After all, this would be his only opportunity to see her this weekend. For he was most assuredly not going to Walsingham for the National Pilgrimage on Monday. He'd been to the National Pilgrimage once in his life, just to see what it was like, and that was one time too many.

He was so glad to see her, looking springlike in a primrose-yellow flowered dress, that he smiled in spite of himself, greeting her with a decidedly unplatonic kiss. Then he took her case and steered her toward the exit. "Good trip?"

"All right."

"I missed you, Lucy."

"So I gathered." The corners of her mouth turned up.

"Did you miss me?" he fished.

"Of course." But he was not reassured.

They got to the car and, once inside, he kissed her again. Someone who was prowling the short-term car park looking for a space honked his horn impatiently. "Oh, all right," David muttered, putting on his seat belt and turning the ignition key. "You're sure about this, Lucy?" he asked. "You're still determined to go to Walsingham? You won't come home with me instead?"

She shook her head with regret. "Darling, you know I'd love to. But this is frightfully important. I'm sure that the answer is there, and this may be the only way to find it."

"Won't you even come home for a coffee?"

Lucy laughed. "You know as well as I do where we'd end up if we did that. I'd like a coffee, but I think it would be safer to stop somewhere along the way, don't you?"

They arrived in Walsingham some time after twelve. Already, though the National Pilgrimage was two days away, the narrow streets were congested with cars and people. "We should have had lunch before we got here," David said, threading the car through the bunches of pilgrims. "Everything is bound to be crowded."

"I'm sure we'll manage," Lucy assured him. And indeed, the tiny village was well provided with tea shops and pubs, all for the convenience of the pilgrims. They had a sandwich at a little cafe across from the Shrine church before getting Lucy checked into her room at the hospice.

To David's undisguised amusement, all of the rooms in the hospice were identified not only by number but by name; each of the names referred to some attribute of Our Lady. He was even more amused to discover that Lucy had been booked into

"Our Lady of Purity," and that it was situated next to the communal loo.

The room was strictly utilitarian, with two narrow beds, each with a small bedside table and lamp, one chest of drawers, and a washbasin. On the wall above the chest was a garishly colored print of the Sacred Heart of Mary, and crucifixes hung over the beds. The window overlooked the Shrine gardens. David shook his head in mock despair. "So this," he said dramatically, "is what you prefer to sleeping with me this weekend?"

Lucy put her case down on the nearest bed, smilingly ignoring the jibe. "Thank you for bringing me, David. Will you come to fetch me on Monday evening, or should I make other arrangements?"

"Of course I'll come."

"See you then, darling." She kissed him goodbye, and he was dismissed. But as he turned to leave, the door flew open and a young woman nearly ran into him as she bounced into the room, laden down with a quantity of distinctive red-white-and-blue Tesco plastic carrier bags, each stuffed to the brim.

"Oh, sorry!" she gasped. "I didn't know there was anyone here. Am I in the right place?" She looked at the two beds and the two people already in the room.

"I'm sure you are," Lucy assured her.

"I was just leaving," David said. "I'll see you on Monday, Lucy." He nodded to the young woman as he edged around her, and closed the door behind him.

"Bye, darling," Lucy called after him. She turned to the other inhabitant of the room with a smile. The girl seemed to fill the room with her bulk; she was not only overweight but quite oversized as well, and dressed in clothes that did little to counteract that image. Her brown hair, frizzed out around her head in an uncultured Afro, added to the impression of volume. She had a rather flat, broad face, plagued with residual spots but redeemed by an open and friendly smile; Lucy judged her age to be about twenty. "I'm Lucy Kingsley," she said.

"I'm Monica Cooper," the girl announced, dropping the carrier bags and thrusting out her hand. "I suppose we're going to be roommates."

"It looks that way," Lucy agreed. "I hope you don't mind."

"No, not at all! I'm glad for the company! I always like to have someone to talk to."

"But you're on your own?"

"Well, I'm part of a parish pilgrimage," the girl explained. "St. Wulstan, Basingstoke. But I was the odd one out. Mrs. Phillips is sharing with Miss Whittaker, thank goodness. And of course Father Clive is in with the other priests. We only brought one carload this year."

"I see."

"And you're on your own, Lucy?" the girl asked with friendly curiosity. "Not with a parish?"

"I live in London," she explained, "and I'm here on my own."

"Was that your husband?"

"No. We're not married."

"Your boyfriend, then?"

Lucy smiled. "I suppose you could say that."

"He's not a priest, is he?"

"No."

The girl shrugged philosophically. "Oh, well, you can't have everything. He looked nice, anyway."

"He *is* nice. And I wouldn't want him to be a priest. My father is a priest, and . . ."

"Golly! Your father's a priest!" Monica looked impressed. "Aren't you lucky!" She began rummaging through the carrier bags and dumping their contents into the top drawer of the chest. "Mind if I have the top drawer, Lucy? I'm too fat to bend down very far," she explained unself-consciously.

"That's fine."

"Is this your first time at the National Pilgrimage?"

"Yes. How about you?"

"Me, too. In fact, it's my first time at Walsingham! I'm jolly excited about it! Are you going out now? To look around?"

As nice as Monica was, Lucy didn't look forward to an afternoon of nonstop chatter. She wanted to be on her own, to drink in the atmosphere of this extraordinary place in solitude. "I'm not sure what I'm going to do," she evaded, then added, "Shall we meet for tea later?"

"Oh, yes! That would be smashing!"

Lucy went through the hospice into the Shrine gardens. It seemed an age since that first day that she'd been here—the day after she and David had become lovers, the day that they'd met Stephen. The day that David had asked her to marry him. Eight weeks, she reckoned quickly. Nearly two months. So much had happened in that time. And now it was nearly summer, the roses in bud twining greenly on the trellises and the elder bushes a froth of white blossom. A few pilgrims made their way around the perimeter, stopping to perform their devotions at the Stations of the Cross.

Lucy decided that it was, at long last, time to go into the Shrine church. She was glad to be alone, without even David, so that she could form her own impressions of the place free from his influence. That wasn't really possible, though, she realized as she stepped through the glass doors that led from the gardens into the Shrine church. His contemptuous description of "hacienda gothic" had stuck in her mind, and it made her smile at its aptness; the building was low-slung, featuring red brick pillars and pointed gothic arches relieved by stuccoed walls.

It really was a most extraordinary place, she thought. Her first impression was a jumble of sensations, for a jumble it truly was: a collection of minute chapels, each decorated in an entirely different style, stuck out at crazy angles everywhere she looked. She walked around looking at each one. An austerely furnished altar with a sumptuous fifteenth-century Flemish reredos jostled next to one that was almost flagrant in its campiness; yet another had the blue and white porcelain decor of an old-fashioned bathroom. Each chapel seemed to have a unique theme in addition to a unique style of decoration, she discovered: they commemorated the Mysteries of the rosary. At the back of the Shrine church she marveled at the Chapel of the Ascension, where a pair of brightly painted plaster feet, gory with stigmata but trailing clouds of glory and gilt stars, hovered jauntily overhead. Turning another corner, she gasped at the sight of a plaster representation of Our Lady, transfixed to a pillar with a sword through her heart, arms outstretched in agony, but a look of rapture on her painted face. Nearby was the Holy Well, its gates now padlocked; examination of the little sign affixed to the gates revealed that sprinklings would take place daily at certain times. Lucy peered through the gates down the steps into the well; it seemed to her an almost sinister spot.

The high altar, Lucy remembered David telling her, had been designed by Sir Ninian Comper. It was resplendent with gold leaf, boasting six very tall candlesticks. Before she went into the Holy House, she paused at the bookstall to buy a pale green Pilgrim Manual, a postcard or two, and a small card that proclaimed, "A prayer was said for you at the Shrine of Our Lady of Walsingham." She'd give that to David on Monday, she decided with a little smile.

Built in the center of the Shrine church and dominating it was the actual Shrine, the replica of the Holy House. Lucy went through the narrow door, pausing momentarily as her eyes adjusted to the darkness.

Darkness wasn't quite accurate: rank upon rank of candles burned in blue and red glass holders. Their flickering imparted an air of unreality to the scene, as at least a dozen people—as many as could be comfortably accommodated in the small space—knelt at the feet of the ornate statue of Our Lady of Walsingham, murmuring their prayers.

A most extraordinary place. Lucy escaped into the sunshine of the garden, where she sat for a long time beneath a flowering pink horse-chestnut tree, watching people, browsing through the Pilgrim Manual, and enjoying the earthy smell of the grass after the rarefied incense-and-candlewax scent of the Shrine church.

Monica was waiting for her outside the Sue Ryder cafe at teatime, her round face suffused pink with excitement. "Lucy! Oh, Lucy!" she waved. "Here I am!"

The cafe was self-service; as they moved along with their trays, Monica gazed greedily at the array of homemade cakes. "I know I shouldn't," she wavered. "But . . . well, you only live once." She helped herself to a thick slab of chocolate cake, decorated with hundreds and thousands of dragées, then, after a fractional hesitation, added a fat currant scone to her tray. Somehow Lucy knew that she'd also take sugar in her tea.

She was right. They found an empty table and settled down; Monica poured out her tea and ladled sugar into it, nibbling a few stray crumbs of the cake with her fingers before tucking into the butter-slathered scone. "I'm going to start slimming after the weekend," she explained defensively. "So I may as well enjoy myself while I can."

Lucy wondered how many times that excuse had been used. "Have you enjoyed your afternoon?" she asked.

"Oh, yes!" Monica's eyes shone. "It's wonderful, isn't it? I've never seen so many priests in my life! Every place I look, there are cassocks and dog collars!"

"There's a priest with your parish party, you said?"

"Oh, yes—Father Clive. He's wonderful. He's not our parish priest, though. He has a regular job during the week. He's a chiropodist. You know—a foot doctor."

"And the others who are with you? What about them?"

Monica took a large bite of her scone before replying. "Mrs. Phillips and Miss Whittaker. Mrs. Phillips—well, she's a bit bossy. She used to be a nurse. She's a bit hard to take sometimes. Sort of a know-it-all."

"Is there a Mr. Phillips?"

"Yes, but she never lets him come along on these things. She likes to go off on her own, she says."

"And Miss Whittaker?"

"She's jolly old. She was a librarian, I think. Miss Whittaker—well," Monica explained frankly, "she just likes to go along for the ride. Wherever anyone is going, she signs up to go along. She never says much, but she's always there. I'm so glad I don't have to share a room with her. Or with Mrs. Phillips, either."

Lucy poured herself a second cup of tea. "Tell me about yourself, Monica."

With her customary ability to draw people out, combined with Monica's willingness to be drawn, Lucy soon knew Monica's life story. The girl was twenty—the same age as Becca Dexter, Lucy thought wryly—and had worked full time at the checkout of the local Tesco since she'd left school. Her parents were divorced, and she lived with her mother and her younger sister, a girl whom Monica described without envy as "much prettier than me, and thinner, too." Her family had never been churchgoers, but somehow within the last year Monica had discovered the local Anglican church, and had become involved with all the passion of a convert. This trip to Walsingham seemed to be a milestone in her young life, anticipated for months. "And it's everything I'd thought it would be!" she finished enthusiastically, cramming the last few chocolate crumbs into her mouth. "So, Lucy, I've told you about me. Now tell me about you. What do you do?"

"I'm an artist."

"Golly!" said Monica ingenuously. "Are you famous?"

Modest as ever, Lucy smiled. "No, not really."

"Well, if you're not now, I'm sure that you will be one day." Monica's face shone with sincerity.

Monica seemed to assume that Lucy was now an unofficial member of their parish party, and it was easier at this point for Lucy to go along with that than to fight it. She managed to avoid the Shrine Prayers at six o'clock, but at dinner on the Saturday night she met the other members of the group.

Characteristically, at least as far as Monica was concerned, they were the first to arrive in the refectory. Monica went straight to the table where they'd all agreed to meet. "You see," she said, "there's plenty of room for you at our table. It would be terrible for you to be on your own, when you could be with us." Sitting down, she speculated hopefully, "I wonder what's for dinner?"

Lucy was less hopeful, and thought longingly of her well-stocked kitchen, then of David, on his own. She was beginning to wonder if perhaps he hadn't been right after all about the futility of this exercise. What, to be honest, had she learned so far that could be of any possible use in discovering Bob Dexter's murderer?

Her self-doubts were interrupted by the arrival at the table of a woman who announced herself as Rose Phillips, and who regarded Lucy with uncomfortably intense scrutiny. "This is my roommate, Lucy Kingsley," Monica said.

Rose Phillips's smile was a mere formality that never reached her eyes, a token baring of her prominent teeth. She was a woman in her late sixties, with a strong, bony face, a high-bridged nose, and pale hooded eyes with tiny pupils which nevertheless missed very little. "Where are the others?" she demanded. "I haven't seen Father Clive since we arrived."

Monica craned her neck. "Miss Whittaker is coming now."

It took a long while for the woman to reach them, moving laboriously with her walking frame. She must have been well over eighty, Lucy estimated—Monica had said "jolly old." She looked as though the life had gradually drained out of her, leaving nothing but a tough, desiccated old shell behind; she was as small as Monica was large, and her face was as brown and wrinkled as a walnut, topped with sparse white hair. When she arrived, at long last, the introductions were repeated, and it was immediately evident that Miss Whittaker was extremely hard of hearing. "Tinsley?" she demanded loudly. "I knew a Tinsley once! Gladys Tinsley—I was at school with her! Any relation?"

Lucy shook her head. "Afraid not."

"Eh?"

"No, I'm afraid not," Lucy repeated, raising her voice.

"Well, never mind. I never liked Gladys Tinsley much anyway. Always one for the boys, was Gladys. I shouldn't doubt that she met a Bad End." With that statement, which had heads at other tables turning, Florence Whittaker sat down with a thump. "I'm ready for my dinner," she announced.

"We're waiting for Father Clive," Rose Phillips said into her ear.

"There he is!" exclaimed Monica. "Just coming in the door!"

In contrast to Miss Whittaker, Father Clive's movements were sprightly, and he was with them in a moment. "Good evening, ladies," he beamed genially, rubbing his hands together. "And who is this lovely stranger in our midst?"

"Lucy Kingsley, my roommate." Monica introduced her with pride, as though credit for Lucy's beauty were somehow due to her.

Father Clive gave a funny little half-bow. "How nice to have you with us, Miss?—Mrs?—Kingsley."

"Miss," she supplied.

"How extraordinary that one so beautiful should be unclaimed," he declared in an attempt at chivalry that was sincere if awkward. Lucy took it in the spirit in which it was meant, and smiled. "And I," he added, "am Father Clive Sparrow."

An apt name, Lucy thought—there was something bird-like about him, in his small, wiry frame and his lively way of moving, and even in the bright black eyes that regarded her beneath his graying crew cut. When he smiled, there was a large gap between his front teeth.

"Have you met Miss Tinsley?" Florence Whittaker boomed. "No relation to Gladys, though."

Father Clive sat down across from Lucy. "Monica tells me that you're a chiropodist," she offered as a conversational gambit.

"That's right! Monday till Friday, that is! During the week, I look after people's feet, and on Sunday I look after their souls. A small step, wouldn't you say?" He chuckled delightedly at his wit; Lucy had a sneaking suspicion that he'd used that one before.

During the meal, Lucy found that she wasn't required to say much. Although Miss Whittaker's contributions to the conversation were brief and loud, Father Clive had plenty to say. And Mrs. Phillips was more than a match for Monica in volubility, her conversation exhibiting a curious and seemingly incompatible combination of nosiness and self-absorption.

The food was even worse than Lucy had expected. On the whole, she thought, as a vegetarian, she had fared rather better than her companions: she, at least, was spared the unidentifiable, leathery meat smothered in glutinous gravy, and had instead a full plate of limply overcooked vegetables. What was David eating tonight? she wondered.

"Is there anyone who doesn't want their bread roll?" Monica asked hopefully, sopping up the gluey gravy with the last of her own roll.

Much later that night, lying in the dark before they went to sleep in their respective hard, narrow beds, Monica and Lucy talked for a while.

They'd been to Evening Devotions at 8:15, which Monica had found enthralling; to Lucy it was fascinating if bizarre. The candlelight procession around the Shrine church and grounds, following the statue of Our Lady of Walsingham, she had found unexpectedly moving, though she knew that she would never dare to admit it to David. They were so sincere, these pilgrims—dozens of them, clustered in their little groups, their faces ablaze in the candlelight with devotion to Our Lady. It should have been silent, though, she thought: the Pilgrim Hymn, with its thirty-seven verses, only detracted from the solemnity of the occasion. After the procession the service continued with Exposition of the Blessed Sacrament and concluded, quite late, with Benediction.

Seemingly, though, Monica was not ready to go to sleep. "Isn't this fun? Just like summer camp!" she enthused.

"Very nice, Monica." She thought of David.

As if reading her mind, Monica asked, "Where does your boyfriend live?"

"Not too far from here—near Norwich."

"Are things . . . serious . . . between you?"

"We don't have any plans to marry, if that's what you mean."

Monica hesitated, then pressed on. "I don't quite know how to ask you this, but don't you ever want to get married? You must have had plenty of chances."

Lucy was glad for the privacy of the dark. "I'm happy with things the way they are," she replied evasively.

"I'd like to get married," Monica said. "But I don't suppose I ever will."

"Oh, I'm sure . . ."

The girl rolled over with some difficulty on the narrow bed and squinted at Lucy in the dark. "There's this bloke, Tom Rigby, in the produce department at Tesco," she confided. "He keeps wanting me to go out with him."

"Well, why don't you?"

"Because he's not a priest. He doesn't even go to church!" Monica grimaced. "You see, Lucy," she continued reflectively, "I wouldn't want to marry anyone but a priest."

"A priest!" Lucy sat up in bed. "Monica, priests aren't superhuman beings, they're just men. Men in dog collars. Some of them may be a little better, or a little nicer, than other men, but not necessarily." She frowned, thinking of Mark Judd and the way he'd treated Becca Dexter. "And even the best of them can be sheer hell to live with. My father is the sweetest, kindest man on earth, but the life that my mother had to live as a clergyman's wife—well, I wouldn't marry a priest for all the money in the world," she declared.

"It would be worth it," Monica insisted. "I'm *sure* it would be worth it!"

Now was perhaps not the time, Lucy thought, to shatter the girl's illusions by explaining that the priests who proliferated around Walsingham were not likely to be very good candidates for marriage, not for her or for anyone else.

Long after the girl's breathing had become deep and regular, Lucy lay awake. Perhaps David *had* been right, she thought, and she shouldn't have come. She'd give it until tomorrow night, and if she hadn't discovered anything significant, she'd admit defeat, ring him up, and ask him to come for her.

She missed him, she admitted to herself. She would never admit to him, though, how much she had missed him the last two nights, after spending a whole week together. And tonight was even worse, here in this miserable excuse for a bed.

Had she been honest with Monica—with herself? *Was* she happy with things the way they were? Why couldn't she just grow up, and tell David she'd marry him? What, after all, would be so bad about being Mrs. Middleton-Brown? How much longer could she go on having her cake and eating it? How much longer did she *want* to?

# Chapter 45

*Who going through the vale of misery use it for a well: and the pools are filled with water.*

*Psalm 84:6*

On Sunday morning, Lucy awoke to a very odd sight. Jammed into the narrow space between the chest of drawers and the washbasin was an ironing board and the substantial bulk of Monica Cooper, struggling with yards of recalcitrant white cotton and a very tiny iron.

"What on earth . . . ?"

Monica looked up, smiling sheepishly. "Good morning, Lucy. Sorry if I woke you. I'm ironing Father Clive's alb—he's going to celebrate Mass for us this morning in the Shrine church."

"Why can't Father Clive iron his own alb?" Lucy thought it was a reasonable question, but Monica was aghast.

"But he's a priest!"

Lucy sat up in bed and hugged her knees. "I've got an idea—why don't you marry Father Clive?" she suggested humorously. She smiled to herself at the fanciful wedding portrait that materialized in her mind: Monica, moon-faced and enormous in a white gown, dwarfing her dapper groom, Father

Clive with his bristling salt-and-pepper crew cut that reminded Lucy of an improperly cleaned paintbrush.

"He's already married!" Monica exclaimed, even more scandalized. "He's got four children! One of them's as old as me!"

Lucy didn't feel that she could gracefully escape from attending the Mass—she was, after all, supposed to be a devout pilgrim—but after it was over she couldn't face the rest of the morning's program, the Stations of the Cross followed by Intercessions in the Holy House. She thought of the interesting-looking novel that she'd packed in her suitcase and as yet had not had the chance to begin; perhaps now was her opportunity. "I've got a bit of a headache," she only half-fibbed to Monica. "Perhaps I'll go back to the room and lie down for a while."

"Oh, you poor thing! Sometimes that happens to me, fasting before Mass," the girl sympathized. "Do you want something to eat? Have you got any paracetemol?"

"Yes, I've got some tablets, thanks. I'll just lie down now, and I'll see you at lunch."

At lunch, which was no more appetizing than last night's dinner had been, Rose Phillips lectured to them all about the history of Walsingham, with occasional humorous interjections from Father Clive. "Through the years, how many feet have trod these sacred streets?" he chuckled; he seemed to find feet an ever-rich source of humor and interest. Lucy fantasized whimsically that his favorite service of the year must be Maundy Thursday, with its ritual foot-washing ceremony.

Monica, uncharacteristically quiet, appeared almost feverish with suppressed excitement. "Are you all right?" Lucy asked in concern.

"I can't tell you now," the girl whispered conspiratorially. "I'll tell you later—when we're alone!" Her excitement, however, did nothing to affect her appetite, and she polished off Lucy's unwanted stodgy sweet in addition to her own.

They walked in the garden after lunch. "Monica, are you all right?" Lucy repeated.

The girl smiled shyly. "Oh, Lucy. I don't know how to tell you what's happened!"

"Something happened at the Stations of the Cross?" It seemed highly unlikely, but then Walsingham itself was highly unlikely.

"Well," Monica began, flopping down on the grass, "we were led around the Stations of the Cross by a priest—one of the Shrine priests. He was so spiritual, Lucy. He made it all come so much alive: the scourging, the nailing to the cross, everything! I've never heard anything like it!" She plucked a blade of grass and contemplated it as though it held the secrets of the universe, and when she turned her face at last to Lucy it was enraptured. "After it was over, I stayed behind to tell him how much it had meant to me. We talked for quite a while. Oh, Lucy! He was so nice! So gentle, so kind! And of course so spiritual! And handsome!" she added.

"I see." Again Lucy wondered if perhaps it would be kind to explain a few of the facts of life to this seemingly naive girl, but realized that it would probably be futile.

Monica smiled at Lucy, aglow with happiness. "The best part of all is—he asked me if I'd like to meet him tonight, at the Bull. For a drink. Lucy! I've got a date with a priest!"

Her dream come true. For the first time, a chill premonition sent a shiver up Lucy's spine. "What is he called?" she asked slowly. "This wonderful priest—what is his name?"

Puzzled, Monica replied. "His name is Father Mark. Father Mark Judd."

Lucy knew beyond a doubt that Monica wouldn't hear a word against Father Mark, and so she held her tongue. She tried to convince herself that she didn't need to worry—that by the end of tomorrow Monica would be back in Basingstoke, far removed from the considerable charms of Mark Judd. What, after all, could happen in one evening, in one day? They'd have a drink, perhaps flirt a bit, and that would be that. Her obvious adoration was fuel for his male ego, that was all—a way to pass one evening. But all of these rationalizations failed to banish the small kernel of fear that had lodged in Lucy's mind.

Monica had wanted to be alone, to pray in the Shrine before the sprinkling at the Holy Well at three. Lucy was curious about the sprinkling and had decided to take part, but for now she stayed on in the garden, watching the pilgrims, thinking her thoughts. She thought about Monica, and the look of awe on her plain face at the memory of Mark Judd. She thought about Becca Dexter, and the anguish that had been on her face just a few days ago, the day that Mark had dumped her. She knew, in her heart, that if she stayed in Walsingham another day, the anguish might well be on poor, vulnerable Monica's face also. She couldn't do anything to stop it, but she didn't have to stay around to watch it. After the sprinklings, she said to herself. After the sprinklings I'll ring David. I'll tell him to come this afternoon, and take me home with him. I was wrong, she thought. There are no answers at Walsingham. Only more questions.

Lucy had been half afraid that Mark Judd would be performing the sprinkling at the well, and was relieved to see that it was Owen Osborne who greeted the assembled party in the nave of the Shrine church. The old priest explained, in his mellifluous voice, what was going to happen, and led some prayers, then the pilgrims queued up at the steps down to the well. Lucy watched those ahead of her so that she would know what to do when her turn came. Each pilgrim was given a dipper of water to drink from, was signed with the cross on the forehead, and then had the water poured into cupped hands. Some applied the holy water to afflicted parts of their bodies, while others let it run through their hands. When her turn came, standing before Owen Osborne, Lucy did the latter.

When it was over she went in search of a telephone. It was in fact not easy to find one: apparently most of the pilgrims had more exalted aims than hers, and were not concerned with contacting the outside world. With a feeling of great relief she located one at last, and dialed David's number, suddenly almost breathless with anticipation. There was no reply. Lucy let it ring ten times, twenty times—she knew how he hated to answer the phone. Nothing.

Having made the decision to go, her disappointment now was extreme. Where could he be, on a Sunday afternoon? She'd just have to try again a bit later.

She wasn't up to the Procession of the Blessed Sacrament, she knew that. Perhaps a walk in the countryside would clear her head.

It was a small village, and it didn't take long to be out of it. The countryside here was gently rolling, and alive with May-time growth. The hawthorn was in full bloom, and the fields foamed white with cow-parsley. There was a small stream trickling clear over a bed of smooth stones; Lucy followed along its path for a while.

In a field she saw a van parked: a distinctive blue van, its side painted with the letters BARC. Lucy smiled; perhaps she'd go and have a chat with whoever was with the van. It would be a change, anyway, from the holy goings-on that she'd left behind her. She remembered, too, that there was a question she wanted to ask—a question for Nicholas, or Gary, or possibly even Maggie.

As she walked toward the van, Lucy saw that there were two people entwined together in the sunshine outside. She was not near enough to identify them—certainly not Fiona and Rhys, she thought, but a couple nonetheless, as revealed by their body language, even at a distance, and by the kisses they continued to exchange. It looked like a curly-haired young man and a tall, long-haired girl. Maggie? she thought; it seemed unlikely, but Lucy decided that it was possible. Surely not Maggie and Rhys? That would break Fiona's heart.

Absorbed in each other, they were still unaware of her as she drew near. Lucy felt embarrassed, a bit of a voyeur—obviously they were not expecting to be observed in this out-of-the-way corner of the Norfolk countryside. But she was relieved to see the young man wasn't Rhys—his curly hair was brown, not red, and his face was clean-shaven and unfamiliar to her. Then he saw her, and with a look of sheer panic tore away from his lover, and made a dash for the safety of the van.

The long-haired girl turned around and looked at Lucy with a puzzled frown. It was after all not a girl: it was Nicholas Fielding.

Totally disoriented, it took Lucy a moment to speak. "Nicholas!"

He was equally surprised. "Lucy Kingsley! Fancy seeing you here!" He grinned, unembarrassed. "Caught in the act." Nicholas looked bemusedly at the van, where his lover had disappeared. "I'm afraid that Toby is a bit shy," he apologized. "But we can sit down out here, if you don't mind the grass."

Lucy was glad to sit down; she didn't really know what to say about what she'd seen. After a moment she decided to ignore it—Nicholas didn't seem to expect any comment. She remembered the question that she'd wanted to ask him. "Nicholas," she said, "I wanted to ask you something about the night that you went to South Barsham church, the night that Bob Dexter was killed."

"Yes?"

She hesitated, making sure to frame her question in a way that didn't prejudice the answer. "The three of you—Maggie, Gary and you—were together on that expedition, Fiona told me. Was there any time that you weren't all together?"

Nicholas considered the question carefully, sensing that his answer might be important. "After the young priest came out of the church," he replied at last, "Gary and I thought we should leave right away. But Maggie didn't want to. She wanted to go into that church porch, to put up a poster right in the lion's den, she said."

"And did she?"

"Yes, I think so. We wouldn't wait for her, Gary and I. We took off right away, and she stayed behind. She caught up with us a few minutes later."

So Maggie could have killed Bob Dexter, Lucy reasoned to herself as she walked back toward Walsingham. It would have been possible for her to have slipped into the church and done it. She walked past the telephone with regret: no, she wouldn't be ringing David tonight. This changed things—this was something new. She was going to have to stay.

It wasn't until later in the evening, when Monica had gone off to the Bull to meet Mark Judd, that the other thing registered in Lucy's mind. The name Toby.

That was the name, she realized at last, that had been teasing the periphery of her mind for days. Toby. Someone had said that name, and it had been important. Who was Toby? Who had mentioned him? Had it been Fiona, that day they'd had lunch? She was pretty certain not—it had been after that that the name Toby had been brought up. Lucy squeezed her eyes shut and tried hard to remember. Elayne? No. Alice? No. Gwen? Yes! The scene came back to her, clearly. Alice was talking about Becca and her lover, about Elayne's reaction. And Gwen—Gwen, her face earnest and her golden wig askew, had said, "Elayne thought that it was Toby Gates."

No, it couldn't be. It didn't make sense. Whoever this Toby was, the one she'd seen today, it didn't seem likely that anyone would have chosen him as a candidate for Becca Dexter's lover. Not anyone who knew him, at any rate. He couldn't be Toby Gates. And yet . . .

There was one way to find out. Lucy left the room and went quickly to the telephone, praying that there would be a reply. After a few rings, Rhys's voice answered. "Oh, hello, Lucy," he greeted her. "I'm sorry that Fiona's not here. She's gone off to the gallery for a few hours, to get some paperwork done. She says that she can't work at home—I can't imagine why!" he laughed.

"Actually, Rhys, I just had a quick question, and you can answer it as well as Fiona."

"Fire away, Lucy."

"I saw the BARC van today, outside Walsingham. Nicholas was there, and another young man. Could you tell me his name?"

Rhys replied readily. "Oh, you must mean Toby Gates."

Monica snored away, intoxicated more by love than by the two sweet ciders that she'd consumed at the Bull. But Lucy was very much awake, and Monica was no longer her greatest worry.

Toby Gates. What could it mean? Rhys had told her that Toby and Becca had come to the meetings together, and that Toby's father was one of Bob Dexter's friends, one of the Evangelicals.

It didn't make sense. Unless . . . she thought. Unless Bob Dexter had found out something that no one, up to that point, had known. Did Becca know about Toby? What if she'd told her father that Toby was no danger to her virtue? Would that give Toby's father a motive to kill Bob Dexter? This, she thought, as she finally fell asleep, could be the breakthrough they'd been looking for. And tomorrow—tomorrow they would all be here, here at Walsingham.

# Chapter 46

*Why art thou so full of heaviness, O my soul: and why art thou
so disquieted within me?*

Psalm 42:6

David hadn't been able to concentrate on the Sunday papers;
shortly after lunch he'd given up trying, and had driven into
Norwich, determined to take his mind off Lucy. There were
thirty-two medieval churches surviving in Norwich. David
had decided that he'd try to see as many of them as he could
in what remained of the day.

Some of them were locked, of course, and some were difficult
to find. It had kept his body occupied, but only a small corner
of his mind. Now, in the warm dusk of the evening, he was
walking back through the heart of the city, back toward his
car. He detoured up Bridewell Alley so that he could pass by
the Bridewell Gallery. If he looked in the window, he thought,
he might be able to see if Fiona had any of Lucy's paintings
on display.

There was a light on at the back of the gallery. David peered
through the glass of the window, then tapped lightly on the
door. Fiona came to the door, surprised.

"David! Come in!"

"I'm sorry to bother you," he apologized. "I saw a light, and just thought I'd say hello."

"No bother at all," she assured him with a smile. "I was just doing some paperwork. It was starting to get a bit much for me, actually. I'm ready for a break."

"Would you like to go somewhere for a drink?" he suggested. "Or a coffee?" he amended, belatedly remembering Rhys's prohibition on alcohol.

"If you don't tell Rhys," she grinned, "I'd love a drink."

They found a pub nearby, one that David sometimes patronized at lunchtime. On a Sunday evening it was nearly deserted; they found a cozy table by the window.

"Thanks, David." Fiona raised her glass of white wine. "You have no idea how good this tastes, when it's forbidden fruit."

"Won't Rhys be able to smell it on your breath?"

"Isn't that what mints are for?" she laughed. She regarded David shrewdly for a moment. "Lucy's not with you this weekend?"

"No." He took a sip of his whisky. "She's gone to Walsingham, as a matter of fact."

"Walsingham?" Fiona looked amazed. "Lucy never struck me as the Walsingham type, I must say."

He knew that he'd never be able to explain. "She's not," he said shortly.

"Maybe I'll see her there. I'm going to Walsingham myself, tomorrow," Fiona revealed. "BARC are going to be there to hand out literature at the National Pilgrimage. You know, hunting on church-owned land, battery farming, and all that."

"Rhys is going, too, then?"

"Yes, of course." Fiona paused thoughtfully, moving her glass around in circles on the table. "You know, it's a funny thing, but it seems that everyone is going to be at Walsingham tomorrow. Even Geoffrey Pickering."

"Geoffrey!"

"Yes. He came into the gallery yesterday. It seems that he's in the area doing some research for his latest television series, tracing the whereabouts of Charles the First's private art collection, which has apparently ended up all over the world. He's staying at a stately home just outside Walsingham, he told me."

"Did he mention Lucy?" David asked sharply.

"Well, he *did* ask me if I'd seen her lately."

David frowned. Not only John Spring, but Geoffrey Pickering! At Walsingham, with Lucy. Lucy had been right about one thing, at any rate—everyone *was* going to be at Walsingham tomorrow.

Fiddling with his seat belt, David accidentally dropped his keys into the pocket on the door of the car. He cursed and fished for them, and came up with not only his keys but also an old copy of the *Church Times*. Friday, May 3, he saw—over three weeks ago; he didn't remember having read it. He'd probably stuffed it in there, in a hurry to get to London on the Friday afternoon, thinking that he'd read it later. Ah well, he thought. Old church news is better than no church news. Most church news, he'd found, kept very well. He put it in his pocket to read later.

At home, he poured himself another drink. He knew he'd been drinking more than he should the last few days, since Lucy had gone. He didn't drink so much when she was around.

There was nothing even remotely interesting on television. The Sunday papers had bored him once; he tried having another go at them, with no better results. In the end he gave up and went to bed.

It was no good, of course. There was no way that he could sleep. He got up and found the old *Church Times*, switching on the bedside light. No, he most certainly hadn't read this. David had an idiosyncratic approach to reading the *Church Times*; he always started with the classified adverts at the back (lingering over the announcements of weekly services at various

spiky London churches), followed by the appointments, resig-
nations and deaths in the Gazette, and then he turned to the
Letters page. There were a few letters about Walsingham, he
noted: with quickening interest he saw that one of them had
been written by Bob Dexter.

*"From the Revd. Bob Dexter,"* it was headed, and continued,
"Sir,—At this time of year, many right-thinking Anglicans,
as well as other Christians, begin to turn their thoughts to
that hateful abomination, Walsingham's National Pilgrimage.
I would like to inform your readership that this year a new
organization has been formed to combat this heresy. 'MIS-
SION: Walsingham' will be a forceful presence on May 27 this
year. For further information, or for assistance with travel
plans or accommodation, contact Noah Gates, Gates of Heaven
Printing Company plc, Fakenham, Norfolk, or myself at the
address below. BOB DEXTER, St. Mary's Vicarage, South
Barsham, Norfolk."

David whistled soundlessly and read through the letter
again, more slowly. Forceful? That sounded like trouble. He
remembered, belatedly, that John Spring had told him that
there could be violence.

The ingredients churned around in his head throughout the
night: John Spring's police reports; the conversations with
Miss Barnes and Miss Vernon, with Elayne and Becca Dexter,
with Fiona Crawford; his interviews with Stephen Thorncroft;
memories of their visit to Walsingham, two months earlier,
and to South Barsham church, more recently. But the final
element, like the last, crucial ingredient in a recipe, was the
*Church Times* of Friday, May 3.

In the morning as he woke, with perfect clarity, David knew
who had killed Bob Dexter, and why. There were still a few
questions to be answered, but he knew the answer to the main
one. Lucy had been right: the answer was at Walsingham. And
in being right, she had put herself in great danger.

# Chapter 47

*Gather my saints together unto me: those that have made a covenant with me with sacrifice.*

*Psalm 50:5*

Early on Monday morning, Monica hummed to herself as she once again tackled Father Clive's alb.

"There's Mass again this morning?" Lucy murmured, waking.

"Oh, yes!"

"How soon?"

"As soon as we can get there. Father Clive wants to be early—it's first come, first served for the chapels, and he especially wants the Chapel of the Ascension."

"Ah, yes. The feet." Lucy smiled to herself, picturing those jaunty plaster appendages. "Will there be a lot of competition, do you think?"

"I should jolly well think so," Monica said earnestly. "Don't forget—there are thousands of people on their way here today!"

Due to Father Clive's determination to be among the first, however, they had their Mass in the Chapel of the Ascension, under the plaster feet. It was one of the shallowest of the chapels, and could not have accommodated many more than the four in their party. As it was, they were crowded up against the pilgrims in the adjoining Chapel of the Descent of the Holy Spirit, whose Mass had begun a few minutes earlier. Lucy found it rather confusing, as though she were participating in two services at once.

By the time they finished, however, the Shrine church was well and truly crowded with worshipers. The first wave of coach parties had arrived, and each chapel contained a knot of people with their priest, determinedly concentrating on their responses in spite of what was going on all around them.

"Let's walk around and see," Monica suggested in a whisper, and Lucy agreed. Monica, of course, wanted to have a look at the priests, each in his own sumptuous chasuble, most dripping with lace. They were old and young, tall and short, thin and fat, bald and hirsute. Later they would walk in the Procession as a group, all in their albs and their white stoles, and would concelebrate the Mass in the Abbey grounds. But for now they ignored each other and carried on independently, at the tops of their priestly voices: one was intoning the Gospel, simultaneously another was elevating the Host, while yet another was administering the chalice.

The overall effect was amazing, Lucy thought. As each party finished, another was waiting to take its place, and it all began again.

"If the big Mass is later on, in the Abbey grounds, why does everyone have to have Mass now?" Lucy asked when they were back in the gardens.

Monica looked at her scornfully. "So they can eat, of course. We can go and have breakfast now, in the refectory. Come on—I'm hungry!"

After breakfast Monica had been very vague about her plans for the morning, and had wandered off in the direction of the

Shrine church. Lucy was relieved—she had a few enquiries that she needed to make, and didn't really want to have to explain anything to Monica.

She went in the opposite direction, into the town. It was still only mid-morning, but already the streets were crowded with people. There were families with young children and dogs, groups of elderly spinsters and widows, people in wheel-chairs, a few nuns, decorative young men in twos and threes, mixed groups of parish parties, and, everywhere, priests in black cassocks. Eccentrics peppered the crowd—within a few yards Lucy saw a sandaled and bearded man in a homespun brown monk's robe and a natty youth in an immaculate white suit with a scarlet bow tie, a matching silk scarf in his breast pocket, and a straw boater. To her surprise, outside the sancti-fied air of the Shrine, there was a festival atmosphere.

At the top end of the High Street, not far from the hospice, was the ancient pump which for the past several years had been the headquarters for the Evangelical protesters. Indeed, they were already out in force, with their new "MISSION: Walsing-ham" banner stretched between two tall poles behind the pump. In contrast to the colorful and varied character of the Catholic pilgrims, the Evangelicals, thought Lucy, were all much of a muchness: they were almost all men, with just a few women sprinkled in, and they were all dressed neatly in dark suits, white shirts, and somber ties. To a man, their hair was short and neatly trimmed; most of them carried Bibles, and many bore posters emblazoned with Bible verses. She'd never be able to pick out Toby's father amongst these clean-cut clones without help, Lucy realized. She approached a young man who looked perhaps a little less forbidding than some of his fellows; immediately he thrust a folded slip of paper at her. MISSION: WALSINGHAM, it read on the front. MARY, IDOLS, SAINTS: STAMP IT OUT NOW!

"Ma'am," he addressed her earnestly, "if you will read this,

I'm sure that God will convince you in your heart of the error of your ways. There is but one way to God, and that is through Our Lord Jesus Christ."

"Thank you," Lucy replied automatically, taking the paper. "But I wondered if you could help me."

"I'd be happy to help you, Ma'am. I'll tell you about how I met the Lord Jesus. If you are sincere in your desire to be saved . . ."

"I'm looking for a Mr. Gates," she interrupted him.

"Then you don't want to hear my testimony?" He was crestfallen.

"Not just at the moment, thank you. Do you know Mr. Gates?"

"Why, yes, Ma'am. Noah Gates is in charge, in fact." He pointed to a small, dark-haired man standing directly under the "MISSION: Walsingham" banner.

"Thank you," she said, and walked toward Noah Gates. As she approached, she saw that he was thrusting his tracts belligerently at the passers-by, most of whom were ignoring him. Occasionally a curious pilgrim would take one, only to discard it contemptuously.

"Mr. Gates?" she said, hesitating. He turned. Noah Gates was a man to be reckoned with, she apprehended instantly— much as Bob Dexter must have been. He was like a coiled spring; the vitality of his personality more than compensated for his lack of stature.

"Yes?"

"Mr. Gates, I wanted to ask you about your son. About Toby . . ."

Noah Gates's small black eyes blazed momentarily, then went dead. "I have no son," he said in a soft, controlled voice, then turned his back on her and walked away.

David had left home just after eight, allowing more than adequate time to reach Walsingham by mid-morning—it was, after all, only about thirty miles away. But it was a bank holiday, and traffic was heavy; at that proximity to Walsingham the roads were virtually choked with coaches full of pilgrims and mini-vans overflowing with protesters. He found himself part of a crawling queue of cars. And then disaster struck: a mini-van emblazoned with "Jesus is the Way" collided with a farm vehicle, strewing Evangelicals and fertilizer across both lanes of the road, and traffic stopped altogether for more than an hour as the ambulances, then the recovery vehicles, and finally the men with shovels arrived.

Nicholas Fielding maneuvered the BARC van through the crowded streets of Walsingham. "Where are you going to park it?" asked Toby nervously.

"Rhys has been around to the Bull and chatted up the owners—slipped them a fiver, I wouldn't doubt," he added. "They've said that we can put the van in the little square in front—near the outdoor beer stall."

"But that's just across from the pump."

Nicholas shot a look at Toby. "Do you mind?"

"My father . . ." The young man set his jaw determinedly. "No, I don't mind," he said. "If my father doesn't like it, that's his problem."

"Have you talked to him at all, since . . . ?"

"No."

"Do you think . . . ?"

"No."

Looking out of the corner of his eye at Toby's set profile, Nicholas didn't dare to ask any more questions.

The remainder of the BARC contingent was already waiting in front of the Bull: Rhys and Fiona, Maggie, Gary, and Karen. All were dressed in BARC T-shirts—even Fiona, though she wore hers stylishly, belted and bloused out over an elegant skirt rather than with jeans like the others. In short order they set up their eye-catching display and began passing out leaflets to the pilgrims who were already flocking to the beer stall, well before noon.

"It's a smashing location," Nicholas congratulated Rhys. "Right across from the Bible-thumpers, and next to the beer stall! We can catch them coming and going!"

Some of the Evangelicals were beginning to call out slogans. Gary decided to retaliate. "Stop animal experimentation!" he shouted in his best Berkeley protest voice. "Ban blood sports!" He looked around for Maggie, expecting her to add her strident voice to his. But Maggie was nowhere to be seen.

Lucy saw the BARC van arrive, watched them set up their display and begin handing out leaflets. After a few minutes she approached Fiona. "Hello!" Fiona greeted her. "David told me that you were going to be here. I wondered if I'd see you. Though with all these thousands of people . . ."

"David?" The sound of his name made Lucy catch her breath with longing. "When did you see David?"

"Last night." Fiona laughed. "He was wandering around like a lost soul without you, if that makes you feel any better."

Lucy smiled wryly. "It does, actually."

"He didn't really tell me what you were doing here. It doesn't seem like your scene, as Gary would say."

"It's a long story." Lucy hesitated. "Fiona, could we talk—privately—for a few minutes? Can Rhys spare you?"

"Of course. Where shall we go?"

Lucy thought quickly. "The Shrine garden." It would be full of people, of course, following the Stations of the Cross, or just having a moment of rest, but they could sit on the grass and have a private chat.

When the two women had found a relatively quiet spot, Lucy turned to Fiona. "I wanted to ask you about Toby Gates," she said.

"What about him?"

"Well, Rhys said that he'd started coming to the meetings with Becca Dexter."

"That's right."

"Were they . . . I mean, did it seem like there was anything going on between them?"

"I never thought so—never picked up any vibes, if you know what I mean. Rhys wondered, but I didn't think so." She gave Lucy a searching look. "Why are you asking me these questions?"

Lucy remembered, too late, that Fiona had been married to a solicitor for over twenty years; she decided to be honest. "Bob Dexter's murder," she said. "David is acting for Stephen Thorncroft."

"The priest who's been charged with the murder," Fiona concluded. "And you're helping him."

"Yes. Just a bit of information-gathering, really. There seem to be . . . quite a few people who had a much better motive to kill Bob Dexter than Stephen Thorncroft had."

"And you think that Toby Gates might be one of them?"

"Or his father," Lucy replied quickly. "How does he . . . get on with his father, do you know?"

"I know that they're estranged at the moment."

Lucy twisted a curl around her finger. "Estranged?"

"Right after . . . after Dexter's death, as a matter of fact. Toby wasn't with us that night, as you know. But the next day he rang Rhys. He said that he'd had a terrible row with his father, and that his father had thrown him out of the house. He had nowhere to go. Rhys said that he could live in the van for a while, until he got himself sorted out. He was terribly grateful."

"And he's been staying in the van since then?"

"Yes. Most of the time with Nicholas. They've been out on the road quite a bit in the last few weeks."

Lucy plucked a blade of grass and split it in half with her
fingernail. "Do you have any idea . . . why he and his father
quarreled?"

"No," Fiona replied definitely. "It wasn't my business. I
didn't ask."

"I wonder if . . . if I might talk with Toby sometime."
That was the only way, Lucy realized. The timing fitted, and
if it were true that Noah Gates had learned the truth about
his son from Bob Dexter, it gave him a powerful motive for
murder. But Toby Gates was the only one who could confirm
her theory—Noah Gates certainly wouldn't tell her.

"I envy you," said Fiona suddenly. "You're so lucky that
David trusts you to help him. Graham never even told me
about his cases."

"I *am* lucky." She wondered what David was doing at that
moment.

And at that moment he was sitting on the B1146, wondering when the hell he was ever going to get to Walsingham.

Maggie was having a look around Walsingham. All these
religious freaks, she thought: it was amazing. To get so heated
up about something as irrelevant as religion. And there was a
lot of money here, one way and another.

She walked down the street, skirting the Shrine grounds.
They were completely enclosed, bordered on the south side by
the hospice and walled the rest of the way. Impelled by curiosity, she poked her nose into the Shrine church to see what was
going on. The scene within was so alien to her that it might
have been taking place on another planet. Everywhere she
looked, people were genuflecting, crossing themselves, kneeling in prayer, lighting candles. There was a long queue at the
Holy Well, and another one waiting to get into the Holy
House. Maggie squeezed past the pilgrims to stand for a moment before the gilded, coped and flower-bedecked figure of
Our Lady of Walsingham, for this morning only moved out

from her customary place in the Holy House to sit in the place of honor before the high altar. She shook her head: too weird, she thought. Totally bizarre. And all those stinky candles. She couldn't breathe—she had to get out. Pushing her way back out again, she continued her anti-clockwise progress around the perimeter of the grounds.

On the north side was a large building, unmarked: the College. Maggie stopped in her tracks as she approached it; in front of the building sat a delivery van with the distinctive logo of Fielding Farms. Fielding Farms! The loathsome stuffed chicken thighs confronted her from the side of the van. She watched for a moment; a young chap was unloading tray after tray of chicken thighs and carrying them into the building.

After a minute Maggie followed. She was stopped by an officious man in a black cassock. "This is a private residence, young woman. I'm afraid I shall have to ask you to leave." His voice was reedy, and rather petulant.

"Maybe I'm staying here," she blustered. "With friends."

He looked inexpressibly shocked. "I should very much doubt it. No one but priests may stay at the College."

Maggie laughed. "That's a lot of food for a few priests. All those stuffed chicken thighs."

"There are a good many priests here today, and that will be their supper. And now I must insist . . ."

"Don't get your knickers in a twist," she sneered. "I'm going." But I'll be back, she said to herself as she went out past the Fielding Farms van. As soon as I can get by that self-righteous shit-head.

She would come back later and steal the chicken thighs. Liberate them, as she had liberated their live sisters at Fielding Farms a couple of months ago. And Rhys be damned—he'd gone absolutely spare when he'd found out what she'd done on that occasion, she remembered with perverse satisfaction. Maybe this time he'd realize that she was the guiding intelligence behind BARC.

# Chapter 48

*Their eyes swell with fatness: and they do even what they lust.*
*Psalm 73:7*

Shortly before noon, the pilgrims, clutching their official blue National Pilgrimage booklets, were beginning to stream through the gates into the Abbey grounds, staking out prime seating spots for the Mass.

The ground sloped gently, forming a natural amphitheater in the Abbey grounds, centering on the great arch that was nearly all that remained of the once-massive Abbey church. The platform was in place, canopied for the bishops who would be in attendance; an air of anticipation gathered momentum with the rapidly swelling crowd.

It was a perfect day; the sun was shining in a cloudless sky and the grass was warm. Cardigans were very quickly discarded as people sat in the sun for a few minutes; the hillside was dotted with their variegated hues, though there might have been a slight predominance of Marian blue. The clever ones had worn sun hats; others less forward-thinking shaded their faces with their blue programs.

Rose Phillips and Florence Whittaker had arrived very early and had prudently found seats in the shade. They had even saved space for Monica and Lucy. "Though I don't know why we should, when they don't even have the courtesy to come with us," Rose Phillips said sharply. Father Clive, of course, would be concelebrating the Mass with the other priests.

Florence Whittaker, settled in the shade, looked longingly at her walking frame. "I have to go to the toilet," she announced.

Rose Phillips frowned. "Well, go on then," she snapped. "I don't know why you didn't go before we came in!"

"You'll save my spot?"

"Of course!"

Lucy opened the door of their room; perhaps Monica would be waiting for her there. She hadn't seen Monica since just after breakfast. But the room was empty. It would be worth looking for her in the Sue Ryder cafe, she decided—she might be lingering over elevenses. Just outside the hospice, though, she found her. Monica was standing near the wall that enclosed the Shrine grounds, supporting a huge sign that seemed to be painted onto canvas on a wooden stretcher. "The Parish of St. Mary the Virgin, South Barsham" the sign proclaimed; Lucy assumed that, like many others that she'd seen people transporting, it would be carried in the Procession back to the Shrine at the end of the Mass.

"I've been looking for you," she said.

Monica looked sheepish. "I'm keeping an eye on Father Mark's sign for him, while he gets ready for the Procession," she explained. "Why don't you go on without me?"

Lucy looked at the sign. It was crudely painted—Miss Barnes and Miss Vernon, with their calligraphic expertise, would have done a better job of it than that. Why hadn't Father Mark asked them? "All right. I'll save you a spot, if you like."

Before Lucy reached the Abbey gates, though, she saw a totally unexpected sight: Geoffrey Pickering strolling rather purposefully up the High Street. Lucy ducked into a doorway. What on earth was Geoffrey doing in Walsingham? The only credible reason for him ever to be here was his nephew, and Stephen Thorncroft, as she well knew, was absent today. If the National Pilgrimage was not, as Fiona had said, "her scene," it was most certainly not Geoffrey's either. What was he up to? She decided to follow him and find out.

At long last David arrived in Walsingham. Needless to say, all of the car parks were full and he'd had to park over a mile away and walk. So when he arrived he was tired, hot, and more than a little put out.

He went straight to the hospice, to Lucy's room. It was locked. As he tapped on the door, an official came down the hall. "If you don't mind, sir," she said, "we'll be locking the building in a few minutes."

"Locking the building?" he repeated stupidly.

"Yes, sir. During the Procession and the Mass, the Shrine grounds are locked. No one's allowed in. Not until the Procession comes back."

John Spring leaned against the door near the College which led into the Shrine grounds. The door was locked—he had the key himself. The instructions were that no doors were to be opened, and no one was to enter, until the Procession had returned. It was going to be a long two hours, he thought. Probably even more.

The weekend had been fully as grim as he had anticipated. There hadn't been any violence, and there hadn't been any excitement. He'd scarcely seen a good-looking woman all weekend, let alone been to bed with one. As he'd told David, the Anglo-Catholics were a rum bunch, and the Evangelicals were worse. Holy, the lot of them. More interested in their souls than in having a bit of fun. Not that he would have had any of them, anyway, even if they'd been interested.

And so when the blonde came up to him, he couldn't believe his luck. She was not only the best-looking thing he'd seen this weekend, she was the best-looking thing he'd ever seen in his life. Legs up to here, and masses of blond hair down to there, and in between the most gorgeous pair of knockers he'd ever laid eyes on, straining against the thin fabric of her blouse like succulent melons. "Hello, sweetheart," he said, showing his white teeth in a predatory smile.

Tiffani had her orders. Distract the cop, whatever it takes, Geoffy had said. Get him to unlock the door, and get him out of the way. And take your time, he'd said. The cop was kind of cute. This could be fun, she thought. "Hi-ya."

"What's your name, sweetheart?" His eyes devoured her ripe lusciousness.

"Tiffani. With an 'i,' ya know," she added breathlessly. "And who are you?"

"You can call me John."

"I'll call you Johnnie." She looked at him through her eyelashes.

"You're not from around here, are you?"

Tiffani gave a tinkling laugh. "No. I'm from Beanblossom, Indiana."

"Is that anywhere near San Francisco? Or New York?"

"Only a few thousand miles, ya know." She laughed again.

"So what are you doing so far away from home, sweetheart? Aren't you homesick?"

"Well, I'm pretty lonesome, ya know, Johnnie." She sighed and put her hand on his arm. "But my mom always told me that the policeman is your friend. Are you my friend, Johnnie?"

"Abso-bloomin'-lutely, sweetheart." His hand, as if by accident, brushed her breast.

Tiffani moved closer. "You're what they call a bobby, aren't you?"

"That's right, my love."

"Is it true that bobbies don't carry guns?"

Spring grinned. "I may not have a gun, sweetheart, but you can squeeze my truncheon any time you like."

Tiffani moistened her very red lips with her tongue and moved even nearer. "Can't we go inside, Johnnie?" she breathed. " 'Cause I'd like to take you up on that."

Lucy watched Geoffrey walk nonchalantly toward the door. What on earth was he about? The Shrine grounds were locked—he had no business going in there now. Whatever he was doing, it was bound to be no good. She took a deep breath and determined to follow him in there if necessary, and find out.

Geoffrey Pickering tested the door: it was unlocked, with no cop in sight. Good girl, Tiffani, he said to himself. I knew you could do it. He pushed the door open and stepped inside the Shrine grounds, moving quickly toward the College.

He pretended that he didn't know that Lucy was following him. Damned interfering nuisance of a woman, he thought. He'd take care of her—he'd have to, or she'd ruin everything with her prying nosiness.

Geoffrey passed through the dining room; at its far end there were two doors flanking the huge sideboard. He went through one of them, and waited quietly on the other side, concealed behind the door.

A moment later Lucy followed. She was wary, but quite unprepared for what happened as Geoffrey grabbed her roughly, pinning her hands behind her back and clapping a hand over her mouth to stifle her instinctive scream. "What do you think you're doing, you stupid bitch?" he hissed. Before she could react, or attempt to struggle, he bundled her into a nearby linen cupboard and locked the door from the outside with the conveniently left key, which he then pocketed.

"Geoffrey!" she cried, banging on the door. "Let me out! You can't get away with this!"

He laughed unpleasantly. "Scream all you like, my dear ex-wife. In case you didn't realize, there's no one here to hear you. And won't be for quite a while. So if I were you I'd save my breath. I'll be back to deal with you later."

She banged on the door for a little longer, but realized that it was useless. Geoffrey was right, of course: there was no one else in the Shrine grounds. Whatever he was up to, he was going to get away with it. Lucy choked back hysterical tears and curled up on the floor of the tiny cupboard.

There were policemen guarding all the entrances around the perimeter of the Shrine grounds, Maggie discovered. A lot of trouble to go to to protect a few dozen stuffed chicken thighs, she thought scornfully. But here was a door with no fuzz in sight. She gave it a tentative push and it swung open.

Quickly and stealthily she went through and pulled it shut behind her. She paused a minute to get her bearings, then headed toward the College. There was no need for stealth now—no one else would be inside the grounds. It might be difficult to get all those chicken thighs out on her own, but she could hide them and come back for them later. Or maybe she could do something even more dramatic: arrange them artistically in the church, where that statue had been, or throw them down the Holy Well.

Once inside the College, she had no trouble finding the kitchen—she'd carefully watched where the Fielding Farms delivery man had gone with his trays of chicken thighs. But the kitchen door was locked. Maggie kicked it furiously, and cursed, then went down the corridor into the dining room.

She stopped and stared incredulously at the other end of the room. It was like a bloody temple to food, she thought: the huge sideboard with its candlesticks, and the massive painting above with its barbaric hunting scene. Maggie was enraged. She moved closer, then stopped as she heard a noise behind her.

"What do you think you're doing here?" said a voice. Maggie turned; it was another one of those bloody priests. This one had a fat girl with him, and between them they were carrying a very large sign. They set the sign down. "You have no right to be in here," the priest reiterated.

Maggie was not intimidated by a priest and a fat girl. What could they do to her? "Oh, sod off," she sneered.

"Now listen here . . ." He advanced toward her.

"Eh—what the hell's going on here?" They all turned as a policeman entered the room, looking a bit disheveled and slightly disoriented. "No one's supposed to be in here!"

"Officer," said the priest unctuously, "this young woman is trespassing. She must be ejected, forcibly if necessary."

"Right you are." John Spring collared Maggie unceremoniously and marched her toward the door, ignoring her shouts of rage. "And you, sir?"

"We'll be going in just a moment, officer," said Mark Judd. "The Procession will be beginning soon."

John Spring was quite pleased. If anyone had noticed that he had abandoned his post, and he were to be questioned about it later, he now had the perfect excuse: he was dealing with a protester. So pleased was he that he didn't stop to wonder what the priest and the fat girl were doing in the College, when everyone was supposed to be out.

And Maggie's screams of "Police brutality!" drowned out any suspicious noises that might have emanated from a certain cupboard, just down the corridor.

# Chapter 49

*The singers go before, the minstrels follow after: in the midst
are the damsels playing with the timbrels.*

Psalm 68:25

David decided to look for Lucy in the village, passing the
"MISSION: Walsingham" contingent at the pump. As the
weather had warmed up, most of the men had shed their jackets
and the pump was now awash with clean white shirts and
multicolored posters.

The priests had all departed to robe for the Procession, so
the beer stall in front of the Bull was all but deserted. David
spotted the BARC van and went over for a word. They had
lost most of their audience, and were taking advantage of the
lull to share a few sandwiches.

"Hello, Mr. Middleton-Brown," said Karen, offering him
a cheese sandwich. "What are you doing here?"

David waved the sandwich away. "Have any of you seen
Lucy?" he asked without preliminary niceties.

Fiona looked up with a smile. "Oh, hello, David. Yes, I
saw her earlier—it must have been nearly an hour ago."

"Where was she going, do you know?"

"She didn't say."

"Well, thanks anyway."

Lucy must have gone into the Abbey grounds, David decided. It was clear that the Procession would be beginning soon, and all but a few stragglers had already made their way into the grounds to wait for the Mass.

He was stopped at the gate. "Do you have your pilgrim handbook?" an elderly nun demanded.

"I beg your pardon?"

"I don't see your handbook. You can't go in without your handbook," she amplified testily.

"Handbook?"

The nun brandished a copy of the blue-backed booklet. "It's only one pound fifty, and it includes the order of service for the Mass."

David rummaged in his pocket and produced two pound coins, which he slammed down on the table. "Keep the change."

"Why, thank you, sir, and God bless you." The nun was now all smiles as she handed him his handbook.

Yes, Lucy must be in here, he realized. Why had he wasted so much time looking for her elsewhere? But his heart sank as he saw the size of the crowd. There must be over ten thousand people here, he thought. How will I ever find Lucy?

He murmured his apologies right and left as he walked through the midst of the assembled crowd, searching for an aureole of red-gold hair. Each time that he saw the sun glint on a reddish-blond head his heart lifted, then sank again. He moved around the perimeter of the amphitheaterlike seating area, then began crisscrossing his way back and forth through the crowd.

His eye caught the unmistakable sheen of a golden wig, and David moved quickly to where Gwen Vernon and Alice Barnes sat with another woman. Alice sat primly, knees together, rosary in one hand and blue program in the other, her face shaded by a small sun visor. Gwen seemed to have shed several layers of clothing; the grass was littered with her bits and pieces, and she fanned herself hectically with her program. "Hello!" she greeted David with enthusiasm. "Mr. Middleton-Brown! How nice that you're joining us today."

"I suppose we can make room for you," Alice said, glaring at Gwen's bits and pieces.

"No, that's quite all right," he assured them quickly. "I won't stop. I was just looking for Lucy—for Miss Kingsley."

"We haven't seen her, have we, Gwen?" Alice declared.

Gwen shook her head in disappointed agreement. "No, we haven't, have we, Elayne?"

Elayne! For the first time, David took a close look at the woman who sat between Alice and Gwen. He should have realized that it was Elayne Dexter, but the woman didn't square with his mental image of Bob Dexter's widow. She wasn't beautiful by any means, but she certainly wasn't the dowdy nonentity that he'd expected. Elayne was smiling, and there was color in her cheeks; she had a good figure, and nice facial bone structure, and with a bit more effort could have been quite pretty.

He dropped down onto the grass momentarily. "Mrs. Dexter and I haven't met," he said.

"Oh, I'm so sorry! How rude of us!" fluttered Gwen.

"Mr. Middleton-Brown is Father Thorncroft's solicitor," Alice explained.

"Miss Kingsley's friend," added Gwen archly.

"Oh, yes!" Elayne turned to him with a friendly smile. "Lucy's told me about you. She's here today, then? How is she?"

"I can't find her," he said with urgency. "It's important that I find her. Most important. I'd like to stay and chat—there are some things that you and I need to talk about, Mrs. Dexter—but I must find Lucy."

"We haven't seen her," Alice repeated.

He got up. "If you do happen to see her . . ." He hesitated. "Tell her that I'm looking for her, won't you?"

As it became clear from the loudspeaker that the Procession was about to leave the Shrine church and make its way to the Abbey, David once again moved to the outskirts of the seating area. There in the shade he spotted the girl who had come into Lucy's room on the afternoon of her arrival. He was sure it was the same girl—she was quite distinctive, with her frizzy hair and her massive frame. She was flopped on the grass, breathing heavily even in the shade. David approached her hesitantly. "I'm sorry to bother you," he said, "but I was looking for Lucy Kingsley. Aren't you . . . ?"

"Monica!" she announced, sitting up. "Yes, I'm Lucy's roommate. But she's not here. I don't know where she is." She scrutinized him curiously. "You're her boyfriend, aren't you? David?"

"That's right. But when did you last see her?"

Monica hesitated. "I saw her a while ago. I thought that she was on her way in here, but she hasn't showed up. Maybe she just couldn't find us."

"I've been saving her a place to sit," Rose Phillips said truculently, pointing to the spot where she'd rested her handbag. "Not very good manners, if you ask me."

"Are you talking about that Miss Tinsley?" Florence Whittaker spoke up suddenly and loudly. "I'm sure she was mistaken—she must be related to Gladys Tinsley. Gladys couldn't leave the boys alone either."

"What are you talking about?" demanded Mrs. Phillips.

"When I went to the toilet. I saw her, out there in the street. Miss Tinsley. Following a man, as brazen as you please."

"A man?" David's voice came out in a croak, but somehow Miss Whittaker understood him.

"She was following a man, all right. What's more, it was a man from the television. Might have been that weatherman—

what's-his-name . . ." With a clawlike hand she patted her
thin white hair in agitation.

Rose Phillips rolled her eyes scornfully. "I think she's been
out in the sun too long," she said.

"I know what I saw," muttered the old woman.

"Thank you, ladies," he said hastily, moving away as the
brass band began to play the first hymn.

David stood at the back of the crowd as the Procession entered
the grounds. The congregation sang fervently "Every generation, Mary, calls thee blest," and sighed collectively in anticipation. First came the processional cross and then, borne high
under a canopy and wreathed in clouds of incense, came the
statue of Our Lady of Walsingham, surrounded by a phalanx
of Guardians in their blackout-curtain vestments. Rank on
rank of priests—probably two hundred of them—in albs and
white stoles, followed, and finally the bishops. Everyone was
standing at that point, so it was difficult to see over all the
heads, but the bishops' miters, tall and gold-encrusted, made
them eminently visible. There were eight or ten bishops, David
estimated, though only the celebrant wielded his ring at the
congregation in an episcopal blessing.

The Mass seemed to take forever. There was a long sermon
delivered by one of the bishops, and a number of Marian
hymns, accompanied by the brass band. Administering the
Sacrament to a crowd of over ten thousand was no small feat;
it was accomplished efficiently by the priests who fanned out
and stood around the perimeter as the pilgrims made their way
to the nearest station. David watched the crowd closely as they
moved: still no sign of Lucy.

At the conclusion of the Mass the Procession began to re-form
and David made a quick decision: if Lucy was there, which he
was beginning to doubt, he could spot her more easily if he got
ahead of the Procession, found a spot to stand, and waited for
them to pass by. The Procession would go out the far end of the

Abbey grounds, snake around past the parish church, then go up the High Street and around to the Shrine, where everyone would gather in the garden for Benediction. David slipped out through the gate where they'd all entered. He could see the pump from there; the protesters, after their inactivity during the Mass, were mobilizing for action. Noah Gates passed among them, exhorting them all and exciting their fervor. A number of police had taken their places between the pump and the street, but David didn't see John Spring among them.

Over the loudspeaker, which was set at high volume to blast the Mass to the Evangelicals, he could hear the first verses of the pilgrim hymn: that meant that the Procession had begun. When the first "Ave, ave, ave Maria" was sung by ten thousand voices, a howl arose from the protesters. Noah Gates waved a few of them into formation and they began an unaccompanied chorus of "A Mighty Fortress is Our God," notable more for enthusiasm than for musicality.

David moved toward the BARC van. This would be a good vantage point, he decided—the road was at its widest between the pump and the Bull. The BARC contingent was also at the ready; several of them had put on fox masks.

It didn't take too long for the beginning of the Procession to reach the top of the High Street, singing "Ave, ave," as loudly as they could. It was like a river of humanity, David thought, looking down the street at them, a solid snaking mass of devotion, six or eight abreast, carrying the signs and banners which identified them by parish. On and on they came, singing fervently, verses of the pilgrim hymn interspersed with the spoken "Hail Marys" of the rosary.

The protesters were no longer a group of mild-mannered, clean-cut men. They sang, they shouted, they waved their posters and shook their Bibles. The row of stolid policemen, arms folded across their chests, ensured that there was no physical contact with the pilgrims, but occasionally a protester would lean over and come dangerously close. David saw one earnest young man waving his Bible under the noses of two devout blue-rinsed Anglo-Catholic matrons, shouting, "Ladies, where are your Bibles?"; they smiled serenely and clutched their rosaries all the more tightly.

The pilgrims on the other side of the street from the pump were bombarded instead with shouted slogans. "Ban blood sports!" "Stop battery farming now!" "No more fur!" "Meat is murder for animals, suicide for you!"

And the human tide flowed on, inexorably. "Ave, ave," they sang, and "Hail, Mary," they chanted. Men and women, young and old.

But there was no Lucy. David scanned each face as it passed him. It was like a nightmare: ten thousand pilgrims, but no Lucy. At the end came the thurifers and the candles and the canopied statue, borne aloft by pious young men. The protesters vented their final and most virulent fury on this detested image, their faces twisted with hate, their voices hoarse with shouting. "The Whore of Babylon," they screamed.

Around the corner and into the Shrine grounds went the end of the Procession. David followed them into the garden, where everyone would receive Benediction at the outdoor altar.

He wouldn't have thought that it was possible to get ten thousand people into the garden, but somehow they were all crammed in, filling every inch of space. David edged along the back of the crowd toward the sepulcher. Everyone faced the altar in anticipation; there wasn't long to wait. A bishop came from the church, sumptuously robed and flanked by two beautiful young men in gold vestments. The crowd parted just enough to let them through. As the monstrance was brought to the altar the pilgrims sang, "O Saving Victim, opening wide the gate of heaven to man below . . ."

David stood at the back and watched the faithful sink to their knees, bowing their heads in adoration and reverence as the monstrance was flourished at them. "Therefore we before Him bending," they sang.

Out of the corner of his eye he caught movement. He should not have been looking, he knew: all eyes should be down at the moment of Benediction. But what he saw, when he turned his head and looked, banished all thoughts of the spiritual implications of the moment. He saw Geoffrey Pickering entering the Shrine church via the door from the garden; an instant later he was followed by Mark Judd.

David couldn't move until Benediction was over; he was hemmed in by far too many people. There was nothing he could do but wait, and pray that Lucy was all right.

"Come on, Gary," Maggie hissed. "I'm telling you, you've got to see this for yourself."

"But Rhys—"

"The hell with Rhys! Come on!"

Gary allowed himself to be dragged around the corner. "A picture?" he asked.

"Yes—a great huge picture. It's absolutely obscene! A hunting scene, with a stag being ripped apart by dogs."

"Sounds pretty gross."

"Obscene!" she insisted. "Have you got a knife?"

"Just my pocket knife."

"That will do."

The door to the College was once again unguarded, and its pious inhabitants all in the Shrine garden receiving Benediction. "It's a piece of cake!" exulted Maggie. "Come on, Gary. Give me your knife." She led him into the dining room. "Take a look at that picture!"

"Maybe it's worth a lot of money," he demurred as she clambered up on the sideboard and flipped out the knife blade.

"I don't give a shit." And with a quick movement she slashed the painting from top to bottom; within moments it was hanging in ribbons. "Now," she said, jumping down, "for the chicken thighs. Come on, Gary—the kitchen is this way."

# Chapter 50

*Yea, the waters had drowned us: and the stream had gone over our soul.*

*Psalm 124:3*

It was Monica who found him. She wanted to be the first in the queue when sprinklings resumed at the Holy Well after Benediction, and was surprised to find the gates unlocked.

Her screams cut through the devout murmurs of the pilgrims who once again circulated in the Shrine church. She screamed repeatedly, for it is not every day that one finds a dead body, and the dead body of a priest at that. She didn't know who it was until the police had pulled him out of the Holy Well and turned him over; when she saw that it was Mark Judd her hysteria could not be contained, and a kind middle-aged woman from a parish on the Scottish borders had to take her out into the garden until a member of the Red Cross could be summoned to administer sedation.

The Red Cross could be of no help to Mark Judd, it was quite clear: he was most definitely dead. Drowning, it looked like, though he had also received some kind of blow on the head. The curious gathered around, and the police were too busy to undertake the tremendous effort of once again clearing the Shrine church.

As David came in from the garden, he saw at a glance what had happened. But where was Geoffrey Pickering? Purposefully, he began searching for him. He could not have gone far.

David found him at last in the dining room of the College. The picture etched itself indelibly on his mind; he knew that he would never forget it. At the far end of the room, above the fanciful altar to food, hung the tattered remnants of the mutilated painting. And beneath it was slumped the figure of Dr. Geoffrey Pickering, weeping uncontrollably. Later would come the rage, and the anger, but for now there was only the inconsolable grief, eerily echoing that of the overweight girl in the garden.

"Where is she, you bastard?" demanded David. "Where is Lucy?" Geoffrey lifted his head. Beneath his distinctive swoop of silver hair his face was unrecognizable, distorted with anguish. He flung a key on the floor and indicated the door through to the corridor.

Lucy had heard the commotion and banged feebly on the inside of the cupboard door, leading him quickly to her. He unlocked the door and wrenched it open; she fell out into his arms. "I knew that you'd come," she wept on his shoulder. "Oh, David. I knew that you'd come."

She wasn't hurt, apart from a few bruises inflicted by Geoffrey's rough handling, merely exhausted with her efforts to be heard, and emotionally shattered. David satisfied himself of that. "You're all right?" She nodded. "He didn't hurt you? You're sure?"

She clung to him. "Just hold me, David."

He tightened his arms around her and stroked her hair, murmuring endearments. She seemed to draw strength from him; after a few minutes she took a deep breath. "What about Geoffrey?"

"He's out there. In the dining room."

"You left him?"

"You were more important."

"But . . ."

"I don't think he's going anywhere," David assured her.

"You don't mean . . . ? He's not dead, is he?"

"No." He hesitated. "Mark Judd is dead."

A sharp intake of breath from Lucy. "Geoffrey . . . ?"

"I think he'll be ready to talk."

He was still there, and he was ready to talk. The first incoherent flood of grief was over, and he now had a great need to talk about his feelings.

"How could anyone do it?" He gestured ferociously at the shredded painting. "Barbarians! Goths!"

"It wasn't a very appealing painting," David said.

Geoffrey turned on him. "You bloody fool! It was priceless!"

"Priceless?" echoed Lucy.

His laugh was without mirth. "It would have made me a very rich man."

"You're already a very rich man," David frowned.

"All right, then. I would have been a benefactor to the nation—given it to the National Gallery. They would have made me *Sir* Geoffrey Pickering for that."

"But it wasn't yours," Lucy pointed out. "How could you . . . ?"

"You still don't understand, do you?" Anger blazed from him. "You stupid, interfering bitch! You come walking in here, getting in the way . . ."

"I won't have you speak to Lucy like that," David interrupted furiously.

The anger burned out abruptly and Geoffrey buried his head

348    KATE CHARLES

in his hands. "It doesn't matter," he said in a low voice. "None of it matters, now. That's the whole bloody irony of it—it was all for nothing." He gestured again at the painting. "All for bloody nothing."

"Mark Judd's death?" said David.

Geoffrey raised his head and looked at him. "He's dead, then?" David nodded. "Yes, I thought so."

"Why did you kill him?"

"I didn't really mean to. He would have killed *me* if I hadn't. We struggled, at the well. He fell, hit his head on the step. I pushed him into the well. I suppose he drowned."

"Yes."

"But why?" asked Lucy.

He laughed bitterly. "Because of the painting, of course. As I said, it was priceless. It is . . . was . . . a Guido Reni. An original. *The Conversion of St. Hubert.*"

"I don't understand."

For a moment he looked like the Geoffrey Pickering that all of England knew; the urbane television presence asserted itself as he explained. "Guido Reni, born 1575, died 1642. A Bolognese painter of the Italian Counter-Reformation."

David thought back to Geoffrey's series on Italian paintings, and wished that he'd managed to stick it out beyond the program on the Renaissance. "An original, you say?"

"Undoubtedly. A lost masterpiece, whereabouts unknown for over a hundred years. And it was hanging here, the gift of some pious fool who didn't know what he had. I spotted it when I was visiting Stephen back in March."

"Tiffani said that you spent a long time looking at all the paintings," David remembered.

"Unmitigated rubbish, most of it. A load of bad copies. I wouldn't have given any of it a second look, but I spotted the Guido right away—rather a speciality of mine, the Italian Counter-Reformation," he added with perverse pride. "I had to pretend to be interested in all of the rubbish, so I could get a good look at the Guido. Unquestionably authentic."

"Mark Judd?" said David.

"He saw me looking at the Guido. He said that if I liked it, I could have one just like it. The new Vicar at the church where he'd been working was going to be flogging off everything, he said, and there was an identical painting there. I could have it for next to nothing, he said. That's what gave me the idea."

"Of switching the paintings?" David said slowly, beginning to understand.

Geoffrey smiled appreciatively. "I can see that you're not as stupid as I thought."

"Thanks." David raised his eyebrows ironically.

"I went to the church a few days later, looked at the painting. It was a copy of this very painting, quite worthless. Worthless without the original hanging a few miles away, anyway, just waiting to be switched. I offered him a couple of hundred quid for it, which was more than it was worth. That was my biggest mistake—it made Judd suspicious. He was a clever lad, Mark Judd. He made a trip to the National Art Library, looked at the catalog of Guido's work, found the reference to the missing painting—the lost masterpiece—and put two and two together."

"So he wanted in."

"Yes. He was also an ambitious lad—had his eye on higher office in the Church, and knew that money would help him get there. At first I thought it wasn't a bad thing, cutting him in. It would make things a great deal easier for me to have help on the inside, so to speak. It was a damned bulky painting—it would have been difficult to make the switch on my own. And I wasn't about to involve Stephen."

"Stephen wouldn't have had anything to do with a dishonest scheme like that!" Lucy protested indignantly.

"No, you're right." Geoffrey shook his head with a sickly smile. "My nephew, I'm afraid, has principles." He made the condition sound extremely unpleasant. "Believe me, he didn't get them from *my* side of the family, unless it was a recessive gene. His friend Mark Judd, however, was not hampered by anything so inconvenient."

"But he got greedy?" David surmised.

Geoffrey nodded. "He still had the painting—it was more convenient to leave it in the church at South Barsham until it was time to make the swap. I was traveling on the continent, researching my Charles the First series. I was back in London for a few days, around the time that Stephen was arrested, but I couldn't get back to Norfolk until this weekend. We agreed to do it today, under cover of all the activity. During the Procession, while everyone was away. But you," he shot Lucy a venomous look, "started following me. I had to get rid of you, or you would have ruined everything. And then Judd, as you say, got greedy. He decided that he could have it all to himself. He could make himself a big hero at Walsingham by suddenly producing the original of the supposed copy that they had hanging—by then, of course, it *would* have been the copy hanging here—and donating it to them. That would be even better than the money, he thought. So he enlisted some stupid broad to help him make the switch."

"Monica," Lucy said faintly, remembering the girl's guilty look as she stood guarding the huge sign. A crudely painted sign, disguising an oil painting. Did she know what she was doing, or had the blessed Father Mark spun her some tale? That wouldn't have been difficult.

"But they didn't make the switch." David stated the obvious.

"No. He said that they were interrupted. But he still had the painting. They would have switched it later. And he had to get rid of me. He told me to meet him at the Holy Well during Benediction. He was going to kill me . . ."

"And instead you killed him."

"Where is the other painting, then?" Lucy asked.

Geoffrey shook his head. "I don't know. It doesn't matter. It's not worth the two hundred quid that I paid for it." He laughed ironically. "As a matter of fact, I never actually paid for it. I suppose that it still belongs to the church! They can bloody have it!"

They all turned at the sound of a breathy whistle from the back of the room. John Spring stared at the tatters of the painting, shaking his head. "Crikey! Someone's jolly well done a number on that!" he said with awe. "I wonder if it was that girl that I threw out of here earlier—that animal rights nut?"

Maggie, thought Lucy. Yes, that would make sense.

John Spring had noticed Lucy, holding fast to David's hand. He grinned at her appraisingly. "Well, Dave," he said. "You're a sly one, aren't you? Where have you been hiding this little beauty?"

David glowered. He'd known he couldn't put this moment off forever, but at least he could distract Spring. "I think," he said, "that you might want to take this gentleman in for questioning in the matter of the death of Father Mark Judd."

"No kidding!" Spring's head swiveled to Geoffrey.

"And while you're at it," David added, "you should ask him what he knows about the murder of Bob Dexter."

When Spring had taken Geoffrey Pickering away, David went to look for the other painting. He found it immediately, stashed behind the door in the corridor, its camouflaging sign draped over it loosely. They carried it between them into the dining room and propped it up against the table to have a look.

*The Conversion of St. Hubert.* The saint-to-be was converted in the midst of a hunting party; the painting depicted him kneeling in awe in the foreground as the image of the crucified

Christ appeared between the horns of a stag. Rotund baroque cherubs peered down in approbation from turgid clouds over the stag's head. But in the background of the painting the hunt went on uninterrupted by the vision, and a less fortunate stag was being dismembered by slathering dogs.

"I still don't find it a very appealing painting," David admitted. "Hard to believe that someone would be willing to kill over it."

"Not over this one, though," Lucy reminded him. "Over the real one. This is the copy, remember?"

David looked thoughtful. "I wonder."

"What you said to that policeman about Bob Dexter—you don't think that Geoffrey killed him, do you?"

"Oh, no. Most certainly not. I think that if you checked his story you'd find that he was in Europe when Dexter was murdered, just as he said."

"Then . . ."

"I think," said David, "that Geoffrey didn't tell us the whole truth. Oh, I think that what he told us was more or less the truth, as far as it went. But I think he knows a great deal more than he told us. I'm sure that Spring will get it out of him."

"That was your friend John Spring?"

David looked at her apprehensively. "Yes. Didn't you think he was attractive?"

She laughed. "Why, was I supposed to?"

"Well, women do, you know. I've seen it with my own eyes."

"Oh, David! You must be joking!" Lucy went to him and put her arms around him. "It may come as a great surprise to you, my dear, but I prefer a man who has two brain cells to rub together."

"Anyone in particular?" David raised his eyebrows.

She favored him with a radiant smile. "Come on, darling. Let's go home."

# Chapter 51

*Our soul is escaped even as a bird out of the snare of the fowler:
the snare is broken, and we are delivered.*

*Psalm 124:6*

They were seven at dinner one evening, over a month later.
Seven: a mystical number. David and Lucy, Becca and Elayne
Dexter, Alice Barnes, Gwen Vernon and Stephen Thorncroft
sat around a table together at the Old Schoolhouse in South
Barsham.

It was Stephen who was hosting the meal, as a thank-you
to David for his work on his behalf, and Stephen who had
decided on the guest list. Fortunately Alice and Gwen had
taken Becca to their hearts once again, now that it was evident
that they'd been deceived by Father Mark just as she had.

Gwen hadn't been in the Old Schoolhouse since it had ceased
to fulfill its original function. "Just fancy!" she'd exclaimed on
arrival. "All those years that I spent in this place, and look at
it now!"

The food was delicious, the company was congenial, and
there seemed to be several things to celebrate. Stephen's release
from prison, of course, and then there was the unexpected
windfall from the painting.

To everyone's surprise, the painting that had been destroyed at Walsingham by Maggie Harrison had turned out to be the copy, and the one that remained had been authenticated as the original Guido Reni. Maggie had been arrested for criminal damage to a valuable work of art, but the charges had been quietly dropped when it was discovered that she had instead destroyed a virtually worthless copy.

The crucial question, then, was this: had the two paintings actually been switched by Mark Judd before Maggie did her worst? There was no one who could settle the question definitively; Mark Judd was dead, and Monica Cooper had been so distraught by his death that the earlier events of the day were a complete blank to her. Geoffrey Pickering, too, was dead; he had hanged himself in his remand cell, unable to face the public humiliation of being charged with Mark Judd's death. The only basis for a decision as to the ownership of the valuable painting was Geoffrey Pickering's statement to the police that the paintings had not been switched, and thus the surviving painting was declared to be his, and Walsingham was left with the tatters of the copy. By Pickering's own admission, though, he had not paid for the painting, and thus it still belonged to St. Mary's Church, which stood to be several million pounds richer pending its sale to the National Gallery.

It was David's private opinion that the paintings must surely have been swapped, for although the two paintings might have looked identical to an untrained eye, Geoffrey Pickering would not have been wrong in his initial judgement: he could not possibly have mistaken a mediocre copy for a genuine Guido, and vice versa. His shock at the painting's destruction, its ravaged condition, and his assumption that Judd had not had time to effect the switch could easily explain his misidentification at the time of the crime.

John Spring, over a pint with David, had admitted that Mark and Monica might have remained behind for long enough to have made the switch. Spring was certainly not about to press for investigation of the possibility: a few uncomfortable questions might be forthcoming about his whereabouts during the time he was meant to be guarding the Shrine. So it would never be proved. St. Mary's owned the painting, and the National Gallery wanted it. Their collection was notoriously weak in the works of the Italian Baroque, and they were willing to pay whatever price was necessary to obtain the Guido.

Alice and Gwen accepted the windfall at face value, assuming that the switch had not taken place and that the valuable painting indeed had been at St. Mary's all along. They, naturally, were ecstatic. This meant that the church could be returned to its former splendor, or even improved. It was, understandably, a chief topic of conversation at that evening's dinner, as it had been at Monkey Puzzle Cottage for some time. "I still can't get over that painting," Alice declared, shaking her head. "That old thing that had been hanging there since the year dot—worth all that money. Imagine it!"

"Worth millions!" Gwen rhapsodized. "Just think what we can do at St. Mary's!"

David and Lucy looked at each other, smiling. No one would ever know the truth about the painting, but it was better this way. St. Mary's could do with the money, and Walsingham certainly didn't need it.

Lucy sipped her wine as her eyes moved around the table. Next to her, of course, was David, looking relaxed and handsome. Then Gwen Vernon, flushed and voluble with the unaccustomed wine. Sandwiched between Gwen and Alice was Elayne. Elayne had blossomed since she'd first met her, Lucy reflected. She was smartly dressed: Becca had taken her shopping for clothes, and had overseen the revamping of her image. She'd had her hair highlighted and cut becomingly; in short, Elayne was emerging from the chrysalis in which Bob Dexter had kept her wrapped for years, transformed from a nonentity into an attractive, self-confident woman.

Stephen sat on the other side of Alice, chatting to her

familiarly. Since Alice and Gwen had been so disastrously let down by Father Mark, Father Stephen had become their new blue-eyed boy; he could do no wrong as far as they were concerned. Stephen, too, looked good, Lucy thought—he had lost his prison pallor, his ascetic face seemed a bit fuller, and his eyes sparkled behind his spectacles. Beside him, Becca was quieter than usual, but she seemed happier than Lucy had ever seen her. She inclined her head toward Stephen, and smiled at him with tentative, tremulous joy. Her hair no longer looked roughly hacked; it had grown out enough to be trimmed to a smooth, shining silvery cap which suited her very well, giving her face a gamine look.

Next to Becca, at this round table for eight, was the empty space. Who was the specter at the feast? Lucy wondered. Was it Mark Judd, or was it Bob Dexter?

It was inevitable that the subject of Bob Dexter's murder should come up, for there were still a number of unanswered questions in the minds of various people at the table. Predictably, Gwen was the one who first mentioned it. "I'm afraid I still don't understand," she said after several glasses of wine had loosened her tongue even more than usual, "why Father Mark should have killed Father Dexter. Perhaps you could explain it to me, Mr. Middleton-Brown?"

Alice leaned over Elayne. "Gwen, I don't think that's appropriate tonight," she said sharply. "Think about poor Elayne!"

Elayne shook her head. "I don't mind. We need to talk about it, I think. Settle it once and for all."

David sighed. "Mark Judd was a fairly unscrupulous young man. That's the first thing that you might find difficult to understand. He didn't operate in the way that the rest of us do—all he cared about, in the end, was what was best for Mark Judd."

Becca bit her lip and looked down; shyly, Stephen took her hand and gave it a little squeeze.

"I'm sorry," said David gently. "I know that this is difficult. But I do think it's best that we bring it all out in the open. Then we can put it behind us." He thought fleetingly of his own life: of Mother, of Gabriel, and of Lucy. "We have to come to terms with the past before we're ready to accept the future." Becca nodded almost imperceptibly and he continued. "The second thing about Mark Judd was that he was ambitious. He wanted to get ahead in life. He'd decided that the Church gave him good scope for that, so he'd chosen a career in the Church. He was willing to use any means at hand to achieve his ambitions, and that, also, is something that most of us have a hard time understanding. How could a young man whose churchmanship differed so completely from Bob Dexter's even contemplate using Dexter as a way to get ahead in the Church?" He shook his head. "But that is what he did. When his efforts to obtain a living through Walsingham failed, and Stephen was offered the living instead, he turned to Bob Dexter for his help. Dexter was well connected in London, and Mark thought that Dexter's influence could get him a plum London living."

"But why would Bob want to help him?" Elayne asked.

"Because he had something that your husband wanted," David explained. "He promised him that he could get him an advance copy of the program for the National Pilgrimage. That would have given the protesters an enormous strategic advantage, and Dexter must have thought that that would give him a great deal of influence in 'MISSION: Walsingham.' So he agreed to do what he could for Mark in exchange for the program."

"That's why Daddy wrote the letters about that job in Pimlico," Becca added.

"But Mark Judd didn't get the Pimlico job," said David. "It was in the *Church Times* on Friday, May third, the day that Bob Dexter died. On the Gazette page, in the appointments section. The living in Pimlico had gone to someone else. Mark must have seen it some time that day, and thought that Dexter had double-crossed him."

"Had he?" asked Becca.

David shook his head. "That's something we'll never know. Maybe he had, or maybe his influence wasn't as great as he thought. But someone else got the Pimlico living, and Mark Judd wasn't happy about it."

"So he went to the church that night?" Gwen leapt ahead.

"Oh, yes. He went to the church. I think he was probably there all along, somewhere in the shadows, listening when Elayne came, and you, Miss Vernon, with Miss Barnes, and finally when Stephen came. He heard Dexter accuse Stephen of seducing Becca, heard Stephen leave the church."

"He must have found that quite amusing," Stephen put in bitterly. "That I didn't deny it, even when it wasn't true— when he *knew* that it wasn't true." He spoke quietly, almost as if he were talking to himself. "I thought that Mark was my friend. I never knew how much he must have hated me—for getting the living that he wanted so badly."

"He hated you because things always came easily to you— all the things that he wanted in life, you took for granted," David amplified.

"Was that why . . . why he went after Becca?"

"Yes, because he knew that you wanted her, that you loved her. By taking her out from under your nose, by treating her the way he did, he was getting his own back on you. You told me yourself that he hinted about his relationship with Becca. He wanted you to know, wanted you to suffer."

It was Becca's turn to squeeze Stephen's hand.

"I think, too," David added, "that he went after Becca for another reason: because she was Bob Dexter's daughter. Because he knew that Dexter cherished her, and didn't want any other man to have her. He felt that it gave him the upper hand over Dexter, even though Dexter didn't know about it."

"That night," Gwen reminded them. "We were talking about that night, at the church."

"Yes. Mark was furious with Dexter about the Pimlico job. He'd heard him rowing with Stephen, heard him accuse Stephen of dishonoring Becca. He must have heard them scuffle, and heard Stephen throw the bar aside. When Stephen had gone, he went into the chapel to confront Dexter." David paused, collecting his thoughts. "He told Dexter that he had been Becca's lover, not Stephen—he wanted to watch him suffer. He told him all the details." Becca blenched, and David went on quickly. "He thought that he didn't have anything to lose, because the Pimlico job was already lost. But then Dexter told him that he would ruin him—he would tell the Walsingham people that Mark had betrayed them, had given him the program. That's when Mark decided to kill him. He picked up the iron bar from where Stephen had thrown it, and killed him in cold blood. Then he wiped off his fingerprints on his cassock and walked away."

There was a long moment of silence; no one looked at each other.

At last Alice spoke briskly. "What made you suspect the truth?"

"I should have suspected sooner. It was staring me in the face, really, if I'd had the sense to see it," David said with a self-deprecating smile. "The main clue was staring us *all* in the face: the layout of the church. The chapel is self-enclosed, with a curtain at the back. You can't actually see into the chapel from anywhere else in the church. It had always seemed odd to me, at the back of my mind, that Mark Judd should have found Dexter's body in the chapel the next morning, when he was showing someone something in the south porch. The south porch is nowhere near the chapel—why would he have gone there, if he didn't know that Dexter was there? It was a question that the police never thought to ask."

"Ah." It was a collective sigh of assent.

"I'd seen the evidence of Mark Judd's personality, in the way he'd treated Becca, and the way he'd treated Stephen, who was supposed to be his friend. And I'd had first-hand evidence, as well—the day that I met Mark, at Walsingham, he told me that he admired Bob Dexter's ruthlessness. That should have given me a clue about what sort of chap he was. But the thing that really brought all the bits together was the *Church Times* for the third of May. I read it weeks later, and there on the Gazette page was the Pimlico appointment. On the day of Dexter's murder. I had known about Dexter's efforts on Mark's behalf, but the name in the *Church Times* wasn't Mark Judd. That's when I knew who had killed Bob Dexter."

Again there was silence. "But how did you find out all the details?" Gwen asked with unusual perspicacity. "He was dead—he couldn't have told you all those things."

David nodded. "You're right. He didn't tell me. But he did tell someone: Geoffrey Pickering."

"Ah." Another collective sigh.

"Pickering admitted it, when the police questioned him. That was the real reason that Mark Judd wanted to kill him—not because of the painting, but because he knew too much about Dexter's murder, and was threatening to talk."

"How did Uncle Geoffrey find out?" asked Stephen.

"I think he just guessed, at first. Your uncle wasn't stupid," David admitted reluctantly. "He'd talked to you, after your arrest. And he'd been to the church—he probably realized the implications of the layout, even if the police didn't. He pretended that he knew more than he did, and Mark panicked. They'd met earlier that morning, before Lucy saw Geoffrey. Geoffrey threw out a few hints about Dexter's murder. Mark admitted the whole thing—he thought he was pretty clever to have pulled it off, and was glad to have an audience who could appreciate his cleverness. A great many murderers are like that, I think. But that meant that Geoffrey had to die as well, and so he invited him to meet him at the Holy Well during Benediction. Of course it backfired, and Geoffrey was able to tell the police the whole story."

The evening gradually regained its air of celebration, as Stephen ordered several bottles of champagne and they began to be consumed.

"You're taking up your new living soon?" David asked Stephen across the table.

"Yes, next month," he confirmed.

"And you're looking forward to it?"

"Well, yes." He gave Becca a sideways glance; she looked down demurely. "Though I'm sure I'll be coming back for frequent visits," he added.

"And Elayne?" asked Lucy. "Did I hear you say that you'll be staying on in South Barsham?"

Elayne smiled. "We'll have to be leaving the vicarage soon, but I don't want to leave the village. Gwen and Alice are the best friends I've ever had. There's nowhere else I'd rather be than with them." Both women beamed. "I'm buying the old blacksmith's place, just down from Monkey Puzzle Cottage. It's not as big as the vicarage, but it will do for Becca and me. And I don't expect that Becca will be with me forever."

No, thought Lucy, observing the way that Becca and Stephen were looking at each other. She probably won't be. She was young and resilient—the wounds that Mark Judd had dealt her would soon heal, and who better to help her through the healing process than the man who had loved her all along?

"There will be so much for us to do, fixing the church back up again," Gwen enthused. "Elayne will be a great help with that. All the new statues to be bought . . ."

Elayne's expression became remote as she thought of the old statue, the very old statue, with her lovely serene smile. The statue was safe now, and her own life was changed beyond recognition.

"A toast," said Stephen, standing up with his glass of champagne, "to the finest solicitor in Norfolk! David Middleton-Brown!"

They all drank enthusiastically, then David spoke. "I suppose this is as good a time as any to tell you that I'll be leaving Norfolk shortly." He glanced at Lucy. "Not even Lucy knows this, but I've been offered a position with a firm in London."

"When will you go?" asked Stephen.

"In a few months. I've inherited a house in London, and when the estate is settled, which I'm hoping will happen this summer, I'll be able to move."

Amid the general congratulations, Lucy smiled at him. "You don't have to wait that long, you know," she murmured. "You can move in with me, if you like."

"I was hoping you'd say that," he admitted softly. "Does that mean that you'll marry me?"

She took so long to answer that he wasn't sure she'd heard him.

"Well, no," she said at last in a gentle whisper, reaching for his hand under the table. "But please don't stop asking me. You never know—some time I might say yes!"